# DEPRAVED SINNERS

### SHERIDAN ANNE

**Sheridan Anne**
**MANIACS: Depraved Sinners #4**

Copyright © 2022 Sheridan Anne
All rights reserved
First Published in 2022
Anne, Sheridan
MANIACS: Depraved Sinners #4

Cover Design: Sheridan Anne
Photographer: Korabkova
Editing: Heather Fox
Formatting: Sheridan Anne

# MANIACS

*This is the final book in the Depraved Sinners series, and I can't believe we're already here! The past few months writing this series have flown by. I just wanted to say a quick thank you to everybody who has come along for the ride and fallen for these three twisted men. I hope this final book is everything you'd hoped it would be.*

*I couldn't possibly finish this series without one last stick figure drawing, and with that, please feast your eyes upon my interpretation of you all reading the last cliffhanger!*

# ONE

They're dead. They're fucking dead.

That manic look in Giovanni's eyes as he ran his blade through his sons' stomachs will forever haunt me. The way they fell to the grass, the way life slowly faded from their dark eyes ... fuck. The way Levi begged me not to look.

I whimper, the very thought tearing me apart from the inside out.

How could I not look? How could I have possibly turned away? The three of them held my heart in the palm of their strong, calloused hands, and in one devastating moment in time, they were stolen from me.

My heart aches. I've never felt torment like this before.

*BANG.*

*BANG.*

*BANG.*

The sound of the three gunshots echo through my mind, and my body flinches with each one. It's agonizing. It's as though I can feel the bullets piercing through their bodies and shattering what little was left of my soul.

There's nothing left of me now. Not without them.

Giovanni is a fucking monster. He won, just as he always said that he would.

The boys warned me, but I refused to listen. They said that he would take everything, said that he would destroy what was good in the world and that he wouldn't stop until every knee was dropped before him. I never thought it was them he would take. All this time, I saw myself as his target, truly believing that he would destroy me in order to destroy them.

I believed we could survive. I trusted the three of them would come through. They were supposed to be invincible. They were supposed to be my rocks, my three devils on the coldest nights.

That's all over now, and I have nothing left but the memories that haunt my mind and the scars left behind on my body. How am I ever supposed to be alright? How am I supposed to move on from this?

Tears stream down my face, and I turn my head into the dreadlocked dude's chest, his arms caging around me as he tears off into the night on his motorbike, the convoy of SUVs speeding behind us.

Wind whips through my hair and smears my tears all over my face, but I barely notice it. I'm so numb. Numb to the world. Numb to the fresh hell wreaking havoc over my heart. Numb to ... everything.

It's barely been a few minutes since hearing those gunshots ring through the night, and if I dared to look up over this guy's shoulder, I'd still see the DeAngelis mansion fading in the distance. I'd still be able to hear the fallen soldiers' screams as they slowly died in the pools of blood gathering on the grass.

Roman. Levi. Marcus. No. I refuse to believe they're gone. They can't be gone. I barely got a chance to know them.

Perhaps this is karma ... my own version of hell ... punishment. I took a walk on the dark side; I sacrificed everything good about myself to indulge in that darkness, and now it's caught up to me. Now I have to suffer the very real consequences. This is what I get for falling in love with the three DeAngelis devils.

I will never be the same.

I will never survive.

Tonight wasn't supposed to go like this. I wasn't supposed to get rescued by the woman who claims to be my mother, something I only learned a few short hours ago, and I sure as hell wasn't supposed to see my three kings fall.

Tonight we were supposed to rise. Tonight we were supposed to be victorious.

Dreadlock Dude weaves through the streets and I cling to him as though he's my last lifeline, only lifting my tear-stained face from his chest when his head whips to the right.

Gia's SUV moves in beside us, and I watch as her tinted window lowers to expose her youthful face and her brows pinched with concern. She holds her hand up as her gaze scans over my face, completely void of emotion. A million questions filter through my mind, a million thoughts and suspicions, but then those three gunshots sound inside my head, and every last thought is replaced with nothing but a hollow ache.

All too quickly, her heavy stare flicks away as she takes in the man I cling to. "Pull over up here," she shouts through the open window.

Dreadlock Dude nods, and without sparing me a second look, Gia speeds off in front of us before he even gets a proper chance to respond. He hits the gas, taking off after her at a million miles an hour as nerves fill my veins.

I swallow hard. I'm grateful that she was there to save me just in the nick of time, but how the hell did she know I was in trouble? Had she been watching us? Did she know that the boys needed her help just as much as I did, only to be left defenseless and bleeding out on the ground? I know this is a dark world and everybody only looks out for themselves, but surely she isn't so cold-hearted as to leave them behind like that, leave them barely grasping onto life, especially considering that she knows how I feel about them.

Gia Moretti is nothing but a stranger to me, but she's a stranger who claims to have watched over me my entire life with my best interests at heart. I'm damn sure that she had some fucked-up intel, considering she truly believed I was better off living with my father, and that I had a life any child would dream of. So yeah, she may have been checking up on me every now and then, but she never cared to dig deeper than the surface, and because of that, I can't trust her. You know, apart from the fact that she's the DeAngelis family's number one competition, their greatest enemy. I mean, if that's not the biggest red flag I've ever seen, I don't know what is.

Who knows, maybe this was all some ploy to separate us, to get something from the boys that they couldn't live without. She knows how they care for me, how they'd walk through the hottest pits of hell just to keep me safe. Shit, maybe I'm not even her daughter at all.

The thought has an unladylike scoff pulling from deep in my chest, and the moment the sound passes my lips, Dreadlock Dude pulls back and drops his gaze to mine. "You good?" he questions, his dark eyes narrowed, looking like two deep pits of nothingness.

I slap a grin across my face, my eyes filled with venom. "Peachy," I spit, watching the way he watches me back. It's almost as though he's trying to decide if he's going to make my life a living hell or if he'll take pity on the sad, broken girl.

His jaw tightens and he holds my stare for a moment longer before following Gia's SUV off the side of the road. Dirt spits up under her tires as she hits the brakes, and I clench my eyes as that cloud of dust smacks me in the face. The motorbike comes to a stop behind the SUV, and I peer through the dirt cloud, wondering what the hell is about to happen.

Dreadlock Dude presses his hand to his ear as his gaze settles on the back window of Gia's SUV, and I realize that she's giving him instructions. He gives a firm nod, and before I can ask what's going on, his strong arms scoop under my ass and he hauls me off his bike.

"Wha … What are you doing?" I rush out as panic tears through me. I cling to him, my gaze wide as I frantically search around. Is he going to ditch me here? Put a bullet through my head and leave me for the bears? Shit, if they were just going to kill me all along, I would have preferred to stay with the boys. At least that way I could have died in their arms with their sweet words telling me that it was all going to be okay.

The guy doesn't respond, and as he starts to move away from the bike, my panic only escalates. "Let me go," I spit, struggling against his hold, desperate to get back on my feet to give myself a chance to run. But where will I go? Back to the mansion to fight for the boys? I couldn't, not without becoming fertilizer for the most pristine lawn in the country. Giovanni slaughtered his own sons, sons that I believed to be invincible. If he could do that to them, I can only imagine the shit he'd do to me.

If the boys weren't already dead, they'd kill me themselves for even thinking of going back there. But I have to do something. I have to fight back and make this right, though nothing I do could ever bring them back to me. There has to be some other way.

I mean … Giovanni did mention that he wanted me to become his wife. The thought alone makes me sick, but it's also a way to get close to him.

No. I can't think like that. It's a stupid plan that's only going to end up backfiring on me just like everything else does.

What a fucking joke. Giovanni is delusional if he thinks there's any way in hell that I would willingly marry him, sleep in his bed every night, bear him a child and grant him access to the Moretti empire. I'd sooner die than hand myself over like that. Besides, I couldn't shit all over the boys' memory by giving up now and becoming their father's bride. I won't do it, not even if it means bringing peace between the two families.

Dreadlock Dude holds on to me, caging me like a prisoner between his strong arms, and I resist the urge to claw his face. It would be a low blow. The guy truly does have a pretty face. He's handsome with a sharp jaw and flawless dark skin. He's older than me, maybe in his mid-thirties, and it's clear from the way he holds himself that he's seen some nasty shit, but that only adds to his allure. To ruin that would be a crime against humanity, but a shot to the junk wouldn't go astray.

"I ain't gonna hurt you, baby," he mutters as he starts walking toward the backseat of Gia's SUV. "But you keep fighting me like that, and I'll have no choice but to put you out. You feel me? And trust me, after sobbing all over my fucking shirt, I won't even feel bad about it."

Well, shit.

My gaze snaps up to his, and I fix him with a lethal stare, one the boys would be proud of. "Then put me down."

Dreadlock Dude tightens his hold around my waist before releasing his other hand. "Gladly," he mutters just as he reaches around me and tears open the back passenger door of the SUV. I barely get a chance to scream before he tosses me straight on the backseat and slams the door before my body even hits the leather seat.

The momentum of his throw sends me sprawling against the

backseat, and before I can even right myself, Gia hits the gas and takes off at a million miles per hour. I scramble to keep myself upright as I fly across the backseat and dive for the handle of the door. I pull hard, desperate to free myself, but the door won't budge.

"Don't waste your energy," Gia mutters, her dark eyes flicking to mine through the rearview mirror. "The doors are locked, and trust me when I say, you're going to need your energy."

Pressing my hands against the leather on either side of my thighs, I meet Gia's stare, hating how much it resembles mine. "What do you want with me?" I demand, my jaw clenching as my fingers ball into fists against the leather, quickly realizing that there's no point in trying to run. The DeAngelis family are scary as shit, but the fact that they were all scared of the Moretti family tells me exactly what I need to know—dealing with the DeAngelis family was only a warm-up for what the Moretti family is capable of.

"I thought I made myself quite clear when we met in my warehouse this afternoon," she says, her gaze falling away to focus on the road ahead as I hear the roar of the motorbike falling back into position behind us. "You, Shayne, are the heir to the Moretti empire, and you will take my place when the time comes."

I shake my head, my brows pinching with confusion. "I know all of this," I spit, my frustration getting the best of me as too many questions fly through my mind. "I just … you said that I could stay with the boys. You said I still had time."

"The deal was that you could stay with the three DeAngelis sons while they could guarantee your safety. They're dead now. They failed you, so I was left with no choice but to come save you before Giovanni took you as his own. You are the sole heir to my family, my empire, and I cannot risk you slipping back into Giovanni's grasp."

A lump forms in my throat as silent tears stream down my face. "They're not dead," I murmur, my voice lowering to a whisper. "They can't be dead."

Gia's sigh fills the car as her gaze slices back up to the small mirror. "You saw what Giovanni did. You heard the gunshots. You're only hurting yourself by holding on to the hope that they could have survived. I've been in this world a long time, Shayne. The likelihood of those boys surviving … it's not possible. It's best you move on now. A clean cut."

"A clean cut?" I scoff. "Giovanni murdered them right in front of my eyes. I was in love with them. There's no 'clean cut' about it."

"It was just business, Shayne. Every mafia family experiences losses like this. It's just part of the game."

"This wasn't business," I spit. "It was personal. He killed them just to get them out of the way, so he could have me for himself. You know that, right? He's planning on marrying me to gain access to your family. He killed them to get to you. That's not business."

Gia shakes her head as the convoy of SUVs finally catches up to us and gets in formation, leaving Gia driving directly between them all with Dreadlock Dude on his motorbike up ahead. "I know it's hard for you to understand. You haven't been in this world long enough for the loss to bounce off you yet, but soon enough you'll see that it was a necessary move in a war that's been going on long before your time."

My eyes bug out of my head, the lump getting caught in my throat again. "A necessary move?" I splutter, unable to make sense of why she would say something like that.

"Yes," she explains. "Giovanni's sons were going to die at some point. Whether by their father's hand or my own."

"Yours?" I spit, gawking at her through the small mirror. "What the fuck? Why would you even say that?"

Gia turns onto the highway and hits the gas a little harder before letting out a heavy breath. "In the warehouse this afternoon, I saw the way they loved you. It was real and ran deep, something many of us never get the chance to experience, let alone to be lucky enough to experience it from three men like that," Gia says, keeping her lethal gaze locked on the road before her. "When the time came for me to bring you home, they were never going to let you go. I would have had no choice but to eliminate them, which is a shame because given the time, they would have been great leaders for the DeAngelis family. They would have endured hell to see their family rise to greatness, but now they will never get the chance."

Gia pauses for a minute as my gaze falls into my lap, the fight quickly leaving my body.

"This was always how it was going to be. You were always meant to be with me," she explains. "I tried to give you time. I wanted you to have that little bit of joy in your life before you started training to rule my empire. I'm not going to lie, I thought I could give you a little extra time, but that simply wasn't in the cards."

My gaze snaps back up. "In the cards?" I scoff, a sick laughter bubbling up my throat. "Your timing was all a little too convenient, wasn't it? You just happen to come screeching down the driveway the moment I ran."

Gia's eyes come back to mine, quickly becoming cold and hard, and if I weren't so broken and consumed by grief, I might have been smart enough to bite my tongue. "What are you suggesting, Shayne?"

Silence surrounds me, and as I stare back at her, I wonder if I have what it takes to accuse the most lethal woman on the planet of being a shady fuck, but as those three gunshots ring inside my head, I realize that I simply don't give a shit, not anymore. "You were there the whole time. You knew about the DeAngelis family meeting, and you made a point to be there to see who would walk out of it alive. You knew Giovanni was coming, you knew he was bringing his army, and you sat back and watched it like primetime entertainment. He murdered the three loves of my life, and YOU DID NOTHING!" I scream, my throat immediately going raw as the grief takes my heart and crushes it.

Tears stream down my face, dropping onto the top of my shirt and soaking the soft material. "You could have saved them," I murmur, my voice breaking with the heaviness of each word, "and the fact that you didn't even try, just sat and watched as they were slaughtered only goes to prove what kind of person you really are. I'm better off without you. I want absolutely nothing to do with you or your bullshit family."

Gia watches me carefully, her expression hard and still like a mask, holding back her true emotions. Not a word is said, and the silence grows heavier with each passing second until she finally looks back at the road before her. "Here's what's going to happen," she tells me, her voice thick with authority. "You're going to live with me, you're going to train with me, and then you're going to become me. Those are your only options. I will give you tonight to grieve and as of tomorrow, the DeAngelis brothers will cease to exist in your mind. You are my daughter, and because of that, I am showing a kindness that I have never shown anyone before, but cross me, Shayne Moretti, and you will understand how it is that I became the head of this family. Blood doesn't always run thicker than water, and you are going to have to earn your place in my family. Is that understood?"

My jaw clenches as I stare back at the woman who looks so much like me. "I want Giovanni dead. I want to tear his eyeballs out of his head with my bare hands and listen to his screams. I want to strangle him, slice my dagger across his throat and rip his organs from his body one by one. I want to leave his heart for last just so I can feel it beating in my hand, and only then will I crush it for his sons and feed the pieces to their wolves. Give me that, and I will do or be whatever the fuck you want."

Gia's eyes come back to mine through the mirror, narrowed and full of thought. She considers me for a moment before silently nodding and turning her gaze back to the road. "Perhaps I've underestimated you," she murmurs. "Is that all you want?"

I shake my head. "I want the wolves, Dill and Doe, and Giovanni's newborn son. I made a promise and I intend to keep it. Besides," I say, narrowing my gaze as I lower my tone, letting her taste the venom I spit at her. "It's the least you can do."

"Okay," she says after a long beat, letting my insult bounce right off her shoulders. "The wolves are yours, as for the remaining DeAngelis heir, that child is not my problem, nor do I care for it."

"I didn't ask for it to be your problem," I throw back at her. "I will raise him as my own if I have to. Either way, I intend to keep my promise. So, make it happen, or watch me destroy everything that you've built the same way you stood back and watched Roman, Levi, and Marcus get slaughtered."

And with that, I turn my gaze out the window, ignoring the way her eyes narrow to tight slits, realizing that demanding my cooperation isn't going to be nearly as easy as she thought.

# TWO

The rest of the drive is silent and I hate it. While I'd give anything to keep from picturing the way the long, thin blade speared through their stomachs and drenched the lawn in blood, I'd also give anything not to be stuck in this awkward silence with my mother, especially after threatening to tear her world to pieces. That probably wasn't my finest moment, but she's kidding herself if she expects me to drop to my knees and beg to serve as her loyal yes man.

Gia motherfucking Moretti.

What the hell am I even supposed to refer to her as? Mommy? Mother? Birth giver? Egg donor? Somehow, I feel that she won't appreciate the terms incubator or power-hungry bitch, so I guess I'll just stick with Gia for now.

We've been driving for well over an hour, and not a single second has passed where a tear hasn't streaked down my face. I can't stop remembering it. Hell, at this point, I don't even give a shit what happens to me. Gia can have me for all I care because nothing matters now. They're gone and there's not a damn thing I can do about it.

Sure, getting revenge is going to be the only reason I wake up every morning, but after that, what's left for me in this world?

Gia hasn't spoken a word about my bargain, and I really don't know her well enough to know if she'll come through on that or not. She doesn't strike me as the type to make deals with desperate people, especially deals that could see a war, but she'd be a fool to refuse me. Whether I get revenge with her at my side or by myself, it's still going to happen. Not to mention, she's sick. She told me in the old warehouse that she has a year to live, maybe two, and while waiting two years to tear Giovanni's throat from his body is going to test me like never before, it would also be really nice if I could do it with the Moretti army at my back ... the army that is apparently going to be mine.

It would be the sweetest day, watching as Giovanni scrambles to hang on to life. Running left to right only to realize that he's cornered like a wicked game of cat and mouse. Then watching the color drain from his face as the panic sets in, realizing that his day has finally come, at my hands no less. The thought is what's going to keep me breathing. I just hope Gia isn't going to make me wait.

But if she says no ... fuck. That's one hell of a civil war that she doesn't want knocking on her door.

The vile things I want to do to that man … I hope I can do justice for the boys, make them proud one last time. But will it ever be enough? Will murdering him in the most brutal, savage way make up for the horrors the boys suffered at his hands for all those years, make up for the heartache and pain that he caused? No, probably not, but I can try.

Gia makes a few turns through an expensive residential area, and I know that I should be paying attention to each one of the turns, but it's like a puzzle, and in this state, there's no way I'll be able to remember how to get out of here. It's a gated community and it's private as fuck. It's the kind of area people can't accidentally drive by and claim they got lost, to be driving these streets and have gotten this far would mean that you were here with a purpose. It's the best kind of security system. I'm sure every resident around here knows all their neighbors' cars and exactly who lives in each home, how many people they have on staff, and the exact hours they expect them to come and go. There are no surprises here. I bet all of the other residents are just as powerful and dangerous as Gia, each one of them desperate for privacy.

We weave through the roads lined with massive homes fortified by iron gates, armed guards, and security systems. Each sitting at the end of a long driveway looking menacing in their own right. I gape at the rows of towering houses in disbelief. Who in the hell lives here?

The SUV rolls to a stop at the top of a hill, and Dreadlock Dude pulls his bike over to hash in a gate code. The house is just as big as the gothic prison meant to keep the boys at bay. But, unlike the antique castle hiding amid a forest, this place looks brand spanking new, sitting atop the hill like a modern citadel on full display.

The DeAngelis castle is likely the remnants of what once housed royalty hundreds of years ago. But even in the dead of night, it's easy to see this beauty was built solely to fit Gia's high standards of living. It's a charming, modern, tri-level home, but I've learned that in this world, what you see on the outside isn't always what you get. I wouldn't be surprised if she had her own villainous lair built beneath the home, just as the boys had done to the castle.

*Fuck ... the boys.*

I let out a heavy sigh, and as the massive iron gate draws back, Gia glances up at me through the small mirror. "Welcome to my home, Shayne," she says, gently hitting the gas and following Dreadlock Dude through the gate. The rest of the SUVs enter behind us and take off around the side of the property. "Your home."

Swallowing hard, I grow restless in the backseat.

My home? Who's she kidding? I already have a home with the boys, but I suppose that home no longer exists.

"I have business to attend," Gia continues as she eases up the long driveway and follows the road around the basin of a stunning marble fountain. "I wasn't expecting to have you here quite so soon. Had I known, I would have carved out some time to show you around and get you settled in."

My brows furrow, not really giving a flying fuck about her need to coddle me to make her feel better for the twenty-two years of abandonment. "Zeke will show you to your room," she continues. "Feel free to—"

"Zeke?" I cut in, meeting her stare through the mirror as she brings the SUV to a stop.

Gia gestures toward Dreadlock Dude, who kills his engine and turns to survey the SUV, waiting for his instructions. Ahhhh, so he has a name. Zeke. I like it. It suits him. I lift my gaze back to the mirror. "You're fucking him, right?"

Gia swivels in the driver's seat and turns to look back at me, her eyes widening as she stares at me in stunned silence.

"What?" I spit, a scowl sitting on my lips. "Are you horrified by how obvious it is or the audacity for me to dare ask? Because honestly, you were a dick when asking me about the boys, so I figured this wasn't exactly off limits."

Gia clenches her jaw, her eyes narrowing just a little as she considers how she wants to tackle this. "Zeke and I have a professional relationship, not that that is any of your business. Occasionally I lean on him when I need …"

"To fuck?" I supply, my brow arched high as I peer out the windshield at the mountain of a man staring back at us through the tinted glass. "I bet he fucks like a pornstar. He's an ass man, isn't he?"

Gia lets out a frustrated groan. "If you must know, yes. Zeke and I have a strange … relationship," she admits. "But know that I am only sharing this information because you will be living with me and will no doubt see things that will make you wonder. He is there for me when I need it, and I for him. However, we are not an … item. Nor will we ever be. He is free to sleep with whomever he pleases, just as I am."

My lips twist into a hard line. "Why?" I grunt. "That's fucking

MANIACS

stupid."

"Excuse me?"

"You're clearly in love with the guy, and if he's been hanging around, then obviously he's down."

Gia shakes her head and lets out a heavy breath before quickly gazing out the window at Zeke. "Keeping Zeke at an arm's length is the only thing keeping a target off his back. You don't get to be in my position without having to make sacrifices. I am sure that's a lesson you are already beginning to learn. Besides, why would I do that to a man I loved? Why would I put his life in unnecessary danger just so I could have the right to hold his hand in public? Love is a fool's game, Shayne, one that makes you vulnerable. It's best to simply not fall in love at all."

I hold her stare, pity filling my chest. "Sounds lonely."

Her features harden, and I realize that for just a moment, I had forgotten who the hell I was talking to. "What do you want from me, Shayne? You want me to go and scream at the top of my lungs that I like to fuck the help? You want me to go and start a relationship with a guy who's going to have to watch me die? No, thank you. I'd rather spare us all the heartache. Now, if I can trust that you are smart enough to keep this information to yourself, I'd like to go inside and prepare for my meeting."

I hold my hands up. "Alright, fine. I'll drop it."

"Good," she says, her eyes darkening. "What you're asking of me, about Giovanni and his child. You must understand that is not something I take lightly. You're asking me to put my family at risk for a vendetta."

"Are you telling me no?" I question, my heart rate picking up as I prepare myself to bolt out of here.

"No," she tells me. "I am not. I'm simply trying to say that a request like that will need some careful consideration. I will let you know my decision once it has been made."

I shrug my shoulders. "Just know that we don't have a deal unless you can come through for me. I don't start training as your little protégée until Giovanni's eyeballs are soaking in a jar up on my trophy shelf."

A soft chuckle pulls from deep in Gia's chest. "Remember your place, Shayne. You will commence training with me when I say you will start training. I am doing what I can to show you kindness and understanding, but that will only go so far. Keep pushing my patience and I guarantee you will not like the consequences."

Without another word, Zeke appears at my side, pulling on the handle and letting the soft night's breeze flow through the back of the SUV. "Come on," he mutters, his eyes hard as he peers over the vehicle at his boss striding away, physically needing to put distance between us to keep from wrapping her hands around my throat.

Stepping out of the car, Zeke remains right at my side as he leads me up the staircase, so close that making a run for it isn't even an option. His eyes focus solely on Gia up ahead, watching as she unlocks the front door and enters a security code. "What did you say to her?" he murmurs, his voice low and filled with that overprotective rasp that comes from a man deeply obsessed, kinda like how Marcus would do when defending my honor.

"Nothing," I mutter, refusing to glance up and meet his eye. "We just had a little ... mother-daughter chat. You know, getting to know each other a bit better."

Zeke pauses, his hand snapping up to my elbow with a tight grip. He yanks me back, twisting me to force my stare up to him. "I'm not going to repeat myself," he growls, his quick temper reminding me of Roman. "What did you say to her?"

I scoff, yanking my arm out of his tight grip. "You really are head over heels for your boss, aren't you? Perhaps you should be up there with her, making her feel better, rather than out here making demands of the trash."

He narrows his eyes, leaning into me. "What the hell do you know about it?"

"I know that she's keeping you away when you're clearly both in love with each other, and I know that you're so much of a bitch to stand by and let her keep doing it. Deep down, it's killing you, isn't it? She's dying and you could so easily swoop in and make her last days on earth the best days of her life, but she refuses you, refuses to put herself first because no matter what, her family will always come first." I stare up at him, my brow arching. "Sound about right?"

His already lethal stare tightens, and if I were smart, I would have shut up the moment I stepped out of the SUV, but apparently, the grief consuming me is helping me realize that without the boys, I have absolutely nothing to lose.

"You don't know what the fuck you're talking about," he growls, the sound so low I have to wonder if I even hear it.

"Try me, asshole," I spit, not forgetting the way he kidnapped me out of the DeAngelis mansion only a few hours ago, a crime he still hasn't paid the price for. "What kind of man would stand back and watch the woman he loves die and not step in to show her just how good it can be?"

His jaw tightens, and I scoff before taking a small step back and continuing up the stairs. "Don't bother showing me to my room," I throw back over my shoulder, leaving him standing behind me, glaring at me as though he could kill me with nothing but his stare alone. "I'll figure it out on my own."

Storming up the rest of the stairs, I try to figure out how the hell I got stuck in this bullshit situation for the second time. What is it with all of these mafia families wanting me at their beck and call? I'm not made for this world, but the boys sure as fuck ensured that I'd survive in it. I'm not sure I can though, not without them.

My hand slams against the floor-to-ceiling front door, and the three gunshots immediately replay inside my head, making me flinch with each of them. I gasp for breath, trying to shake it off as I give the door a hard shove, sending it sailing open.

The lights are all off inside except for a few deeper in the home, and while every cell inside my body screams at me to start searching for a way out, I'm too exhausted to even care. But just as Gia said, tonight, I grieve, tomorrow I will rise like a fucking phoenix from the ashes.

Making my way deeper into the mansion, I pass through the wide-open foyer. A double staircase centers the room, one hugging the left side of the expansive room while the other curves up the right. It's the most impressive set of stairs I've ever seen. This place is literally built for a queen. It's insane, but Gia won't catch me admitting that out loud.

I wonder if she expects this to be my home after she's gone.

Assuming the bedrooms are upstairs, I step to the left set of stairs and grip the delicate black railing before making my way up. I barely reach the top before light spreads through the landing from an opening door. My eyes widen as Gia freezes in the doorway, her hand still on the doorknob. "Oh," she says, as though she's surprised to see me actually inside her home. "Where's Zeke? He was to show you to your room."

My gaze drops as I move up the final stair. "He and I don't quite see eye to eye. We had a little falling out."

Gia lets out a heavy breath before quickly glancing at her wrist and taking in the time. "Follow me."

I trail behind her, wanting to keep my distance as she makes her way through the upstairs foyer. We step through an informal sitting area and Gia comes to a stop, glancing back at me. "Your room is just through there," she says, holding up her hand toward the door in the furthest corner. "There's a private bathroom that's fully stocked with everything you should need. I wasn't expecting you here quite so soon, so I haven't stocked your closet yet. However, we look the same size. My staff shouldn't have any trouble finding you something to wear. As for your belongings, if you have anything sentimental that you'd like for us to retrieve from any of the DeAngelis properties, just make a list and I can arrange a suitable time for my men to go and … collect them."

It's not hard to read between the lines on that one, but I nod anyway, appreciating the offer as there is one thing that I've left behind, one thing that would mean the world for me to have back—Marcus' dagger that he gifted me the first night he came into my castle cell. The rest of it can all go to hell.

I move to walk past her when she continues. "I do not use this sitting area, so feel free to claim this as your own," she says, scanning the room that's bigger than my old apartment. "I want you to be comfortable here."

I press my lips into a tight smile, really trying to find gratitude. This woman doesn't have to take me in … well, I guess she kind of does, but either way, it's bound to be weird for both of us. "Thank you," I say, glancing away. "You don't need to do all of this. I'm fine with just a bed to sleep in."

"You are my daughter, Moretti blood—*my blood*—runs through your veins and giving you a roof over your head is the least I can do. Besides, starting first thing in the morning, you will commence your training. It's not going to be easy. It will be brutal and test you in ways that not even those DeAngelis sons could have prepared you for. I do not take this lightly and neither should you," she explains. "Now, go ahead and get yourself cleaned up. You have a big day tomorrow that will require enough sleep to make it through."

With that, Gia walks away, and the moment she turns the corner, I let out a shaky breath.

Feeling too exposed out here in the open sitting area, I push through to my new bedroom, the millionth room I've had since all this bullshit started eight months ago. Though I'm not going to lie, this room is significantly nicer than the one I occupied down in the castle cells or in Giovanni's desert dungeon. But at this point, what does it even matter? I could sleep in a dirty alleyway behind a dumpster and it wouldn't change anything.

The boys are gone.

It hits me harder than I could have known, and as I pull off my bloodstained clothes and stumble toward the private bathroom, the heaving sobs consume me.

The boys are dead.

And I will never see them again.

# THREE

*B*ANG!

My eyes spring open and I fly out of bed, my puffy, sore eyes quickly scanning the room for a threat. Zeke stands in my open doorway, the rising sun barely peeking through my window and glistening against his flawless skin.

My heart thumps wildly as I take in his hard stare. No wonder my so-called mother has been using him as a playtoy. He's got that sexy, alluring thing that the boys had, mixed with that hard edge in his eyes that warns you to keep your distance. He's dangerous in every possible way, the perfect match for my mother.

"Training starts in ten minutes," Zeke spits, not at all happy to see me, and hell, the feeling is mutual. "Don't be late."

With that, Zeke storms out of my bedroom, leaving the door open wide and my heart racing erratically in my chest. Fuck, I need to pull myself together. It's one thing being in a situation like this and knowing the boys are coming for me, but I'm on my own now, and I have to make this work. This is going to be my only shot at getting close to Giovanni. Without Gia and her crew, I'm as fucked as can be.

I take short, calming breaths as the memories of last night come racing back to me like a haunting movie on replay inside my head. It hits me like a freight train and drops me to my knees, the weight of the boys' deaths resting heavily on my shoulders, the grief too much for me to bear.

Grief claims me, and I struggle to suck in a breath. Gia expects me to move on today, to just get up out of bed as though they never mattered, as though I should share in her disdain for the boys. That'll never happen, and she was a fool to even suggest it.

Last night, I spent an hour sitting in the shower as the hot water washed the boys' blood from my skin and down the drain, and as I watched the last pieces I had of them vanish, I replayed their final moments in my mind over and over again. The pain in their eyes as they fell into the grass. The desperation in Levi's voice when he begged me not to watch. I tossed and turned fitfully in a cold sweat, unable to fall asleep without those three gunshots startling me awake. I know it was real, yet every fiber in my body screams for them to walk through the door and tell me this was some sick joke. I mean, sure, Roman would have hated it, Levi would have rolled his eyes, and Marcus would have laughed until he made himself sick … but he would have made it up to me in a way that only Marcus could, and damn it, I would have forgiven him before I even came.

I can't be without them. I can't go on with this pain. I don't know how to exist in this world without them now.

My head falls into my hands as long, painful moments pass by. I can't break like this. I promised myself that come morning, I would rise like a phoenix, but it's too hard. How am I supposed to get up and face the day knowing that they're not here, knowing that I'll never hold them again, never feel their touch or hear those sweet, whispered words?

Fuck.

I have to do this alone. I have to get up and train, I have to become stronger, fiercer, and wiser or I won't stand a fucking chance. If I'm going to make Giovanni pay for what he did, then I have to survive this. I won't have an endless number of chances. There will be only one, and when that time comes, I'm going to be ready.

That cold, hard knowledge pulls me to my feet, and I turn toward the private bathroom, drawing my hands across my face, drying my tears.

I won't back down from this.

Giovanni DeAngelis fucked up when he set his sick, twisted games upon my men, and for that, he will face the firing squad. He pissed off the wrong bitch.

After stepping through to the bathroom, I quickly go through my morning routine. There are no training clothes in sight, but for some reason, I trust that Gia will have something prepared for me when I get down to the training room—wherever the hell that might be.

Knowing damn well that I'm pushing Zeke's limit of ten minutes, I push my way out of my bedroom and saunter down the impressive staircase, finding Zeke standing at the bottom with a scowl on his face and his eyes piercing right through me. If looks could kill … goddamn.

His jaw tightens, and as he looks at me, there's not a doubt in my mind that he can tell I've been crying again, and I instantly hate how weak that makes me feel, but I'll own it. If those tears were for anyone apart from my three devils, then I'd happily stand here and allow him to call me a little bitch, but I won't apologize for tears shed for them.

Zeke turns on his heel, his hands held behind his back. He doesn't tell me to follow him, but the silent demand is there. Every bone and fiber in my body tells me to get the fuck out of here, knowing Gia Moretti's definition of 'training' probably isn't going to be rainbows and flowers. It's going to be brutal, and it's going to have me begging for freedom, but if she wants to turn me into a fucking warrior, then so be it. I'll rise to the fucking occasion just as the boys would expect.

Following Zeke through the massive residence, we step through to an elevator. Tension rolls over my body the moment the door closes, locking us in. This motherfucker could end my life with his bare hands. The last thing I want is to be trapped in a small space with him, especially considering the lethal scowl stretched across his face.

A million comments about having his knickers in a twist try to fly out of my mouth, but I force myself to bite down on my tongue until I taste the coppery, metallic tang of blood. I doubt this dude is very forgiving and if I start off on the wrong foot with him, it's only going to make my training that much harder.

The elevator takes us down to the basement and dread spears through me, my blood turning cold with the unknown. I haven't had much luck when it comes to meeting new people and being invited for a stroll through their basements, yet when the elevator *dings* and the heavy metal door slides back to let in a rush of clinical light, my jaw goes slack, dropping open in surprise.

I step out of the elevator, staring around me in wonder. This place is done up like some kind of combat heaven, and if I were in a vampire hunter movie, this is the kind of place I'd want to train. The basement training level must be as wide as the actual house upstairs, and I'm surprised to find so many people down here.

Men are sparring, fighting hand-to-hand combat while the metallic clash of blades sound across the room. There's a shooting range and a wall of training weapons, but what catches my attention is the pissed-off woman standing in the very center of the room, her glare piercing right through me.

I swallow hard, remembering her words from last night. *You're going to live with me, you're going to train with me, and then you're going to become me.* I'm fucked.

"Prepare yourself, girl," Zeke murmurs, his lips barely moving. "If you thought training with those DeAngelis scum was a nightmare, you ain't seen nothing yet."

He steps away from me as though he didn't just fill my veins with the heaviest kind of fear, his hands behind his back once again. Zeke strides across the training room, only stopping and turning when he reaches Gia's side.

As I get closer, I watch the way Gia's lips press into a hard line, her gaze falling down my body and taking in what little I wear. "You're late," she snaps. "My time is money and you're wasting it."

I don't bother with a response and her stare hardens, her eyes filling with venom as I do nothing but stare back at her. I guess we're doing things the hard way today, but I really don't care either way. If she wants to beat the shit out of me under the disguise of training, then so be it, at least this way, I might feel something.

"You were told you would be training today," she says, stepping toward me, her gaze dropping down my body again. "Why are you not prepared for your lessons?"

My eyes drop to take in my lack of shoes and the baggy tank I slept in that's showing off a little too much side boob. "Oh, um, you see, when I was twelve, I never had some big, hairy dude break into my home and say, '*You're a wizard, Harry,*' so unfortunately, I don't come equipped with the ability to manifest training gear."

Her gaze drops away and a hint of embarrassment flashes through her eyes, realizing that perhaps the little oversight of having clothes ready for me may have been her own fault, despite her declaration of getting me everything that I could need.

"Right," she says, her lips tight. "Get started with Zeke, and I will arrange for one of my guards to bring you something appropriate."

My gaze snaps to Zeke's body and I arch a brow. "Oh, you're going to share your man with me, huh? I've been waiting to feel his body all over mine. Tell me the rules though, do I get to bite him?"

Gia's face reddens with rage, and she places her hand on Zeke's chest, stopping him from doing the exact thing that's probably flashing in her own mind. She looks up at the beast of a man beside her, her eyes dark and angry. "Get the girl some clothes—a training crop, tights, and shoes," she snaps before turning back to me and indicating the training mat to our left.

She walks toward it, each step filled with the kind of authority that makes me want to shrink back, but I don't dare. Instead, I hold my head high and meet her right in the center of the mat. Then without even a breath of warning, her hands shoot out, one gripping onto my shoulder as the other slams a devastating blow right into my stomach. I double over in agony, but she's not quite finished. Her leg waves out, connecting with the back of my feet and knocking me on my ass with a heavy thump.

Gia comes down over me, pressing a knee against my winded stomach and a hand flat against my sternum to keep me pinned. "This is my home, girl," she seethes, her voice low and furious. "No matter how you feel about me, you will show respect. Is that understood?"

With a clenched jaw, my hand shoots up to her throat. Her eyes widen briefly, but before she gets a moment to react, I hook my legs around her waist and rip her off me. Gia's back slams against the training mat, half of her body sprawled on top of mine, and like lightning, I scramble until I'm pinning her down.

"Let's get one thing straight," I spit back at her. "You brought me here. I didn't ask to be here, nor do I *want* to be here. The only reason I haven't stormed out the door is because you're my only shot at getting revenge on Giovanni, but don't get me wrong, with or without you, I'll find a way," I tell her, my heart racing faster by the second. "You are not entitled to my respect simply because this is your home, you need to earn that from me, and right now, you're doing a really shitty job of it. I won't fall in line simply because you tell me to. You were right yesterday, blood doesn't always run thicker than water, and my loyalty to those three brothers will always come before everything else. No matter what."

I push up off her, the rage and emotion pulsing through my veins as I take a step back and watch her get to her feet, all her men on standby, ready and willing to take me out if she were to ask. "You want to train me," I continue, swallowing hard, "then train me, but do not use this as some kind of excuse to make a point. I will bite my tongue and reel in my attitude, but you've gotta drop the bullshit act as well."

Gia studies me for a moment, her gaze narrowed. "I don't think you've got a grasp on just how serious this is," she tells me. "I'm not training you just so you can learn how to defend yourself, and I sure as hell don't have you here as some idiotic way to claim you," she says, stepping closer to me and lowering her voice. "*I will fall.* Whether it be in twelve months or twenty-four. I'm going to fall, and all of this is going to be thrust into your hands whether you want it or not. Looking at you now, I'm not exactly overcome with confidence. You're weak and rely on your attitude to get by, and while it's entertaining to watch you embarrass yourself, it's going to get my men—*our men*—killed."

Gia holds my stare as I step into her, my eyes narrowed and full of fire. The elevator dings in the distance, and I watch over her shoulder as Zeke steps out, his hands full of training clothes and a pair of Nikes. His eyes come to mine and immediately narrow, seeing the distinct tension between his boss and me.

I only have a moment to say what needs to be said before he gets close enough, and the moment fades, so I glance back at my mother, letting her hear the anger, grief, and torment that overwhelms me. "You want me to say what I have to say without the bullshit attitude, then I will," I tell her, piling on the facts hard and thick. "Your first mistake, showing your true colors and standing by to allow Giovanni to murder the men that your daughter is in love with. Your second mistake was assuming that I'd willingly lead and protect the members of your family, knowing that you stood by and did nothing. You want me to stand at the head of your family with their best interests at heart, then you need to find a way to make things right because right now, there's absolutely nothing stopping me from walking away the moment your heart stops beating."

A pair of Nikes hits my chest so hard that I stumble away from Gia, my sharp gaze snapping up to Zeke. "Get dressed," he spits, falling into Gia's side, venom pooling in his eyes.

My hands close around the training clothes bunched with the shoes, and I tear them out of his grip. Stepping forward, I stop right at his side, my gaze lifting to his. "I'm really looking forward to the day she dies and you become my number one yes man," I murmur. "If I were you, I'd be doing everything in my power to make sure that I'm not the asshole left scrubbing toilets day in and day out. Be careful, I'm not the bitch you want to fuck with."

With that, I tighten my hold on my training clothes and walk across the room, my heart thundering in my chest.

# FOUR

"Again," Gia snaps before my back has even hit the training mat.

I drop to the ground with a hard thud, a whoosh of breath racing from my lungs as I groan in pain. We've been going at this for three hours and my body is exhausted. A light sweat coats my skin as my lungs scream for oxygen.

She stands by, watching as Zeke kicks my ass over and over again, demanding me to be better, and damn it, he doesn't hold back, though I didn't expect anything different. To be honest, had he gone easy on me, I'd never have been able to respect him. The boys never went easy on me in training, they never held back, and I was grateful for it, but it's clear from how brutal Zeke is, they trained me with care, with love. Not Zeke. He simply doesn't give a shit if I were to get hurt.

Groaning, I roll onto my stomach, trying to get my hands and knees under me, only when I'm too slow, Zeke's foot sweeps out under my midsection, kicking my knees back out and watching as my body drops to the mat with a loud *oomph*.

"Get up," he spits, irritated to be kept waiting.

My cheeks blow out with a heavy breath as I clench my jaw, desperately trying to reel in my attitude, but the fucker is pushing my limits, and after watching the boys die last night, I can't be blamed for the shit I do.

Zeke stands over me with his arms crossed like the asshole he is, and I quickly get back to my hands and knees, going faster to avoid the wrath of his temper. Only this time, when I pull myself just a little higher, I let my hand shoot out, connecting hard with his junk.

The fucker doesn't even flinch as my knuckles slam against something hard, so fucking hard it feels like metal.

I scream out, agony tearing through my hand as Zeke simply watches me, a cocky smirk on his lips. His hand curls into a fist and he taps his knuckles against his junk, letting me hear the solid sound coming from beneath. "Really, Shayne? You're a scrappy fighter, trained by DeAngelis scum. You didn't think I'd come prepared for a cheap shot to my cock? I'm insulted."

Shaking out my hand, I get back to my feet and throw myself right into his face. "Call them scum one more fucking time and I'll gut you while you sleep."

Zeke laughs and shoves his hand into my shoulder, forcing me back a step. "That's a mighty roar for such a little cub."

The insult stings, but I try to hide it, not wanting to give him more ammunition to use against me. If there were any way for me to get through to him and make him hurt, I would have done it long ago.

Zeke immediately gets back into my training, not taking it easy on me at all. I block his advances, each of my movements getting sloppier by the second, the exhaustion quickly creeping up on me. "So, tell me," I spit, watching his every move. "Where were you while the brothers were being slaughtered? Watching the show with a fucking grin on your face?"

"A dead enemy of mine is another fucker who can't hurt my woman and another night that I get to rest easy, so you bet your fucking ass that I was watching every moment of it, making sure they went down hard," he says with a smirk, his fist shooting straight through my defenses and landing a devastating blow against my ribs, no doubt one that will turn them black and blue within minutes.

Tears sting my eyes, but I refuse to let them fall. How the hell am I supposed to stay here with people who would have happily killed the brothers had their father not already done it? Fucking hell. It won't be long until one of these assholes pushes me a little too far and I accidentally slit their throat in return.

Anger pulses through my veins as fire burns in my eyes, making each of my movements harder to control. "Focus," Gia growls, "you're not going to improve as long as your mind is stuck on those boys. I have told you already, Giovanni's sons were not my problem, nor will I make space for their memory in my training room."

I scoff, my gaze quickly flicking her way as I duck under Zeke's strong arm. "Oh, but it was your fucking problem the second Giovanni wanted to make me his bride," I spit. "Tell me, if the boys were still alive, would you have bothered to step in or did you plan to let them handle your fucking dirty work?"

Zeke pulls back, his brows furrowing as he turns back toward Gia. "The fuck is she talking about?"

Lesson number one. Don't turn your back on your enemy.

My hand curls into a tight fist, and with everything I have, I rear back and throw my arm forward, letting it fly free and slam against the side of Zeke's face, cracking his nose and sending a spray of blood hurtling across the training mat.

A strangled roar tears from deep in his chest, but before I can even congratulate myself on such a good hit defending the boys' honor, his hand shoots out and curls around my throat. He rips me up off the training mat, my feet dangling for only a moment before he throws me down with his whole body weight. My head rebounds off the mat so hard that I feel the solid ground through the protective cushioning.

My vision blurs, and I don't hear a damn thing apart from a sharp ringing in my ear. But judging by the way the veins protrude from his throat as his face reddens, he's definitely saying something.

Only a moment passes before my vision clears and my lungs begin to ache. I struggle around his hold on my throat, gasping for air, but it never comes. My head starts to spin and I'm not sure if it's from the lack of oxygen or the hit I took, but when Gia steps in beside us and places a calming hand on Zeke's shoulder, he immediately releases me.

The loud ringing begins to ease, and I can hear her murmured voice as Zeke pushes up off the ground. "Go and get yourself cleaned up," she orders. "That's enough for today."

Without a backward glance, Zeke takes off, leaving me with the incubator. She crouches down, her eyes raking over the bruises marring my skin. "Zeke is not a man whom you want to make an enemy of," she tells me. "You will do well to remember that."

I swallow hard, pushing up onto my palm as my other hand searches the back of my head, feeling a lump already forming, and damn, it's going to be a nasty one. Gia watches me cautiously. "You're going to need to ice that," she says. "Zeke's given me plenty of those over the years, and trust me, it's going to get worse before it gets better."

I glare up at her, shakily getting to my feet. My brow arches and I cut in front of her, desperate for the water bottle sitting across the room. "Do I need to give you the number for the domestic abuse hotline?" I mutter. "Or do you guys just like playing dirty?"

With my back to Gia, I don't see her response, but I can all but feel the sharp glare digging into the back of my head. I scoop up my drink bottle and take a quick gulp before crumbling down to the sparring mat, every last ounce of my energy depleted.

The water is like a gift from the heavens, and I go through nearly half my bottle before Gia rolls her eyes and slowly walks back toward me. "Take small sips. You'll give yourself a stitch if you continue gulping it down like a pig."

My gaze snaps up to hers. "Am I supposed to assume that you

actually care? Because you've fucked up that ruse at least a hundred times since I've been here."

"I am not foolish, Shayne. I don't expect you to care about me or want a mother-daughter relationship, but don't assume I don't care for you because I'm pushing you to be a leader. Sending you away after your birth was the hardest decision I ever made, but I truly believed that I was doing the right thing back then. Perhaps I was wrong," she adds. "Perhaps sending you away wasn't what was best for you. You could have grown up in this home, and I could have molded you into that strong young woman I see hiding inside you. You sure as hell would have been smart enough to keep from falling for those DeAngelis boys. You may have even been the one to end them yourself."

I gape at her. "Is that your version of an apology? Because it sucked."

"Look, Shayne. I want us to be able to get along. I know you don't see it now, but I want you to succeed. I want the best for you, and I believe that given time, you'll come to love it here. However, this training is necessary. When it comes time for you to step into my shoes and rule over my empire, I want you to be able to make the right decisions, I want you to be able to rise up and take the challenge with both hands. I want you to make this role your bitch, just as I did when my father passed."

Letting out a sigh, I take one more small sip before capping the bottle and meeting her softening gaze again. "Then tell me everything. How did you find out that Giovanni had taken me, and how the hell did you end up striking a deal with the boys?"

Gia presses her lips into a hard line before letting out a sigh and moving just a little bit closer. "To be completely honest with you, I didn't know Giovanni had taken you until his sons held that party in their home. Giovanni had been off my radar for a while so when whispers sounded of his sons having themselves a new girl, I made it my business, and the shock of realizing it was you … I had to play the game carefully. I wanted to storm their castle the moment I realized, but if Giovanni caught wind that I knew of his plans, he would have ended your life before I had a chance to save it." She pauses and takes a subtle breath, watching me too closely for comfort.

"My men watched you carefully. Those boys had quite the reputation. They weren't gentle with their girls, and I hated that they would use you in the same way, but my blood runs through your veins. I knew you would be strong enough to withstand their abuse. You were fine where you were, nor did I wish to start a war over something so … trivial."

My nerves grind at her calling my kidnapping trivial. Nothing that I suffered through, the guns, stab wounds, the bathtub, felt trivial to me.

"We followed your every step, until you went off the radar. The boys were making quite a lot of noise and news quickly spread that Giovanni had taken you. Believe me when I say that there were a lot of people out there looking for you, however only a small handful with good intentions."

I swallow hard, the memories of what happened in that cell haunting me, but I keep quiet, desperate to hear the story.

"I have the kind of resources that those boys didn't have access to, and I was able to get a location on your whereabouts, which is where things got tricky. I had a decision to make. It was clear to me at that point that you had formed a *bond* with the brothers, one I will never understand, however I didn't wish to strip you of that quite so soon. I know of your ... *issues* with the Miller brothers and how fiercely the DeAngelis boys fought to protect you. It was clear that you were safe with them, despite their reputations. There was also the risk that had my men stormed Giovanni's desert cells, you wouldn't have gone with them. There is only so many times a girl can be kidnapped before she loses her mind. The timing wasn't right, so I arranged a meeting with the brothers and gave up your location considering they would ensure your safety and release you when the time was right. The deal was that I didn't want any complications. They weren't to harm you or fall for you in any way. It was to be a clean break."

I shake my head, knowing just how scared they were, and that they would have agreed to absolutely anything if it meant getting me back—they would have given up their own lives had she asked. "I can imagine," I tell her. "Though you know they would have never given me up. They were well and truly in love with me by then."

"Well, they certainly didn't give me that impression. It wasn't until I saw you with them in person that I realized the bond you shared was much more than mere friendship."

I scoff, a smirk stretching across my face. "Apparently you're easily fooled," I murmur. "That's good to know. I'll keep that in mind."

Gia narrows her eyes. "I won't forget you said that."

A soft smile plays on my lips, thinking of just how crazy in love they were, though in their own strange way. "You know, they would have gone to war just to keep me by their side."

A sparkle hits Gia's eye as she presses her hand to my shoulder. Her lips pull into a wicked grin. "I know. I was looking forward to it."

Gia gives me a tight smile, one that certainly doesn't reach her eyes, and as she starts to walk away, her words hit me like a wrecking ball. She said that despite the boys' reputation, she was willing to leave me with them. She's known since that very first party that they kidnapped me, yet she refused to rescue me when I needed it the most. Before the bathtub, before Marcus got shot, and before my captors became my everything. I was terrified, waking up in the middle of the night, certain that death was knocking on my door, yet she still didn't come.

Scrambling to my feet, I turn on my heel, and hurry the few steps to catch up to her. My body aches from my brutal training session with her playtoy, but I put it to the back of my mind and hold my head high so that when she turns, I can look her dead in the eye. "Gia," I call after her. "Wait."

She spins around, her brow arched, and if I look close enough, I swear I can see a hint of impatience. "What is it, Shayne? I have a nose to set."

Guilt flurries deep in my gut but remembering the cruel words Zeke spoke of the boys, I push it away. "Yeah, that sounds like a you problem," I tell her, taking one more step to put me right in her way. "I just need to know ... this whole arrangement we've got going on, it's purely because you need an heir, isn't it? Nothing else."

"Shayne, I have already told you how I feel about this. I am glad that I have the chance to get to know you as my daughter."

I shake my head. "Any mother who truly gave a shit, would have done everything in her power to save her daughter the moment she knew that she was kidnapped by a man like Giovanni DeAngelis, yet you thought of it as a holding cell, somewhere to shove me until it suited your schedule."

Her gaze flickers, cutting away from my heavy stare, so I continue, knowing damn well that she feels uncomfortable having this discussion. "Tell me this," I say. "If you weren't dying, if you still had another fifty years as the leader of the Moretti family, would you have bothered to rescue me at all? If there were no need for an heir …"

Her brows furrow as she looks at me in shock. "Of course I would have. When the timing was right and when Giovanni least expected it, I would have found a way to take you back. My blood runs through your veins, Shayne. You are a Moretti and therefore, you belong to me."

"Yeah," I scoff. "As a possession."

Gia sighs, reading the words I haven't spoken out loud. "It is the same for how I feel about Zeke," she starts. "Love is weakness. Love makes us vulnerable and puts targets on people's backs while giving our enemies something to use against us. I will not love you, Shayne, if that is what you are asking of me. I sent you away so that you couldn't be used against me. You are here solely to become my heir, the leader of my family, and nothing else. If we happen to connect in that time and create a … comradery, then that is wonderful. However, do not hold out hope for something deeper because you're only setting yourself up for disappointment."

I shrug my shoulders. "What does it matter? I've been let down my whole life by the people who I called family. I'm not going to magically expect that to change now."

Her lips pull into a tight line and a swirl of anger flares within her eyes, one that she does a shitty job of concealing. "If that is all," she says.

"One more question," I rush out before she gets the chance to leave. She watches me, waiting impatiently, so I take a shaky breath, terrified of what her answer is going to be. "Am I a prisoner here?"

Gia's eyes widen in shock. "No," she says, her brows pinching together as she stares at me through a horrified gaze. "Absolutely not. I have explained to you that you are here for training. I thought I made that quite clear."

"So, I can walk away from this at any point?" I challenge, my brow slowly arching. "I can decide that this life isn't for me, that I don't want anything to do with it and go home to my shitty apartment, live my life the way that I'd planned?"

Gia swallows hard, her gaze dropping for a brief moment, telling me exactly what I want to know. "No, Shayne," she says. "You cannot walk away from this. As long as you have my DNA, you will be the heir to the Moretti empire. Your name is whispered on my enemies lips, so know that the moment you decide to run from me, they will be searching for you. This is not a prison, and I am not your warden. However, you cannot leave without my explicit say so. Don't be foolish, child. I am giving you free rein of my home, full access, but if I get even the slightest hint that you will make a break for it, I will not hesitate to lock you up."

An unladylike scoff tears from the back of my throat as I walk forward, knocking my shoulder against hers. I stop right beside her, anger rolling off me in waves. "The last person who pissed me off accidentally lost their organs to a chainsaw," I tell her. "If you say this is not a prison, then don't treat it like one. If you bite me, I will bite back."

With that, I walk out of the training room and take myself back to my room where I'll stay until Zeke comes barging through my door first thing in the morning.

# FIVE

My body aches as I lower myself down into the bathtub, and I suck in a sharp hiss between my teeth when the freezing water hits my skin. I've been training for a week, day in and day out. Gia's men will barge into my room at any damn hour they see fit and demand my presence down in the training room, sometimes only letting me sleep a few hours at a time. Gia warned me that training would be brutal, but I never imagined this.

Tears of exhaustion leak from my eyes, and I hate myself for not being stronger through this, but if I just keep pushing, just keep showing up, it'll eventually get easier. I can feel myself starting to improve. I'm still far from being able to protect myself the way my boys could, but I feel the muscles in my arms getting stronger, my reflexes faster, and my ability to read someone's movement is more precise.

The boys had years of training and no amount of early morning sessions is going to bring me up to their level, but I have to keep trying, despite how much I hate it here.

I haven't spoken a word to Gia since my first training session, though I'd bet anything that Zeke has been reporting back to her every day. Either that, or there are cameras in the training room, probably all over the property. Perhaps I should check that out when Zeke inevitably drags my ass back down there in a few hours, at least that way I'll know which direction to flip the bird every time I walk in.

I've gone over everything—combat skills, weaponry training, Moretti family politics—and it's all fucking bullshit. The last thing I want is to be initiated into this family, though like everyone keeps reminding me, Moretti blood pulses through my veins, so I don't get a choice in the matter.

Lucky me.

*Insert eye roll here.*

As much as I hate to admit it, Zeke is a good trainer, crooked nose and all. He pushes me to my limits, and when my body begins to fail, he takes me straight across to the shooting range, always keeping me moving, always training, always pushing me to go past the point where I want to give up, and damn it, I've learned to keep my mouth shut around him. The more I bitch at him, the harder his hits become, but at least they make me feel something.

When I'm not training, when it's just me alone in this massive room, I'm dead inside. I don't feel a goddamn thing.

Scooting down in the oversized bathtub, I let the ice water cover my whole body, blowing out my cheeks as the chill seeps into my bones. I hate this, but my body needs it to help recover from the intense sessions I've been suffering through for the past seven days. I sink lower and lower in the tub until only the important parts of my face are protruding from the water, and I try to relax, try to loosen my taut muscles, and hell, after a while, it even starts to feel good. Or perhaps the water is just cold enough that I've gone numb and lost all feeling. It's hard to tell the difference when my soul no longer exists.

Just like every time I'm alone, my mind filters through everything that went down that night. I've cried more tears than I thought possible, yet they just keep coming when I least expect them.

The grief is too much, too hard to push through. I need them here to hold me, to tell me that I can get through this. I've been living in complete darkness since the moment their bodies crashed into the grass, like I've been asleep this whole time and nothing will wake me until I know they're okay, but that's never going to happen. There's no way Giovanni would have allowed them to survive after that. His plans have changed, and the boys' betrayal was the final straw. He's going to rise up just like everyone kept warning me, and it's going to be brutal.

The water's surface reflects the sunlight streaming through the floor-to-ceiling window, and as I blow out all the air in my lungs, I slip further into its icy grip. The cold water burns my face, but I don't dare move.

What's the point? There's nothing here for me, only a life filled with tragedy. Giovanni is always going to win. Even if I somehow manage to get through this and end his miserable life.

I don't want to be here. I don't want to be Gia's little protégée, and I sure as hell don't want to live a life with targets constantly on my back. I just want to find peace.

My lungs begin to ache as my body screams at me to resurface.

I've never felt so low, so hurt, so full of despair.

A little voice spears its way through my mind. *The boys would be so mad at you right now. Look how weak you are, giving up on yourself, letting Giovanni win. They didn't love you so you could lose the fight, lose everything that they worked for. Ten years in their prison castle and a lifetime of abuse just for you to give up on them now. I'm so ashamed of you. Are they not worthy of your fight? They saved you, they brought you back from the brink of death time and time again. Now it's your turn to take everything they so carefully laid out for you. Take what you're owed. You're not this weak bitch. They made you stronger than this. Send them off with what they're owed.*

Fuck.

I push up out of the bathtub, my arms hooking over the edges as I gasp for air, my lungs straining for relief as their faces appear in my mind.

How could I have been so fucking stupid? I can't give this up now. I have to push through. I have to make this right and somehow survive.

Fuck Gia. Fuck Zeke. And fuck Giovanni DeAngelis. That prick will die by my hand whether I have help or not. I have to get out of here. I have to find a way because that's exactly what Roman, Levi, and

Marcus would expect of me—no. That's what they'd demand.

Though, if they're rotting down in the deepest pits of hell, I can guarantee that they're already too busy ruling over the other assholes down there to be bothered thinking about the bullshit life they endured up here on earth. They'd be right at home down there, even the devil himself would be kneeling to my men.

Reaching through the bottom of the ice bath, I release the drain and pull my aching body from the tub, stepping out onto the soft floor mat and grabbing the massive towel from the heated rack. I pull it around my freezing body, holding it tight as I dry off and promptly drop it back to the pristine tiles.

Strutting out into the bedroom, I pull open the walk-in closet's big double doors and rifle through all my new clothes. There are so many things in here, shirts, leggings, jeans, summer dresses, gowns, not to mention the vast array of shoes, heels, and boots. I've never ventured further than the top two drawers—underwear, training crops, and workout tights … plus my Nikes. I have no need for all the other crap, and as much as I appreciate the thought, none of this shit is my style. My clothes are back in the DeAngelis mansion, and I won't stop until I'm right back there, taking ownership of every last one of them.

In order to get out of here, it's time to step up my game. I need to be strong. I need to be ready, but more than that, I need a fucking plan.

Despite not seeing Gia since my first day here, I still have no idea what her intentions are when it comes to Giovanni or his newborn son. She hasn't given me any indication on whether she plans to help me, and so I have no choice but to assume she's keeping quiet to avoid telling me no, simply because she doesn't want to deal with the outburst that will follow.

Slipping out of my bedroom, I creep down the hallway and to the stairs. I don't see anyone below, but that's not unusual. Though, how would I really know? The only times I come up and down here is when I'm being dragged to the training room, apart from that, I've never bothered to search around.

The elevator for the training room is to the right of the stairs, so when I reach the bottom, I take off to the left instead. Gia gave me free rein of this place, as long as I play by her rules, so what could a little snooping hurt?

The home is bigger and nicer than Giovanni's place, though I didn't even think that was possible. Gia defied all odds when building this masterpiece. It has everything a woman could ever need. Two massive ballrooms, one of them the size of Giovanni's, while the other is even bigger. There are formal and informal living rooms, meeting rooms, and three separate dining rooms ... though room is probably the wrong term for them, they're more like dining halls.

Everything is glossy, white marble, and I'm struck with the thought of the kind of place both Gia and Roman could build had they ever been given the chance to work together. Roman had an incredible eye for detail, and I'm sure in another life, he would have made an amazing architect. Gia, on the other hand, has the type of interior design skills that any homeowner would dream of. Every corner of every room has been meticulously thought out and flows perfectly from one space into the next.

I can't imagine how much this place would have cost to build. It's insane … but it's also quiet. Too quiet.

When I was with the boys, I could always hear something, whether it be the sounds of the wolves racing through the long hallways, Marcus maniacally laughing as he thought up new ways to kill someone, or the heavy thumping of Levi's drums through every corner of the home. Roman though, no one ever heard from him. When he made a noise, it was meant to be heard. He was always so broody, it made me wonder about the things that tormented his mind while he was alone.

The soft murmur of voices trail down a long hallway and I stand at the top of it, staring down as I bite my lip. The hallway is decorated with big doors on either side, all of them closed apart from the one at the very end. Something screams at me that this is Gia's personal office, the space where she conducts all of her shady business deals and makes the kind of decisions that change people's lives, sometimes for the better, but I'd be lying if I said the majority of those changes were good ones.

Curiosity flares through me, but do I really want to risk going down there and listening to a conversation that wasn't meant for me? Especially a conversation that's intended to be behind closed doors.

Hell to the motherfucking yes, I do.

Call me a fool, but I'm not going to get anywhere from shying away.

I sneak down the long hallway like some kind of ninja, feeling like the baddest bitch who ever lived. Only every breath I take makes me want to strangle myself. I've never tried to breathe so quietly before, but the more I do it, the louder it seems to get. What the fuck is wrong with me?

My heart thunders like it had a bad dose of crack, and as I move further down the hall, the tone of the voices becomes clear. There's a female and a male, the woman clearly being Gia but the man … I don't know, his voice is so low that I can't quite make it out.

I haven't spent enough time with any of Gia's guards to really recognize their voices, but as I hear the name 'DeAngelis' murmured through the open door, I suck in a breath, straining to hear every last word.

"That's not possible," Gia says as my brows furrow, desperate to know what the fuck is going on and why they need to be talking business about the DeAngelis family. Has something happened? Are they preparing an attack on Giovanni? "Not even a whisper?"

"Nothing," the man says, his tone suggesting that it's possibly Zeke, though I could be wrong. "No one has heard a thing since the attack last week, at least where the brothers are concerned. Funeral arrangements have been made for Victor's four sons."

"But nothing for Giovanni's?"

There is a painful silence and I struggle to listen over the sound of my pulse thumping heavily in my ear drums. "You don't think …" Gia lets the words fall away as though she doesn't want to risk voicing her thoughts, as though what she's about to say could ruin everything.

"No," the other voice says, his tone firmer, confirming my suspicions. It's definitely Zeke. "They couldn't be alive. It's not possible. Not after what Giovanni did to them. Plus, those three gunshots that rang out as we were leaving. We'd be fools to assume they weren't kill shots right through his sons' skulls."

Bile rises in my throat at just the thought of those bullets penetrating the boys' heads, but I swallow it down, needing to put it aside to hear what's going on in that room. "They're the biggest players in the DeAngelis family," Gia says. "If they were dead, people would be talking. The DeAngelis family swore loyalty to those boys. If Giovanni truly killed them, the remaining family would be scrambling for their lives, begging for forgiveness, but you're telling me there's nothing but silence?"

"That's right," Zeke returns. "Unless Giovanni hasn't made it public. They could be dead and the family simply doesn't know it yet."

"No," Gia says, her tone forceful and strained. "There were too many guards. Even if they were sworn to silence, information would have been leaked by now. There's only one possible outcome of this."

"The fuckers are still alive," Zeke finishes for her, his voice a breathy whisper, full of disbelief, and if I'm not wrong, a hint of awe.

Hope spurs through my chest as I suck in a shaky breath. Could they really think my boys are alive? Is there truly a chance?

Silence fills the room again, and I find myself edging closer to the door, needing to hear every last word. "It's just not possible," Gia murmurs, her tone filled with confusion, and it sounds as though she may be talking to herself, thinking out loud. "You saw those injuries. They couldn't have survived that, but then—"

"Those boys have defied much worse odds than that."

"So, you think we should work off the assumption that they're still alive?"

Zeke scoffs. "My assumption is that if they are alive, if those three gunshots weren't aimed between their eyes, then they're barely holding on."

Fuck, fuck, fuck. FUCK.

That darkness that has consumed me for the past seven days explodes inside my chest, waking up the devil who lives inside me. I haven't felt a damn thing since they crumbled into the grass and for the first time, that small ray of hope begins to flicker deep in my chest.

My boys. I fucking knew they wouldn't give up without a fight. They wouldn't leave me like that. They aren't done here yet. They have too much to accomplish, too much to give.

My hands shake at my sides as the need to barge into Gia's office flutters through me. I have to get out of here. If there's a chance they're still alive, I have to make it to them. They've saved me more times than I can count, and now it's time to return the favor.

Tears of happiness streak down my face as I try to contain myself. I know there's a good chance Zeke is wrong, that they really are dead, but I have no choice but to believe because, without them, I have nothing.

There's a soft thud, possibly Gia dropping down into a large desk chair as she lets out a heavy sigh, the sound filled with thought and unease. I have to pull myself up, holding back as I hear footsteps. Zeke makes his way around her desk, putting himself at her side, probably offering her what little comfort he can. "What's the plan, boss?" he says, his voice muffled and low.

Silence follows, and I don't doubt that Gia is weighing all of her options, figuring out the best course of action to ensure that every possible outcome keeps the Moretti family on top. "There is no plan," she finally says, my back stiffening. How could she have no plan? There is only one obvious answer to this. We go in and we save them. "Do not speak a word of this. If Giovanni has those boys, they'd be locked up and slowly dying. We keep quiet and let nature take its course. Soon enough, they'll be riddled with infection to the point they'll probably beg each other to take their lives. They'll die, and when that happens, we break the news to Shayne, tell her there was nothing we could do to help them, that we tried, but it was too late. Vengeance will spark in her, and she'll push herself until she's up to the task of taking out Giovanni herself. We won't even need to lift a finger."

"What then?" he questions, amusement shining in his tone. "Does she return here? It won't be long until she realizes that you're not sick."

The fuck? Not sick?

"No. We let her take out Giovanni. Without him or his sons to continue the line, the whole DeAngelis family will crumble. Once she's completed her task, we put a bullet through her head and take Giovanni's newborn son as our own. The Moretti family was built on my blood and my blood alone. I sit on the throne, and I will not risk her swooping in here and trying to take it out from under me. So, for now, we turn her into a warrior to do our bidding. She knows the inner secrets to that family, and we will corrupt every last one of them until they finally fall. Keep your enemies close, Zeke. The Moretti family is only just getting started."

Well ... fuck.

# SIX

**W**hat the actual fuck just happened?

I sit up in my room, my mind reeling from everything I just learned downstairs.

One. Gia is a lying sack of shit who will do absolutely anything it takes to get what she wants—cross anyone, stab them in the back, betray her own blood. She's a coward and a fool, and at some point, I'm going to make her pay for what I heard through her office walls, but I have bigger problems right now.

Two. There's a good chance that my boys are still breathing, and if they are, ain't nothin' gonna stop me from getting to them.

Watching through my bedroom window, I spy Gia's guards and

begin to take note of their schedules and faces. There are about fifteen of them who are regulars here, working in shifts every day and night. I see them down in the training room and around the house every now and then, but there are maybe another ten who I've only seen once or twice over the past week.

I get Gia's need for having guards at her constant disposal, but it's kinda embarrassing. The boys never needed hired help to get a job done. They had each other and that's all they ever needed. I doubt Gia would have gotten anywhere without the line of hired muscle at her back. The Moretti family may be bigger and stronger than the DeAngelis family, but at least the DeAngelis family can stand proud knowing that its rightful leaders are the kind of men who would bleed to protect it. I can't say the same for Gia.

She's a spineless bitch and I can't wait to crush her.

My bedroom door slams open with a BANG and my head snaps back, taking in Zeke standing in my doorway. His gaze travels over my body, no doubt surprised to see me dressed and ready for today's training session. "You're ready," he states, his brow arching as a flicker of surprise crosses his face.

I push away from the windowsill, not needing the usual ten-minute warning, swallowing down every bullshit comment about what I heard downstairs that wants to come flying out of my mouth. "Wow, you're observant today," I say, striding straight past him, hating the thought of having my back turned to the man who will most likely be responsible for ending my life. But as long as they don't know I overheard them in Gia's office, I should be safe. I hope.

My hands pulse at my sides, curling in and out of fists as I do what I can to relax. Ever since finding out the boys could be alive, I haven't been able to concentrate. The desperation to get out of here drives my every move and sitting still simply isn't possible.

I need to run.

I need to make a plan.

I need to find a way to get to them.

Nothing else matters to me, not anymore.

The boys could be suffering; they could be laying in dirty cells in agony, slowly bleeding to death. Maybe I'm their only chance at survival. Fuck, even if it means ending my own life just to save theirs, I'd do it. I need to play Gia's game more now than ever because the alternative ... shit, I can't even think about that.

Skipping down the steps, I beat Zeke to the bottom, but I feel his hard stare digging into my back the whole time. I grip the railing at the bottom and catapult myself around the corner, leading toward the ridiculously expensive elevator. Hitting the button, I wait patiently for it to arrive and by the time the door opens, Zeke is there, moving in beside me. We move silently into the elevator together, and as the door closes us in, his suspicious gaze slowly turns on me. "Why?" he questions, his tone low and curious.

I shrug my shoulders, avoiding his piercing stare. "Couldn't sleep. Figured I'd get a head start on the day."

I sense his eyes narrowing further, but when the *ding* sounds our arrival at the training room and the door begins to open, it releases the tension in the small metal box, and his gaze finally falls away. I stride into the room with a sharp eye, taking note of every man here, where they stand, who they spar with, and what weapons they have at their disposal.

I won't allow myself to be ambushed in this house. I've been prey to assholes of this world too many times, and that shit sure as fuck won't be happening again.

"Where do you want me?" I murmur, feeling Zeke hovering far too closely.

He glances over at the shooting range, his lips pressing into a tight line when he finds all the lanes full. "Training mat," he mutters, a hint of disappointment in his tone. "We need to work on your speed and agility. They're lacking. We'll shoot this afternoon."

Irritation burns through me as I turn on my heel and march across the room. Not only because of his comments about my lacking skills, but because I'd had my heart set on shooting or at least some form of weapon training. Don't get me wrong, I'm not a whore for shooting, I don't particularly love it, but when I'm on the training mats and my body starts to ache, this bitch gets a little too emotional. I can't always trust myself to bite my tongue.

Zeke has a particular fire about him when training, he pushes me to my limits and then keeps going until I break. He's ruthless, and right now, I can't trust my emotions not to get in the way. It's going to be one of the hardest things I'll ever do, especially because the few hours I stay down here are another few hours the boys will suffer.

"Alright, in position," he says as we step up onto the training mats. He pauses for a brief moment, watching as I cross the mat and turn to meet him head on. My gaze quickly flicks over his shoulder as I take note of my new position in the room, where guards now stand, how quickly they could get to me, and just how many I'll need to fight off if it comes down to it.

Zeke sees the quick calculation and his gaze narrows just a bit, but he decides not to say anything about it. Perhaps he thinks I'm just getting better at knowing my surroundings, a lesson he taught me himself, or perhaps he thinks I'm a shady bitch and I'm up to something. The asshole can read me like a book, so I wouldn't be surprised if I've already screwed myself over.

I'm so fucked. So fucking fucked.

Keeping my gaze on Zeke, I try to appear as the broken, frustrated girl I was before overhearing his conversation with Gia, and I plaster a scowl across my face, waiting for his instructions. His eyes remain narrowed. "I'm going to come at you," he tells me, not shrugging off his suspicions, but definitely putting them aside to do the job his boss has demanded of him. "I want you to block me. You'll need to read my every move. Watch my feet, watch how I advance toward you. Be prepared. My moves are going to get faster, more precise, and the moment you see a chance, I want you to strike back."

Swallowing hard, I give a firm nod, not needing much more instruction than that, but I don't know why he bothers with the long, drawn-out explanation when he could sum it up with a simple, *I'm going to kick your ass for the fun of it, try and stop me.*

Zeke moves toward me, and I brace myself, watching his every move. I've gotten pretty used to his style over the past week, but my head has never been as clear as it is today. Today, I'm ready for him.

His weight shifts onto his right foot, and just like that, his hand shoots out and I throw everything I have into my defense. His hit slices straight past my face, and without even a hint of warning, my hand that just blocked him flies back up in a scrappy, backhanded whack to the side of his face.

He blinks quickly, taking a step back as though he's never been so confused in his life. He hadn't expected me to get through, especially when he had his full attention on me. So far, the only hits I've been able to land are the bullshit ones that happen when his back is turned. "You're focused today," he says, trying to sound as though he's giving me the nod of approval, yet the suspicion is still deep in his tone.

My brows furrow, and I watch him carefully as his jaw ticks. I bet the asshole wants to rub his face, but he won't dare lift a finger to his jaw in my presence and silently admit that it actually hurts. "Would you prefer that I wasn't?" I throw back at him, holding my fighter's stance, more than ready for him to come at me with a harder, more brutal edge. "I didn't realize that beating the shit out of unsuspecting young women is what got you hard, but I'll keep that in mind."

He snaps out at me, his hands moving like lightning and proving just how much I still have to learn. His big hand closes around my throat, squeezing tight. "Don't push me, Shayne. I am not in the mood for your bullshit today."

I keep myself calm, having learned that panicking in situations like this doesn't help anybody. So instead, I throw my hand up, bracing my fingers together as I spear them right at his throat in a wicked blow.

He immediately releases his hold around my neck, and I suck in a desperate breath as he stumbles back, clutching his throat and trying not to cough. Rage burns through his gaze, but I stand tall. "You're a scrappy fighter, Zeke, trained by Moretti scum," I say, mimicking the words he'd used on me during our first training session. "You didn't think I'd come prepared for a cheap shot? I'm insulted."

I walk around him, keeping my sharp stare on him at all times, watching the stillness of his body and waiting for him to strike. His eyes never leave mine and that suspicion only grows until something finally snaps into place. Whatever he thinks he knows, he doesn't say a damn word, and I briefly wonder just how much shit I've put myself in, but he lashes back out at me, throwing his whole body into it.

My eyes are wide, focusing on his every movement, but he's too fast and keeps getting through with devastating blows, but I don't give up. I've learned what giving up means over the past week and that's not something I want to put myself through again, so I keep fighting, keep blocking, even when my aching lungs scream for it to end.

Zeke advances on me, every step he takes bringing him closer and closer. He's trying to force me back, get me trapped between him and the wall with nowhere to run, but I've been trapped far too many times to allow that kind of bullshit to go down. So, with every step he takes toward me, I sidestep, moving me across the mat and forcing him to turn until he's the one with his back to the wall.

He meets me blow for blow and I block his vicious strikes against my forearms, but when he gets past my defenses and slams his strong fist against my ribs, I go down like a sack of shit. Rolling myself away from him, I scramble to my feet as Zeke saunters after me, but I'm too slow, feeling his tight grip curl around my back. Now, if the boys hadn't taught me exactly what to do in this position, I might well and truly be fucked, but unlucky for Zeke, I don't allow assholes to grab me from behind, not anymore.

I slam my elbow back into his gut, winding him just like Roman taught me, and before the asshole even realizes what the fuck is happening, I slam my ass back into his groin before doubling over and using the momentum to my advantage. Grabbing his arm, I yank hard, flipping his body right over my head until his back slams onto the training mat with a heavy thump.

I drop on top of him, my knee pressing against his throat as I make a pistol out of my fingers, pressing it right to his temple. "BANG! You're dead," I tell him, arching my brow. Despite this session being just like all the others, he doesn't know why I'm extra pissed off and worked up. He knows I've bested him though, and that definitely hasn't happened before.

He narrows that sharp gaze again, and before I know it, his hand is wrapping around the knee that's crushing his windpipe, and with impressive strength, he throws me right off him. I barely catch myself, stumbling for a moment before balancing on two feet, and by the time I brace myself for more, Zeke is already standing before me.

Something catches my eye on the ground between us and I risk dropping my gaze to find a set of keys. They must have fallen out of his pocket when I threw him over my shoulder. He doesn't look down at them, but a man like Zeke is aware of his surroundings at all times.

He doesn't go after them, doesn't even comment about them, just stares at me, knowing that I know they're there, knowing that I know that he knows I know … fuck. I sound like an old episode of Friends.

Neither of us make a move. "You know," he says, watching me like a hawk as he slowly begins circling me. I move with him, never allowing him to get behind me.

A breathy scoff tears from the back of my throat and I arch a brow, letting him know just how ridiculous I think his question is. "That you dropped your keys on the ground and are now trying to use them as some form of bait. Yeah, I fucking know. They're right in front of my face."

"No," he says, his tone darkening, making me swallow with unease. "That's not what I'm talking about, and you know it." Zeke keeps circling me, and I watch him closely, not liking this one bit. The tension in the room has changed. I'm no longer his student, I'm his prey. He lowers his voice, keeping our conversation private from the other guards using the training room. "You're focused. You're alert, aware of your surroundings. Your reflexes are sharper than they've been since arriving here. You've counted the men in this room five times since we started, and you've been more interested in protecting yourself rather than lashing out, almost as though you won't risk an injury. Plus, you're looking at me as though I might decide to pull the fucking trigger at any given point." Zeke gets back to where he started, looking me dead in the eye as he positions himself directly in front of the security camera. "You know."

I shake my head, my eyes narrowed on him as my body screams

with unease, unsure where the fuck I'm supposed to go from here. My heart races, every other noise in the training room fading away. "I don't know what you're talking about."

Zeke scoffs. "Anyone ever tell you that you're a shitty liar?"

A wicked grin pulls at the corner of my lips. "All the fucking time."

Zeke's gaze drops to the keys on the mat before slowly coming back to mine, and just like that, his muscles tighten, and I brace myself for another attack. He races toward me, and I meet him in the middle, his hits harder, more forceful, and coming at me a million miles an hour. I groan and grunt, trying to keep up with his advanced level but he quickly gets his hands on me, throwing me down to the ground.

He comes down on top of me, his heavy body slamming into mine and forcing the air out of my lungs with a quick whoosh. I cry out, the pain all too real as my eyes widen with fear. I might not have admitted to knowing about the boys, but he's made it all too clear that he knows I showed up here ready to fight. He knows that I'm ready to bust my way out of here, and he knows that I'm prepared to burn this fucker down to the ground to make it happen.

I'm fucked.

Zeke pulls back, flipping my body and slamming me back into the cushioned mats, pressing my face into the ground, the keys right in front of my eyes. His knee comes down on my spine as his hand curls around the back of my neck, pinning me down. And although I'm pressed into a soft training mat, I can assure anyone who'll listen, there's nothing comfortable about this shit.

Zeke leans down, his movements putting more pressure against my spine. He doesn't stop until he's hovering right by my ear, his big body blocking both me and the keys from the security camera by the elevator. "Run," he murmurs, his voice so low I have to strain to hear it. "Take the fucking keys and run. Don't ever come back here unless it's to put a bullet through her fucking head."

My eyes widen, my breath coming in sharp, pained gasps, and no sooner than he slammed me down onto the mat, he tears away from me. "We're done here," he snaps before turning his back and walking away. He doesn't look back at me and I'm wondering if I just heard what the fuck I think I just heard.

Not taking any risks, my hand shoots out like lightning, scooping up the keys left abandoned on the mat.

# SEVEN

Fuck. This is stupid.

This is so fucking dumb, but what choice do I have?

I pace through my bedroom, my finger slipped through the circle key ring, flipping the keys back and forth in my hand, exactly as I've been doing since the moment that I arrived back in my room over twelve hours ago.

Zeke is Gia's second in command, he is her most loyal follower, her soldier, and lover, and now I'm supposed to trust that he would give me the resources I need to get away with a warning that if I were to come back, it better be to murder the woman who's supposedly my mother.

## WHAT THE EVER-LOVING FUCK IS HAPPENING HERE?

One. I can't trust Zeke. I don't know enough about him to assume he has my best interests at heart. Nor can I trust the key in my hand. The thing could have a GPS tracker in it, same goes for the car it belongs to. If I were to somehow get out of here, I'd have to ditch the car and find something else, but that shouldn't be too hard. At least, I hope.

Two. What if this is some elaborate set up? What if I try to make my escape only to find Zeke and Gia waiting for me on the other end, gun in hand and a bullet in the chamber?

Three. Gia Moretti isn't a woman I want to cross. No one in their right mind would want to cross her, but I don't know what choice I have, not after hearing the bullshit I heard last night.

Four. Roman, Levi, and Marcus need me more than anything and there's absolutely nothing that's going to stand in my way. To hell with Gia and her snake-like tendencies. My mind is made up. I'm going to rescue my boys, I'm going to save their lives, and when they're strong enough to stand with me, we're going to tear down the whole Moretti empire.

The familiar rumble of a motorbike sounds through the walls and my head whips around to my bedroom window. I race across the room, my eyes wide and alert as I continue to fidget with the keys, the anticipation and anxiety almost too much.

Night fell a few hours ago and darkness swept across Gia's property, but there's enough light coming from the house to showcase the motorbike screeching out of the underground garage and down the long driveway.

I have to strain to see out of my window that overlooks the side of the property, but I don't miss the convoy of black SUVs that trail behind it.

My breath catches in my throat.

Nobody said anything about Gia going out tonight, but why the hell would they? It's absolutely none of my business, especially considering that she has no intention of ever handing me her fortune. I race to my door, peering around the massive upstairs area. I never see anyone up here apart from Zeke and Gia, so I assume the guards aren't permitted on Gia's private levels, but I'm not stupid enough to not check first.

The coast is clear, and I break out across the upstairs area, dashing toward the window that overlooks the front of the property. I keep myself hidden behind the big pillars so that if Gia takes a look behind her, she won't be able to see my silhouette standing front and center, watching her leave.

At some point, she's going to make her move. She'll tell me that my boys are dead and then expect me to fight back. The longer I can delay that, the better. I don't want to give her any reason to doubt me, especially not now.

The convoy of SUVs take off through the iron gates, and Zeke waits behind on his bike, probably in charge of securing the gate after they leave. Once the last SUV is out of the way, I watch as Zeke enters the code into the keypad and as the gate slowly closes, I swear he looks back at the house, his eyes finding me hidden behind the pillar, but he's too far away for me to be sure.

The motorbike roars, and not wasting another second, he takes off after the SUVs just as the gate finishes closing. But just as the heavy iron closes the final gap, it bounces back as though something was blocking its locking mechanism.

My brows furrow as I watch the gate, waiting for someone to come back and secure it, but they never do. The remaining guards in the house don't race out to fix it, and the two guards who usually stand by the front gate day and night aren't even there.

Realization hits me like a wrecking ball. Plausible deniability.

Zeke did this to give me a way out, and when Gia has her men go over the records, they'll see that Zeke put in the code just as normal. Just like down in the training room when Zeke all but handed me those keys without the camera ever catching it.

Fuck me. Maybe I should trust him after all.

All I know is the gate isn't going to stay open like that for long. This is my shot, and fuck it all to hell, I'm taking it.

My gaze drops to the level below me, skimming over the two massive sets of stairs and lower into the foyer. I don't see any guards, but Gia would never leave her home without protection. The guards are here, it's just a question of finding out where.

Needing nothing but the key in my hand, I make my way down the steps, taking long, shallow breaths to keep as quiet as possible. I don't hear anyone, but I have to assume that anyone hired by Gia Moretti would be ready to strike at a moment's notice.

My feet hit the marble floor at the bottom of the steps and I pause. Gia's private garage is to the right, but the main garage where the black SUVs park is to the left. My gaze drops down to the key. It has a symbol on it that I don't recognize, but I'm not exactly a car person. What I do know is that there's nothing fancy about this key. It's just a regular car key, and I have to assume that anything parked in Gia's personal garage would be a little fancier than this.

I go to the left.

My feet barely brush the ground as I walk, stealthy and silent like the boys trained me to be, like a lion preparing to pounce. There are three rooms I need to go through to reach the garage—a formal living area, the help's kitchen, and a library. This shouldn't be too hard. If anything, the remaining guards should be held up in the security room, wondering why the fuck the front gates haven't closed properly.

Nerves flush through my body as I cross through the opening of the first room, and I do everything I can not to flip the keys around in my hand like I'd been doing up in my room. That bullshit isn't going to do me any favors. The room is dead quiet just as I expected, and I turn my gaze, quickly scanning everything in sight.

Safe.

I move toward the help's kitchen and my anxiety doubles. If anyone is going to catch me, this is probably where it'd be. There's a soft whirring sound, and my eyes go wide as I spy the microwave across the kitchen. Someone's cooking their dinner, but there's no sign of that someone.

I keep creeping, my eyes darting from left to right when a voice cracks out behind me. "And where the fuck do you think you're going?"

I whirl around, the key immediately slipping inside the small pocket at the back of my workout shorts. A guard stands before me, covered head to toe in tattoos, and if I weren't madly in love with three psychotic devils, this might even be the kind of guy I'd let rock my world.

Arching a brow at him, I indicate around the kitchen. "Getting a glass of water," I tell him, crossing my arms over my chest. "I was under the impression that I had free rein of this place. Am I wrong to assume that, or shall I give my mother a call to let her know her guards are interrogating me in my own home?"

The guard steps toward me, his eyes raking up and down my body. "Come on, baby, ain't no need for hostility. I was just asking a question. This is the guard's kitchen. If you're hungry, you should be using your private kitchen."

"Forgive me," I say, an idea sparking as I lower my voice to a seductive whisper. "Would it be bad if I admitted that I don't actually know where that kitchen is? This is just the first one I found."

The guard watches me for a minute and takes a step toward me. I roll my tongue over my bottom lip, backing up and putting a nice sway into my hips as I do. His lips twist into a wicked smirk, seeing the hunger in my eyes. "Not gonna lie, this place is a fucking maze. Took me a minute to find my feet when I first started."

"Yeah?" I question, my eyes lighting up as I move another step back until the cool stone counter brushes against my skin. I suck in a gasp, letting him see me as an innocent young woman with big doe eyes, the perfect damsel in distress. A soft giggle slips from between my lips. "You know, I think you're the first person here who's bothered to say a single word to me that wasn't an order."

He moves in even closer and there's no doubt in my mind that out in the normal world, this guy is nothing but a predator. He shrugs his shoulders, that cocky smirk spreading wider. "What can I say?" he questions. "I'm here to serve."

"Really, now?" I purr, my hand coming up to his chest. "A big man like you ... I don't know. You seem like trouble, and I'm not sure if you've been paying attention, but I've been in a little too much trouble lately."

He moves in even closer until his chest is pressing up against mine, his hardening cock rocking against my stomach. He takes my hips and lifts me up onto the corner of the counter before letting his hands fall to my thighs, pushing them wide as I hold back a gag. "What's a little more trouble?" he questions, ducking his head and letting his nose skim up the side of my neck, inhaling deeply. "I promise, I'll make it worth your while. Besides, who knows how long you're going to be staying here. We might as well make it interesting."

A grin tears across my face and I let him see just how willing I am. "Oh, yeah?" I tease. "I'm not sure you can handle it. I like a man who can throw me down, dominate me, make me scream until my legs give out."

"Trust me, babe. You ain't got no problems here. I can make you come so hard the fucking neighbors will know. You won't need nothing but my cock. I bet you're fucking tight too."

"Yeah?" I question, biting my lip and watching the wicked

temptation burning in his dark eyes. "Prove it. Show me what that tongue can do and if you can make me scream, then I'll let you bend me over and fuck me right here on the counter."

He groans low, his tongue rolling over his bottom lip as his fingers dig into the waistband of my tight shorts. He starts pulling them down to my hips, his gaze dropping to my cunt in anticipation and before I even lift my hips to help him remove my pants, my hand curls around the back of his head, and with all my might, I slam his head down on the corner of the counter.

A hollow thud sounds through the kitchen, and the guy doesn't even get a chance to cry out before he crumbles to the ground like a sack of shit. I laugh, jumping down from the counter and skirting over his fallen body, rolling my eyes as I go. "Yeah fucking right, asshole," I mutter to myself. "Credit for trying."

And with that, I hurry out of the room, fixing the waistband of my shorts back up around my waist.

Reaching the internal garage door, I turn the handle and slip inside just as I hear a loud curse flowing from the kitchen. "Jason? Jase, man? Wake up." There's a short silence before a loud, "FUCK. The little bitch is gone."

Oh, shit.

I scramble for the key in the back pocket of my shorts and hold it up, furiously pressing the little button as I hastily close the door behind me and flip the lock, hoping that somehow spares me a few extra seconds.

A soft *beep, beep* flows through the garage and I race toward the

MANIACS

black SUV as scrambling sounds from the other side of the garage. "Oh, fuck, fuck, fuck, fuck, fuck," I chant, racing toward the car, unsure just how many guards there might be coming after me.

Tearing open the door, I immediately hit the button for the automatic garage door as I frantically search the car. The seat is as far forward as it will go, and just as I find the push start button and bring the engine to life, the interior garage door flies open.

"FUCK," one of them roars. "GET HER."

Three guards race for the SUV, and one of them presses the garage door button, trying to pause it from opening, while the other runs out in front of the car like I won't crush his dumb ass.

Stupid fucker. Bad move.

I hit the gas and the asshole's eyes widen in terror before darting out of the way, barely clearing my pathway before the car screeches out of the garage, leaving thick black lines marring the pristine garage floor.

My heart races erratically as my gaze shoots up to the rearview mirror, finding the three guards scrambling, knowing it's certain death for them if they let me get away. I almost feel bad for them. Almost.

It won't be long before they send word to Gia. This is my one shot, and I have to make it count.

Flying down the long driveway, I pull my seat belt over me. This could be one hell of a bumpy ride, and as I speed through the open front gates, a wave of hope surges through my chest. I can do this. I can save them.

I barely get twenty seconds down the road before a set of headlights

79

appear in my rearview mirror and hot panic courses through my veins. I don't know where the hell I'm going and barely remember how to exit out of this stupid gated community, but I have to give it my all. The boys are relying on me, and I won't dare let them down.

Hitting the gas even harder, I fly through the streets, hoping to God that no innocents come barreling down the road in the opposite direction. I go left then right, and with so many corners, these assholes don't stand a chance at catching me, at least not yet.

After what feels like a lifetime, I finally exit out of this corrupt little community and floor it down the main road. I pass by angry drivers desperate to get home, and I swerve and weave through the traffic, horns blasting in my wake.

I'm not a confident driver. I lived close to the bar where I worked and never had a reason to drive very far. My reverse parking skills are as shit as they come, but tonight, I'm putting it all to the test. I follow the street signs, barely getting a chance to read them before whizzing past.

My gaze flicks up to the rearview mirror to see the guard's SUV ducking and weaving through the traffic, just like me, but I push faster, hoping that there are no red lights or head-on collisions in my future. It's not quite rush-hour traffic, but I also couldn't have picked a worse time to stage my getaway. They're only a few cars back, and I have to do something fast. I have to lose them, otherwise, I won't stand a chance. My gut is telling me to get onto the highway, but I'm too vulnerable there, too easy to ram right off the road. I need to lose them before that, and I need to do it now.

Breaking out through the intersection, I hastily make a left from the inside lane, cringing as the oncoming traffic slams on their brakes with horns blaring, cursing me out. It was well deserved, and if I were in their position, I would have done the same thing.

The cars make a mess of the road, and I watch through the mirror as the other SUV struggles to get through. I take a right, my heart racing so fast that it begins to hurt, or perhaps that's just the sickening anxiety pulsing through my veins. I go right and right again, going faster with each turn and hearing the reckless sound of the tires screeching around the corners. Glancing up, I don't see the other SUV, but I don't doubt that it's only moments from showing up in my mirror.

I turn again and my eyes widen, finding a mall up ahead. It's risky. The mall will slow me down, but I can ditch the car and steal someone else's. It'll take them too long to sift through all the other cars, and by the time they know what they're looking for, I'll be long gone.

Nerves race through me, but I forge ahead, pulling into the busy mall parking lot, my eyes darting from left to right until I find a dark corner. Bringing the SUV to a hasty stop, I quickly abandon it. I'd be fucked if it were the middle of the day, but the night sky above does nothing but aid me in my escape.

Not even bothering to slam the door behind me, I take off, throwing the car key onto the road and watching it skim under a row of cars. Losing myself in the crowd, I slow my pace so as to not stand out. It'll be like some twisted version of *Where's Wally*.

A woman walks ahead of me, her black hoody hanging over the back of her handbag. Going against everything I am, I follow her deeper into the rows of cars just as the other SUV appears at the parking lot entrance.

My stomach twists in knots as I duck my head, trying to keep hidden while the woman in front of me darts between an old Corolla and a Porsche. She comes to a stop—*please be the Porsche*—and turns toward the old Corolla. I let out a frustrated sigh. It'll have to do.

She catches sight of me just a moment too late, and my arm comes up around her throat, curling around it as I grip my other arm in a tight lock. "I'm so sorry," I murmur as she struggles for air and slowly crumbles. "You're going to be okay."

It only takes a moment until the woman passes out, and I gently lower her to the ground, completely ashamed of myself, but there's nothing I won't do to get to the boys. I don't waste any precious seconds yanking her handbag off her arm and rifling through it until my fingers curl around her keys. Unlocking the car, I thumb through her wallet, taking what little cash she has as I keep my head ducked from the SUV that's starting its lap around the lot. Placing her bag back by her side and leaving all her credit cards intact, I turn the key and let the small Corolla drum to life.

With the SUV stopping by my abandoned one, I watch as the guards bail out around the other busy shoppers as I slowly back out of the parking spot, doing everything I can not to draw attention to myself. Nerves wreak havoc on my body and my hands sweat, but before I know it, I'm taking off out of the exit with the guards left scratching their heads, completely dumbfounded, and absolutely fucked.

# EIGHT

It takes me two hours to reach the famous DeAngelis mansion. I pull up outside, keeping a good distance to give me some kind of vantage before moronically storming in there. The driveway is long, but even in the dead of night, there's an eerie silence about the place.

Not a single light shines through the property. Not even the ones that line the driveway at night. When I stayed here, they were always on, no matter what, even in the middle of the day. There's a coldness, but I suppose that's expected after a fucking massacre took place in the front yard.

I worry my lip, staring ahead at the property as my hands shake by my sides. My gut is screaming that they're not here. It's too silent, but I have to check, I have to know for sure even if it means searching every last room of the ginormous property.

Killing the headlights, I drive the shitty Corolla around the side of the property, silently impressed that the old heap of metal has made it this far. Unease rattles me as I take in the thick bushes surrounding the DeAngelis mansion. I don't have a good track record with these bushes, but it's the only option I've got.

Slipping out of the car, I let out a shaky breath and start my trek through the thick bushes, listening for any signs that I might not be alone. Swallowing hard, I forge forward, one foot sneaking down in front of the other. The last time I saw these bushes, Marcus was hiding out in them, shooting the enemies that came for us. It's only been a week, but in that time, so much has changed. I'd give every last part of myself to be able to go back and change what happened that night.

By the time I reach the clearing at the edge of the bushland, I'm covered in sweat, not from the fifteen minutes of hiking, but from the sheer anxiety of what I might find on the other side.

Up close and personal, I see the DeAngelis home for what it is—a mass grave. Blood still stains the concrete and there's a raw odor surrounding the property that sticks in the back of my throat. No bodies have been left behind, but that shit would be too obvious. One quick FBI drone over the top of this place would have every kind of law enforcement coming down on all of their asses, and that's not something any of them can risk.

Fuck, that night ... It wasn't only the boys' cousins that were slaughtered, but many of Giovanni's men, men who probably showed up for work unaware of what Giovanni had in store for them, men who probably had families waiting for them back home.

The whole thing was a shit show, and it never should have gone down like that. Hell, never should have gone down at all.

Taking a step toward the property, I swallow down the fear of exposing myself. There's at least a two-hundred-yard sprint between here and the actual house, until then, I'll be out in the open, no trees, no shrubbery, nothing to keep me concealed, just me and the manicured grass.

My foot presses down into the lawn when a soft branch cracks behind me and I whip my head around, more than ready to scream until my lungs give out, but before a sound can creep up through my throat, two sets of jet black eyes sparkle through the thick trees.

I catch my breath, my eyes going wide.

It can't be.

A moment passes and I squint through the trees, wishing I could see better, and within a breath, Dill and Doe step out of the darkness. I sink to my knees, relief washing over me as they bound toward me. I crumble onto the forest floor, sticks and moss pressing against the backs of my arms as the murder puppies get right into my face, their own version of checking me over.

"I know, I know," I whisper, curling my arms around their big heads and meeting their haunted stares, hating the grim darkness that reflects back at me. These assholes have been through hell, just like the rest of us. They've had to witness things that no animal should have to see, and for that, my heart breaks for them. "We're going to find our boys. They're going to be alright."

Shakily getting to my feet, I feel a million times better knowing that I have Dill and Doe at my back. They won't let anything happen to me. Dill is proof enough. The big bastard has already taken a bullet for me, a debt that I will never be able to repay, though I'll give him absolutely anything he wants. Endless supply of treats, tick. Scratches behind the ear, tick. A big, fat juicy steak at three in the morning, your wish is my command.

I absolutely love these wolves. They've become my family, my home, and knowing they're safe and unharmed has a weight falling off my shoulders.

"Okay, guys. Are you ready?" I question, looking out across the clearing to the big house. Doe whimpers as I scratch the top of her head, but nonetheless, they fall in behind me, just as the boys trained them to do, flanking me, always having my back.

We break out into the clearing as one, and I grip the fur on the backs of their necks as they propel forward, their raw speed helping me storm across the grass so much faster than I would have managed on my own.

Within moments, we're under the safety of the mansion, and we head around the back, sticking to the shadows. There are three back entrances, and all three are locked. I cringe at the thought of setting off an alarm, but I do what I have to do.

Grabbing one of the outdoor chairs, I hold it up and let out a shaky breath. If someone is inside, surely something would have happened by now. I use that wishful thinking as I run full steam ahead at one of the many back windows, letting the metal leg of the chair pierce through the fragile glass.

It shatters into a million pieces, the tiny fragments spreading through the back room like rain as I swallow hard and stand as still as a statue, silently listening for any hint of a disturbance inside. Nothing comes, and after a moment, I head in, gasping when the wolves follow me. "No," I rush out, my eyes widening like saucers, but it's too fucking late. The wolves traipse over the shattered glass as though it's merely sand beneath their bare paws.

I gape at the big assholes. "Are you two stupid?" I demand, watching as they strut past me, their tails low and still as though they're listening to the noises of the house just as I am. "Don't come crying to me when your paws get all cut up and you need someone to kiss them better."

Dill stands in front, his body taut and still, assessing the situation, and after a short moment, that tightness fades and he moves deeper into the home, Doe trailing after him. Dill glances back at me, and I wonder if he's trying to send a message, trying to let me know that the house is safe. "Okay," I murmur, keeping my voice low just in case. "Let's find the guys and get out of here."

We search for an hour and come up blank, and the more minutes that tick by, the more aware I am of the fact that Gia's men will be out there looking for me. Their first stop should have been here and honestly, I'm a bit concerned as to why they haven't shown up yet … unless Gia has specifically asked them not to. After all, she knows I plan on going after Giovanni. Perhaps I'm playing her game and I don't even know it.

Doe sniffed out two hidden rooms, one behind the bookshelf in Giovanni's office, while the other was located behind the fireplace in the main living area, both I never knew existed, but either way, they were both empty.

We found cells beneath the house just as I expected, and my blood ran cold as we made our way down there, but Dill and Doe didn't seem phased. They kept walking, kept searching, until finally coming to the conclusion that they weren't here.

I let out a heavy sigh as we moved back across the lawn, my feet dragging through the manicured grass. A part of me knew they weren't going to be there, but I'd hoped for it, needed it to be true. The very idea of them lost out in the world, alone and in pain ... fuck. I can't stomach it.

The last time Giovanni had anything to do with making someone disappear, it took the boys days to find me, and that was with a lifetime of training and resources to use. I'm all alone out here, and if Giovanni has taken them somewhere like his desert cells, then I'm fucked—we're all fucked.

Heaviness sweeps over me, and Doe pushes into my side, her big body pressing against mine. My fingers twine into her fur as my nails scratch behind her ear. "Where the hell are they?" I ask the big wolves.

Doe tilts her big head up, the jet-black eyes boring into mine as we slip into the cover of the bushes. I give her a tight smile, unsure why I'm trying to comfort the wolf as though she can understand human gestures, but on the off chance that she can, I want her to know that it's all going to be okay.

Thinking back to everything that I know about Giovanni, I try to put the pieces together. He kept Felicity at his home cells for months before taking her to the desert cells, he put me in the desert cell with Ariana, but before that …

The boys had once mentioned that their father was using their underground playground at the castle for his own sick games … What if he's taken them there? That would be the cherry on top of this already fucked-up shit storm. Keeping them locked up in their own fucking cells, using their own tools against them, using the space they created, it's sick and screams of Giovanni.

They have to be there.

A newfound hope burns bright in my chest and my pace kicks into gear, rushing through the thick bushes. The wolves stick with me, helping to lead me through the dark until we finally break out the other side to find the shitty Corolla exactly where I parked it.

Tearing open the driver's door, the wolves barrel in, cutting through the middle to find enough space for their big furry asses in the back, and before the car door has even closed behind me, the engine is roaring to life and I'm peeling off the side of the curb, anxious to get to the boys.

The drive is long, and despite the many hours that it's taken me to get to this point, I fear that those few wasted hours today have cost me dearly.

Tension rises as if the wolves know that this is it, that what we're about to walk into could be fatal. Silence fills the car while the wolves remain alert, their bodies held taut as though they're ready and prepared for any kind of war, ready to make things right.

The castle approaches and nerves settle deep in my stomach.

I have no idea what I'm supposed to do, no game plan, only that I have to get in there and somehow get them out, assuming they're still alive. Fuck, I could be walking headfirst into a trap. The boys could have died on that battlefield that same night, but I refuse to give up now.

Assuming that Giovanni is there somewhere, I don't drive down the main road. Instead, I head straight for the thick bushland surrounding the property, desperately searching for the discreet dirt road the boys carved through the trees. It's well after three in the morning, and the events of the night are already weighing down on me, but just the thought of being near them, getting to see and hold them, spurs me on. I'd face down absolutely anything just to hear those deep, authoritative voices one last time.

The week of thinking they were dead has wreaked havoc on my soul, and now it's time to take back what's mine.

Finding the narrow trail, I turn off the road and dive headfirst through the thick trees. The wolves sit up even straighter, watching the fresh hell before us as though they're terrified that I'm about to send us hurtling off a cliff, and honestly, with the way my heart is racing and the anxiety that's pulsing through my veins, it's a very real possibility.

"Come on," I mutter, my eyes snapping through the bushes, scanning every dark corner. "Where is it?"

Desperation twists my stomach into knots as I search for the small shed the boys built out here as their escape. I only got to use it a handful of times, and those few times I did, I was either on the brink of death or already out cold. I have no recollection of how long this trail is or just how deep it goes into the thick trees.

Minutes pass, and just as I'm convincing myself that I've made the wrong turn, the headlights reflect off a dark green shed, camouflaged to keep hidden within the trees. Had the light not hit it just right, I would have driven straight past. My foot slams on the brakes, tires screeching to a halt. I cut the engine and rush out of the car into the dark shed, with nothing but the soft moonlight showing me the way.

The wolves bound after me as I scramble through the shed, slipping past an old Escalade, which probably hasn't been used in months. A few bottles of water lay forgotten on a low riding bench, and I quickly crack them open, giving both the wolves something to drink before finding the hatch that leads down into the long tunnel.

It's pitch black, darker than night in the long, winding passage, and I search around for a flashlight or an old lamp to light the way but come up blank. I guess it's just me and my memory on this one.

The wolves follow me down into the tunnel and we walk for what feels like forever, each step bringing me closer and closer to discovering my fate. The boys built the tunnel beneath the staff kitchen, leading up into the castle, and I have no idea how I'm supposed to actually get down to the playground without giving myself away. If Giovanni is inside the castle, I'm fucked. My only hope is that the place isn't locked up like Fort Knox.

My hands shake as I reach the end of the tunnel and I groan, finding the heavy bookshelf the guys kept at the opening to conceal the tunnel. "How the fuck am I supposed to move that?" I murmur as the wolves hang back, leaving me to figure out this one on my own.

Gripping the old shelf, I suck in a breath and push with everything that I have. The fucker doesn't budge, doesn't do shit apart from breaking my nails. I stifle a cry, the frustration quickly getting the best of me as I try again and again, until I finally begin to inch it out of the way.

My fingers bleed, my palms ache and blister, but I don't stop until there's a space big enough for me and the wolves to squeeze through. We push through it, the wolves right on my heels, and we all listen hard, trying to figure out what's going down in this prison.

The DeAngelis mansion was dead silent, but unlike that, there's the soft vibrating whirr of the refrigerator, the subtle hum of the air conditioner, and if I listen close enough, maybe even the faint cries of a newborn baby.

My back stiffens. I hadn't considered that. All I'd been focused on was saving the boys, but if the baby is here too, if there's a chance that I can save him ... fuck. There's nothing I won't do.

Making my way up to the staff kitchen, I peer around, resisting the urge to flick on the light. It's late, there's a good chance that Giovanni is fast asleep, but what about his guards? There's no way a man like that could sleep in peace knowing his sons are down in the playground, each of them dreaming up the most brutal ways to murder him. No, Giovanni will need men surrounding him at all times and watching the property like hawks.

Not wanting to risk cutting through the house, I lead the wolves straight out through the staff exit. The door is unlocked, and I sigh in relief as a light sheen of sweat begins to coat my skin. The wolves follow me right out the door, and as if already having the boys' scent, they storm around the back of the property. I hurry to keep up with them, my desperation knowing no bounds as I try to stick to the shadows.

I don't see anyone around, no guards or cameras, so I race like a fucking maniac to the entrance of the underground playground. The wolves sail down the long, winding road with ease, and I push myself to keep up, each stride longer and more urgent than the last.

The downward plunging hill quickly levels out toward the bottom, and I stumble, falling straight to my knees. A soft cry forces it way through my clenched jaw, but I get back to my feet, my knees cut up and bleeding. I don't turn on the big overhead lights, that's way too obvious, but there are old oil lamps hanging along the row of cells lining each side.

The wolves take off far ahead of me to the point I don't even see where they are, but that doesn't matter right now. I have to find them. I have to know they're okay.

Grabbing one of the oil lamps, I hurry through the cells, looking left to right. I find dead bodies of men I never knew, people demanding that I stop and free them, others calling me a filthy whore and trying to grab at me through the cells, but I don't let it phase me. We can work on saving people once I have what I need. Hell, who even knows what these people did to end up down here in the first place. All I know is that these cells were empty when we left them a few short weeks ago.

The cells begin to empty out, and I shake my head, not liking this one bit. If they were down here, I would have seen them by now. I should have found them, but I keep going, refusing to stop until I've checked every last one.

There's only a few more to go, but no more oil lamps light the way. There's nothing but darkness up ahead, and with a shaky hand, I swallow hard and continue, not knowing what I might find.

Holding out the oil lamp, I try to light as much of the cells as possible. The first one on my left is empty, and dread sinks heavily into my gut as I turn to the right and hold up the light. The cell is used, dirty with pools of dried blood smeared across the cold, concrete ground. I shake my head, terrified of what I might find when a soft groan sounds through the remaining cells, deeper into the darkness.

My head whips around, my eyes wide, my heart frantic.

I know that fucking moan. I know it like I know my own fucking soul.

"Marcus?" I rush out, tears filling my eyes as I storm to the left, throwing myself up against the cold, metal bars. Thrusting the oil lamp forward, the dim light shines through the cell, and I find Marcus laying on the ground, his skin clammy and pale. "Marcus?"

He peers up at me through small slits, barely having the energy to open his eyes properly. "I knew it," he says with a heavy, defeated sigh, sadness thick in his tone. "This is what heaven looks like."

His eyes are glossy, and I quickly realize that he's not really looking at me, but through me as though he doesn't even see that I'm standing here in front of him. "Marcus, please," I cry, dropping to my bloodied knees and reaching through the bars, trying to take his hand.

My fingers brush over his clammy skin, and his eyes open a little wider, a soft smile pulling at the corner of his lips. "So fucking beautiful."

Fuck, fuck, fuck.

What should I do?

I squeeze his hand tighter, tugging on it, pulling, letting it drop heavily to the ground, anything to try and get his proper attention. "Come on, Marcus. It's me," I beg, tears streaming down my face. "Look at me. You're not dead. I'm here. Snap out of it. *I'm right here.*"

"Empress?" The sound is whispered like a question from behind me, and I latch on to the oil lamp again, releasing Marcus' hand and all but bolting to the dark cell over my shoulder.

I slam into the bars, my chest immediately aching as I find Roman sprawled in the back corner, slumped down against the back wall, his head hanging heavy. "Roman?" I cry, my eyes scanning over his broken body.

His head slowly rises, and the effort looks painful, but he doesn't stop until his obsidian eyes are locked on mine, the very weight of his stare dropping me to my knees. "Told you ... to run," he breathes, letting his head fall back against the brick wall, refusing to take his eyes off mine.

I shake my head, hastily wiping my eyes. "I'm not leaving you," I tell him, letting him hear the determination in my voice. "I'm not leaving you here to die. Where's Levi?"

"Look at us, Empress," he breathes, not bothering with my question. "We're as good as dead. Save yourself."

I shake my head, my gaze sailing over the bars, trying to figure out a way to get them out. There must be a key … something.

Spinning around, I race to the final cell in the back, dread resting heavily in my gut as I shine the oil lamp toward the bars. A body lays across the ground and I suck in a breath, finding Levi sprawled across the concrete, not moving … not … No. "Levi?" I snap, gripping onto the bars. "Levi. Oh, God, no."

His head pulls up off the concrete, his eyes opening to tiny slits. "Shayne?" he murmurs as though he can't believe what he's seeing. "That you, little one?"

Relief slams through me like a fucking rocket, and I fall to the ground once again. "Yeah, Levi," I breathe. "It's me. I'm going to get you out of here."

"You should have run," he tells me, groaning as he tries to get up off the ground, only it's too much, and he settles for half crawling, putting one knee in front of the other before collapsing to the ground. It's just close enough for him to reach through the bars and take my hand.

I squeeze it tight, gripping on to him with everything that I can as the memory of him begging me not to look crushes me from the inside out. "Not safe for you here," he tells me, his skin just as clammy and pale as his brothers' … only Marcus … fuck.

Tears stream down my face as I look to the cell directly across from Levi's to find Marcus right where I left him, murmuring sweet nothings about how beautiful I look in heaven. "He's dying, isn't he?"

Levi nods, and it looks as though it takes all of his energy to look up at me, his dark eyes brimming with grief. "Yeah, Shayne. It won't be much longer now. He's got an infection. But I'm glad he got to see your face one last time."

I shake my head. "No," I demand, pulling my hand out of his failing grip and scrambling to my feet, the desperation getting to me. My gaze flicks from left to right, from Levi's cell to Roman's and back to Marcus'. "I'm going to get you out of here. We didn't go through everything we did, just for you guys to give up now. I won't let you. I'm going to get you out."

Levi gives me a sad smile, and I gape back at him, but just as horror washes over his face and his eyes widen with fear, a sharp sting slams down against the side of my neck and a body steps in behind me. "Well, well, well. It seems my new bride has returned to me."

"EMPRESS," Roman roars, his body crashing into the bars with a desperation that I've never seen from him before.

And just like that, I crumble into a broken heap at Giovanni's feet.

# NINE

## LEVI

"Don't fucking touch her," I growl, my chest slamming up against the cold, metal bars as my fingers curl around them, holding so fucking tight my knuckles threaten to split right through my skin. I pull against them as if I could tear right through them, but there's no fucking use. We built these cells to withstand a nuclear bomb.

Shayne collapses, the oil lamp crashing to the ground and sending short licks of flames sprawling across the opening in between the cells as my father laughs with a wicked enjoyment. "What a shame," he says, his eyes glistening as he kicks his foot out, slamming into her ribs and watching her lack of response.

"I swear to fucking God," I roar, tearing at the bars again, desperate to get to her. "If you fucking touch her, I will tear you limb from limb with my fucking teeth."

My father scoffs, his sick gaze slowly turning to mine. "Look what's become of you, son. You've turned into such an animal." He laughs, crouching down and making a show of brushing Shayne's hair off the side of her face, trailing his fingers down her cheek and across the soft skin of her neck. "I bet my new bride will be an animal, too. Tight and fucking slick. It's going to be my fucking pleasure destroying her. I should thank you boys for warming her up for me, training her for what's to come."

Bile rises in my throat as panic courses through my veins. She's right there in front of me, only two short steps away, and there's not a goddamn thing I can do about it. She's never been so fucking far away in her life.

Roman's horrified stare flickers toward mine, mirroring the exact same bullshit that's etched on my face. The fucker can barely hold himself up, but I'll be damned if he doesn't give everything he's got left as he turns his ferocious glare on my father. "You're going to die for this, old man," he growls, his tone full of venom, deep and booming with a raw intensity that I've never witnessed from my eldest brother. He pulls against the bars of his cell, and I swear for just a moment, I see them rattle, but I could be seeing things.

We've been down in these fucking cells for …. fuck, I don't know how long. We're in a constant state of darkness, unsure when the sun rises and falls. My guess, maybe four or five days. All I know is that my father has done everything in his power to keep us suffering.

Our bodies had barely hit the concrete of our cells before Marcus started showing signs of infection. We all were, and true to his fucked-up nature, my father went and offered us antibiotics and gauze to dress our wounds, but the asshole only supplied enough for two of us, so no matter what, we were going to sit here and watch our brother die.

"SHAYNE," I roar, knowing there's no point. She can't fucking hear me. Whatever he shot into her system knocked her out cold, but I have to try. She has to fight back. It's our only fucking chance.

Marcus' head whips up from the ground, drenched in sweat as his dying eyes take in the scene before him. "Shayne?" he questions, his eyes widening in fear, snapping out of his hallucination, and quickly realizing that this isn't a fucking dream, that she's right here in front of us. So close, but so damn far out of our reach. It's a cruel fucking game. He may have made it this far but, watching him hovering over her with a sick delight sparkling in his eyes, he's going to wish he were dead.

Terror rips across Marcus' face, feeling that same wave of helplessness that Roman and I have been riding since the second she showed up down here. "No," he breathes, shoving his hand beneath himself to drag his heavy body across his cell, trying to get closer to the bars, closer to our girl.

My father has done everything in his power to draw out his death. Giving him just enough water to keep him alive, but not enough to help his suffering. Every minute he gets worse, every minute begging for the sweet relief of death.

If I could, I'd fucking do it for him. I'd curl my hands around my brother's head and snap his neck in an instant, putting him out of his misery, and fuck, I know Roman is thinking the same damn thing. He's my blood, my brother in every definition of the word. He's had my back my whole fucking life, and as much as it'd kill me to do it, I'd do it for him.

I watch in horror as my father's arms slip under her body, and I shake my head as he lifts her from the ground, threatening to take the one thing that truly matters in this fucked-up world. "No, no, no," I breathe, the fear like nothing I've ever felt before.

Shayne lolls in my father's arms, her head back at an awkward angle, and I want to fucking scream as helplessness courses painfully through my veins. Not even when she was held in my father's dungeons, did I feel this helpless. I knew she would survive that, but this … this is going to destroy her.

Marcus stares up at my father, tears in his eyes. "Don't do this," he begs. "Take me. I'm dead anyway. Torture me, slit my fucking throat, play whatever sick games you have to play, just leave her out of this."

My chest aches with his fucking words, but I don't dare force him to stop. As sick as it sounds, Marcus is a dead man, and if he's willing to spend his last hours on earth in the worst kind of torment to save the love of his life, then I'm not one to tell him no. He knows that when the time comes, we will make good on our promises and our father will pay for this. Marcus has an unwavering faith in us, just as Roman and I would if we'd been in his position.

But fuck … to lose Marcus?

I can't. The idea of losing him to my father's hands, having him suffer more than he already is, sends a hollow ache through my chest. It needs to be quick. He needs to be put out of his misery.

My father turns to leave, and I feel myself crumble, knowing exactly what he plans for her. He's done nothing but torment us with his games, explain to us in grave detail what he plans on doing to her, and it's a reality I simply can't take.

He looks down at Marcus with pity, but I don't miss the laughter in his eyes. "Such a waste," he says, looking at his son as he adjusts Shayne in his arms and pulls his gun. A surge of hope fires through me. All he needs to do is pull the trigger and Marcus will be free from this agony. "I should put you out of your misery," my father says, holding the gun directly toward Marcus in a kill shot. "I should put you down like a fucking animal, but I'm not nearly done with you yet. Not for a long time, son."

And with that, he disappears into the darkness, taking our girl with him.

Roman crumbles, dropping to his knees as he desperately clutches the bars, his head falling forward as Marcus weeps in the cell beside me. It fucking kills me.

I stumble back in my cell until my back slams against the concrete, my head falling back with a heavy thud.

"We failed her," I murmur, knowing they're thinking it and feeling it just as hard as I am.

There's not a goddamn thing we can do. She should have fucking listened when we told her to run and never look back. She's fucking stubborn, and despite not voicing our fears, we knew there was a possibility this could happen, that she'd foolishly risk it all just for the off chance that she could save us from this hell.

"He's going … to kill …" Marcus lets his words fall away, not having the strength to keep fighting, but he doesn't have to, I know exactly what he intended to say because I feel it just as strongly as he does, the words are all but fucking burned into my skin.

My father is going to kill Shayne Mariano, and he's going to fucking enjoy it, but only after he's stripped her of every last piece of dignity and will to live that she possesses. He's going to destroy her.

Roman slowly shakes his head as he calls on all of his energy just to look up and meet our eyes across the dark cells. "No. No," he says, refusing to believe it. "Shayne is strong. She defies all odds, has since the beginning. She'll get through this. She'll save us from this, all we have to do is give her the chance to do it."

I shake my head, the idea like poison in my chest. I can't afford this kind of hope to pull me down, offering me some kind of peace that's never going to come. Maybe he's saying it for Marcus' benefit, to give him something to fight for. Give him just the smallest ray of hope as he slowly fades away. It's a kindness we should have offered him days ago.

"Not … possible," Marcus says, struggling to get the words out.

"It wasn't possible for her to survive the bathtub or the fucking shit I did to her after you got shot, but she did. She's a fighter, Marc. Believe it. She's coming for us, and when that happens, you better be alive because after what she's about to suffer through, she's going to need you. We're all going to fucking need you."

Roman turns his dark gaze on me, silently demanding that I believe his every word. "You really believe that?" I question. "You think she can pull through this?"

Roman nods, his skin growing clammy again. "If anyone can do it, it's Shayne. She's coming for us, brother," he says, the conviction and complete faith in her clear in his eyes. "And ain't nothing standing in her way. She made it this far, Levi. She won't give up now."

Letting out a heavy breath, I nod. On some level, I know that he's right, despite my fear of what she has to go through in order to get to that point. "She's not going to come out of this the same girl she was."

"No, she won't," he admits. "Which is exactly why we need to save our strength. We need to be ready for her when she comes because she will burst through here, guns blazing, and she's going to need us at her back, prepared and ready to take what's ours.

# TEN

## SHAYNE

A piercing cry cuts through the darkness, and my eyes snap open to a familiar room that instantly sets me at ease, until I remember that I'm not supposed to be here.

I'm in my room, the one I occupied at the top of the boys' prison castle, and for just a moment, I almost convince myself this is all a shitty dream, that we're back at the castle with the boys asleep in their bedrooms, that the war at the DeAngelis mansion was just a bad dream, and that they weren't taken from me, that my mother isn't a lying piece of shit … that Giovanni didn't just shoot up my veins with some kind of bullshit and take me prisoner, yet again.

My head aches and my body is heavy, but when the cry sounds again, determination spears through me. I try to sit up, but the heaviness in my arms and legs is much worse than I feared. Realizing that I've been tied down, the panic immediately begins to rise.

"What the fuck?" I breathe. This can't be happening again. I was so close. All I had to do was get their cells open and find a way to break them free, then we would have been out of there, but Giovanni had other plans.

Pulling against my binds, tears spring to my eyes knowing exactly what he intends to do to me. After all, he doesn't call me his new bride for nothing.

I have to get out of here. I can't become a slave to his sick desires, I won't.

I'm alone in my room, and while everything feels so familiar, there's something off about it. The afternoon sun streams through the small window, but I can't quite put my finger on it. Perhaps it's the loneliness. Before, I had the boys just down the hall. I had Levi's incessant drumming and Marcus' howling laughter, but all I hear now is a crying that's so fucking loud it makes me fear for the innocent soul it's coming from.

A fucking newborn cry.

The baby. *Roman's baby.*

Hope surges through me. Maybe being here is a good thing. This might be exactly what we've been needing to get close to Roman's son. It takes all of two seconds for the daunting memories to come slamming back to me, remembering the wicked words Giovanni spat at his eldest son, taunting him with the truth.

It's not Roman's baby at all.

It's Giovanni's, and despite having no right to swoop in and try to save that little angel, I sure as hell am going to try. What other choice do I have? The boys are down in the cells dying. Roman and Levi looked like they were struggling, but they still have time. Marcus though … I've never seen someone quite so close to death.

*It won't be long*, Levi had murmured to me. Those four words gutted me.

The rush of emotion I felt as I searched through those dreadful cells was overwhelming, and the surge of hope when I found them was short-lived. They were alive, but not knowing how to free them or get them to safety made me feel like a failure. Their bodies, starved and depleted, weren't strong enough to get back to the car. The long tunnel would have been too much for them to handle, and Marcus? How was I going to help him? Drag his ass the whole way? The boys would have tried to hold him up, but it would have been too much. The walk alone would have killed him.

All those unknowns meant nothing the second I felt Giovanni's presence, and I knew I was fucked. I could see it in Levi's eyes, the fear and agony in knowing what lays in store for me. Fuck. I should have taken Giovanni out first. I should have made a better plan, but I was too caught up with needing to see the boys alive. I was an idiot, and now I'm here, tied to my old fucking bed with a newborn screaming in the next room.

Someone please tend to that fucking baby. He's in distress, he needs food or a new diaper … or … I don't fucking know. I don't know shit about babies, but I know they need attention and love, something he's clearly not been getting. He would have been so happy with us. We would have been able to offer him a nice, loving home, but now I don't know if Roman even wants to try. Does he still want him? Would he still want that final piece of Felicity even knowing the baby is his brother?

Shit. So much has gone down, so much that I haven't had a chance to work through shit with the boys, but what's the point? What's the point of suffering through all of this if it's only going to end in tragedy?

My heart races with the unknown as I worry my lip, biting it until it begins to swell. I have no fucking idea how all of this is going to go down. I don't know if it's going to be violent or if I'll be drugged. I don't know if he's going to claim my name and then throw me aside, or if he intends to destroy me on a much deeper level. Perhaps he'll just sign the marriage papers and immediately put a bullet through my head … A girl can only dream.

I can't find it in me to give a shit about what a marriage between us truly means for the Moretti family. Maybe a week ago I would have given a shit, but I'm being used as a pawn in a war that was never mine, and I simply don't give a shit anymore. If Giovanni wants to infiltrate the Moretti fortune, then that's Gia's problem. As for me, I'll fight my own fucking war the only way I know how—me with the fucking boys at my back. That's all I've ever needed in this world.

Hours pass as I lay in this stupid bed, a bed that holds so many of my darkest secrets and memories with the boys, but I don't dare allow myself to fall victim to them. Time and place, and this isn't it.

The quiet footsteps of servants pace up and down the hall to tend to the baby, but no one comes to check on me. His raspy wails calm momentarily, only for him to be left alone again to scream. His poor cries play like a torturous loop over and over again.

There are murmurs outside my door which quickly fade away, only to return minutes later. The soft voices in the hall come more often, and I can't help but feel that something is happening. My time is quickly running out.

My fingers bleed from trying to break through my binds, and by the time my wrists and ankles are red and raw, my bedroom door flies open, three of Giovanni's men storming toward me. My eyes widen, and I let out a piercing scream as a blade catches in the light.

Fuck, I'm dead.

The guards bear down on me as sheer panic and terror take over me. I watch the guy with the knife as his friend grabs hold of me and presses his weight down. "GET OFF ME," I scream, certain that I'm about to become a toy for them to pass around.

The third guard strides through to my private bathroom as the big one keeps holding me down, my eyes flicking from left to right. The one with the knife steps into my side and I watch him like a fucking hawk, waiting for the right time to bring my knee up and crush his nose back inside his skull, but it never comes. Instead, the sharp blade slices through my binds.

For a moment I stare in surprise, wondering if these are Gia's men coming to take me back to her prison, but when the big guy grabs me and hauls me off my bed, all sense of false security falls from my mind.

I barely get my feet under me as he shoves me hard toward my private bathroom, jabbing me in my bruised ribs. "STOP," I scream, fighting his hold, but my body is too weak, too heavy from whatever Giovanni shot into my neck. "GET OFF ME. LET ME GO."

The asshole rears back and slaps me as I dig my nails into his face, then he shoves me through the bathroom door with a grunt of disgust. Hot steam flows through the room, and I hear the familiar sound of a shower. The biggest guard holds me still as the third man steps in behind me and grips the back of my training crop, tearing it down the center. While I struggle against my assailant's hold, desperate to keep the scrap of fabric in place across my chest, the third man fists the material of my shorts and slides his blade straight through them. The big guard rips the dangling scraps of clothing from my body until I'm bare in front of them.

All three of them look at my body with disgust before the big dude grips my arm and launches me into the scalding water. I try to scramble away from the burning water as the big dude glares at me, letting me know that the task he's been given is clearly beneath him. "Bathe," he spits. "You have two minutes."

Not one of them goes to move, and humiliation washes over me as I commit their faces to memory, knowing that I will take sweet pleasure in ending their lives when the time is right. Having no choice, I quickly wash myself and shampoo my hair. Just when I think I'm done, a razor bounces across the floor of the shower, clattering against the tiles. "Shave," the big guy says, his eyes sparkling with a silent, wicked laughter. "Everything."

Clenching my jaw, I cower in the corner as I scoop up the razor, doing everything I can to keep my most private parts hidden. I drag the razor over my legs, trying hard not to think about what they're preparing me for.

With humiliation brimming high in my chest, I make quick work of it, knowing damn well that if it were any of the boys I was preparing for, I would have put a lot more care and attention into it, but I honestly couldn't give a fuck right now.

Insisting that I've been in the shower long enough, the dude who stripped me reaches in and grips my arm, yanking me back out, scoffing as I slip across the wet tiles. A towel falls over my head and I quickly collect it, wrapping it around me the best I can. "Can I pee, or do I need an audience for that too?" I snap.

Big dude waves his hand toward the toilet. "By all means, princess. Ain't nobody stopping ya."

Fucking hell.

If I thought I'd get a chance to pee later, I'd hold it, but it's been hours, and my body is starting to ache. It's well into the late afternoon and Giovanni took me in the early hours of the morning. I've already lost all sense of dignity after having these assholes standby to watch me shave, what else have I got to lose?

I make it quick, dropping down on the toilet and using the towel to cover me as I try to tune them out, but that's easier said than done. Three sets of leering eyes are hard to ignore at the best of times, but when those leering stares are from assholes like this, all I want to do is slit each and every one of their throats.

Scrambling off the toilet, I quickly flush and pull the towel tighter around me. The big guy in charge grips my arm again, pulling me through the door and into the bedroom as my hair drips all over the shitty carpet. I'm thrown down against the bed as one of the guards moves into my closet and appears a moment later with a big box. He dumps it at my feet before pulling out a hair dryer and curling iron and thrusting them at me. He tips the box upside down, letting hair pins and makeup sprawl across the floor. "Get ready," he says, looking at all the stuff as though he has no idea what any of it is actually for.

Letting out a huff, I rifle through the contents, knowing all too well that if I don't look a particular way, I'm only going to be told to start again. I hesitantly rise and move across the room to the dresser, dumping everything on top of it and staring at myself through the mirror. The guards hover way too close, but as long as they keep their hands to themselves, this is a task I can oblige without argument.

After drying my long hair, I plug the curler into the outlet and picture how good it would feel to shove the searing hot tongs up each of their asses and burn them from the inside out, but then the smell of burning shit would probably scar me for a lifetime.

I make quick work of putting my hair up and slathering on a face that doesn't reflect my own with false lashes and smokey eyeshadow. I don't bother with lipstick, just put a soft gloss over my lips before brushing a light blush over my cheeks. I don't put much effort into it, but they look at me with dead eyes, having no idea if what I've managed to achieve is actually considered good or not.

Turning to face them, I cross my arms over my towel-covered breasts. "What now?" I spit, not wanting to prolong the inevitable. The sooner I face my demons, the sooner I can figure out how to defeat them.

The guard who came in with the knife indicates toward my closet, and I see a white garment bag hanging over the open door. My stomach sinks.

A wedding dress.

"Fucking hell," I mutter, shaking my head in understanding. "That asshole doesn't waste any time."

"Just get dressed," the big guard says, clenching his jaw in irritation. "And don't skimp on the lingerie. Giovanni is very particular with how he expects his women to dress. Lace is best," he spits. "Oh, and don't forget to smile. A DeAngelis wife must always smile."

"Fuck you."

"If you weren't about to become my boss's bride," he says, his eyes darkening, "I would have fucked you the moment I walked into this room and found you tied down."

I scoff, crossing the room and trying to ignore the heated stares coming from him and his asshole friends. "What's the matter, asshole? Couldn't get a woman on her knees without the need to rape her? Tough break. Don't blame them though," I say, letting my eyes drag up and down his body in disgust. "You're certainly no treat, and don't act like I didn't see your micro cock straining through your pants while I showered. No woman in her right mind would want that. Now, your friend," I say, glancing at the dude who released me from my binds.

"He has something to work with."

He roars in anger, and as he storms toward me, I step into the closet and wait just a moment before slamming the door so hard it crushes against his face. Sick laughter tears through me as I pull the zipper down on the garment bag and get the first look at the stupid silk wedding gown that Giovanni expects me to wear, only the laughter dies down as the piercing wail of the baby in the next room tears through the walk-in closet.

My heart shatters.

*Hang in there, little guy. I'm coming for you, and then I promise, you'll get to meet all three of your big brothers. You'll be safe, and loved, and warm. You'll never want for anything. Just give me a little more time.*

After rifling through my underwear drawer, I pick out the most hideous lingerie I can find before taking the dress off the hanger and reluctantly putting it on, hating how it fits me perfectly, and damn it, it's really fucking beautiful.

A tear streaks down my face.

Today I get married to the wrong DeAngelis.

Letting out a heavy sigh, I quickly wipe my face and pull on a pair of heels that work nicely with the gown. The matching veil slides effortlessly into my hair, and I let it fall over my face before opening the closet door and preparing to face the devil.

The boys told me that I should have run and never turned back, and up until this very moment, I refused to hear them. I wanted nothing more than to come back here and do what I could to save them, but I hear them now. I hear the agony in their voices, the desperation for me to allow myself a better life, even if that meant being on the run forever.

I didn't hear them until now.

Now, I've never wanted to run so fast in my fucking life.

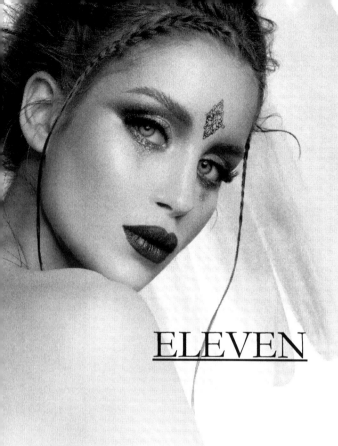

# ELEVEN

The church is massive, and I immediately hate it.

Grandfather DeAngelis sits at the very front, a sick grin resting on his old, decrepit lips as familiar faces fill the pews around me. The whole DeAngelis family—or what's left of it—must have shown up for Giovanni's big moment.

He stands at the top of the aisle, watching me like a hawk, his eyes glistening with a million dark secrets, and with each step I take down the long aisle, bile rises higher in my throat.

My heart races, erratically thundering in my chest, and I barely hear the soft music over the loud thumping of my pulse in my ears. People stare at me left and right, and I can only imagine what they've been told of the union, of what it could mean for the DeAngelis family to secure the only living heir to the Moretti fortune, plus the added kick in the famous DeAngelis sons' balls that their father has stolen the one remaining thing that's important to them—me.

With each step down the aisle, I remind myself that without getting through this, I stand no chance at getting close to the boys again. If I run now, I risk it all. Plus, I have maybe two or three hundred mafia men to deal with in this very room. Running isn't an option, not unless I want a bullet in the back.

The priest standing in the center of the aisle to Giovanni's right looks like he's going to be sick, and I hope to God that this guy is on my side, that he's maybe written some loophole into the vows, some way for me to get out, but Giovanni is too smart to be played like that. I can guarantee that the whole *does anybody object to this union* part is probably going to be accidentally forgotten. And hell, where the fuck is Gia? I know she doesn't give two shits about me, but surely it's in her best interests to do something about this. On second thought, it's also in my best interests for her not to be here right now, at least not yet. She's more than welcome to come and 'rescue' me once I have the boys safe and sound.

Stepping up in front of Giovanni, my stomach twists, and I bite the inside of my cheek to keep from lashing out. A man like this won't hesitate to put me in my place, especially in front of all these people.

The soft background music begins to fade, and my hands grow clammy with sweat. I swallow hard, my stare locked on Giovanni's as he watches me, his hard, dark eyes are so similar to Roman's that it kills something within me. "Don't play any games," he warns me, his tone low and private. "Nobody needs to get hurt today."

My jaw clenches and I resist the need to cry as the priest begins to speak, welcoming the guests to the grandest wedding of the year, uniting two families for the sake of peace. Realizing that this whole thing is going to be a pile of flaming bullshit, I let my mind wander back to the boys and the happy memories we shared. We'll get back there again. I know we will. There's just one more hurdle that we need to make it over before we can find our peace.

I don't hear another fucking word the priest says as I do my part at the front of the church. Giovanni holds my stare hostage the whole time. Minutes pass, or it could be hours, I honestly don't know. I'm so fucking numb that nothing matters to me right now.

Marcus … that spark in his eye. It was gone.

I whimper.

Giovanni reaches for my hands, gripping them in his own so fucking tight that an agonizing crack fires through my pinky. "Careful," he warns me as I hold back a ferocious scream. "Don't force me to break another."

Tears well in my eyes but I don't dare let them fall as the priest steps closer between us. "Your vows," he says, glancing toward Giovanni expectantly before turning to me, a flicker of sadness in his closed off stare.

"Indeed," Giovanni says, the darkness fading behind his eyes as he puts on a show for his loyal guests. He adjusts his hold on my hand and fire burns through my finger as he fixes me with a soft smile, fakeness tearing across his features. A moment passes before he steps a little bit closer, unable to keep his smile from turning into a sneer. "I, Giovanni Roman DeAngelis, take thee, Shayne Alexandra Moretti, to be my lawful wedded wife, to hold from this day on. Till death do us part."

His grip tightens on my hands, and it doesn't take a genius to realize that there was a whole lot of *to love and to cherish and in sickness and in health* left out of those vows, but what else should I have expected? Giovanni has literally just vowed to hold me as his wife, in any uncertain capacity, until I die, and that knowledge has dread sinking into my stomach.

He releases one of my hands and digs into the pocket of his tux before withdrawing it again. A thin gold band rests in the palm of his hand, and he quickly jams it onto my finger before gripping my hand once again.

The priest turns to me with arched brows, silently inviting me to declare my vows, but I bite down on my tongue. It's not like I'm going to stand by what I'm forced to say today, but I also thought that the first time I recited these words would be when I was standing in front of the love of my life—perhaps I would have ended up marrying one of the boys, assuming they would be able to decide between them which one got to do the honor. But this … I never wanted any part of this.

Giovanni's hands tighten around mine and a pained squeal escapes my lips. "Do I need to remind you of what is at stake if you were to fail here today?" he says, my mind immediately going to the three loves of my life down in the castle cells. "Get on with it."

I swallow hard and a single tear falls down the side of my face as I glance out at the hundreds of DeAngelis family members gathered in the church, not one of them with the balls to do anything about this. Turning back to Giovanni, I give him exactly what he wants. "I Shayne Alexandra Mariano—"

"Moretti," Giovanni snaps, his eyes blazing with fire. "Shayne Alexandra Moretti. That is what's on your birth certificate, and that is the name in which you will make your vows. Start over."

Murmured laughter fills the big church, and the sound echoes up into the high ceilings as humiliation washes over me. I've never seen a copy of my birth certificate, so really, how the fuck am I supposed to know what's written on it? Taking a slow, deep breath, I start over, my tone filled with a thick, lethal venom. "I, Shayne Alexandra Moretti," I spit through a clenched jaw, "take thee Giovanni Roman DeAngelis to be my wedded husband."

Another tear streaks down my face and my gaze falls away, feeling absolutely dead inside. A moment passes before Giovanni squeezes my hand again, sending searing hot pain shooting right up through my arm. "Get on with it."

I can't fucking do this.

Anger pours through me, and I yank my hand out of his hold, tearing the ring off my finger and throwing it down to the ground, letting it roll far beneath the pews to never be found. "Fuck you."

Murmurs rumble through the church and I expect a hand to slap across my face or a gun to be lodged into the side of my head, but Giovanni just smiles with a twisted enjoyment. He indicates to a man sitting in the front row, holding out his hand.

The guy smirks and stands before passing him a phone and retreating back to his seat, straightening his suit jacket in the process. Giovanni doesn't speak a fucking word as he silently turns the phone around to show me the screen, laughter brimming in his dark eyes.

My world falls as I take in the phone, looking at the live stream from down in the playground. I shake my head, my chest rising and falling with rapid breaths. "No," I cry, yanking the phone right out of his hand as I find Marcus beaten and bloodied, slumped in the corner of his cell with a man standing over him, gun aimed right between his eyes.

Failure tears through me, and as I look back up at Giovanni, I know that he wouldn't hesitate to take the final shot to end Marcus. He's always been the one to challenge Giovanni, always the one to call him out on his bullshit in the most infuriating ways. Levi has learned to keep his mouth shut while Roman would just do whatever his father requests of him in order to keep the bullshit from falling on his brothers' shoulders. But not Marcus. He's brave … or maybe just really fucking stupid, and I know that deep down, maybe letting the man shoot him and put him out of his misery would be a blessing for Marcus at this point, but I can't bear the thought of losing him. Marcus is strong, he can pull through this. He just needs someone to save him, someone to give a shit. He needs a fucking guardian angel, and that's exactly what I plan to be.

My mind swirls with grief as I stare down at Marcus, broken and bleeding, and I barely even notice Giovanni's hand snapping out toward the phone before it's already gone. "Shall we?" he demands, knowing damn well that he's backed me into a corner, forcing my hand, and there's not a damn thing I can do about it.

Tears fog my vision, and I blink them back as a lump forms in my throat, making it nearly impossible to speak. Giovanni slips the phone into his suit pocket and takes my hands once again, squeezing them tight. But this time, I don't feel the pain. I am completely numb.

Trying to remember where I was in my vows and what comes next, I glance at the priest who looks as white as a ghost, clearly having seen the screen of the phone and realizing just how deep this shit goes. "I … I can't remember the words."

The priest nods and glances toward Giovanni, his jaw clenches before looking back at me. "Repeat after me," he says, before starting the vows over. "I, Shayne Alexandra Moretti, take thee, Giovanni Roman DeAngelis, to be my lawfully wedded husband."

Swallowing over the lump in my throat, I speak the words that will crush everything that I am. "I, Shayne Alexandra Moretti, take thee, Giovanni Roman DeAngelis, to be my lawfully wedded husband."

"To have and to hold from this day on," the priest continues.

"To have and to hold from this day on."

Giovanni's grin widens and I listen to the next part of the vows. "For better, for worse, for richer or poorer, in sickness and in health."

My stomach churns at the thought of having to say this, but thinking of Marcus down in that cell, I force the words through my teeth. "For better, for worse, for richer or poorer, in sickness and in health."

The priest looks grim, but reluctantly continues. "To love and to cherish until death do us part, according to God's holy ordinance, I pledge myself to you."

Closing my eyes, I let the words consume me, break down every little piece of myself that I have left and allow them to turn everything to dust, leaving me as nothing more than a hollow shell. These words are binding, and while I have no intention to stand by them, they make me feel as though a leash has been tightened around my throat. But the boys …

I say the fucking words. "To love and to cherish until death do us part, according to God's holy ordinance, I pledge myself to you."

Giovanni grins, his eyes glistening with untold secrets and plans for what my future may hold, each one of them, I'm positive, is worse than the next. "That wasn't so hard now, was it, wife?" Giovanni taunts. "It's what comes next that's really going to make you squirm. Only from what I hear, you like being held down and fucked, don't you? You're a whore, but from this day on, you're mine to do with as I please."

Darkness swirls through me, and I choke back the tears, knowing there's no way in hell that I'll be able to escape this unharmed, untouched. No matter how quickly I can find my freedom, Giovanni won't wait to dirty me, won't wait to hammer that final nail into his sons' coffins. It'll be his sick game and it will destroy me.

The priest glances at Giovanni. "You may kiss your bride," he says flatly, disgusted with the events that just took place, though something tells me that there's absolutely nothing he could have done about it. I don't doubt he's got skin in the game too, a precious life being threatened to ensure his cooperation.

Giovanni wastes no time, stepping into me. He twists my hand around my back, bending my broken finger in the process, forcing a cry out of my mouth, and just as my lips part, he presses his mouth to mine, sinking his tongue into my mouth as tears of pain and disgust stream down my face.

It doesn't last long but leaves a foul taste in my mouth. The need to hurl pulses through me but before I can, Giovanni is forcing me back down the aisle as his loyal family applauds his new marriage.

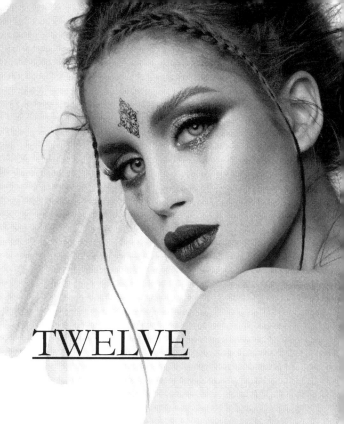

# TWELVE

The black SUV pulls to a stop at the top of the big circle driveway, and I stare up at the castle. There used to be a time that I liked being here. I liked waking up in this prison knowing the boys were there, and that despite everything shitty in the world, I had a place to call home.

Not anymore. I'm dreading walking back into that castle more than I hated it those first few weeks as the boys' prisoner. I was petrified and certain that death was knocking on my door, and now, I'm right back there, only I know exactly what's in store for me.

Giovanni is going to consummate the marriage. He's going to hold me down and fuck me until I bleed. My only saving grace is that a man like Giovanni would most likely have a micro cock and last less than five seconds. It'll be over quickly, but that doesn't take away from how brutal and painful it's going to be, the havoc it will rain down over my mental wellbeing, the pride I'll lose, or the way I'll be left with no dignity.

How the hell am I supposed to walk back in there knowing what's waiting for me?

The driver, who doubles as one of Giovanni's many guards, pushes out of the car and storms around to the back as my heart thunders. Giovanni took his own car, leaving me with a two-hour drive to stew on everything that just happened … everything that's going to happen.

Fuck.

The door opens and I shrink away as the guard leans in and grabs my arm. I pull back but the fucker is too strong, and I'm too defeated. He drags me out of the SUV and my body drops heavily to the asphalt. My knees scrape through the white silk, and as he hauls me to my feet, the dress catches on the loose stones, tearing the fabric with ease.

"No," I cry, pleading with everything that I am. "Please. Please don't take me back there. Please."

The guard ignores my every cry as he drags me up the big entrance steps of the castle. Dread sinks heavier with each step, and by the time we reach the top, I'm clawing at his arm, all but shredding his flesh to ribbons.

The guard presses his hand to the scanner, and it flashes green before the automatic lock clicks and the door releases. The guard struggles to hold on to me, and I use it to my advantage, remembering every last thing Zeke and the boys have taught me.

I bring my elbow around in a quick arc and slam it down over his arm, hitting him right in the soft spot below his bicep. The guard cries out in agony and I tear my arm free from his strong grip before hightailing it back down the steps.

Not today, asshole!

My feet slam against the stairs, taking two at a time, and I concentrate with everything that I have, knowing damn well that coordination simply isn't my thing. The likelihood of misstepping and sending my ass flying over my head is too great. I haven't exactly had the best luck lately, and now really isn't the time to test that theory.

The guard bounds after me, and I don't dare waste a second looking back, but if the sound of his feet against the steps is anything to go by, the fucker is gaining quickly.

My heart thunders wildly, and I resist the urge to scream, needing to conserve whatever energy I have left. I haven't eaten or drank even a sip of water since leaving Gia's home. That was barely even twelve hours ago, but so much has happened since then, so much of my energy has been drained and I won't get far before this asshole is bearing down on me.

My feet hit the asphalt and I sprint like a motherfucker, but the guard is behind me in seconds, his arms locking around my waist as he throws us down to the ground. My jaw crushes against the hard driveway, and I cry out, certain that something is broken. "You think I fucking enjoy this?" the guard spits in my ear. "You're not the only one with something to fucking lose. Stop fighting me."

My elbow barrels back into his throat and he releases his hold on me just enough for me to begin scrambling out from under him, but he's not having any of my bullshit today. Apparently, it's been a long day for everyone, and I almost feel sorry for the prick. I can only imagine what Giovanni is holding against him to force him to do his bidding, but I can't force myself to care. His problems are his alone. I have my own issues, and I won't be blamed for the position he got himself in.

He lashes out, gripping my ankle and yanking me back before I get a chance to take off, and my body crumbles back to the driveway, my white gown well and truly fucked now. He gets a good hold of me, pulling my arms behind my back and I fear that my shoulders may pop out of their sockets. Pain tears through me as the guard hauls me up off the ground, keeping at my back and disabling any chance of getting away. "Fucking grin and bear it," he spits in my ear. "Whether you like it or not, you're his now. There ain't no escaping it. So do yourself a favor and just get it over and done with. The sooner you let him fuck you, the sooner he'll leave you the hell alone."

I swallow hard, knowing he's right, but I can't accept it. He's going to destroy me. He's going to take everything that I have and he's going to use the boys to do it.

I can't ... I can't allow this to happen.

A sob tears from deep in my throat as he forces me back up the stairs. Every step feels like lead in my soles, dragging me down as tears stream down my face. Fear settles deep into my gut, and for a moment, I wonder if this is what Jasmine felt like, terrified of what was about to happen to her.

No … no, I shouldn't compare this to the fresh hell Jasmine suffered through. She was bound and gagged, stolen out of her home and brutally raped. This is … it's different. I came back here to save the boys knowing there was a possibility that Giovanni would get me. I knew what he wanted, and I still came, risking it all just to see that the boys were alive.

They're going to hate me for allowing myself to get into this position. They told me to run, and I refused to listen, but in the end, if I can get them out, if I can save them, it'll all be worth it, right?

Fuck.

The guard gets me through the front door and the massive castle seems so much smaller now. He doesn't waste time getting me back up to my room and the soft cries of the baby deeper in the castle are the only thing that can take my mind off what's going to happen.

He throws me down on my bed and I crumble, my will to fight quickly dissipating, but when he comes down on top of me and flips me over, I stare up at him with wide eyes. "What are you—"

His thighs press down on either side of my chest, locking my arms by my side as he grips my jaw with one hand. I try to pull away, terrified of what he might want from me when a small pill appears in his other hand. He forces it into my mouth and before I can even attempt to spit it back at him, a jug of water pours down over my face. I sputter against the water, but he keeps my mouth open, forcing me to swallow or risk drowning in it, and only when the pill effortlessly slides down my throat does he let up.

Water drenches my face and my bed as the prick places the jug back on the small bedside table. "You're going to thank me for that," he mutters, climbing off me.

He doesn't say another word, just simply turns his back and walks out the door, locking it behind him.

I gasp for air and throw myself off my bed, my head already beginning to feel woozy. What the fuck did he just give me? A roofie? Or something so much worse?

The door handle jiggles, and my eyes bug out of my head, terror raining down on me. I hear the deep tones of Giovanni's voice and race across the room, slamming the door of the private bathroom and shoving my face over the toilet, forcing whatever the fuck I just swallowed to come right back up. It's one thing being drugged and raped, but not being able to fight back … hell no.

Violent heaves take over my body as I shove my fingers down my throat, forcing it up while listening to the sound of a key sliding into the lock.

Fuck. FUCK. FUCK. FUCK.

I hurl again and again, my body quickly growing weaker by the second. Whatever he gave me is dissolving into my body fast, and I can only assume that it's something so much worse than a roofie.

I shakily get to my feet, falling forward and catching myself against the tiled wall of the bathroom. My head spins, my body growing weaker and weaker. One foot presses in front of the other and I stumble again, barely gripping on to the towel rack to keep myself up.

I come out into the bedroom and my eyes go wide, finding

Giovanni standing before me, a twisted smirk stretched across his face. "You're mine now, Shayne. There's no point fighting it."

My jaw clenches and I push forward, determined to fight for everything it's worth. "I'll never be yours," I spit, tearing the ring from my finger and throwing it at his stupid face, the momentum of my movements sending me crashing to the ground, my scraped knees crushing against the plush carpet. "You'll never amount to what they are. Never."

Giovanni laughs and strides toward me, my fear screaming at me to get up and run, but my body is too heavy. My muscles strain to get up, but I fail with every attempt. Giovanni twists his hand into my hair, curling it around his wrist before pulling hard and dragging me across the room.

Agony tears through my scalp, and I grip his hand frantically, digging my nails into his tough skin, desperate to release the ache. "You're a fighter," he says with a sick pride, a laugh brimming deep in his chest. "I like that. Felicity was too easy, too willing. One threat from me had her spread eagle on my bed practically begging for it. She was a fucking whore, but she served her purpose. I have my son, a soldier to mold into my image, but one soldier is not enough. I need a fucking army."

He pulls me up off the ground, throwing me across the bed as easily as if I were nothing but a soft toy. My body falls against the wet mattress, and I do what I can to scramble away, pissed off with how easily my body has succumbed to his drugs. "Don't fucking touch me."

Giovanni laughs, slowly stalking closer and closer. "You're my wife," he says, spitting the word with venom. "Now, what kind of husband would I be if I didn't fuck you until you screamed?"

My body struggles, fighting to push myself up the mattress and failing over and over again. I've never felt so weak and pathetic. The drowsiness creeps up and a tear slides down my cheek. It won't be long until I can't fight anymore, until my body gives up and I pass out, succumbing to his every sick, twisted desire.

He moves to the end of the bed, watching me like a lion watching an injured bird. "It won't be long now, Shayne," he murmurs, his voice growing deeper … colder. "Give in to it. Give yourself to me."

I shake my head, my jaw clenching as the tears fall even harder. "I do not belong to you."

Giovanni laughs. "Very well," he says, making his way around the side of my bed. I watch his every step, swallowing hard over the lump in my throat and gasping as a blade catches in the light. He grips my arm, and I don't even have the strength to pull back. The tip of the blade presses against my skin, high on the inside of my arm. "Resist me, and my sons will suffer the consequences," he says. "Do what is required of you, and I might even spare their miserable lives."

"They'd rather die than allow you to have what belongs to them."

Giovanni roars, his grip tightening on my arm. "YOU BELONG TO ME."

My eyes widen with fear and just as his face twists into a wicked smirk, the tip of the blade digs down into my skin. I try to cry out, but the scream never comes, slipping from my lips like a pathetic whimper. All I can do is watch as the sharp blade sails down my inner arm.

Giovanni pulls back and then digs the blade back in as though he's searching for something.

"Uh-huh," he declares, digging his fingers right into my open flesh. He pulls hard and this time the scream comes tearing from the back of my throat like a motherfucking sailor. A small stick comes out in his fingers, and I quickly realize it's my contraceptive rod. "You won't be needing this," he laughs, tossing it over his shoulder and letting the blood pool beneath my arm on the wet bed.

He releases his hold on me, only to grab the material of my dress. He tries to tear it straight down the center, but the fabric holds tight, and he's forced to use the knife again. I can't help the smirk that dances across my face, my eyes gently rolling from the dizziness. The fabric tore so effortlessly when I fell, but now this asshole can't even split it in two. "Any one of your sons would have had this dress shredded into ribbons with their cocks already buried deep inside of me. What's the matter? Waiting for your little blue pill to kick in?" I spit. "Got some news for you, old man, ain't nothing you've got is ever going to compare to them. You could fuck me until the sun comes up, but nothing you do to me could make me feel your little pin dick." Bile rises in my throat and my face twists into a disgusted scowl. "I bet it's old and wrinkly, isn't it? Loose gray pubes that I'm going to find in my bed for days, wrinkly ball sack down to your knees."

His hand flashes out like lightning, slapping hard across my face, but I barely even feel it. Instead, I fucking laugh. "Hit a nerve, did I?" I taunt, feeling sick as he tears his suit jacket off to find big sweat patches under his arms.

I gag, digging my feet into the mattress to try and shove myself away but get nowhere.

He tears the dress from my body and slices the blade straight through my white lingerie before grabbing the front of his pants and freeing his hard cock.

Giovanni grabs my legs, pulling me across the bed and forcing my legs apart as tears stream down my face. "They're going to fucking kill you," I growl, the lump growing harder in my throat.

He. Fucking. Laughs. And as his eyes darken and his lips twist into a foul smirk, I know that this is it. The moment I've been dreading.

The drowsiness gets worse, and I will it to just take me out, but for some goddamn reason, my body is holding on, forcing me to be witness to his vile game. All I know is that one day, karma is going to burn him alive. Once all is said and done, once the boys are safe and thriving, I'm going to return here, and I'm going to make this motherfucker pay.

My eyes roll and my head begins to loll to the side, my body quickly giving up the fight.

And then he's there, slamming into my bruised and abused body, trying to claim something that already belongs wholeheartedly to his sons.

Tears pool in my eyes and I blink them out, letting them stain the sheets by my head.

He slams into me again and again, gripping on to my heavy thighs as I just lay here, unable to fight, unable to scream for help. He groans and grunts as darkness washes over my soul, picturing exactly how I'm going to take his life from this world, picturing how I will tear him limb from limb, how I will cut his fucking dick off with a serrated knife and feed it to him, how I will tear his intestines right out of his body and listen to his scream.

Giovanni quickly grows sweaty, and I realize that this is going to be a quick game. "Is that all you got?" I mutter, my fingers clenching in the sheets. "You're like a fucking jackhammer. This is embarrassing. No wonder Ariana was so desperate to fuck literally everyone but you. I bet you've never got a woman off in your life."

He growls, trying to block me out as he focuses on fucking me raw.

"If I had to guess, I'd say Levi has the biggest cock, a million times bigger than that little jack rabbit you're trying to fuck me with. I didn't realize they even came in size micropeen. But Levi, he's a girthy motherfucker. Angry veins with a long shaft that I have to use two hands on. I bet you've never made a bitch even gag before."

Anger burns in his eyes, and I feel his dick quickly start deflating and I laugh. My DeAngelis men would never face such an issue. In fact, they'd use my taunts as a fucking weapon, desperate to prove they can get me off harder and faster than their brothers, but there is no competition. They all come with individual gifts, but it's when all three of them have me up against a wall … that's when the magic happens.

Giovanni fucks me harder, desperate to hold on to his erection, but with every snorted laugh that tears from deep in my throat, his will to fuck quickly dies. By the time it feels like nothing but a floppy cock trying to jam itself into my cooch, the second-hand embarrassment is too much. "Fuck, man. Give it up," I laugh. "This is just shameful, but don't worry, it'll be a good story to share with your sons when we're standing over your dead body."

I don't see his fist before it's too late, but one second I'm laughing, and the next his fist is slamming into my temple, knocking me out cold.

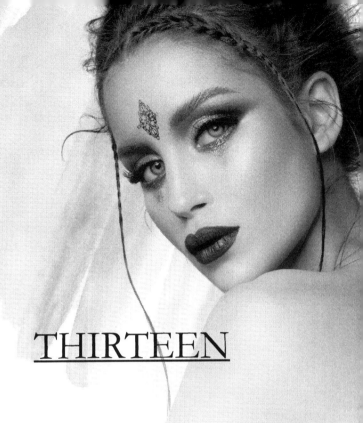

# THIRTEEN

A heavy thump sails through my room, so loud that I feel it vibrating in my chest and my eyes pop open. A gasp tears through my lips, remembering exactly what happened, and within moments, the emotions hit me hard.

Guilt. For allowing it to happen.

Anger. For not being able to fight.

Sadness. For not being able to save myself for only the men I love.

Shame. For having that vile man use my body for his own wicked games.

I don't know what happened after he knocked me out. I don't know if he kept fucking me, if he somehow got his limp dick hard again, if he even had the stamina to keep going. But it doesn't matter if he made himself finish or not, all that matters is that it happened against my will and that the fucker will pay for it.

My fingers brush past my temple, and I wince at the sharp pain. There's definitely a killer lump there that's going to seriously fuck with my day, but at least I've regained some kind of control over my limbs.

Another loud thump comes from deeper in the castle, and my head shoots toward the door, certain that someone is going to come for me again, but when the door remains shut, I give myself a chance to breathe.

Pushing up from the stained mattress, I rest my back against the headboard and pull my knees into my chest, holding them to me as though curling into a ball could offer me some semblance of safety. Minutes pass, and I drop my forehead onto my knees as tears flow freely down my face.

He raped me.

He took my body and stole from me, abused me, held me down and forced himself inside of me without my consent. How am I ever supposed to be okay after this? I know I fucked with his head, took away his power over me, but that doesn't change the fact that it still happened. Doesn't ease the ache between my legs, doesn't help the bruises to fade any faster.

Giovanni ruined me, and for that, I will destroy him and his whole goddamn army, but to do that, I have to put this behind me. I can't break down into a sobbing mess every time it's thrown in my face, every time the memories come back to haunt me. At least, not until he's dealt with. I can break after that, once I have the boys to lean on. They'll help me to find my value just as they've done in the past. They're my rocks, and I won't be able to do this without them.

They have to be okay.

Marcus ... he ... there's not enough time.

Fuck.

Raising my head from my knees, I hastily wipe my tears. I've already wasted so much time. The boys are locked up in the underground playground with no food or water, no way to help one another. Roman and Levi have to just sit there in their cells watching Marcus slowly fade away. Hell, it's been hours since the wedding, since I saw that live footage, he could already be ... No. I can't think like that. I have to believe that they're going to make it because, without them, I won't survive this. They hold three equal parts of my heart and without them, I'll never be whole again.

They're my everything, even Roman's broody assholery.

Quickly taking note of my body, I check over my injuries. I'm bloodied and bruised. No one has bothered to come in and tend to the gaping wound in my arm, but on some level, I'm glad. I don't think I can handle anyone else coming in here uninvited. As for the rest of me, I'm mostly unharmed. Lines of blood decorate my skin and matted hair, and there are bruises mainly on my thighs and hips. My jaw stings from the guard crash-tackling me like a fucking linebacker. My finger is swollen, but it doesn't feel broken like I'd originally thought.

I'm going to be okay. I can work with this.

Grabbing the shredded material from the wedding dress that lays scattered across the bed, I wrap it tightly around my arm where my contraceptive rod used to be to stop the bleeding before shakily getting to my feet. I'm as naked as the day I was born, only now I'm sporting a shit load more scars and bruises than any woman should ever have to bear.

I don't dwell on it. Instead, I wear them with pride because these are the marks of a survivor.

Stopping by the massive walk-in closet, I grab some clothes and fresh underwear while trying not to think about what happened in this room. I don't even look back at the bed. From this point on, it lives in the past. I'll close it out the best I can. I've had a few minutes to cry, to grieve for my lost innocence. When the little reminders come to destroy me, I'll be ready and waiting to shoot every single one of them down.

Giovanni DeAngelis will not define me. Only I get the right to do that.

My head spins and my body still feels heavy, but I refuse to dwell on it. I can break down and crumble once I get out of here, but until then, I need to remain strong, remain the woman my mother insisted I become, the woman she feared returning. After all, there are three men who need to rise from the dead, and they can't do that until someone gives them the strength to do it.

Their warrior hearts are still beating rapidly, they're just buried under mounds of bullshit, pain, and torment. But not for long. My warriors are going to fly free, and it's going to be fucking spectacular.

Fuck, I can't wait to watch them rise. They're going to burn this whole fucking family to the ground.

With a renewed courage and determination burning through my veins, I make my way into the bathroom. I close the door behind me, and to give myself the illusion of privacy, I flick the little lock on the back of the door before stepping into the shower.

Hot water cascades down over me, and I quickly wash myself, being extra thorough between my legs. When I first stood, there was no rush of fluids dripping out of me, so I can only assume that he didn't finish, but I have to be careful. It would be the worst thing in the world to become pregnant with Giovanni's child. There are a lot of things I can handle in this life, but that would not be one of them. There's a risk that Giovanni could kill me at any time, but to be pregnant with his baby means that he will never let me go, never stop coming for me or my child. I'd sooner die than inflict that kind of hell on a child. That's why it's so imperative that I find that baby and free him of this shit. Not to mention, I promised Felicity that I would protect him with my life.

Finishing in the shower, I quickly dress and make sure I'm completely covered. There's nothing in my room that can be used as a weapon, but I need to make sure that if he comes again, he's going to have one hell of a hard time gaining any type of advantage over me. I won't be drugged again, and I sure as fuck won't become his playtoy, but if he somehow gets past my defenses again, I'll be more than ready. Besides, he made it pretty damn clear that his precious little ego bruises easily. It shouldn't be too hard to hammer the final nail into that particular coffin.

Can't blame the guy. I'd have a dick complex too if I had to compete against men like Roman, Levi, and Marcus. Now, they're real fucking men. Tall, broad shoulders with piercing eyes that hold a woman captive. Not to mention their rock-hard bodies, sharp jaws, and a darkness that screams dirty alpha bad boy who'll fuck you until you call them daddy. They take care of their business, and they protect what's theirs with an animalistic possessiveness and fierce loyalty that does things to me I've never felt before.

They're my family. It's as simple as that.

Damn. I need to get them home.

My head pounds as I walk out of the bathroom and cross to the main door. If I have any hope of breaking out of this fucked-up little prison, then I have to know what I'm working with. Getting up close and personal with the door handle, I peer over the lock, wondering just how hard it's going to be to pick it, or if I should just break the whole damn thing off.

Pressing down over the handle, I test just how sturdy the lock is. I expect resistance, only it never comes. The handle keeps turning and my eyes widen further and further the lower it gets.

Holy mother of all things sweet and sexy. This is not happening. Surely I'm seeing things. I must be so fucked in the head that I'm hallucinating.

I suck in a gasp, my heart leaping right out of my fucking chest as I stare at the handle in shock. The softest click sounds through the room, assaulting my eardrums with the sweetest sound.

*The door is open. It's fucking open.*

Giovanni must have stormed out of here in such a huff that he forgot to lock the door behind him.

He fucked up. He fucked me, screwed me over, and then he fucked up in the kind of way that is going to see the end of his miserable life.

Holy fucking shit.

Let me say that again for the assholes in the back.

*HOLY FUCKING SHIT.*

Why didn't I try the door before? Why did I waste all that fucking time having a shower and sobbing about what Giovanni did to me? I could have been out of here ages ago, could have already had the boys halfway through the thick trees by now.

A wicked grin spreads across my face as my heart thunders a million miles an hour, the hope swelling inside of me like a fucking cancer, infecting every part of my body. Millions of thoughts and plans swirl through my mind like a fucking hurricane, each one demanding attention. The possibilities are endless, and all of them are centered around finding that fucking prick and putting a dagger right through his chest before his yes men drag me back here kicking and screaming.

I shake my head. I can't lose myself to that. My only priority is finding that baby and getting the boys out of here. We can deal with Giovanni later. Hell, I might even put Gia against him and let her clean up her own fucking mess.

Calming my racing heart, I slowly peel the door open a little wider and hold my breath, terrified that this could be some sick, twisted joke. Perhaps they're lying in wait, ready to screw me over again. Perhaps Giovanni is watching me through cameras, predicting my every move.

Fuck, it's a risk, but I'm willing to take it.

My gaze flicks from left to right before turning to the left once again. Something was out here before making loud, heavy thumps, and whatever it is, I need to keep as far away from it as possible. I don't see anyone, but I'm not taking any chances. This whole thing has the potential to backfire in the most absurd, hideous ways, and I don't want to hang around to discover what they might be.

Swallowing the fear, I remind myself that I was trained by not only Gia Moretti's right hand, but by the three grim reapers, the infamous DeAngelis sons. If I can make it this far, I can sure as fuck keep going. I lived in this very castle for months. I know its ins and outs, its little secrets ... secrets that perhaps Giovanni hasn't discovered yet. I have the upper hand here.

Not wanting to waste time, I push out into the empty hallway, going as slow as possible and trying to remember where each of the creaks are in the old flooring. My heart thunders so loud that I swear I can hear it on the outside of my body, but if anything is going to give me away, it's the rapid, heavy panting that sounds like some old bitch frothing over the Magic Mike live show performers, who I may or may not be following on Instagram. I've got to reel it in.

Creeping up to the room directly beside mine, I swallow hard before gripping the handle. I've got one fucking shot.

Get the baby. Grab a few diapers. And get the fuck out of here. The rest we can worry about later.

Pushing the handle down, I storm into the room, more than ready to put some old bitch flat on her ass, but I get hit with the worst kind of déjà vu—racing into the room only to find an empty crib.

"No," I breathe, my eyes wide as I look around the room, my sharp gaze flicking from corner to corner. Where the fuck is he?

"The baby is gone, girl."

I spin on my heels and my hands immediately go up to defend myself. An older lady hovers in the doorway, her eyes narrowed and unsure. There's something familiar about her, and as she takes a hesitant step into the room, I realize that this was one of the many staff who worked down in the castle kitchen, caring for the boys over the past ten years—seen and not heard. She's not here to hurt me, but who knows what kind of orders she's under.

I swallow hard and slowly lower my hands, unsure of what she plans to do. "Where is he?" I snap, standing to my tallest height despite the older woman towering over me.

She watches me with sharp eyes from years of watching her back around Giovanni's sons, always terrified that they may snap at any moment. Hell, the kind of guests they invited over would be enough to scar anybody. "Master took him for a drive thirty minutes ago," she says, eyeing me warily as she slowly walks deeper into the room. "You will not be able to get your hands on that child," she adds as though she can read every thought pouring through my head. "He is heavily guarded, all hours of the day. It is unclear when Master shall return. So, if you are going to run, now is your only chance. He believes you to be … indisposed for another few hours."

My eyes widen, but before I can get a word out, she moves out of the doorway. "Go now, child."

My gaze falls back to the empty crib, my heart breaking with the thought of leaving him behind. "I—"

"Don't be foolish, girl," she seethes. "Forget the baby. You cannot save him. Go before he …"

I read her unsaid words loud and clear.

*Go before he rapes you again.*

Shame settles over me once more, realizing that every last person in this fucked-up castle knows exactly what happened in that room, but I push it aside. She's right. If that baby is with Giovanni right now, I don't stand a fucking chance. I have to come back for him, and I'll do it with a fucking army at my back, until then—it's time to get my boys.

# FOURTEEN

My hands shake as I take off out of the nursery, bypassing the older lady. I'd do anything to be able to stop and thank her or somehow offer some type of freedom from this hellhole, but all I can manage is a quick smile before I whiz past her. The determination to get my boys the fuck out of here is the only thing keeping me going.

My eyes dart from left to right, forward and backward with every step I take, knowing all too quickly how fast one of Giovanni's men could catch me making a break for it. Nerves pulse through my body, and I wish that I were stronger, that I had regained all of my strength after those drugs completely fucked with my system, but beggars can't be choosers. Had I waited until I was feeling like myself, I might have missed this chance completely.

Fuck, I just need to get to Marcus, need to know he's doing alright. Roman and Levi are strong, they would have been able to push through the last … shit. I don't even know how long it's been. All I know is that any amount of time could be too much for Marcus. He needs to get help, and he needed it days ago.

Hitting the stairs, I bring myself to a standstill, listening for any noises below and forcing myself to calm down. My pulse is drumming so fucking loud in my ears that it's almost impossible to hear, but I won't be fucking this up.

Taking slow, calming breaths, I briefly close my eyes and concentrate, the way the boys had taught me to do that first night we visited the home Roman built, the very home we burned to the ground.

There's soft chatter coming from the opposite direction in the castle, maybe guards discussing shift rotation while shuffling papers. There's a clanging of pots and pans, maybe even the soft murmurings of the kitchen staff as well, but more importantly, the foyer at the bottom of the staircase and the areas around it are free.

Taking a breath, I start to move, keeping a quick pace as that clear path could change at a moment's notice. My feet hit the floor and it's all I can do not to shout out in success before I hook around to the left and make my way through the grand ballroom to the door that leads down to the castle cells.

I don't have the best memory of being down in those cells, and I'm sure that I'm probably going to see some things down there, but I remember the boys telling me about a passage down there that leads to the underground playground. Not wanting to risk being in the castle and out in the open any longer, I push through the door and trail down the big concrete steps before coming to a stop in front of the heavy medieval-looking door.

I hate this fucking thing. I could never get it open when it mattered the most. It's heavy as fuck, but I'll stand before it all fucking day, clawing at it until my bones break to get where I'm going.

Gripping on to the big iron handle, I pull hard, clenching my jaw and using all my body weight. Shit, if I weren't so fucking thin right now, maybe my body weight might actually do the trick, but it seems I'm left with nothing but pure muscle strength.

Fuck.

I keep trying until my forehead is coated in a sheer layer of sweat when it finally budges. Tears sting my eyes as exhaustion threatens to claim me, but I push hard, determined to get this fucker open enough to slip through. I try and try again, biting down to avoid screaming at the stupid thing, moving it inch by inch until I can finally slip my hand through the gap.

A chill blows through the air and sails straight down my spine, remembering how the boys would torture me with white noise and the sounds of the metal cell doors opening and slamming once again, but then those images are quickly replaced with ones of Marcus holding chains.

Slipping my hand through the small gap, I use it to push against the door, and as I tug on it one more time, it finally inches enough for my body to slip through the gap. I don't hold back.

My feet pound against the concrete floor, flying past all the cells. I don't dare look up, terrified of what I might see … or *who* I might see. I have no idea where I'm going, but I spent one awful night racing through here and I use everything I know of these passageways to lead me deeper.

It takes four wrong turns until I finally break out into the open space where I stood all those months ago, determining which path to take. That night, I went straight ahead and that led me into a small room where Roman was waiting for me. He knocked me out with barely a moment's notice, but it was enough time to realize that's not where I need to go.

I mentally try to map out the castle above me, trying to place myself. If I were upstairs now, I'd be somewhere near the main dining room … I think, which means any path to my right is going to be short, it's not going to lead far, but the path to my left; that has the potential to lead anywhere.

Knowing I could be wrong, I turn to the left and take off like a fucking rocket, the darkness beginning to overwhelm me. The path leads down, and before I know it, I'm tumbling over a steep set of stone steps. "Fuck," I grunt, my already aching body barely able to handle the abuse.

My palms bleed, and I thank whoever is looking out for me that I didn't smack my face against the ground again. Hastily getting to my feet, I keep going with hope surging through my veins, the stairs confirming that I'm heading in the right direction.

It's almost a five-minute hike before I finally reach a door and have to feel in front of me for the handle. The deeper it gets, the colder and darker it seems to get as well. The door is large and made out of a hard metal, telling me that I'm right where I need to be, only the fucking thing comes fully equipped with a keypad entry.

Dread fills my veins as a small screen lights up the dark passageway and I squint into the darkness, the harsh, bright light of the keypad sending a searing pain right into the back of my head.

What's the fucking code?

0000? 1234? 4321?

Fuck. No. They wouldn't make it that easy. Well, Marcus would make it that easy, but Roman and Levi would demand something more complex. Something their father would never remember. A birthday maybe? No, he'll have each of their birthday's memorized … but not their mother's.

I put myself back on that beach all those weeks ago when I sat up on the highest hill, watching as the boys dug a hole for their mother. We sat and talked until the sun went down. They told me everything they could remember, and I cried silent tears listening to the way they poured out every broken emotion clouding their hearts.

But what was it they said about her birthday? The twenty-something of April.

My hands clench into fists.

"Come on," I mutter to myself, pacing the narrow passageway in front of the metal door. "You didn't come all this way just to get stuck now."

My hands run through my hair and clench into fists, desperately trying to recall the moment. I doubt the keypad will reset if I get it wrong. It's not like my social media passwords that are going to give me three attempts before sending me a convenient email with a link to update it. If I get it wrong, I'm fucked.

With shaking hands, I move toward the keypad and go with my gut.

April 26th.

I start typing the code, pressing each number with care and accuracy.

0 … 4 … 2 … 6

A shaky breath expels from my lungs. "Oh, fuck, fuck, fuck, fuck," I breathe, watching and waiting, feeling absolutely sick to my stomach until the whole fucking keypad flashes green and the automatic locking mechanism releases inside.

"Holy shit," I sigh, filling my cheeks with air before letting it rush out between my lips, my relief knowing no bounds.

I don't wait another second, pushing against the door and letting it swing open into a dark room. I follow it through, no doubt that I'm exactly where I need to be. The door slams behind me with a heavy *BANG* and I jump before shaking out my hands, trying to get a fucking grip.

The room is small and, judging by the drain in the center of it, I can only assume that this is one of the many torture rooms the boys had built into the underground playground, a room I so hope to get to use against their father one day.

Rushing out of the room, I try to get my bearings, glancing around the darkened playground. The open space where I'd learned how to use a chainsaw is to the left, with all the cells to my right. I'm about halfway through the playground, and I have to keep myself from racing straight to the other end. Instead, I go to the left and start scrambling through the vast array of tools on offer, shaking my head as I really have no fucking idea what I'm supposed to use to cut through the metal locks.

I search high and low, my frustration quickly getting the best of me. There are guns and knives, every kind of weapon under the fucking sun, but my aim isn't nearly good enough to try and shoot out the locks the same way the boys would. But then …

I grab the guns and every silencer in sight, not sure which is best suited to do the job, or which even fits with what gun. Hell, I can barely even think straight, and the idea of such a loud gunshot going off makes me nervous, but what other option do I have? Bolt cutters maybe? If I knew where to find them, then maybe, but time is running out.

I've seen Roman do this before and I trust his shot better than I trust anything, even in the worst of times, he'll be able to get the job done. I know he will.

The boys were right at the far end of the cells in the darkest corner, so I get a move on, storming down the long line of cells, my desperation controlling my every move. My heart races, the fear of getting caught so close to the finish line is crippling my ability to think clearly.

Cells whip past me, and I push myself faster.

*I'm fucking coming.* I chant it over and over again like a mantra, willing them to hold on just a little while longer.

Ten more cells.

Eight.

Five.

Fuck, so close.

*I'm coming. I'm fucking coming.*

Three.

Two.

One.

# FIFTEEN

"Roman?" I cry, throwing myself down in front of his cell, immediately dropping to my knees, not giving a shit that it opens old wounds. The guns spill out in front of me with a wave of bullets and silencers before I've even looked up into that angelic face.

I swallow hard, seeking him out in the dark, but he's right there on his knees in front of me, his hand curling over mine as I clutch the metal bar. "Empress," he says, the exhaustion in his tone killing something deep inside of me. "I knew you'd be back here."

"Like I could stay away," I cry, fat tears falling down my cheeks.

Roman reaches through the bars and cups the side of my face, and

I instantly lean into him. "You're a fucking warrior, Shayne," he tells me, his thumb striking out to catch a falling tear before gently wiping it away, and within a moment, just one glance into my eyes and he can see right through me. He knows exactly what kind of hell I've been through at his father's hand. "Shayne——"

I shake my head and push the guns and silencers toward him. "Don't," I cut out, refusing to meet his stare.

He nods once, a silent acknowledgment, telling me that we won't speak of it now, but in time, he'll expect me to come to him, to tell him exactly what went down and exactly what I plan to do about it. And I can do so with my head held high because no matter what, he and his brothers will have my back every step of the way.

Roman immediately gets to work, scrambling through the weapons, picking up what I'm throwing down and figuring out what bits and pieces can somehow be useful to us.

Glancing back over my shoulder, I see the slightest outline of Levi and Marcus through their cells. They sit together, each of them slumped with exhaustion. Their cells share a wall of bars, and it kills me to see Levi pressed right up against them, holding onto Marcus with everything that he has, willing his brother to hold on just a little longer.

I can't make out his face, but I know he's looking at me, know the overwhelming relief coursing through his veins because I feel it just as strongly as he does. "Is ... Marcus."

"Still holding on," Roman tells me, his voice rising higher behind me, standing to his full height to wreak havoc over the lock holding him in his cell. "Do you really think the fucker would die before he gets the chance to eat your tight little cunt just one more time? It's all he's been able to talk about since you stormed through here last night."

Not having it in me to laugh, I simply step out of the way, letting Roman do his thing. He doesn't hesitate nor does he waste a single moment, squeezing the trigger and letting the bullet fly free. A soft pew sounds through the cells, echoing down the long playground before the heavy lock clatters to the ground.

He grips the cell doors and slides them back before racing out and falling into my arms, letting his brothers wait just a moment longer. "I fucking knew you'd come for us," he murmurs, his fingers gripping my aching jaw. Tears continue falling down my face as he briefly crushes his lips to mine before dropping his forehead. He takes a calming breath, holding me close, and I hate how fucking weak he feels in my arms, lethargic and broken. I've seen him walk away from bullet wounds as though it was nothing more than a papercut, but this time it's different. It's been just over a week, and while his stab wound has slowly begun to heal, it's nowhere near where it needs to be for him to be in the clear, not even close.

Barely a breath has passed between us before Roman releases me, knowing there's a fucking job to be done before we get a chance to celebrate. He cuts across to the front of Levi's cell, and before I can even catch up to him, he's already taking aim and firing off the quick shot to free his youngest brother.

His aim is perfect even in this horrendous darkness, and as I move in to grip the metal and pull the bars free, Roman is already moving onto Marcus' cell.

Levi watches me with wide eyes, refusing to get up and leave Marcus, so I race in after him, dropping down in front of him as Roman takes his final shot and darts to his brother's side.

I drop down in front of Levi, being careful not to hurt him as my hands cradle his face. "Are you okay?" I breathe, the tears getting fatter by the second.

"Peachy," he lies, the softness of his tone giving away just how much agony he's really in. He reaches up and grips my chin, forcing me to look up from my scan of his body and meet his dark eyes. He pulls me in closer, his breath brushing against my bruised skin. "Did he touch you?" he demands, swallowing hard as though just the idea of what happened in the castle could kill him.

I shake my head. "No," I murmur, the white lie breaking something deep inside of me, but I need him to focus on getting better. If I admit it right now, Levi might just insist on hanging around here a little longer just so he can get his hands on his father, but he needs to heal first. Nothing is more important than seeing the boys get better. After that, they can rain down hell over whoever the fuck they want. The right time will come, and when it does, I'll let him know, but in the dark corner of this cell, he can't read me as clearly as Roman had. "I'm okay. I just want to get you out of here. Can you walk?"

Levi groans as he shifts his weight, and I meet Roman's stare through the cells, both of us thinking the same thing—how the fuck are we supposed to get them both out of here?

Reaching through the bars, I find Marcus' hand and hold it tight.

"You're going to be okay," I whisper, wondering if I truly mean it. Right now, the confidence in my tone doesn't match the fear I feel inside, not even close.

A breath escapes Marcus' lips. "Shayne?" he murmurs, his voice barely audible in the deathly silence of the dark cells. "That you, baby?"

"Yeah, Marcus," I say, trying not to let my voice break as the fear begins to cripple me. Seeing him like this … this is something that will forever haunt my mind, a million times more than the vile abuse I went through at Giovanni's hands. "I'm here. Everything is going to be alright. I swear, I'm going to get you out of here. You're not dying on me yet."

Roman leans down in front of Marcus and slips his arms under his brother's lifeless body. "Come on, brother," Roman murmurs, clenching his jaw and lifting Marcus up off the ground. "It's time to go."

Levi grunts as Marcus' weight is lifted off his side and I reach down, slipping my arm around the back of his ribs and pulling his arm over my shoulder. He grips onto the metal bars and pulls himself up off the ground, his weight bearing down on me.

We move out of Levi's cell, and I pause by Roman's. "Give me a second," I warn Levi, making sure he's got his balance before I dive to the filthy ground, shoving the sheathed daggers and bullets into my pockets and tucking the gun into my waistband. Bouncing back to my feet, I grab Levi again and fall in behind Roman.

We're on the home straight, but it's going to be a fucking hike back to the stolen Corolla, and another two-hour drive back to civilization to get help. I try to pull it together and think positive for the boys, but we're not even close to being out of the woods.

We're only halfway down the long row of cells before a light sheen of sweat begins to coat Roman's skin. "What's the plan?" he grunts, already breathless.

My heart shatters. Marcus is a heavy fucker on his best day, but with open stab wounds and no food or water for a week while slowly bleeding to death, asking Roman to carry him all that way would be cruel. He's weak, all three of them are knocking on death's door, only Marcus has already been invited in. Making it all the way back through the woods to the car would be … fuck.

"I have a car," I tell him, breathing heavily while trying to support Levi's weight, terrified with just how much he's declined since last night. "It's out in the woods, where you guys dug that escape tunnel."

"Shit," Levi grunts. "If we could get back through the castle and use the tunnel, we could hide out, take breaks."

Roman pauses, leaning his back against a cell while adjusting Marcus in his arms. "Can't," he grunts, the exhaustion already showing on his face. "Too risky. They'll catch us. We have no choice but to make a break for it across the fucking lawn and hope we make it to the woods before bullets start flying."

I meet Roman's worried stare, my chest heaving with heavy pants. "Giovanni doesn't know I've slipped away. The guards aren't looking for me yet, but it won't be long until someone realizes I've gone. This is our only shot. We won't get another chance to do this."

He tips his head back against the bars as Levi grips onto one behind us, giving me a moment to catch my breath. "We take turns," Levi suggests. "You can't carry him across the whole fucking property, not without collapsing."

"Look at you," Roman spits. "You can barely even stand. You can't take him. Don't fool yourself."

I begin pacing, my hands pressing against my temples before the pain slices through me and I remember the fucking beating my head took only a few short hours ago. I glance up at Roman, an idea beginning to form. "We need something to take Marcus' weight," I tell him, my brain spinning in desperation to make this work. "If I could … I don't know … push him, like a shopping cart, or something like that, then you can support Levi and then maybe … just maybe we might have an actual shot at getting out of here."

Roman glances at Levi, doing that silent conversation bullshit they do that I often find endearing, except for right fucking now. I need to know what they're thinking, need to know how this is going to work … *if it will work.*

"No," Roman finally says. "It's too fucking risky."

"Do you have a fucking brighter idea?" Levi shoots back at him. Roman's lips press into a hard line before he catches his breath and pushes off the bars of the cell, ready to walk a little further. Levi loops his arm over my shoulder once again, but this time he doesn't quite need as much help. "That's what I thought."

Roman mutters something under his breath that sounds a lot like, "If you weren't already dead, I'd fucking kill you myself."

"Okay," I cut in before this goes any further south. "Just tell me whatever the fuck it is you're refusing to tell me, and I'll get it done."

Roman clenches his jaw, side eyeing his brother before letting out a pained curse. "We had this big guy, Big Tony. Weighed about 450 pounds. We needed a cart to haul his ass around. It's hidden way out back in a storage shed, not visible from the castle. But you'd have to cross the fucking property, putting you at risk, and I'm not okay with it."

I scoff. "You think I was okay with you being stabbed right in front of my fucking eyes? You think I was cool with watching you fall to your knees and listening to you screaming at me to run? No, it fucking killed me, but sometimes, we don't get a fucking choice. So, screw you and your need to be an overprotective asshat. I'm getting the fucking cart. I'm the only one who's got the stamina to do it right now. I'm getting the fucking thing and then we're getting this big motherfucker out of here. Got it?"

Roman glares at me, not liking the idea one bit, but he doesn't have it in him to argue. He knows it's our only shot, and as much of a stupid idea as it is, it's got merit.

It takes us almost twenty minutes of agonizing steps to finally see daylight, and by the time the late afternoon sun is shining down on our faces, blood has already begun pooling on Roman's shirt, but the stubborn fucker hasn't said a word.

The boys quickly find somewhere to hide, and without a backward glance or even a semblance of a goodbye, I take off like a raging bull, knowing damn well that time is running out. Giovanni is bound to have noticed my absence by now. He has a bruised ego, and men like that can't handle it. He'll be determined to destroy me, to prove something, and he'll do it as many times as it takes to get me to either change my mind or suffer enough that I simply never want to mention it again.

Keeping to the shadows, I run as far as I can around the perimeter of the castle, only breaking out into the open at the very last moment. My heart races from more than just the strenuous run, and by the time I reach the hidden garden shed right in the back of the property, I'm certain that I would have been seen.

My back presses up against the storage shed and I listen out, trying to clear my mind and focus just like the boys taught me and when no shouting or bullets seem to come flying my way, I get back to work. It takes only a moment to find the cart, and just to be safe, I grab a rope as well. On my way out, a small refrigerator catches my eye, and I nearly sigh in relief when I find it filled with water for the groundskeepers.

I load up everything there is and quickly search for a first aid kit. It's doubtful that a man like Giovanni, or even the boys would be OSHA compliant with safety supplies for their workers, but there's bound to be some fucking bandages somewhere. Finding a small kit near the entrance, I toss it in with my other supplies. It won't be enough for what the boys need, but it should at least give them a sliver of hope.

Not wanting them to have to wait another second, I grab hold of the cart and race through the property like a fucking bat out of hell. I stare down the castle in the distance, hating just how far I still have to go and knowing that all it would take is one guard to walk across a single window to see me racing through the yard.

The run takes me only a moment, but it feels like a lifetime before

I'm able to dive back into the shadows of the castle. The boys have managed to walk a little further to meet me in the middle and without even a moment of hesitation, Roman dumps Marcus' heavy body onto the cart before switching him out for a bottle of water.

Levi does the same, and they each take small sips despite their need to down the whole fucking thing. As they do, I can't help but hold Marcus' stare. He looks absolutely defeated, and it kills me. Leaning over the cart, I gently press my lips to his. "We're going to make it," I murmur, giving the guys a second to catch their breath.

Marcus captures my lips in his, his skin clammy and pale. "Bet that sweet ass we will."

A smile pulls at my lips, and before I can respond, his head is lolling back again, too exhausted to be able to hold it up. They dump water over their faces, refreshing themselves as they prepare for something not one of us is mentally or physically prepared for. They rinse off their open stab wounds, cleaning out the dirt and grime, and before I get a chance to really think about just how hard this is going to be, I look up at two of the greatest men I've ever had the pleasure of falling in love with.

"Come on," I tell them. "We have to get across to the woods before they come looking for us. We're running out of time."

Roman nods, and a small spark of hope begins to burn deep in my stomach, seeing just how much better he looks for having that small break and a sip of water. Hell, there's even that familiar glint of fierce determination shining through his obsidian eyes. He holds my stare for a moment before turning back to Levi, clapping him on his back.

"You good?"

Levi nods, clenching his jaw and staring out at the woods as though picturing every step he's about to take, envisioning himself getting across the property and into the thick bush like a football player envisioning his team scoring the winning touchdown right on the buzzer. "It's now or never," he says, his shoulders bouncing with anticipation. "Let's fucking do this."

And just like that, Roman gently pushes me aside, takes the handles of the cart, and takes off across the property. Levi and I follow closely behind him, and even with their injuries, their long strides carry them across the property a million miles faster than I could ever dream.

Levi grips onto my hand, pulling me along with him, keeping the four of us in a tight group, not letting one of us fall behind for even a second.

Sweat coats my skin, and I can only imagine what fresh hell the boys are feeling right now, but we forge ahead, pushing ourselves to limits we never knew we were capable of.

It takes forever to cross the wide expanse of manicured lawn, and I'm more than aware of the tire mark the cart has left in the grass. I'm sure the run isn't as long as what it feels, but the thick woods can't come quick enough.

Once we finally break through them, we continue running just enough so that we're completely concealed in the bushes, and only then does Roman collapse into the hard ground. I go down with him, grabbing a water bottle from beneath Marcus' ass and cracking the lid.

Roman takes it greedily as Levi drops to the ground beside us, his knees crashing into the mossy earth as he grips his stomach, his hands instantly stained with blood.

"Shit," I pant as my arm weaves around the curve of Roman's head, holding him close to my chest as he closes his eyes, his desperation to save me and his brothers almost costing him his own damn life. Reaching across to Levi, I pull his hand away from his stomach and raise his shirt, getting a good look at his wound. "It looks infected."

Levi nods, giving me a grim stare. He's known that it was infected for a while and just never said anything. "Why?" I question, knowing he knows exactly what I'm asking.

He shrugs his shoulders and takes the water bottle right out of Roman's hands. "We got bigger things to worry about," he tells me. "Marcus is our priority. Once we know he's going to get through this, then we can worry about this shit."

I nod, knowing he's right. The boys might be in pain and barely holding themselves together, but they can handle it, what they can't handle is losing their brother, and that's not about to happen on my watch.

Catching my breath, I scramble back to my feet and focus on Marc. He looks terrible. The jolting of the run and the uneven ground of the woods couldn't have been good for him. I press a water bottle to his lips, and he barely opens his mouth enough for me to pour water into it.

"I heard my magical pussy has been the one thing keeping you going?" I tease, not feeling it but wanting to keep his spirits high.

He shakes his head as I place the water bottle back down and switch it out for the first aid kit. "Never been a magical pussy," he mutters so quietly I have to strain to hear the words. "Magic is for children."

"Oh yeah?" I grin, finding some antiseptic wipes before pulling up his shirt and gaping at the infection eating away at his stab wound. "And what would you call it?"

"Call it as I see it," he says, swallowing hard and trying not to wince as I begin to clean his wound. "It's a tight fucking cunt."

My brow arches and I pause for a moment, glancing up to meet his eyes and find him watching my every move as though he still can't believe that I'm standing right here in front of him. "A tight cunt, huh?"

"Nothing short of perfect, made for the filthiest of men," he tells me, making my thighs clench which only serves to remind me what happened back in that castle. I flinch at the thought, and if Marcus weren't so fucked up, he might have even noticed, so instead, I focus on his wound and let him continue, knowing that talking about my pussy is a sure-fire way to spark that fire that burns within him.

"No other cunt could squeeze my cock the way yours does," he continues. "It's the real fucking deal, Shayne. Ain't no fucker without a goddamn hair on his chest would even know how to handle that sweet pussy, know how to fuck it just right, how to make it come apart with nothing but a single finger. But nothing, *nothing,* compares to the sweet taste of your cum on my tongue. *That's* what's keeping me going, babe. Mark my fucking words, the moment I'm able to spread those pretty thighs and bury my face into that tight cunt, I will."

I lean in closer to him, bracing myself against the side of the cart. "I'm going to hold you to that," I warn him, the seriousness flooding through my gaze as I stare deep into his glassy eyes, ignoring the fact that half of his rambling doesn't make sense while the rest of it seems slurred. "And if you don't come through for me, if you fucking die on me and don't give me exactly what you've promised, I'm going to be pissed. Is that understood, Marcus DeAngelis?"

Marcus holds his hand up, using every last ounce of his energy to salute me before his arm falls heavily back into the side of the cart. "Your wish is my fucking command," he tells me. "Now get me the fuck out of here."

With that, Roman and Levi get back to their feet, and with the boys barely holding it together, and at least an hour trek through the thick woods, I take over pushing Marcus while doing everything that I can to distract them from the burning agony tearing through their weakened bodies.

# SIXTEEN

The guys barely fit in the Corolla, but for now, it's the best we've got.

Roman sits beside me as I drive, holding a bandage to his bare waist as Levi sits directly behind me with Marcus' head resting in his lap. Levi is the closest thing to a doctor we have and he's doing everything that he can, but with limited resources at our disposal, it's not a lot. At least, not until we get some decent pain killers and the strongest kind of antibiotics, and even after that, it'll be one hell of a scary waiting game. It could take days until we start seeing a difference, but until then, all we can do is keep him hydrated and comfortable.

"He's going to pull through," Roman says, reading me as easily as though I had the words stamped across my forehead. He reaches across the front seat, his big hand gently pressing down over my thigh and squeezing, while being careful not to cross any boundaries that I might have erected since the last time he was freely able to touch me. There's no doubt in my mind now, he knows what his father did.

I weave through the thick trees, my foot all the way down on the gas, trying to put as much distance between us and the castle while also desperate to get Marcus the help he really needs. Shit, the help all three of the boys need. The sooner we can get back into civilization, the better.

Letting out a sigh, I try to hold it together. It won't do us any good to get in a major car wreck right about now. God, that's the last thing we need. "I know," I tell him, starting to believe it more and more with every passing minute. Marcus still looks like he could drop off the face of the earth at any moment, but the water and that bit of fresh air and sun on his skin has already done wonders for him, though the race to the car only served to exhaust him more. I've never seen him so lethargic, but all that matters is that he still grips tightly onto his will to live, and that's so much more than I could ask for.

Glancing across at Roman, a weight presses down over my chest, and before the words can even come out of my mouth, his eyes are narrowing. "Out with it," he says, not one that likes to be kept waiting in the dark ... the last week of literally waiting in the dark more than proof of that.

I give him a tight smile, not wanting to break his heart any more than it already is. "The baby was there," I finally tell him, not sure how he feels about the baby right now. Hell, I doubt he's even had a real chance to figure out his emotions after his father so kindly dropped the 'he's not your baby' bomb on him. "I could hear him crying in the room directly beside mine. It was non-stop, like he's not happy … or I don't know. I don't exactly have any experience with babies, but I'm sure they don't cry that much … or *that* loud," I add, glancing away, unable to take the weight of his stare. "I, umm … when I left, I went to his room. I wanted to bring him with us. I promised Felicity that I'd take care of him, you know, keep him safe and all that, but he wasn't there. Giovanni took him somewhere, and I had no choice but to run without him."

Roman's lips press into a hard line and it's more than clear he's struggling with what he wants to do about this baby. On one hand, this is Felicity's child, the one he so desperately wanted to bring into the world, the one he wanted to father and care for. He was so happy knowing he was going to be a father, and when that baby was finally born, this overwhelming protectiveness kicked in. Without even laying his eyes on that child, he would have given up his life just to know he would thrive. But now … knowing that baby was never his, that his father constantly raped the woman he loved with the goal to conceive another son … yeah, I don't exactly feel great about it either. No matter what though, that baby is still their biological half-brother. The blood that runs through his veins also runs through theirs, and there's no ignoring that.

The boys have a chance to give this baby the life they should have always had, and something tells me that they're going to fight for this.

No matter what, they won't be able to push the baby away because it's simply not in their DNA to do so. They're kind and loyal, and if they have a chance to save this child from the same hell that they suffered … well shit, it's a no-brainer.

"It's okay," Roman finally says, his hand falling away from my thigh as the heaviness of the topic begins to plague him. "You were already risking everything to get us out. It would have been impossible to do it with a baby hanging off your—"

Roman cuts himself off as he peers out into the thick bushland around us, his hand falling to the gun that's been stashed in the cup holder between us. I glance out through his window and don't see a damn thing, but any gut feeling that has Roman reaching for a weapon is a feeling that shouldn't be ignored.

His hand pauses, squinting at something deeper through the thick trees that I'm clearly missing. "Is that …?"

My brows furrow and I try to peer through the trees but only allow myself a moment before having to look back at the dirt trail marked out through the bush. "What?" I rush out, needing to know if I have to adopt some epic drag racing skills in the next three seconds. "What do you see?"

A grin pulls at Roman's lips and his hand relaxes over the gun. "No fucking way."

Just as the words leave his mouth, a flash of black fur cuts through the trees, sprinting alongside the car and keeping up with us as though it was born to run, and hell, maybe it was. Levi laughs, his eyes lighting with joy as I hit the brakes and allow the car to come to a screeching halt just as the two big wolves break out onto the trail before us, narrowly avoiding becoming roadkill.

My door swings wide and I climb out of the driver's seat, glaring at the big furry bastards staring back at me with their tongues lolling out of their mouths. "You big assholes," I screech, holding my hands out, yet struggling to actually be mad at them. All I feel is pure relief knowing they're okay. "Where the hell have you been? I've been worried sick about you."

They took off down in that playground and I'm not going to lie, it would have been nice of them to stick around, perhaps give me just a few seconds of warning that Giovanni was about to jam a needle into my throat. I have no idea how they escaped the playground without detection or where they even ran off too, but they've lived at the castle and in the surrounding woods for years. They would know this property better than anyone.

Staring back toward the small Corolla, I realize that we have no choice but to squish Dill onto Roman's lap while Doe will have to lay across the floor space of the backseat, doing what she can not to wriggle around and bump Marcus in the process.

"Come on," I tell them. "Get in."

The big wolves saunter over to me, and I don't miss the way their noses rise high into the air, no doubt smelling the fresh blood spilling through the car and knowing that this is so much more than just some bullshit broken nose or stab wound through the center of a hand. The wolves are intuitive, far more than any human could ever be, and they know this is serious.

"Could it have killed you assholes to stick around?" I question as I open my driver's door for Dill to jump in. "I could have really used you guys after you abandoned me down in those cells. I don't know, maybe a quick heads up that Giovanni was about to knock me out with a fucking syringe to my neck would have been nice."

Dill bounds across my seat and awkwardly tries to push Roman out of his while acting as though he doesn't understand a damn word that I'm saying. Doe looks up at me with those big wolfy eyes, demanding I forgive and forget, and damn it, when my family is whole like this, there's not a damn thing I'm not willing to forgive and forget.

My heart swells, and I scratch her behind her ears before ducking down and pressing a quick kiss to the top of her head. Her tongue lolls out the side again, and I roll my eyes as I open Levi's side door. Doe immediately climbs into the car, keeping her body low until there's enough room for her to drop down onto her stomach and try to find a position that offers even the smallest bit of comfort.

After closing Levi's door and getting back into the driver's seat, I glance over my shoulder to find Doe's big head resting on the seat, her stare locked onto Marcus' while Dill is half sprawled across Roman's lap, his big head against the center console, watching through to the backseat just as Doe does.

They really care about him, just as we do, even though they're wild animals. They consider Marcus their family, and if we were to lose him, they'd feel that grief just as strongly as we would.

Swallowing over the lump in my throat, I turn my attention back to the road and floor it, not willing to waste another second between now and getting the boys the help they need.

----------

"**A**re you sure about this?" I question, bringing the small Corolla to a stop around the back of the building, right where Roman had parked the last time we were here.

"I'm sure. It's the only place we can go without question."

I shake my head, my eyes wide with fear. "But Marcus ... he needs a hospital, a surgeon ... meds. How is he going to get that here?"

"There are sterile bunkers underground," he tells me, gripping the handle and moving to get out of the car. "One call is all I need to get a doctor down here. Trust me, Empress, this is where we need to be."

He's fucking crazy. Perhaps he's forgotten what this place is.

Roman glances over the massive building with unease, though he doesn't voice his concerns, just demands that I trust him without question. Though, he's never given me a reason to doubt him ... you know, apart from the whole dragging me through the woods and torturing me when he thought I shot Marcus all those months ago. Hell, that seems like a lifetime ago now. Too much has gone down. I can't wait to just spend my days watching Netflix and chilling with my guys, not even a hint of this bullshit drama floating in the air. Whatever happened to uneventful boring days anyway? I'd give anything to have that back.

Letting out a heavy breath, I push out of the car as Roman moves to the backseat, helping Levi to lift Marcus out of the car. My heart breaks watching them like this, seeing the care and fear in their dark eyes, the horror knowing that Marcus might not make it through this. He's always been so strong, indestructible, but right now, he's barely holding on.

Dill and Doe flank the boys, watching their surroundings and having our backs as we move toward the alley door of the massive warehouse ... the big fucking warehouse that just so happens to be used as Giovanni's main production center. "He'll find us here," I say, moving in closer to the boys, my spine stiffening with unease.

Levi shakes his head. "He'll look here," he confirms, "but he won't find us. Mick is good at his job. He'll wipe the surveillance cameras and cover our tracks. We'll be okay to lay low for a few days, let Marcus regain enough energy to move him again, but after that, we need to start putting a plan together."

I swallow hard and nod, not liking it one bit but if we could get a doctor here, someone to help Marcus, then I'm willing to do whatever the hell it takes.

We make our way to the back door and Levi slides his hand on the keypad, quickly hashing in the code before letting the retinal scanner do its thing and stepping back as the industrial sized door opens. It pulls back and we quickly move inside the warehouse, but not before Roman spares another glance up and down the back alley.

We move through to the second door and by the time it's opening, Mick is there, meeting us on the other side. Confusion settles across his face, not having expected to see us here today, but the second he gets a good look at the three boys with the wolves flanking their sides, his eyes widen in horror.

"FUCK," he curses, his eyes darting from left to right, trying to assess everyone and their injuries. "What do you need?"

Roman nods back toward the door we just came through. "Lose the car and wipe the cameras," Roman orders. "I don't want a fucking trace of this ... and get me a fucking doctor who knows what they're doing."

Mick nods and gets a move on, his phone already out of his pocket. We move past him as he hashes in the code and brings the phone to his ear. He quickly disappears through the door, surely to lose the car as instructed, but the second the door closes behind him, Mick is already gone from my mind.

We weave through the warehouse. It's creeping up to eight in the evening and I'm relieved not to find many workers here tonight. The less people who know we're here, the better. I don't doubt that Giovanni has realized we're gone by now, and the fucker would surely be coming after us already. Despite being out of there, our time is still running out.

We need to get ahead of this. We need to get the boys back in good shape and figure out how we're going to move forward.

The boys cut through stacks of rebranded pills, and I resist the urge to grin at their logo on the front of the small packets. Obviously, Giovanni hasn't thought to make a trip out here in the past week and has no idea what the boys have done, though that is only going to make this even more entertaining. Oh, to be a fly on the wall when he figures it out.

High piles of cash keep us hidden as we move through the

warehouse and come to a stop outside an elevator. Levi presses the call button, and the soft ding that sounds through the warehouse is enough to send anxiety pulsing through my veins.

I quickly glance around, but no one seems to be paying any attention to what we're doing. Letting out a sigh of relief, we step into the elevator, and I'm surprised to find so many different levels on offer. Most buttons are the standard, plain silver buttons, but at the very bottom, separate from the others, there are three black ones, none of them labeled, and each requiring a retinal scan to select.

My brows furrow as I watch Levi hit the middle black button and lean into the retinal scanner. There's no *ding*, no digital screen telling us that the scan was approved, no button lighting up like they do at the mall—just one minute, we're closed off in a metal box, and the next, the doors are opening into a world of disbelief.

We step out into a clinical hallway with large metal doors on either side and heavy, industrial locks in place. It smells weird, like we must be deep underground. I don't like it one fucking bit. "Is this some kind of bomb shelter?" I breathe, the place sending chills down my spine.

It looks like the kind of bullshit you get in a scary movie right before the crazy psychopath begins chasing you with a knife. The only difference is, in this particular situation, we're the messed-up psychopaths.

We walk down the long hall until Roman turns toward a door. "In here," he says, nodding at it, silently telling Levi to hurry the fuck up and open the damn thing.

Levi cuts in front of me, quickly pulling back on the heavy bolted lock before pushing the thick metal door open. The room leads down a steep stairwell, and as we pass the door, Levi quickly closes it behind us again. We get to the bottom only to find another locked door, this one seeming much heavier and resistant than the one before, but it's nothing that Levi can't handle.

The door slides open, and we step through to a clinical bunker that looks more like a surgical room. There are narrow beds at the far end, a small bathroom with a shower, and a wall of weapons, filled with everything anyone in our position could possibly need.

Roman immediately moves toward the surgical table in the center of the room and lays Marcus down, blood instantly spilling over the side and dripping onto the clean, sterile floor. I move in beside him, curling Marcus' hand into mine, hating that I don't know how to help him. Letting him know that I'm here is all I can really do for him right now.

He slept for most of the drive, and I'm not going to lie, the way Levi would constantly shake him awake just to check he was still with us didn't bother me one bit, despite how desperately he needed to rest.

Roman tears the shredded shirt off his clammy body and tosses it to the ground, while Levi begins rifling through the vast array of medical supplies, only judging by the grunts and shallow curses, we may not have exactly what we need.

Levi comes back with a stack of supplies, though I can tell he's anxious for the actual doctor to arrive. He doesn't have much energy of his own, and soon enough, all three of them are going to be passed out. "He's burning up," Levi mutters, handing me a washcloth. "Wet this and dab it over his face, we need to keep that under control."

I do as I'm told, hurrying toward the small bathroom and quickly drenching the washcloth before wringing out the excess water and hurrying back to Marcus' side.

The boys start cleaning him up, but he needs hardcore antibiotics to fight the infection and a surgeon to stitch up the internal wounds. Who knows what kind of hell their father's dagger wreaked on their organs? With each passing minute, my frustration only gets worse.

Where is that doctor?

It feels like a lifetime ago that Felicity shot Marcus. That night, Levi didn't hesitate to dive straight through the wound to retrieve the bullet and stitch him up, but this is different. Marcus' body is too weak to fight it. He needs the right kind of medical help to ensure that he makes it through the other end.

I go back and forth, keeping the washcloth cool on his head before grabbing another and sponging off the dried blood from his skin. I know it won't help him in any way, but I always feel better when I'm clean.

After what feels like a lifetime, a quick rap sounds at the door and Roman quickly rushes across to open it. Mick appears holding a box, with a woman by his side. My gaze falls to the woman, and I've never seen anyone look so wary and terrified. It's clear Mick hasn't given her any details as to why she's here, but when she gets a look at Marcus on the table, understanding flashes in her eyes.

I can only assume this is the doctor.

She doesn't hesitate, moving across the room and finding a pair of gloves. She quickly chats with Levi, getting as much information as possible as she begins loading Marcus up with something that will hopefully put him out of his misery.

As the doctor tends to Marcus, Roman spouts off a list of things he needs for Mick to organize: food, medication, a car, more weapons, and cell phones. He goes over everything as Mick places the box down at his feet and I can just see the tip of the contents spilling out. There's no mistaking the vast array of medical supplies in there, extra bandages, gauze, tape, syringes … and thank fuck, a shit load of what I hope to be the strongest kind of medication anyone could ever need.

We're going to be okay.

Mick scurries away, determined to get a jump on wiping the surveillance footage and logs from the scanners before Giovanni has a chance to find it, but he doesn't leave without assuring us that he'll be back with everything that we need. Roman sends Dill and Doe with him, giving him instructions on where to stash them for the time being, and my heart breaks just a little more watching the massive wolves follow him out.

The door closes behind him and just as Roman collapses down onto one of the small beds and goes to close his eyes, a sharp gasp tears from deep in my chest. "What is it?" Levi spits, his eyes wide as he looks to me in concern.

My gaze travels over his body, my brows furrowing in confusion.

"The gunshots," I say, feeling like an idiot for not having even thought about this sooner. "I heard them when I was leaving. Three of them. Giovanni shot you all, but …" My gaze flicks to Roman, scanning him from head to toe, just as I did with Levi. "Where are the bullet wounds?"

Roman holds up his hand and I see a chunk of flesh torn out of the side of his hand, big enough to cause a shitload of pain, but not enough for a man like Roman to concern himself with. "Warning shots," he mutters, closing his eyes and allowing his hand to fall back onto his chest. "Three shots into the grass, one just a little too close."

"Fuck," I breathe, falling against the wall of the bunker and slowly sliding down to my ass. "I thought they were kill shots. Those first few days after," I start, tears forming in my eyes, remembering the grief at thinking I'd lost them. "I thought … I thought you were gone."

"It'll take a shitload more than a fucking bullet to take us out," Levi murmurs before dropping down onto a bed and falling back, his head crushing against the pillow. His eyes immediately close, and within moments, he falls into a deep sleep, and hell, maybe Roman already is too.

Wanting them to get as much rest as possible, I keep my torturous memories and comments to myself, sitting in silence and listening as the doctor tirelessly works on Marcus. It takes long, tormenting hours before she declares that he's going to be okay, and only then does she move onto Roman and Levi, cleaning out their wounds and ensuring they're alright. After the boys have been treated, she digs through the box that Mick had left and hands out medication like it's candy.

She gives strict instructions on how to care for Marcus, and I commit each one to memory. She quickly looks over my bruised jaw and fixes a proper bandage to the slice on my arm. She doesn't ask how any of this happened, nor does she question our names. Just simply does the job I can only assume she's being paid a shitload to do.

Once there's nothing else for her to help us with, she spares me one last curious glance, probably wondering how a girl like me could fit in with these three guys. She doesn't ask and I don't bother offering her anything before her heavy stare falls away and she slips out the door, hopefully to never see us again.

# SEVENTEEN

Three days.

Three fucking days is all it takes for Marcus to get back on his feet and declare that he's some kind of indestructible god. Fuck, the asshole is close to assuming that he's immortal, but in reality, he still has a long way to go. All three of them do. They're each fighting different levels of infection, Marcus obviously has the worst.

Mick came and went, offering us everything we needed to get through the few days underground before explaining where we could find the car, cell phones, and enough cash to keep us going. He confirmed that everything had been wiped from their system and that on day two, Giovanni had raided the place like a fucking psychopath, just as we thought he would, and Mick had shown him a live feed from the bunkers to prove we weren't down here, which he then explained was a mirror image of the empty bunker across from us.

The boys pretty much rested the entire time, and I did what I could to keep them comfortable as they healed, while also avoiding every lingering stare that came from Roman. He knows too much, and I feel him waiting, anticipating the moment that my grief will all come crashing down around me. He hasn't said a damn word, but soon enough, he's going to push me to talk, and the moment I open the floodgates, I'm scared I won't be able to stop. Not to mention, we're in a cramped space, the second I speak about it, Marcus and Levi will know and then nothing will be able to reel them in. Hell, I haven't even shared the big news—I'm their new step-mommy.

Fuck.

This is wrong on so many levels.

Hell, at this point, I don't really know if I'm scared to tell them because of their reactions or if I'm just too afraid to face it, to admit what happened in there, to own it and start the process of learning how to move past it. I'd do anything to not have to go over those details, to say the words out loud and see the looks on their faces.

What are they going to think of me? Will they see me as dirty? Used goods? Will they pull away from me, not being able to even touch me without imagining what their father did to me?

Shit.

For now, all I want to focus on is them getting better. Once we get out of this bunker and find somewhere to stay, somewhere to lay low and figure out our next move, then we can address the ugly details.

Marcus passes in front of me for the hundredth time over the past few minutes, and I roll my eyes, leaning back against the wall of the cramped bunker. It was one thing when the three of them were bound, but after three long days, they're getting just a little agitated. I don't blame them though, after being locked up in those cells, they're probably desperate for freedom.

"Stop fucking pacing," Levi grunts, playing with a gun, pulling the bullets out before putting them straight back in, the same routine he's been following for the past hour. But hey, I'm not one to judge, whatever passes the time. "You're going to tear your stitches."

"My stitches aren't your fucking problem," Marcus fires back, his ability to keep calm long gone.

Levi scoffs, shooting a nasty glare at his brother. "Right, because I'm not going to be the one that has to restitch them like I did yesterday and the day before that. Sit your bitch ass down."

A smirk pulls at the corner of my lips, and I glance up from under my lashes, watching the show, a sick excitement drumming in my veins. Levi might pass his time by loading and reloading a gun, but I get my kicks from watching these assholes lose their shit at one another like three caged animals. Then they have to spend the next hour acting as though they're not bothered by their close proximity. What can I say? It's been a long three days.

Marcus glares at his brother, and I get a thrill out of how fired up he is. It's a dangerous game. He isn't exactly known for being able to control his reckless emotions, but seeing that fire burning through him, getting stronger each day, makes me feel like I'm on cloud nine. He's not my usual, ready to fuck at the drop of a hat, Marcus, but he's sure as fuck on his way.

"Can't we just get the fuck out of here?" he questions, glancing back at the clock that sits high on the wall above the door. It reads 8 pm, and I let out a sigh, predicting the next conversation that's about to go down.

"No," Roman murmurs, laying back on his bed, his eyes boring a hole into the ceiling with his laser-sharp stare. "We leave at nine."

"What difference does it make?" he grumbles, his frustration building and coming out clear in his deep tone. He crosses the bunker and slams his fists against the wall before leaning into them and letting out a low groan. "I can't take this anymore. I need to get out of this fucking shoe box."

"9 pm," Roman reminds him for the millionth time, taking absolutely no pity on the brother who he almost lost only three days ago. "Not a minute before. Not a minute after."

Reaching out, I press my hand to Marcus' hip, wanting to offer him what little comfort I can. He immediately drops his hand to mine and shuffles just a little bit closer, needing that closeness just as much as I do.

Roman has his reasons for wanting to leave at nine. The whole plan he's carefully constructed with Mick to get out of here unscathed and undetected all starts when the clock strikes nine, and Marcus knows that. He knows it's imperative to wait, but he's not exactly a patient guy. He likes to act first and deal with the consequences later, and if they weren't still healing, maybe we would have taken the risk.

I don't know how Mick intends to pull this off, but Roman insists that he's as good as he says he is, and I trust Roman's instincts. He's never let me down … except that one time when he jumped to conclusions and decided my word wasn't worth trusting, but that's all in the past now.

The thought has my gaze shifting across the room to Roman to see the perfect outline of my bite tattooed on his forearm. Every now and then, when he's caught deep in a thought, I catch him looking at it, staring as though his will alone should be enough to change the past. His finger traces over the bite mark, and it only lasts a moment before he sighs and drops his hand away. Those moments kill me. I've been able to block out those memories, been able to replace them with new ones, but not Roman, he holds on to everything.

"That's still a fucking hour away," Marcus mutters, relentless with his demand to get out of here. "What the hell am I supposed to do for another hour?"

"The same thing you've been doing for the last seventy-two hours."

Marcus sighs before a grin begins pulling at his lips, and he slowly angles his head down to meet my gaze.

"No," I say before the words even get a chance to come flying through his full lips. "Absolutely not. I've told you a million times already, you're not fucking me until your stitches have healed properly. I've fallen victim to that bullshit before, and it won't be happening again. You can wait."

"Come on, babe," he says, crouching in front of me, his hands falling to my knees. "Promise I'll make it worth your while."

Rolling my eyes, I capture his hands in mine and push them off my knees, grinning back at him. "I don't doubt that, but the answer is still no," I tell him, not daring to let on that the thought of being vulnerable like that right now scares the absolute shit out of me. I know it's irrational and the boys would never hurt me like that, never take away my consent, but it's too soon, too fresh, and if I had the guts to actually speak up about it, I know Marcus wouldn't dare press me on this right now.

His eyes narrow, and for a split second, I fear he's reading my mind and trying to put the pieces together, but the moment his eyes light like it's Christmas morning, I let out a soft sigh of relief. "What about this," he says. "What if, instead of me fucking you, you fuck me. I can just lay back and let you take control, let you do your thing. It's a win all around. My stitches won't tear, you'll get to take control, do whatever the fuck you want to do to me, and the boys get a fucking show." He grins wide, pausing as if to give me a chance to think it over. "Why didn't I think of this before? It's pure genius. We should have been doing this all along and those seventy-two hours would have flown by."

Marcus shakes his head, his smile faltering. "Actually, it's kind of depressing. What a wasted opportunity."

I scoff and his brows shoot back up, meeting my stare once again, the question still lingering in his eyes. "You're insane if you think I'm about to fuck you, but I'll definitely take a raincheck on that one. Besides, that camera up in the corner looks far too suspicious. I'd bet a week's worth of orgasms that Mick has been watching us this whole time with his dick in his hand, just waiting for us to start fucking."

"Nah," Marcus says, falling down on his ass and leaning back onto his hands, not willing to push me any further. I said no the first time he asked, and if he were seriously trying to convince me, he would have played me with those dark bedroom eyes that he knows I can't resist. He's a gentleman like that. "Mick's not like that."

A laugh bubbles up my throat and I raise a brow. "How do you know that? Have you met the kind of people you like to keep company with? Don't think for one second that I've forgotten that party you guys threw in the castle. Literally, all your friends are either serial killers, on the FBI's most-wanted list, or have done hard time in the past few years. What's a few perverts added to the list? Or is there only room for one serial killer pervert around here, Marcus DeAngelis?"

My eyes sparkle and he immediately picks up what I'm putting down. "If you didn't have such a tight little ass, then I wouldn't have to be such a fucking pervert around you. You bring it all on yourself, Shayne Mariano."

"Damn," I say, batting my eyelashes, feigning adoration. "All this time away from you made me forget just how sweet you can be. I bet you tell all the girls that right before you slit their throats, just to watch the blood stain their pretty white dresses."

Marcus grins at me, slowly shaking his head as his dark eyes sparkle with mirth. "You better wash those filthy words out of your pretty mouth, Shayne. You're getting me hard, and you've already told me no. Don't set me up for disappointment."

"Sorry," I laugh, patting the space beside me and watching as he instantly moves into my side, curling his arm over my shoulder and pulling me into the safety of his warm body. I relax into him. I've been sleeping in their arms every night and remaining as close to them as humanly possible just to have that warmth and feeling of home that I get when I'm close to them. When they hold me, nothing can hurt me, not even the bad memories, and over the past few days, I've become dependent on it. "Tell me something."

"Like what?"

I shrug my shoulders. "I don't know … anything. We have an hour to kill. Tell me something I don't know."

Marcus grins and shoots his stare across the room to Levi who has done nothing but sit across the bunker minding his own damn business. "Have I ever told you about the time I caught Levi jerking off to Ronald McDonald?"

What the actual fuck?

Levi's head snaps up as Roman groans from his bed, knowing all too well what the next hour is going to consist of. "I was not," Levi demands, his eyes wide as he looks at me, shaking his head. "I swear, babe. I don't have a fucking clown fetish. I was getting off to the chick on the opposite page. It's not my fault there was a full-page McDonalds advertisement on the next page."

A grin pulls at my lips as I pinpoint my entertainment for the next hour. "Really? Are you sure? Because if you need me to wear a red wig and paint my nose red, I will, but I draw the line at the big, floppy clown shoes."

Levi shakes his head. "Fuck me," he breathes, leaning back against the wall as he glares at Marcus. "Thirteen fucking years we managed to never bring that up. *Thirteen years, bro.* I thought you had my back."

Marcus laughs, his eyes twinkling with the type of secret he knows will bury him. "It's cute you think that over the space of thirteen years, I haven't told every motherfucker who came my way."

Levi's face drops, mortification taking over his sharp, handsome features. "I swear, dickwad, if you weren't barely holding on right now, I'd fucking shred you to pieces."

Marcus winks, taunting his brother. "That's cute too."

The boys get into it, throwing insults back and forth as I relax deeper into Marcus' side, feeling truly at peace for the first time in over a week. Their insults are perfect, deadly, and wicked in all the right ways, and it makes me wonder just how many long nights they spent in that big-ass castle doing this exact thing, forcing themselves to get creative to keep on top of the game.

It's not long before Roman stands, and I gaze up at the big clock. 8:59 pm.

He moves into my side, offering me his hand, and I take it greedily before he pulls me up from the ground. "You ready?" he questions, leading me toward the heavy, metal door as Levi cuts in front of us and slowly pulls the lock out of place.

Taking a deep breath, I look up into Roman's adoring eyes as Marcus subtly moves in behind me, his hand pressed to the back of my hip, ready to propel me forward if needed. "I'm ready."

"Good," he says, looking up at the clock once again. "It's game time."

Not even a second passes before the power cuts off, and if Mick is as good as he says he is, then it's not just the warehouse that's out—it's the whole fucking city. Every camera, every scanner, every streetlight, completely out, making it nearly impossible to track our movements.

The door swings wide and we take off like fucking bats out of hell, having only two minutes and sixteen seconds to race up six flights of stairs, break out of the warehouse, and get to the new ride Mick stashed in the storage facility halfway down the block before the city generators kick in and the power restores.

From there, we'll be able to start a new life. At least, Mick promised that he would fill the car with everything we would need to start fresh if that's what we decide, but I can't see that happening any time soon. Not going to lie though, I appreciate that he went and bought us each new clothes and made sure to have refills of all the medication the boys are dosed up on.

Levi runs out in front as Roman grips my hand, pulling me along. The door of the stairwell has been left unlocked, and I can only assume that the one at the top has been too. It takes less than four seconds for us to hit the very first step, and even less for the boys to start racing up them like it's their greatest challenge.

The noise of our feet thunders in the hollow stairwell, echoing up and bouncing off every wall. Levi takes them two at a time as Marcus keeps right on my heels, his hand still on my hip, propelling me up the stairs at a speed that scares the shit out of me.

The need to comment on just how strenuous this is on their bodies rattles me, but every sentence I try to form gets replaced with silent chanting. *Don't fall, don't fall, don't fall.*

The first floor passes with ease, and by the time we're reaching the top of the second, my thighs are starting to burn. I'm sure the boys could do this kind of shit all day. Fuck, I bet they even used to practice it up and down the castle steps, but not me. Running really isn't my thing, but an elliptical? No, absolutely not. No sir. There's a reason I've never had a gym membership, but if this is what my future is going to look like, then perhaps it's about time I sign up.

"Don't slow down on me, baby," Marcus says, feeling the resistance as he tries to push me up the stairs. "I've seen the way you fuck. Those thighs have more fucking endurance than mine. You can handle this."

He's right. I can ride those fuckers for hours on end, even with my thighs burning. It's just mind over matter. When I'm riding them, I'm pushing for that sweet release at the end, and this is no different. If I put in the work, I'll be rewarded on the other end. It's just a different kind of reward this time.

I push myself faster, matching Levi's steps in front of me. "You're a fucking goddess, Shayne," Roman says, noticing the newfound fire burning through my veins as he silently keeps track of the time.

We pass the third floor.

Fourth floor.

Fifth floor.

Ignoring the ache, I push through it, forcing myself faster until I can barely feel Marcus' hand at my hip, and before I know it, we're crashing through the door at the top, bringing us right out into the pitch-black warehouse. I can't see shit, but the guys seem to have this place mentally mapped out as though they have spent every waking hour of their lives preparing for this very moment.

Voices call out across the warehouse, and I strain to hear them over the rapid beating of my pulse against my eardrum. I don't doubt they can hear the sound of our feet slamming against the warehouse flooring as we storm through here like a fucking tornado, but before I can give them a second thought, we're racing out through a side door and into the cold night.

"Time?" Levi calls over his shoulder.

"A minute, twenty-eight," Roman calls back, his hand tightening in mine.

"Fuck," Levi growls, picking up his pace.

That took too long. We still have to get down the street and break into a storage locker. It's probably been left unlocked, but that doesn't change the fact that there's only so much we can do within the space of two minutes and sixteen seconds.

My feet pound against the ground, and I push myself harder, determined to make this happen. My chest rises with sharp pants, and I feel myself beginning to slip, but Marcus is right there, pressing against me and taking the strain. As long as I keep my legs moving, he can propel each of my steps further and further.

It won't be long. All we have to do is get inside that storage locker and then I can stop. After everything we've suffered through together, I refuse to allow a quick sprint to be my downfall. Hell no, if I'm going down, it'll be during a fucking war with a crown on top of my goddamn head and my men at my back.

"Twenty seconds," Roman grunts just as I see the storage facility up ahead, the very sight of it lighting a fire under my ass and giving me a target to aim for. It's not so bad. We can make that … I think.

Ten seconds pass before we're finally sprinting into the complex and rounding the corner. All the storage garages look exactly the same and my eyes dart from side to side, conscious of the big lights and cameras surrounding us. They're still out, but it won't be long now. Only a few more seconds.

"There," Levi calls out, pointing across the lot. "Number eight."

We sprint, all too aware of our time quickly dwindling. "Five seconds," Roman calls as Levi reaches the old roller door. He doesn't hesitate, reaching down and gripping the little handle before tearing the door up.

"Three," Roman says. "Two."

Panic tears at me as Marcus pushes against my back, taking us that final step and crossing into the safety of the storage shed just as the power flickers back to life.

I collapse against the brand-new Escalade, my face squishing against the shiny midnight paint. "Holy fuck," I pant, unable to catch my breath as Marcus braces his elbows against the hood, his forehead dipping into his hand. "Are you good?"

His jaw clenches and he glances down at his waist, gently pulling his shirt up to see a trickle of blood sailing down his tight abs, dripping along the harsh curve of his V. "Shit," he says, pressing his shirt against the wound to mop up the blood before it can make much more of a mess. "I'll be fine. I just need a minute."

I nod, feeling it more than he could know, and that's without a stab wound or a life-threatening infection. If I were in his position, I would have given up by the second flight of stairs, yet every fucking moment of this he proves to me just how strong he really is.

Fuck, I'm seriously out of shape.

Roman walks to the driver's door as I quickly look around the small storage garage, double checking that we're not about to be sprung. "There are no cameras in here," Roman says, reading my thoughts, "but that doesn't mean the night guard hasn't been alerted to an open door. We have to move. Now."

My tongue rolls over my dry lips, and I nod, knowing he has a damn good point, but actually getting my legs to move again is going to be a struggle. My knees give out and I stumble around to the back passenger door as Marcus and Levi take the other side. "You know," I say, passing Roman as I reach for the handle. "I could always drive."

Roman laughs, tearing open the door and instantly climbing in before quickly searching out the keys. He reaches up and drops the visor down, grinning as the keys fall directly into his waiting hand. "No chance in hell," he tells me, watching me through the rearview mirror as I get comfortable behind him.

All four doors close, one by one with heavy thuds, and before I can even ask where we're heading, the shiny Escalade is roaring to life, the vibrations of the engine rocking the whole damn thing.

Roman doesn't waste another damn second and hits the gas, the momentum pressing my back flat against my seat. The tires squeal and all too soon, we're peeling out of the storage facility and racing past Giovanni's warehouse like criminals on the run.

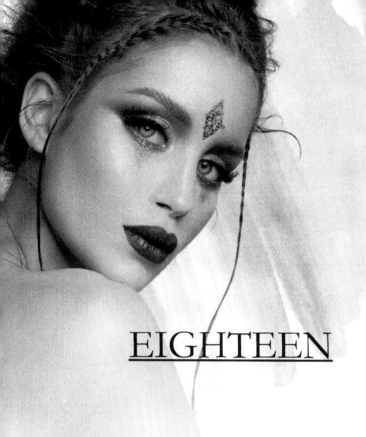

# EIGHTEEN

The Escalade pulls to a stop outside a large country property, and I stare out the window, my brows furrowed in confusion. "Is this where we're staying?" I question as Roman pulls the small button to put his window down.

"Hell no," Marcus says, his face scrunching up at the small cabin-style home that looks as though it's about to fall over. "Even in desperation, I still have five-star taste."

I scoff, suppressing the comment sitting on the tip of my tongue as Roman leans out his open window, pressing his fingers to his lips and letting out an ear shattering wolf whistle that immediately has my head pounding.

"What the hell was that—"

The words fall away as I see Dill and Doe come bounding through the massive country property, their tongues lolling out the side of their mouths while their tails wag from side to side like two happy little murder puppies. They're so carefree that I find myself watching them with awe, my chest constricting with a fierce jealousy. God, what I'd give to have that.

Soon. *Really soon,* I promise myself.

Levi climbs out of the Escalade, and by the time he reaches the trunk and has the door wide open, Dill and Doe are already there, jumping into the massive trunk space and shoving their enormous heads through, their hot, meaty breath slamming into my face.

I hold back a gag, unable to push their heads away simply because of the happiness in their eyes at seeing the boys alive and well. Levi gets back in, and within seconds, Roman is pulling the car around and hitting the gas, leaving nothing but dust in our wake.

We drive for another few hours, and it doesn't take long before Marcus is uncomfortable and fidgeting in his seat. He twists around, reclining his chair and trying to stretch out. I don't blame the guy, there's nothing wrong with me except for a bruised ego and a shitload of dark thoughts that plague my every waking hour, and even *I'm* ready to get out of this car.

Only a few short days ago, I would have killed to be able to spend long ass hours cramped in a car with these three guys. Now that I know they're on the brink of being perfectly fine, that reckless desperation inside of me has begun to ease.

Now, I'm only plagued with a deep anger and hate. It fuels me like never before.

By the time Roman is pulling down a familiar driveway, Marcus is sprawled across the backseat, his head in my lap and my fingers knotted in his messy hair. "Here? Really?" I ask in surprise, glancing out the window at the big mansion I thought I'd never see again.

My question stirs Marcus to open his eyes and sit up. He glances out the window, his brows arching just as mine had. "Shit," he mutters under his breath, looking to the front seat of the car and studying the hard set of Roman's jaw. Concern laces his dark eyes, but it's clear that Levi and Marcus are just as surprised to be here.

Roman doesn't answer my question and realizing that one is never coming, I turn my gaze back to the charred remains of the home Roman built. It was only a few short weeks ago that we burned this fucker to the ground … with their uncle inside of it.

The fire decimated the front half of the massive property, but there's still plenty of it left for us to hide out in until we find our bearings. At least, I hope there is. Who knows what it actually looks like inside. It's definitely a risk being here, but what other options do we have? I don't think Giovanni would come here. He would have written this place off the moment it burned to the ground.

Roman brings the Escalade right to the top of the circle driveway and cuts the engine. He pauses for a moment, taking in a deep sigh that the boys don't notice, but I do. It's clear that he hates what we did here, that this project he loved so much was destroyed, despite it being taken away from him. But he would have done it a million times over if it meant keeping me and his brothers safe.

Levi walks around the Escalade and opens my door for me, unintentionally robbing me of the chance to grill Roman about his headspace. Slipping out of the car, Levi takes my hand, and just when I think he's about to lead me around the back of the Escalade to let Dill and Doe out, they come bounding out after me, jumping straight over the backseat.

Marcus leads the way with me and Levi just behind him, but it's not until we hit the bottom step of the charred mansion that I hear the final door of the car open and close. Roman is silent as he follows us up the grand entrance, but despite not saying a damn thing, I feel him there. His presence can't be ignored. He's just that kind of guy who walks into a room and has the eye of every last person without even trying. He's a natural born leader, just like Marcus and Levi. But unlike his brothers, that alpha bullshit seems to radiate out of him without even trying.

Marcus stops by the remains of the front door, and honestly, there's not much to look at. He gives it a gentle push and the expensive charred wood crumbles. Not wanting to dwell or twist the knife already protruding from Roman's chest, Marcus silently continues, stepping over the front door burial site and continuing deeper into the foyer.

He sucks in a breath, and that's the only warning I get to prepare myself as Levi tightens his hold on my hand and leads me into the mansion.

"Shit," I say, letting out a shaky breath of my own as Levi follows. I come to a stop in the center with Levi stepping in behind me, his hands at my shoulders as we each take in the destruction. It looks bad from the outside, but in here, it looks so much worse.

Marcus moves around in a wide circle, needing to take a closer look as I hear a soft "Fucking hell," murmured from the non-existent door.

My heart breaks and as if sensing that need in me to question him, he silently moves away, avoiding me like the plague as he makes his way through the foyer. He passes the sitting room to our left which was used as Victor's personal barbeque room and deviates his stare before moving through the front portion of the mansion, his back stiff and taut as waves of emotion roll off him.

Glancing up at Levi with a wide, concerned gaze, I silently ask him what the hell I'm supposed to do. I hate that Roman is feeling this so heavily, that his heart is most likely shattering inside his chest as I stand back and do absolutely nothing.

Levi gives me a tight smile and pulls me into his chest, his strong arm curling around my body. He dips his head toward me, and I close my eyes as his warm lips press against my temple. "Go," he murmurs, his words so low that Marcus and Roman, who are barely a few steps away, won't hear. "I don't know what he needs, but I know you're a part of it."

His soft lips move away enough for me to raise my head, and without skipping a beat, I push up onto my tiptoes and capture them in mine. Our kiss is brief and gives me just a fraction of the closeness I've been craving over the past week and a half.

Stepping away from his side, I move through the charred remains of the foyer, passing Marcus, who gives me a tight smile, his fingers softly brushing mine as I go. By the time I catch up to Roman, we're moving through the back portion of the foyer and into a wide-open living space. It's just as charred and ruined as the grand entrance, but it holds a little hope that things might get better.

His sharp gaze travels over the living space as we walk through it, not stopping to take in the minor details, but I don't doubt that he's silently working out a game plan to restore it.

Moving into his side, I allow my fingers to brush up against his, and he greedily takes my hand, linking our fingers before looping our joined hands over my shoulder and drawing me into his side. Looking up at him, I take in the sharp set of his jaw, his deep, dark eyes that look so broken, and the slight frown resting on his lips.

Pulling him to a stop, I reach up with my other hand and curl it around the back of his neck, my thumb resting along his jaw. His eyes drop to mine, and for only a moment, he lets me see just how deeply the devastation burns within him.

My thumb moves back and forth over his jaw as I slowly move closer into him, his other hand dropping to my hip as his forehead gently presses against mine. "Are you okay?" I murmur, the heaviness between us weighing us both down.

Roman scoffs and raises his head just enough to press his lips against my forehead. "It's a home, Shayne. Four walls and a bit of interior design. It's nothing that I can't rebuild, but that's nothing compared to what you're going through." He drops his gaze, letting it bore into mine just enough to prepare me for where he's going with this. "I should be asking you the same question."

I immediately look away, not ready to go there. Not even close.

I begin pulling out of his arms, and despite his better judgment and every little need to hold on to me, he lets me go. I've been scarred enough over the past few weeks, and there's no way in hell that he'll try to add to that in any way.

"The fuck is he talking about?" Marcus' stern tone sounds through the heavy silence. Glancing back over my shoulder, I find Levi and Marcus, both watching me and Roman with furrowed brows, anger and confusion swirling in the dark depths of their eyes.

Fuck.

"It's nothing," I say, picking up my pace and moving through to the next room. "I'm fine. Roman shouldn't have said anything."

Roman scoffs, which only sets off the boys even more. If there's anything they despise, it's being left in the dark, especially where I'm concerned. Finding out that one of their brothers knows something and they haven't had the decency to share? Now that is a betrayal of the most epic proportions.

"Shayne," Levi demands as I try to scurry away, the memories of that day coming back to me in haunting waves, image after image assaulting my mind.

I push through a door and move into a room that didn't get hit so hard from the fire, letting me know that maybe this mansion can be saved after all, but right now, it's the furthest thing from my mind.

A hand curls around my elbow and I'm spun around to face all three angry DeAngelis brothers. Well, two of them are angry, the other looks a little sheepish—so fucking sheepish that he deserves a goddamn stiletto heel slammed up his ass. The fucker knew what he was doing. I've seen it on his face for days, desperate to question me, desperate to know the details just so he can dwell on them and fuel his hatred for his father. But bringing this up right now in front of his brothers, fuck. He's going to get it, and it's not going to be pleasant. This is all a ploy to avoid his own feelings about his home, and for that, he's right at the very top of my shit list.

"The fuck is going on?" Marcus spits, his emotions always getting the better of him. "What are you keeping from me? From us?"

I clench my jaw, my heart racing like a fucking jaguar through the thickest jungle. My gaze snaps to Roman's as I tear my elbow out of Levi's strong grip. "Dead to me," I spit, loving the way my words make him flinch. I don't mean it, not really. Despite his moody assholish tendencies, I'm crazy in love with the fucker, but damn, do those words make me feel better, even if only for a second.

I storm away knowing all too well that there's no way I can avoid this now. The boys will get the answer they want whether I'm ready to share it or not, and there's not a damn thing I can do about it. But if I can make Roman hurt during the process, then that's more than alright with me.

The boys storm behind me, and I barely even get a step away before Levi's tone fires through the open room, betrayal thick in his voice, mixed with a sadness that pulls me up short. "We don't keep secrets," he murmurs. "Not here. Not now. Not after everything we've already suffered through. If there's something you're hiding from us

…"

He lets the words fade away, but I still hear them loud and clear. He's asking me why I don't trust him, why after everything we've been through I still feel as though I can't share part of myself with him, but that's not it at all.

Agony spears through my chest, and I slowly turn to face him, hot tears stinging my eyes. "You seriously think that after all this time, after everything we've been through, that I still don't trust you? That I would purposely keep secrets from you?" I question, the tears falling down my cheeks and staining the top of my tank. "Have you considered that maybe I'm not ready to discuss it? That I needed to see you guys get better before I thought about what I needed? That maybe I haven't even come to terms with what happened? That I can't even get the words to come out of my mouth because I'm so damn scared that they're going to tear me to shreds all over again?"

I drop to my knees, my head instantly falling into my hands as heavy sobs tear from the back of my throat.

"Fuck," Roman says, dropping down with me, pulling me into his arms and holding me close to his chest. "I'm sorry," he murmurs, his lips brushing against my neck as he speaks. "You've just been so strong over the past few days I thought maybe it wasn't affecting you or that you'd just brushed it off as not being a big deal. You've always been so open with us, and you didn't say shit. I almost convinced myself I'd imagined the whole fucking thing. I … I wasn't thinking. I'm sorry, Shayne. Fuck. I shouldn't have—"

"I'm not asking again," Marcus demands in an authoritative roar, forcing my eyes up to his. "What the fuck is going on? Did someone hurt you while we were locked up? Gia? One of her men?"

Roman gently rubs my back, his other hand coming up to wipe away one of my many tears. "They need to know, Shayne. At some point, they're going to try and get you alone. They're going to kiss you and touch you and you're going to let them because you don't want to let them down, but you'll be dying on the inside. We can't take care of you if we don't know what happened."

My eyes flick to Levi, seeing the pieces beginning to fall into place. He watched his father's syringe drive through my skin, he watched me fall to the ground, watched him take me away, but Marcus, he would have absolutely no recollection of what happened down there.

Levi shakes his head, horror flashing in his eyes while also a hint of self-loathing for not having questioned it sooner. "Tell me he didn't put his hands on you," he growls, his hands shaking at his sides.

"The fuck?" Marcus spits, his stare coming straight back to mine. "What the hell are they talking about? Who put their hands on you, and why the fuck am I just hearing about this now?"

Taking a few deep breaths, I try to calm myself. As much as I want to tell Roman to go and eat a flying dick, he's right. I might not be ready to discuss it, to have to face everything that went down, but sooner rather than later, Marcus or Levi are going to touch me, and it's going to send me into a world of devastation. They need to know, they all do, and from there, we can figure out a way to help me move forward.

Wiping my eyes, I get to my feet and take a hesitant step back, leaning against the wall that was once pristine and white, but is now covered in soot, burn marks, and dirt.

Reaching out, I take Marcus' hand, wanting to ease the fiery desperation pulsing through his veins as Roman gets back to his feet. The three of them crowd me, and despite wanting all the space in the world, I let them be close.

My gaze cuts across to Roman's. "It's not just what you think it is," I start, the ugliness pulsing through my veins and pooling deep in my chest as his brows furrow in confusion. "After he, you know," I start, rubbing my hand over the side of my neck where Giovanni had shot me up with drugs. "I woke up in my old bedroom. I would have only been out for a few hours. My wrists and ankles were tied down to the bed and—"

"No," Marcus breathes, moving even closer as his hold tightens on my hand. "My father raped you, didn't he?"

My gaze falls away, not having the strength to look any of them in the eyes. "Yes," I finally say, swallowing over the lump in my throat.

Marcus lets out a pained breath, dropping his forehead to my shoulder as Levi turns away, slamming his fists against the wall and bracing himself there. He takes rapid breaths, barely holding on to his last shred of self-control, while needing a moment to himself to come to terms with what I just said. But I can't let them fall apart yet, if they're going to hear me, then they're going to hear it all.

"It's more than just that," I tell them, my hand slipping under Marcus' shirt and pressing against his chest, needing to feel the solid beat of his heart beneath my palm, reminding me that somehow, through all of this, we're still alive.

"What more could there be?" Roman questions, moving closer to my other side and gripping my hand in his like it's his only lifeline.

My gaze remains down, and I focus on Levi's back, watching the way his shirt strains against his body, the material stretching over his muscles. There's a small sliver of skin peeking through at the bottom of his shirt, and I can't take my eyes off it, focusing hard as I let the words fall from my mouth. "I was bound to the bed when three of your fathers guards came in."

Marcus sucks in a breath, his hand tightening in mine to the point of pain. "No," I rush out, "not that."

He immediately relaxes his hold, but not quite as much as it was before. "What happened?" he prompts.

Letting out another breath, I continue. "They came into my room and cut me from my binds. Stripped me bare and forced me into a shower. They watched as I washed myself then threw a razor at me. They made me shave everything while their filthy stares lingered on my body. I didn't even get privacy to use the toilet. I … even after what your father did to me, I think that might have been the most humiliating part about it."

Tears fall from my eyes again as Roman kisses my temple. "You're okay now. You're safe."

I hold on to his words, closing my eyes and allowing them to sink in and find purchase somewhere deep inside of me.

*I'm safe now.*

*I'm safe.*

Keeping my gaze locked on that small sliver of skin that peeks out from beneath Levi's shirt, I watch as he slowly turns and watches me back. "I was told to make myself look nice, given a whole bunch of makeup and hair products, and after twenty minutes, I was told to dress in the silk wedding gown hanging off the closet door."

All three of them curse as another tear rolls down my cheek, but I tune them out, knowing if I were to stop one more time, I probably won't be able to keep going. "I was taken to the church. All of your family was there, and they watched me with sneers on their faces, as though they knew I was Gia's blood. They didn't give a shit that I was just a regular girl being forced to marry a man three times her age. They didn't care what was going to happen to me, or even gave a shit when he hit me in front of the whole fucking congregation."

I let out a shaky breath and avert my eyes lower to the ground. "When it came to the vows, I refused. I wanted to fight it, but he forced me to do it. He ..."

"What did he do?" Marcus spits through a clenched jaw.

My broken and scared gaze lifts to Marcus' dark eyes, looking back at me with nothing but love. He doesn't pity me, doesn't look at me as though I'm dirty or used. Don't get me wrong, he's pissed. Fucking pissed to be finding out like this days later, pissed that I wasn't open straight away, pissed that it even happened in the first place, but that love in his eyes gives me just that little bit of strength I need to push on. "He had a live feed of you in your cell. One of his guys ... they were hurting you. They were going to kill you if I didn't go through with it, and I ... I couldn't let that happen. There's nothing that I wouldn't have done to save you guys. You have to know that."

"Shhhhhh," Roman soothes, wiping at a tear. "You don't have to explain yourself to us. We would have done exactly the same thing had you been in our position. You are our number one priority. We love you, Shayne, like that deep gut-wrenching type of love that is definitely going to kill us one day. We know you'd save us even if it meant giving up your own life because we would do the same fucking thing for you."

He presses his lips back to my temple, and I take a few calming breaths, letting my heart slow once again. Closing my eyes, I try to focus. "He shoved me in a car and I was sent back to the castle. The driver dragged me back inside, and I swear, I tried to fight it. I tried to get away, but the dress and his size … I just … I couldn't. He took me back up the stairs and forced a pill down my throat and then walked away."

A chill sails down my throat, remembering the feel of the guard on top of me, forcing the pill into my mouth and then pouring the water. "The second he left, I ran into the bathroom to throw it up, but by the time I came out, your father was already there and the pill … I don't know what it was, but I was already dizzy and my muscles … I couldn't control myself. I fell and your father grabbed me by my hair and dragged me to the bed."

Tears fall down my face, staining my shirt as my voice breaks, the pain quickly catching up to me. "I tried to fight him off, I swear. He cut my contraceptive rod out of my arm and was talking shit about how easily he'd taken Felicity and—"

I cut myself off. There's no point in telling the rest. They know what happened.

Levi meets my stare and pushes off the opposite wall, walking into me. Marcus and Roman inch aside and I fall into his strong chest, closing my eyes as his arms curl around me. "You got out of there, Shayne. That's all that matters. You survived to tell your story and now, you get to be the one who destroys him."

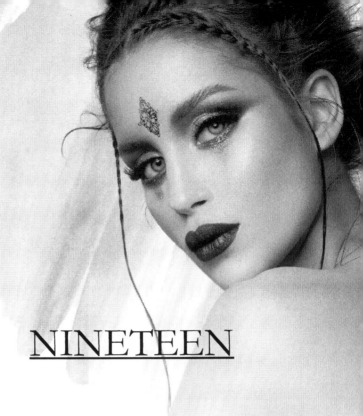

# NINETEEN

The deeper into the mansion we go, the more we find that survived the blazing fire. There are cars in the underground garage left completely untouched, a fully stocked kitchen, bedrooms and living areas. If this mansion had been smaller, maybe it wouldn't have lived to tell the story, but as it is, there's enough room for us to lay low and piece together a plan to destroy Giovanni DeAngelis… and hell, if that plan just happens to fuck with Gia too, then I'm good with that.

Naturally, the power to the mansion is about as fucked as Giovanni is going to be, but as long as we have food and water, then we're going to be just fine. Though, I'm not going to lie, the fully loaded armory that survived the fire is also a bonus.

We sit in a dark living room with a blanket over my lap as I curl into Marcus' side on the couch. Levi disappeared to the only surviving kitchen ten minutes ago, while Roman has been searching the mansion for some kind of lighter or matches to start the fire in front of us.

It's a cold night, and while we could each go to separate bedrooms, all of which look as though they've never been lived in, the thought of being separated right now doesn't sit well with me. Despite us basically living on top of each other for the past few days, I still can't bear to let them out of my sight. So, a living room couch slumber party it is.

Marcus scoots down on the oversized couch, adjusting the thick blanket over his lap as his fingers draw small circles on my shoulder. "You good?" he murmurs, turning his face into me and pressing his lips against my head in a lingering kiss.

I smash my lips into a tight line and snuggle deeper into his side. It's only been an hour since the four of us stood in the charred hallway and I spilled my deepest shame, and since then, the boys haven't left me alone for even a second. One of them has always been with me, holding me, watching me, checking that I'm not about to break.

"I'm alright," I murmur, my gaze shifting to the massive fireplace directly in front of us, finding it easier to relax in this darkness. "I just … I wish you guys didn't have to know all of that. It makes me feel … I don't know, kinda dirty."

His body tightens beneath mine, and without hesitation, Marcus grabs me and sets me down over his thick thighs so he can stare right into my eyes. "You listen to me, Shayne Mariano," he demands, gripping my chin and holding my stare as my hands fall to his waist, knotting into the soft fabric of his shirt. "You are a lot of things. When we first took you, you were innocent—"

"Innocent?" I scoff, cutting him off. "I was hardly innocent. I let you chain me up and fuck me with the handle of a knife, and if I recall correctly, I was begging for more. That hardly screams innocent."

Marcus grins. "No, you're right. You definitely weren't innocent, but you were sure as fuck a different, softer version of this woman you are now. You've been through hell, and yes, some of that was at our hands. You've got scars no woman should have to bear and the kind of nightmares that would scare even the devil himself. You're fierce, loyal, destructive, and fucking gorgeous in every possible way. Me and my brothers have never been so lucky to have stumbled upon you. You've made us whole again and given us a purpose when we were on the cusp of giving up. You are a lot of things, but *dirty* is not one of them."

I glance away, his words equally spreading warmth through me while also making me feel cold and empty. "I am," I insist, taking his hand and placing it on my thigh. "When you touch me here, all I picture is *his* hand. When you lean into me, I remember the feel of his body against mine. I'm so scared that when I finally feel you inside of me again, I know exactly what's going to go through my head, and nothing can take that dirty feeling away. I know you don't see me that way, none of you do, but I can't help feeling it. When I'm with you guys, I'm willingly handing my body over, but with him ... he stole it and abused it as though he had every right, and the body I received back doesn't feel like my own ... not anymore."

Marcus trails his fingers over the side of my face, pushing my hair back before I lean into his touch, wishing there were some way for him to strip me of that pain.

Tears threaten to spill as I lift my gaze and meet his stare once again. "I don't know how I'm ever going to be able to give myself to you guys again without feeling … that."

Marcus' hand slips lower on my face before curling around the back of my neck and pulling me down to him. He's gentle and gives me the chance to pull away if I need it. But I go because being close to him, being close to any of them, is the only thing keeping me from falling apart.

My hands brace against his strong chest as my forehead comes down on his. "You know I love you, right?" he questions. "You are my whole fucking world. There's not a goddamn thing I wouldn't do to make you happy. I will do whatever it takes to help you feel comfortable in your own skin again. If that means not touching you, or sleeping in different beds, then I'll do it. Just say the word, babe. I'm not going to push you, and you need to know that Roman and Levi won't either. The ball is in your court, and we don't want you being afraid to speak up about what you need because you're too caught up worrying about what we want. Do you understand me, Shayne? All we want in this whole fucking world is to see you rise like a phoenix and get everything you deserve and more."

A soft sigh escapes and I raise my chin just a bit to feel my lips resting against his. I kiss him softly, his words meaning more to me than he will ever know. "I love you, too," I murmur, my lips moving against his.

A silent moment passes between us, each of us simply living in the moment of being in each other's arms until I finally push back up onto his thighs. My eyes remain on his as Roman walks back into the room, heading straight for the fireplace and giving us our moment together. "What about you?" I ask him. "That was a lot of moving around we did today. That sprint up the stairs and to the storage facility couldn't have been easy on you."

Marcus shrugs a shoulder, his hand still on my thigh as he moves his thumb back and forth. "I'm fine, babe. Nothing a few days with you in my arms won't fix."

A grin tears across my face, and I quickly shake my head. "Don't even try to butter me up with that bullshit, Marcus DeAngelis. I just spent three days locked in a bunker with you. I know when you're trying to distract me." His eyes darken just a bit and I raise my brow. "What's wrong?"

He lets out a sigh and reluctantly pulls up his shirt, showing me the angry redness spreading around his wound and the dried blood from where he tore his stitches during our frantic run. "Shit," I gasp as Roman works on the fireplace behind me. I drop my fingers to the angry swelling and gently prod at it, hating the way Marcus hisses under the pressure. "Why didn't you say anything?"

Marc gives me a look that suggests I should be able to figure this one out on my own, but I simply stare right back, forcing him to say the words out loud just to hear how ridiculous they sound.

He lets out a sigh and peers down at the wound. "What can I say, babe? You will always come first."

Rolling my eyes, I let out a heavy breath and peer toward the entrance of the massive living room, but with no sign of Levi, I turn back and take in Roman who has a warm fire steadily building. "Have you seen Levi?" I ask. "Marc—"

"Marcus doesn't need that asshole poking and prodding at him anymore," Marc cuts in. "Just slap a Band-Aid on it and I'll be fine. I swear," he adds, seeing the look on my face. "I won't move from this spot all night and I'll be as good as new come morning."

Letting out a huff, I climb off his lap and cross the room to the box of medications and first aid supplies that Mick gave us. I return to his side a moment later with everything he needs, not hesitating to crawl back onto his lap. Pulling his shirt right over his head, I do my best to concentrate on the wound and not the masterpiece beneath me.

Getting straight to work, I spread an antiseptic cream over his wound, slowly massaging it in before bandaging it up, knowing all too well that he's over being stitched up. There's enough there to hold the wound and with a few more days to just chill, he should be as good as new. I don't know anything about internal wounds, but Levi has assured me that as long as they all take it easy from here on out, we should be on the home stretch.

Grabbing the bottle of water by the side of the couch, I force medication down Marcus' throat, grinning as he scrunches his face. "What's the matter? Not enough practice having things shoved down your throat? I could give you some pointers," I laugh as Levi waltzes back into the room, his arms full of food, though from what I can tell in the dark, it's nothing nutritious, but it's probably the best we've got.

Marcus grins right back at me and the best kind of warmth spreads through my chest. I hate that my issues are going to keep him from having me the way he really wants and needs, but he'll keep his hands off at all costs because that's just the amazing kind of guy he is. Doesn't change the fact that I want to … I just don't know how it's going to go. I owe it to them and myself to at least try.

My tongue rolls over my bottom lip as nerves settle into my stomach. "What's wrong?" he asks, sitting up a little straighter, sensing the change in me. His question instantly gets the attention of Roman and Levi, and all three of them watch me as though I'm about to break all over again.

Quickly shaking my head to ease their worries, I reach forward, nervously biting my bottom lip before swallowing hard. "I want to try something," I murmur, leaning closer and closer. His brows furrow, having absolutely no idea where I'm going with this, but willing, nonetheless. "I want to kiss you," I tell him. "Like *really* kiss you, but you have to promise to let me be in control. You can't reach for me, can't grab me, or deepen the kiss beyond anything I'm already doing. Not even a groan, Marc. I know you have a hard time handing over control, but I … I need to know."

He nods, his eyes focused on mine, and for a moment, I swear he looks just as nervous as I feel, something I've never seen in him before. "I'm not going to hurt you," he whispers, remaining as still as a statue, letting me slowly move into him. "I've got you, baby. Anything you need."

Fear and anxiety build in my stomach, and the closer I get, the harder it becomes to push past it, but I trust Marcus with everything that I am. If I need to stop, he won't think twice about it or be upset about not getting what he needs from me. He won't hold it against me for even a second.

My breath becomes shaky as I press a hand against his chest to brace myself. His hands fall away from my body, making me aware of them the entire time.

My hand shakes against his chest but I don't dare stop, determined to see exactly what Giovanni has cost me.

I swallow hard over the lump in my throat, and then just like that, the gap closes and my lips press down on his. So far, so good. This isn't anything I haven't already explored with them, so I close my eyes and allow myself to sink into him, slightly deepening the kiss.

I feel Roman and Levi's curious stares, each of them more than ready to pull me away if Marc even looks like he's at risk of losing control and pushing my boundaries. But a second passes and as my tongue pushes inside his mouth and I melt into him, the fear dissolves.

I kiss him greedily, taking everything that I've missed from him over the past few days. He matches my hunger, but doesn't dare push me further than what I'm ready to give. His hands remain where they are until I physically reach down and place them on my body. He pulls me in tighter but doesn't hold me flush against him like I know he's dying to do, giving me space to pull back if and when that time comes.

Seeing that I'm perfectly fine, Levi and Roman get back to what they were doing, leaving me to kiss Marcus with everything I've got.

I haven't dared kiss any of them with more than a small peck since finding them in the cells, and I don't doubt the jealousy is eating at Roman and Levi, but they're also very patient men … not Marcus though. He's a different breed.

My body melts into his, and I kiss him a moment longer until a soft groan pulls from the back of my throat. I don't intend on pushing my boundaries, only exploring where they are, so I gently pull back from him, my breath coming hard and fast.

Marc holds me just in front of him, our eyes meeting through the darkness. "You good?" he murmurs, his fingers brushing against the side of my face, pushing back that same strand of hair he only moved a few minutes ago. The nervousness still shines in his eyes, and he looks unsure if he did the right thing.

Swallowing hard, I nod, feeling the warmth exploding through me, spreading through my veins, and strengthening something I thought I no longer possessed. "Never been better," I whisper, a smile playing on my lips. "Thank you."

"Wow," he says, that nervousness fading away. "Can't say I've ever had someone thank me before."

Levi scoffs, jamming a crisp chip into his mouth. "Probably because you've never actually listened to what a woman wants before," he says, before adding with a wicked smirk. "Or maybe because our girl here didn't realize you were actually capable of satisfying her without the use of your cock."

Marcus grabs the water bottle by the side of the couch and launches it at Levi's head, his aim perfect as always. I laugh and slide off Marcus' lap, moving back in beside him and curling into his side, feeling a million times better about myself. It was only a kiss, a fucking good one at that, but I don't doubt that my issues finish there. There's still one more important test, but I'm not ready for that, not yet.

The fire crackles and lights up the room with a soft orange hue that somehow helps me to relax. The boys sink into their couches, laying back and enjoying the silence, each of us lost in our own thoughts. My eyes grow heavy, and just as I'm about to fall into a deep sleep across Marcus' lap, I hear Levi's soft murmurs across the room. "This is our last chance," he murmurs, his eyes locked on the blazing fire. "Whatever we decide to do, we need to make it count. We cannot fail this because the alternative … him winning and taking Shayne again. I won't accept it. We do this, or we fucking die trying."

Roman nods. "No more fucking around."

"So, what's the plan?" I murmur on a yawn. "Find the baby, kill Giovanni, destroy what's left of the DeAngelis family and rise up in its spot?"

Levi scoffs. "Close, but no. We can't take that baby, not anymore."

I push up off Marcus' lap, my brows furrowed in confusion. "What the hell are you talking about?" I question, looking to Roman for some kind of back up, but getting nothing. "We're rescuing that baby no matter what. That is your brother we're talking about."

Levi's lips press into a hard line, and for a moment, he looks sick with what he's about to say but pushes through it. "No, Shayne. I know your heart is in the right spot, but before, we thought that child was Roman's son, our nephew, but he's not. Since finding out that child is biologically my father's, it's not rescuing him, it's kidnapping."

I scoff. "Since when do you assholes have an aversion to kidnapping?"

Levi glances at Roman who leans forward, bracing his elbows against his knees and dropping his chin into his hands. "I don't know, Empress. I think we need to focus on taking out Giovanni first. The rest will follow. Going after the baby, it's too risky."

I stand and shake my head. "Absolutely not. Think about the childhood you had. That man is about to inflict that same hell on your brother, your blood. He needs you three more than ever. I made a promise to Felicity as she died in my arms. I told her that I would protect her son, that I would save him, and as long as he remains in Giovanni's care, I'm failing. We are going after that baby no matter what it costs. Even if I have to do it on my own."

I give the guys a hard stare, letting them see just how serious I am. "So, what's it going to be? Are you with me, or against me?"

Roman clenches his jaw. "That child was born out of deceit and betrayal."

"Yeah," I scoff, anger boiling deep inside of me. "He was. The woman you loved, the woman you wanted to marry was manipulated and raped over and over again, and all three of you missed it, just as we all missed the fact that she was being held down in Giovanni's desert cells. She might have lied to you to protect herself, but she also loved that child, and because of that, we owe it to her to save her child, your brother. I know you're hurting. I know you had hopes for that child to be your son, but you need to put that aside to see what's important in life. You have a chance to make a difference, and fuck, Roman, if you don't, I don't think I'll ever be able to look at you the same."

Then with that, I turn on my heel and stalk out of the room, leaving the guys to stew on it, knowing damn well that in the end, they will do the right thing.

# TWENTY

A chill sweeps through the big living room and I lift my head off Marcus' chest, my eyes squinting into the night. The fire is barely holding on, and I let out a soft groan, pulling back the blankets and peeling myself away from the warmth of the couch and Marcus' wide chest.

It must be somewhere around four in the morning. I don't really know, but what I do know is that the three boys are all but dead to the world. Despite not being in the comfort of their own home with their own beds, they were long overdue for a good night's rest where they could truly relax.

Padding across the big living room, I crouch down in front of the dying fire and reach for a few pieces of wood to feed the flames, hoping to not wake the guys.

Sitting for a while, I watch as the new wood catches and the flames grow larger, already beginning to re-heat the room. An undeserved pride tears through my chest, and I smile to myself as I stand and walk back over to the couch.

While the boys are doing much better and can just about withstand anything this fucked-up world throws at them, I can't fathom how horrendous a man-flu would be to add to our list of things to conquer. Fuck, three of them with the man-flu at the same time…

A shiver trails down my spine.

Hell to the motherfucking no.

Quickly checking over the guys, I make sure they're still asleep and let out a soft sigh. The week without them was hell, especially the first three-quarters of it when I thought they were dead. But seeing the lines on their troubled faces soften as they sleep—sprawled out on the couches and totally relaxed—that's a feeling I will never tire of.

*They're okay. They're safe. They're healing.*

*We're going to be alright.*

Moving back to Marcus' side, I reach over to the coffee table and grab some more painkillers and the antiseptic cream. Taking the blanket, I pull it down just enough not to disturb him before gripping the hem of his shirt.

Why does it always have to be Marcus? It wasn't so long ago that he was healing from the gunshot wound. Don't get me wrong, I will sit up night and day to help him get better, but it shatters my heart seeing him wounded.

As I remove the old bandage from his injury, my fingers brush lightly over his skin. His eyes flutter, and he drops his hand over mine. "You okay, baby?" he murmurs, too tired to open his eyes.

"Yeah," I whisper, holding the painkillers to his mouth and tipping a bottle of water to his dry lips. "Take these and go back to sleep."

He doesn't need to be told twice.

Marcus swallows the pills and lets me poke and prod at his wound, slowly massaging more cream into it before I quickly rebandage everything, wanting to disturb him as little as possible. He keeps his eyes closed, and while he looks as though he's sleeping, I know better.

Once I'm done, my gaze raises to his face, and I reach for him, brushing my fingers over the soft skin of his forehead, my heart pounding with overwhelming fullness. "You know I'd burn down villages just to be able to have one more day with you?" he murmurs into the night, his voice so soft that I can barely make out the words.

A grin pulls at my lips, and I relax back into his side, folding my arm over his chest. "You know, when men make declarations like that, most women would roll their eyes at the dark promises they know their man would never actually follow through with, but you ... you'd do it without even thinking twice, and that's what scares me."

A breathy laugh slips through his lips, gently vibrating against his chest. "Nobody ever said love wasn't complicated," he tells me, unashamed by his declaration of cold-blooded murder as his thumb brushes back and forth across my waist.

"Do me a favor," I murmur, raising my head up off his chest to look at him. He peers back at me through tired eyes, a subtle smirk resting on his soft lips, patiently waiting. "Don't burn down any villages."

"Can't make any promises," he says with a wink.

Rolling my eyes, I drop back to his chest, the warmth of his body spreading through to mine as I grip the blanket and pull it up to my shoulder, more than ready to slip into a deep sleep. At least I would have if Dill hadn't shot to his feet, his ears pricked and alert.

I watch him, my back stiffening as Marcus slowly drifts off again. "What is it?" I question, pushing up and watching as Dill crosses the big living room to the window, his tail dipped low, sending a wave of unease pulsing through my body.

A soft growl tears through his chest, and within moments, Doe is joining him, standing at his side, both their sharp gazes locked out the window. My hand falls to Marc's thigh and I give it a rough shake. "Something's wrong," I say, pushing up from the couch and cutting across the room, joining the wolves by the window.

"What's wrong?" Marcus questions, his sharp tone making Roman and Levi snap out of their deep slumber, all three of their heads whipping toward me, their laser-focused stares on my back.

I shake my head, having absolutely no fucking idea as I watch out the window, unable to see or sense whatever it is that has the wolves' attention. "I don't know, it's too dark. I can't make anything out, but something ... I don't know, something has the wolves about ready to attack."

Strong hands press to my hips, and I suck in a surprised gasp as a hard chest presses into my back. I hadn't heard any of them get up, but by this point, I shouldn't be surprised. Roman hovers over me, staring out the window with a sharp gaze. Silence fills the living room, the only noise I hear is the heavy thumping of my pulse in my ears.

"Fuck," Roman grunts just moments before I see it—a dark shadow cutting across the manicured lawn. But it's more than that. My eyes adjust to the darkness and I'm finally able to see it, men everywhere, shadows moving through the property, surrounding us at every angle.

Roman grabs my elbow and pulls me back. "Keep away from the windows," he rushes out, and before I can even respond, he's gone, already across the room with his brothers, digging into the pile of weapons they ransacked from the armory for this very reason.

"How many?" Levi questions, preparing for a fucking battle that they're not strong enough to endure, not yet. They're still healing, Marcus especially.

Roman shakes his head. "Impossible to tell. It's too dark. They have us surrounded."

Fear rocks through me as I move toward the boys. "No," I tell them. "It's too soon. We're not ready for this."

Roman looks back at me while checking over his gun. "What do you want me to do, Empress? Shall I run down there and request they come back at a more convenient time? They're going to come whether we're ready or not, and we have no choice but to go out there and face this head on."

"I know that," I spit back at him, frustration quickly claiming me.

"I just … I can't lose you guys again."

Roman sighs and steps away from his brothers, taking my hand. "You're not going to lose us," he tells me, pulling me into his chest and pressing a kiss to my temple. "We'll get through this just as we've gotten through everything else. Now get yourself ready. I don't want you out there unable to defend yourself."

I swallow hard and nod before stepping out of his arms and between Levi and Marc. I grab all my favorites, strapping knives to my thighs and checking that my guns are fully loaded. How many times is a girl supposed to do this? Why is it so hard to hold on to my happiness?

Levi double-checks everything I go over, and it grates on my nerves, but I know he's only doing it because he's adamant about keeping me safe and protected, not because he doesn't trust me.

Marc saunters over to the big window, watching the property with a keen eye, his sniper rifle slung over his shoulder. He glances down at the big wolves, and they watch him, waiting for some kind of command. Marc's eyes sparkle with excitement, the very thought of shedding blood making his own pump faster through his veins. "Wanna go hunting?"

Dill makes an odd *harumph* sound, and without a backward glance, the two wolves bolt out of the living room, their favorite game about to be played in epic proportions. Marc turns back and meets my stare before looking at his brothers. "I'm going up to get a better vantage point," he explains. "He wants her. He's not here for us. You know that, right?" he adds, sending chills sweeping through my body. "If anything happens to her while I'm gone, I will tear your organs out through your mouths. Is that clear?"

"Got it, brother," Levi snaps, almost offended that Marc would assume that I wouldn't be perfectly safe with Roman and Levi ... though, considering what happened last time, can I really blame him?

Marcus spares me one last lingering glance, and without so much as a goodbye kiss, he sprints from the room, determined to see this through. Roman and Levi move next, Levi's hand falling to my lower back and leading me through the mansion, back through the charred remains that we'd painstakingly trudged through only a few short hours ago.

Roman shakes his head. "He shouldn't have found us this fast."

"He could have been watching the property," Levi says.

Roman scoffs. "Or worse, he could have gotten to Mick."

Levi curses as we reach the massive, charred foyer that used to be so spectacular, but now is nothing but destroyed soot and ruins. Roman moves toward the front window, peering out at the lawn, his brows furrowed. "What's wrong?" Levi questions.

"I don't recognize any of these guards."

I move in beside Roman, peering out to get a better look at what we're about to face down. "Father has had nearly two weeks to replenish his guards after the last attempt on our lives. Just be prepared. Who knows what hole he dug these assholes out of," Levi states.

My brows furrow, watching the dark shadows on the lawn slowly creep closer. They're so formal, so in sync. "They're not your father's guards," I tell them. "They're Gia's."

"How do you know that?" Roman demands. "Do you recognize

them?"

I shake my head. "No, but watch how they move. They're well trained and have been working together for a while. Your father's guards were always sloppy and didn't know how to work as a team. Plus, look at their uniforms. They're all exactly the same, like tin soldiers moving under one command."

As if to confirm my theory, Gia Moretti, the bitch otherwise known as my mother, steps out of the darkness, Zeke at her side and a shitload of nerves break through my tough exterior.

"Fuck," Roman sighs, his gaze coming back to mine. "I can only imagine what she wants."

Swallowing hard, I meet his heavy stare. "I'm not going with her, no matter what," I tell them. "She was training me to kill your father and then she was going to kill me once her dirty work was out of the way. She had no intention of me taking over her empire. The bitch isn't even sick."

Levi lets out a heavy breath and I realize that I've been an idiot not bringing this up until now. I should have told them all of this the second I found them but getting them better was all that mattered to me. "I knew her 'sickness' was too fucking convenient."

Looking between the two brothers, I try to calm my racing heart. "So, what's our plan?"

Roman shakes his head. "We go out there and see what the fuck she wants," he says as though it's as easy as that. "Let her show her cards and use them against her. All that matters is that she still needs you alive, at least for now."

My lips press into a hard line. "Not unless she assumes that you're going to kill your father. Then technically, she has no use for me."

"FUCK," Levi grunts, his hands going to his head. "Why does every motherfucker we meet want to see you in a goddamn grave?"

"You're telling me," I scoff before moving to the door. "Let's just get this over and done with. Hopefully, we can get her to fuck off without having to put a bullet through someone's head."

"Marcus isn't going to like that," Levi says under his breath, letting out a heavy sigh before reaching for the door and giving me a tight smile. "What do we have to lose?"

Roman lowers his tone, darkness seeping into his obsidian eyes. "Absolutely everything."

Stepping out into the cold night to face down Gia's army isn't exactly something I want to get used to. Until now, it's always been Giovanni's army that we've faced down in the dead of night, and though that's not a great feeling either, Gia's army is something different. They're stronger and fiercer than Giovanni's men. They play by their own rules and are well versed in the art of manipulation.

The soft breeze hits my face as Roman and Levi flank me, no longer demanding that I stay behind them as they have in the past. Tonight, we stand as equals.

Gia's men stop the moment they notice us, and we immediately begin descending the stairs, not allowing their presence to intimidate us.

Gia continues forward with Zeke at her side, and my gaze flickers toward him, capturing his hard stare with nerves. The last time I'd seen him, he was giving me keys to a getaway car and telling me that if I ever returned, it should be to put a bullet in Gia's head. If it weren't for him, I never would have gotten away. I never would have found the guys, and I sure as fuck wouldn't have been able to get them the help they so desperately needed.

Without Zeke, the boys would be dead and for that, I owe him my life, but he's also the man who keeps Gia's bed warm at night. He has other intentions at play here, and I'm not sure he can be trusted.

We hit the bottom step and Gia watches me like a hawk, keeping a fair distance, but not too far that we have to shout to be heard. She glances over Roman and Levi, scanning them from head to toe, probably mentally tallying how many weapons are on their bodies and where their weaknesses may lie. "You're missing a brother," she comments, her gaze sharp and controlled.

"We are," Roman states, allowing her to believe the worst rather than explaining that the third brother is currently propped up on the roof of the mansion with a rifle pointed right between her eyes.

Gia narrows her gaze, not believing it for one second but having nothing else to suggest otherwise. With her whole army at her back, what does it really matter? We're only a small handful up against a fucking empire. We don't stand a chance.

Gia's gaze comes back to mine. "You ran from my home," she states. "You know the consequences. I explained to you what would happen if you were to run."

I nod my head. "Yeah, I heard you loud and clear. I heard the threats rolling off your tongue as though you'd dipped them in poison, but you know what? Your threats don't mean shit to me … and neither do you for that matter."

Gia's gaze darkens in a similar way that Roman's does when he's being tested, and it's damn clear that she doesn't appreciate it. "Do you see how this looks?" she spits. "What position you've put me in? My daughter, my heir, has willingly risked her life to save DeAngelis scum."

I laugh. "And I'd do it again."

Roman groans at my side. "Stop provoking her," he mutters under his breath.

Whoops.

"Your foolishness has come to an end," Gia spits. "You are embarrassing me and the legacy that I will be leaving behind. You will be coming with me whether you like it or not, so I suggest that you march your ass over here before I am forced to come over there and take you."

Levi flinches at my side, and I brush my fingers against his, allowing my pinky to hook around his thumb and feeling him slowly begin to calm. "So you can train me to kill Giovanni, turn me into one of your soldiers, only for you to fake a sickness and kill me once you've used me for your sick games? Yeah, fuck that. It was a nice idea while it lasted, but I'll pass. Catch ya on the next one."

Gia's eyes blaze, realizing that her carefully structured plan to fake a disease and rule the fucking world is imploding in her face. She scrambles, trying to think of how to play me, but it won't work. I'm not interested. I have too much to lose to risk being tangled up in her twisted little web again.

"I'm going to give you three seconds, Shayne Moretti. You're going to cross this lawn and stand behind me. You're going to say goodbye to your lovers and then walk away."

A smile pulls at my lips, and I hold back a laugh. "I applaud your confidence, really, I do. It's impressive, but I'm over it. You're not my mother. We may share the same blood, but you do not hold a damn thing over me. I'm over playing by other people's rules. I'm the puppeteer now, and you just stepped into my world."

Zeke presses his hand to his ear and in an instant, we have every gun on the property turned toward us. "You want to play games, Shayne? Then that is what we will do."

Her gaze drops to my chest, and I glance down to see the red, glowing dot on my chest, and I laugh, glancing up to find an identical one right between her eyes.

"Two can play that game," I say, watching as Zeke's head snaps up to the top of the mansion, seeking out Marcus' rifle with shock on his face. He hadn't expected us to be so prepared, and that's on them. They should have known that no matter what, we have each other's backs. "You know, I'm surprised you bothered making the trip all the way out here. After all, don't you have bigger issues to worry about other than tracking your degenerate daughter all over the state?"

Her gaze shifts over the property, taking in Marcus' exact location, taking her time as she tries to figure out how to play this, though something tells me that she's considering ending us all right here and now. But then, I'm sure she knows just how unhinged Marcus can be.

He won't hesitate to pull the trigger, and he sure as hell won't wait for a reason to do it.

Gia's stare falls back to me, narrowed and showing just a hint of confusion.

Hook. Line. Sinker.

"What are you talking about?" she demands, inching forward.

Roman and Levi follow her movements, not saying a damn word, but they don't need to, their intentions are clear in their dark eyes. They won't be giving up tonight. Gia is nothing but a small hurdle that stands in the way of what they really want, and they won't hesitate to take her out and start a war if it will get them one step closer to victory.

"Oh, didn't you hear?" I taunt, knowing just how much my bullshit is grating on her nerves, and honestly, with this little red dot hovering over my chest, it's not the smartest idea, but she needs answers, and until she gets them, the red dot is nothing but an empty threat. "You must be so proud. Your baby girl finally got hitched. I'm a DeAngelis now."

Gia's face drops, her eyes going wide as she gapes at the boys at my side. She storms forward, her men following her without question. She puts herself directly in front of me, jabbing her fingers right into my chest. "I don't know what kind of game you're playing, but I'll see to it that marriage does not stand, even if I have to slit their throats myself."

A full-on belly laugh tears through me as I shove a hand into her shoulder and push her back a step. "That's cute you think one of these assholes is my husband. I mean, I wish. Could you imagine just how possessive they'd be if they got to legally call me theirs? But think again, Mother dearest. You were right; running from you did come with its consequences because now there's a ring on Giovanni's finger with my name on it."

Her face falls again and she stumbles back a few steps, her eyes wide, quickly calculating her every move and what this could mean for her empire. But I just grin. "That's right, Giovanni DeAngelis has just opened a back door right into the heart of your empire, and there's not a goddamn thing you can do about it."

Panic tears through her gaze, wild and unpredictable, and in a flash, she tears her gun from the holster strapped to her thigh. My eyes go wide as time seems to slow.

A million things happen at once.

She raises the gun and aims directly between my eyes, just as Roman's hand curls around my arm, yanking me hard. Marcus pulls the trigger just as Zeke shoves Gia out of the way, but not before she fires her own weapon, sending a bullet hurtling toward us. Levi throws himself forward, catching the bullet in his shoulder just as Zeke drops to the ground, the bullets meant for Gia now plunging through his chest.

A tortured scream tears from my chest as Gia looks at Zeke, horror in her eyes for only a moment before she disregards him and scrambles to her feet.

Roman throws himself protectively in front of me and Levi, standing fearlessly before those he loves. "MAKE SURE HE'S ALIVE," Roman yells back at me, his gun stretched out in front of him, prepared and ready to take as many shots as he can, if that's what it comes down to, but there's too many of them. If Gia decides to turn this into a fucking war, we would crumble.

Dropping to my knees, I scurry to Levi's side. Blood coats the ground as fear rockets through me. "LEVI?" I cry, slamming my hand over the bullet wound and trying to stop the bleeding. "Please be okay. Please be okay."

He grunts, the pain tearing through me. "FUCK," he roars, spitting the word through a clenched jaw. "I'M FINE. I'M OKAY."

"There's too many of them," Roman calls back at us as Gia holds up a hand, a silent signal for her army to start descending on us. "LEVI," Roman calls, desperate for some kind of backup other than Marcus hidden up on the roof.

Levi scrambles to his feet, and as I race in between them, their big shoulders force me back. Blood soaks the back of Levi's shirt, and I know he's not going to be able to deal with this for long, especially after the shit he's still healing from.

Gia's army stands at her back, two men gripping onto Zeke's arms and dragging him back into the crowd as she looks back at us in a pure rage. "Hand her over," Gia commands, momentarily forgetting who the fuck she's speaking to.

Roman scoffs. "Come and get her."

Well fuck.

And that asshole was warning me against provoking her. He's just given her an open invitation to attack.

Bracing myself, I prepare for what's bound to be the fight of my life when Gia slowly begins looking between me and the boys. Curiosity dances in her eyes and my back stiffens, realizing the games are far from finished. She's had her moment of panic and an added bonus tantrum, but now the fierce leader of the Moretti family is back, and she can see the world clearly once again.

"I'll make you a deal," she says, her eyes on me, but her words aimed at the two men standing before me. "One of the famous DeAngelis brothers comes with me, and I will spare her life ... for now."

I scoff under my breath. "She's fucking insane."

There's no way in hell.

I look through the boys' shoulders, preparing to tell her to go and fuck a donkey when Roman's shoulders sag and Levi turns to me. My brows furrow, looking up at him as he steps into me, taking my face in his big hands and pressing his lips to mine. "I love you," he says, meeting my eyes with a loyal fierceness that kills me inside.

"What the fuck are you doing?" I demand, looking at him as though he's lost his mind. "Don't you dare walk away from me. She's playing us. She's only doing this to lure me out."

Levi smiles, pulling me into his chest and holding me tight. "I know, Shayne. I fucking know, which is why you can't come for me."

I search his eyes, desperation filling my veins like lead, weighing me down. He pulls back, and before I know it, Roman's arms are around my waist, gripping me tight ... too tight. Levi steps away and I shake my head, my eyes filling with tears. "No," I yell at him. "NO. LEVI."

"I'm sorry, Shayne. I fucking love you with everything that I am and if sacrificing myself to the likes of Gia Moretti is what it takes for you and my brothers to walk free tonight, then that's what I'm going to do. Do you understand me? I love you, Shayne. Don't do anything stupid."

I pull against Roman's hold, but his grip tightens, and he begins dragging me back toward the steps. "LET ME GO," I scream, clawing at his arm as Levi watches me, his heart on his sleeve.

"Say it," Levi says.

I shake my head, tears spilling down my face. "Don't you dare do this. Don't do this to me."

"Say it," he demands.

My heart breaks and a heavy sob tears from the back of my throat. "Please." He just watches me, silently waiting to hear those three words he knows have been plaguing my heart from the very moment we met. He takes a backward step as Roman pulls me even further away, and the desperation overwhelms me. "Please, Levi. Don't do this. We can survive this. Don't leave me. I love you so fucking much."

His dark eyes bore into mine, filled with everything we've refused to say out loud, everything that he's held back on sitting right there in his beautiful eyes. "There's nothing I wouldn't do for you, Shayne." He holds my stare a moment longer as a silent goodbye lingers in the air between us, and with that, he turns his back and walks into the waiting arms of Gia's army.

"LEVI. NO. DON'T DO THIS TO ME," I scream, the raw intensity of my cries tearing at my throat. I struggle against Roman's hold, watching as Levi is lost to the crowd of soldiers, his arms pulled tightly behind his back and bound as he's smacked down to his knees.

"LEVI. NO. DON'T TOUCH HIM. DON'T FUCKING TOUCH HIM."

Roman drags me up the stairs, lifting me off the ground as I fight against his iron grip. "No," I sob, watching the way Gia just stands there with a fucking smirk on her lips, watching me break into a million little pieces. "Don't do this."

"I'll be seeing you, Shayne," Gia tells me, her smirk widening as her eyes dance with laughter. "Mark my words. I'll be seeing you."

"If you hurt him," I spit, hot angry tears spilling down my cheeks, knowing that being a prisoner of Gia Moretti's is a fucking death sentence. "I swear to God, I'm going to fucking kill you."

"I welcome you to try." And with that, she turns her back and walks away with her army while Roman pulls me into the mansion, slamming the heavy door between us.

# TWENTY-ONE

"Let me go," I cry, clawing at Roman's arms as he carries me back into the massive living room where we'd only been fast asleep forty minutes ago. I try to pull free, slamming my elbow back into his neck, anything to get free, anything to race back out there and save Levi. I'll give her anything, anything she fucking wants, even if it means my own fucking life.

Hot anger boils within me, overwhelming my senses and filling me with a devastating rage that I have no chance in hell of trying to control.

My body aches, my heart cries, and my fucking will to live is gone.

I need him back.

Why did he have to do that?

Roman drops down onto the big couch, his arms still so tight around me. He adjusts his hold, turning me in his arms until I'm straddled over his lap. "It's going to be alright, Empress," he promises me, his words whispered but somehow still holding so much emotion that it only serves to kill me that much more. "We're going to get him back. No matter what, I promise you."

Sobs spill out of me, forcing their way over the painful lump in my throat. My head falls into the base of Roman's neck, trying to breathe him in, trying to desperately calm myself. "He's gone," I cry, my pain knowing no bounds. "Why would he do that? He just walked away. He just gave up everything and let her destroy us. He didn't even fight, just let her take him."

My tears stain Roman's shirt but he doesn't dare push me away, just simply holds me, letting his hand roam up and down my back as his other holds me tight to his body. "Because he loves you, Shayne. You heard what he said. There's not a damn thing he wouldn't do for you, even if it means giving himself up to keep you safe. You're the most precious thing in his life. You're his whole fucking world, just as you are to me and Marc. Had you been taken again, had they hurt you ... or worse. It would have killed every one of us. If he didn't walk, Empress, then I would have. The same goes for Marc."

I pull my head up, wiping at the tears that just keep coming. "She's going to kill him," I warn him. "Don't you understand? We're never going to see him again."

Roman shakes his head. "You can't think like that, Empress. Levi is strong. Look at what he just survived. We'll get to him, and he'll make it through it with us by his side."

My head falls against his shoulder just as Marc comes back into the room and drops onto the couch beside us. I don't see the look on his face, but I can feel it. He's just as broken as I am, barely holding it together, knowing exactly what lies in store for his brother.

Marc's hand finds mine squished between me and Roman, and he grips it as though it's his only lifeline. "It's going to be okay, babe," he tells me, but the words sound more like he's trying to convince himself. "We're going to get him out of there."

Taking slow, deep breaths, the sobs finally begin to ease and the intense, crippling thoughts circling my head start to slow, making it easier to come to terms with everything that just happened. "He's gone," I breathe, repeating the words I'd cried only moments ago.

Neither of the boys respond, feeling the ache just as much as I do.

Roman's hand slides up my back until his fingers are curled around my neck, slowly massaging as if trying to calm me. "We're going to figure this out."

"How?" I murmur, pulling my face out of the crook of his neck. "She wants me. As long as her blood runs through my veins, then she's never going to stop coming for me. She's going to kill me. And as for Levi, she's going to use him to draw Giovanni out, but it's not going to work, and when she finally realizes that, she'll destroy him and boast about it. We can't survive this. She's too strong. I've seen her home, and I've seen the kind of empire she runs. The family your father has built doesn't hold a match to the power the Moretti's have. We don't stand a chance."

Roman pulls me in, pressing his lips to mine in a lingering kiss, and the moment he pulls back, his forehead comes to mine. "Hear me, Empress, we are going to find a way to get through this. Levi needs us more than ever, and I'm sure as fuck not about to start letting him down now, and I know you're not about to either."

"How?" I ask him, searching his dark eyes. "Zeke was our only shot, but we don't even know if he's going to make it."

"Zeke?" Roman questions. "You mean the asshole hanging off Gia like a bad smell?"

"Yeah."

Roman holds my stare a moment longer. "That's how you got out, isn't it? He helped you?"

I swallow over the lump in my throat and nod. "He was put in charge of training me, and he slipped me a set of keys when we were sparring. The last thing he said to me was that if I were to return, it better be to put a bullet between Gia's eyes. That night, Gia had business to attend to and the front gates were left open. All I had to do was find a way from my room and to the front gate and I was free."

Marcus laughs, shaking his head. "Fucking knew that asshole was with the feds."

"The feds?" I ask. "You think he's undercover, working with the FBI?"

"We always had our suspicions," Roman says. "But helping you escape … no real member of Gia's family would ever risk such a betrayal. He's walking on eggshells. But that doesn't mean that we can trust him. Just because he'd rather see us live than her, doesn't mean that he still won't lock our asses up."

"Shit," I sigh. "So, what do we do? We have to get in there somehow."

Roman shakes his head. "For now, you tell us everything you remember from her home. The cameras, levels, where the rooms are. Do you think you could draw up some kind of blueprint?"

I shrug my shoulders. "I mean, I didn't see it all. I don't know what was hidden behind even half of the doors, but I can draw up the bits that I remember. I don't know where she keeps her prisoners though, or if she even has them at her home."

Marcus nods. "She will. Her number one priority is getting my father's sticky fingers away from her empire, meaning that Levi just became her most important prisoner ever. She won't let him out of her sight. Our only saving grace is that she can't kill him until she draws out my father, and my father isn't the kind to just show up when being called. We have time."

"But how much time does Levi have? He's already weak, he's still trying to heal. There's only so much torture one man can go through before he gives up."

"Levi is strong," Roman reminds me. "He's been trained for this. We just need to be prepared for the fact that he might not be the same man who walked away from us tonight."

My heart shatters into a million pieces, and I try to hold back the tears, taking slow, deep breaths before finally meeting Roman's gaze again. "Okay," I finally say, the lump growing in my throat. "So, we plan for a raid. We do our homework and figure out the best time to go in. But what happens if that doesn't work?"

He shakes his head, and I hate that he doesn't have the answers I need. I have to remind myself that just because he doesn't have the answers now, doesn't mean that we're screwed, it just means we have to think harder, we need to play our pieces and figure it out. "We'll figure it out, Empress. No matter how hard it is, or how long it takes. I won't let him down. *I won't let you down.*"

He kisses me again, his lips so damn soft against mine it's almost criminal, and I don't know what kind of voodoo bullshit he's pouring into this kiss, but he has the ability to calm me, even during the most torrential storm. He holds my lips hostage, giving me a moment to breathe before pulling away just a fraction, barely a breath between us. "I love you, Empress. You are my fucking rock. I live to please you," he says, his fingers gently brushing over the side of my face. "Yes, Levi is my brother, and I'd do everything in my power to get him home safe. But knowing that his absence kills you just as much as yours killed me, it pushes me to try harder. I can't stand seeing your heart broken like this. Hear me, Shayne. Really fucking hear me when I tell you that no matter what it takes to bring him home, I'll do it. He's my baby brother. You, Marcus, and Levi—you're all I have in this world, and I'm not about to let some two-faced bitch take that away. And you can bet your fucking sweet ass that Marc feels the same way."

My gaze falls to Marc, and he nods, squeezing my hand in his before bringing it to his lips and pressing a soft kiss to the tops of my knuckles. He lets it fall, landing against Roman's thigh as he meets my teary eyes. "Whatever it takes," Marc promises me, his heart on his sleeve, looking just as broken as mine. He gives me a tight smile. It's one thing for Marc to express his feelings for me, but when it's one of his brothers, it hits differently. He goes to get up and holds my stare. "I need a drink," he says. "I'll give you guys a minute."

I watch him make his way out of the big living room, wishing that I could do something for him, but as much as it kills me, he wants to be alone. He's going to find a bottle of the most expensive whiskey, drain it, and once the effects wear off, he'll be ready.

My gaze falls back to Roman's to find his eyes haven't left my face the whole time, and I can't resist throwing my arms around his neck and folding into him just as I was before. "I trust you, Roman," I tell him, my words a breathy whisper brushing against his warm skin. "I know you'll bring him home. I've known it since the moment I met you. You're their protector, both Levi and Marcus. You've always shielded them from the worst your father had to offer, and a part of me wonders if they're even aware of just how bad it really got."

His arms tighten around me, pulling my body in flush against his. "You're too observant for your own good."

"And you're too loyal for yours," I tell him.

"Not possible," he murmurs, brushing his fingers through my hair.

Silence falls between us as I rest my head against his chest, soft tears still falling down my face thinking about the hell Levi is going to endure at the expense of saving me from harm. It's barely been ten minutes, and I already fear what Gia's men could have done to him. He's still healing, still hurting, despite the brave face he wears every time he meets my eyes.

Fuck, I love him so bad it hurts.

"I love you, Roman," I whisper. "I know I've told you that before, but I need you to know just how much I mean it. I was so stubborn for so long, and I refused to admit it, even to myself, but the thought of Levi being taken like this and not knowing just how much I love him … I swear. Every chance I get … I need you to know."

Roman's embrace seems to soften around me as he lets out a gentle breath. "Even if you hadn't said the words, Levi knows. We all know because we can see it in your eyes every time you look at us. It's part of the reason I'm not beating them black and blue and demanding that you'll be only mine. I wouldn't take that kind of love away from them, and I sure as fuck wouldn't take it from you."

I pull up from his chest, looking into his dark eyes, listening intently as he continues. "The way you screamed those words, despite your fear and the desperation in your voice, I can guarantee that those words are repeating over and over in his mind. Your words are what's going to get him through this."

My lips press into a tight line, the smallest spark of hope rising deep in my chest. "I can only hope," I tell him before falling back into his arms and watching as the sun slowly rises, casting long shadows across the big living room and reminding me that today is a new day—a new day to survive, a new day to thrive, and a new fucking day to take what's ours.

# TWENTY-TWO

D ays. It's fucking days before the call we've been desperate for finally comes through to Roman's phone. He jumps on it, scooping it up off the kitchen counter and immediately taking the call. He hits the speakerphone, and his voice booms through the big kitchen.

"Mick. Where are we at?"

I jump down off the counter, my eyes wide as I walk over to Roman, needing to be closer as if that's going to somehow help me hear the conversation clearer. "I'm sending you a video now," Mick says, his voice filled with a strange emotion that I can't read. "Gia sent this through to your father."

My chest heaves with heavy, frantic breaths as Roman's phone dings with an incoming video text. Marcus steps into my side just as Roman opens the video. He adjusts his position so that we can all see the screen, and the second the video begins to play, my knees fall out from under me.

Marcus grips my elbow, keeping me up as we watch Levi on the screen, his wrists cuffed and held by heavy, thick chains above his head. His feet barely touch the ground as his beautiful head hangs forward, already exhausted and ready to give up.

"Shit," Marcus says, his other hand falling to my hip as he moves in closer to me.

Tears fill my eyes, and I take the phone out of Roman's hands, holding it closer, studying every inch of his skin that I can make out in the darkened room. It doesn't look like a cell. It's more open than that, but it's definitely not the five-star castle I lived in while being held captive.

Roman's hands knot into his hair, his eyes darkening as he begins to pace across the narrow walkway between the kitchen island and the cabinetry behind it. "Tell me you didn't forward that video to my father."

"No, I didn't," Mick says, reminding me that he's still on the line as my eyes remain glued to the screen, watching Levi dangling by his chains. "Figured you'd want to keep it private. It came through a minute ago and I called you straight away."

"Did you get anything from it?" Roman says as a man steps into the frame, his face covered by a black mask. My back straightens as I suck in a terrified gasp, the sound bringing Roman to a stop at my side, peering over my shoulder at the screen again.

"Yeah, my team is working on it now," Mick says, unaware of the horrors overwhelming my heart, making it nearly impossible to breathe. "We've managed to open a back door into the Moretti surveillance system. We might be able to get a live feed set up, but it's not going to be easy. Whoever she has working her tech is good, but not better than me."

"Good," Roman snaps, his eyes glued to the screen. The masked man moves toward Levi with a whip in hand, and like lightning, strikes out at him, leaving a red, bloodied mark right across his chest, the sharp snap cracking through the phone speaker. Levi cries out, his head throwing back in agony as the sound paralyzes me. "Get it done."

My hand slaps over my mouth, trying to stifle the gasps that tear through the back of my throat, unable to pull my gaze away from the video. The masked fuckhead strikes him again, and I crumble back into Marcus' chest, barely holding myself together. Tears swarm my eyes watching Levi's anguish and hating the torment that must plague him right now.

Marcus lets out a soft curse, his fingers digging painfully into my hip as he watches his brother go through hell. "Levi is strong," I whisper, unsure who I'm trying to convince. "He can make it through this."

Who am I kidding? He's just been through hell, just watched his brother almost die. How much more of this can we all take? This isn't Gia's first rodeo, and I don't doubt that she has broken men much worse than Levi. He's not in the right headspace, his body is already broken, and judging by the angry red markings on his tanned skin and the dried blood coating his body, he's already been through a world of hell before this video was taken.

Gia isn't going to make this easy, and what's worse—the bitch is baiting us. She's drawing us out and she knows it's going to work. She has all her fucking ducks in a row, and we're going to storm in there with targets on our backs.

We're fucked.

Levi is fucked.

*We can't save him. But I'll fucking die trying.*

"Roman?" Mick says, his tone lowering with unease and something a little darker, something filled with nerves and horror. "We might have a location. We're still waiting on confirmation, but I think it's time you start making your way back here."

"You've got two hours," Roman snaps down the line. "You better have something solid."

He ends the call without so much as a goodbye, and within moments, we're breaking out into torrential rain, more than ready to leave this hellhole behind. Storms have wreaked havoc over these mountains for the past few days, and I can't help but feel as though the fucking sky is in tune with my shattered soul. It's like a sick fucking joke, but at some point, there has to be blue skies.

Dill and Doe bound down the stairs, passing us in no time. The rain glues my hair to my face, but nothing matters to me except getting into that Escalade and flying down the fucking road, one step closer to getting him back.

We pile into the SUV, and before the door has even closed behind me, Roman's foot slams down on the gas. We fly back out through the destroyed property, each of us in a deathly silence. My mind replays the video over and over like some sickening way of torturing myself.

No one says a damn word, and before I know it, we're pulling into the familiar streets of the city. The past two hours have both flown by while also feeling like a lifetime. Every minute that Levi is left in her hands is another minute of me clawing at my own skin. But it's almost over, it has to be.

It won't be long before she realizes that Giovanni isn't going to respond to her efforts, and soon enough, she'll tire of the game.

We're only a few streets away from the main warehouse when my back stiffens and my head snaps up, meeting Roman's sharp gaze through the rearview mirror. "What is it?" he says, recognizing the fear in my eyes and spitting the words out before I can even articulate my thoughts.

"Gia knew exactly where to find us," I say. "On the one night where we were out in the open with no extra protection. Is that not too coincidental?"

Marcus turns in his seat, looking back at me, his brows furrowed as he thinks it over. "She would have been tracking your movements since the second you left her home."

"But how?" I question. "I ditched her guards at a mall parking lot. They didn't see me leave, didn't see the car I was in or where I was headed."

"Maybe she's got men on the inside. My father goes through guards like he goes through toilet paper. Any one of them could have come right out of Gia's pocket. He could have led her right to us."

"How could he have led her to us if your father doesn't even know where we are? Don't you think he would have come for us if he knew where we were?" I shake my head. "Your father doesn't know, so Gia couldn't have known either."

"She could have someone staking out all of our properties."

I shrug my shoulders, my gut telling me that it's something much more sinister than that. "Maybe," I say. "But if that were the case, she would have grabbed me when I went to your father's place. It would have been a shitload easier. I was alone."

Roman watches me for a brief second before his eyes bug out of his head. "FUCK," he spits before slamming on the brakes and pulling off to the side of the road. He storms out of the car, walking around to the backdoor and ripping it open.

"What the fuck is going on?" I demand as he reaches in and grips my elbow, yanking me across the backseat. He pulls me out of the car, his hands roaming over every inch of my body as traffic flies by us, honking horns and screaming curses out their open windows.

"You're right," he says, as Marcus watches us from the open door. "She has been tracking you, but not by following your every fucking move. She's got a fucking GPS tracker on you, just like we had."

My eyes bug out of my head as I frantically begin searching my body. "What the fuck?" I screech as Marcus curses softly to himself. "No. No, that can't be right. I would know. I was never knocked out and never ... no. I would know if she put something into me. It's not possible."

Marcus scoffs, shaking his head. "Trust me, babe. It's very fucking possible."

"Here," Roman says, his hands pausing on my back, just below my ribs in the fleshy part of my skin. He pokes and prods at something hard, his face grim realizing that he was right. "I have to get this out," he tells me, his stare coming back to mine. "She'll know we're coming."

I nod, agreeing wholeheartedly and letting out a sigh as he leads me around the other side of the car to block our view of the traffic storming by. Marcus' hand falls out the window with a knife resting between his fingers and Roman gingerly takes it.

This is gonna suck, but at least it'll be done quick ... a shitload quicker than when it was me trying to cut it out of my own freaking arm.

We step right up to Marcus' window, and I grip on to his hands as Roman braces me against the side of the car. "On three—"

"No," I rush out, clenching my eyes. "Just do it."

He doesn't need to be told twice. The sharp tip digs into my skin, and I bite down on my lip, squeezing Marcus' hand and trying to think of anything that could distract me from the agony.

"Sorry, Empress," Roman murmurs, his tone dark and pained, not liking the idea of hurting me any more than I do, but Roman isn't the kind to back down. He'll do what needs to be done, no matter what it costs him.

I swallow hard, forcing the pain out of my head. "You know this means that Gia knows where the warehouse is," I spit through my clenched jaw. "She could destroy your whole operation with just a click of her fingers. She'll use it against you."

Marcus' thumb moves over my knuckles, drawing my attention to his gentle, calming touch. "Not if I have anything to do with it."

The sharp tip of the knife pulls away from my skin, and I let out a shaky breath as Roman holds a tiny little device between his fingers, blood covering both the tracker and his hands. He studies it a moment before flicking the small device through the open window of a passing car. He wipes the blood from the blade onto his dark pants and hands it back to Marcus before glancing back at me. "Turn around. I need to stitch that."

I shake my head and move out of his hold. "We don't have time. We need to get to the warehouse and see what information Mick has found. It's just a small cut. It can wait."

Roman's lips press into a hard line, and before he gets the chance to argue, I'm already around the other side of the car and slipping back into the open door. I close it with a heavy thump and not a moment later, Roman is back in the driver's seat, pulling out into the midday city traffic.

----------

The back roller door is already open and waiting for us as we barrel into the warehouse. Mick stands by a controller and as soon as the Escalade has cleared the door, he hits a button, bringing the roller door down.

We're out of the car within seconds, following Mick to his office in the center of the main floor. "What have we got?" Roman asks as the warehouse workers watch on with wide eyes, curiosity getting the better of them. By just the look on the boys' faces, it's clear that something is about to go down.

The last few times we've come through here, we've been secretive, hiding in the shadows, but not anymore. Right now, we don't give a shit. We have one goal in mind, and not a damn thing is going to stand in our way.

We step into Mick's tech room, and I'm not surprised to find the big space swarming with computer dudes, their hands moving over their keyboards like lightning. The room is completely closed off to the workers on the opposite side of the wall. I remember walking in here the first time and being in complete awe by the one-way glass surrounding this room. We could watch over the warehouse while the workers busily went about their day, oblivious to our stares. But now, the room is cloaked in darkness, complete privacy locking us in. We don't see through, and they don't see in. This right here is all about focus, no distractions.

Mick leads us over to a massive computer screen, but another catches my attention.

Levi's face rests on the screen, his eyes closed with blood matted in his short hair, only the angle of his chin is different from the video I replayed over in my mind during the long trip here. "Is this more footage?" I question, gaining the mens' attention. Their heads snap up and I indicate to the screen. "This is different."

"We got into Gia's surveillance system," Mick explains. "That's a live feed."

I all but fall at the screen, rushing in closer to rake my eyes over him. "Can you zoom out? I need to see his body."

The computer tech at the desk does exactly as I ask, and my heart shatters seeing the angry welts across his chest from the whip. There are six of them, each one staring at me like an accusation, dropping weight after weight down on my shoulders. "Shit. Is he alright?" I ask. "Have they done anything else to him since then? Given him food or water?"

"Nothing," the tech dude beside me says. "He's just been hanging there. Maybe this whole time."

Roman stands behind me, his eyes narrowed and filled with questions as Marcus fidgets, his hands balling into fists at his side. "I need to fucking kill something."

"You'll get your chance, brother," Roman mutters darkly before turning to Mick. "Have you nailed down his location yet?"

Mick nods, getting straight back to business. "We have. But you're not going to like it." Roman gives him a hard stare and Mick hurries to give him the information that he needs. "You were right, she's holding Levi in her private residence an hour out of the city. From the fifty cameras within the home and the layout Shayne was able to draw up, we were able to determine that Levi is being kept in a padded cell under the mansion. We're unsure how to access the underground portion of the property or just how big it might be, but if you take the rest of her home into consideration, you can guarantee that she put a lot of thought and cash into it. These cells were not meant for people to come out of."

Roman and Marcus nod as if simply discussing what toppings they're having on their pizza.

"I'm not sure of Gia's usual day-to-day security, but there are a lot of guards swarming her property. It looks as though she's anticipating an attack and she's ready for it. I don't know how you guys are going to get through this one, but if anyone can make this happen, it's you crazy fuckers."

Mick goes on to show us a shitload of tech gear that we'll be using as if we're in some kind of James Bond movie, and I gape at it all. I've never known the boys to need anything apart from themselves and a gun, but to have a tech dude in their ears, watching their movements with heat signatures and a shitload of other stuff I don't understand only goes to show just how fucking dangerous this really is. Hell, there's even a hint of nervousness buried deep in Roman's eyes, while Marcus looks like he's about ready to slaughter every man who stands in his way, and I can guarantee that's exactly what he'll do.

The boys are preparing for one hell of a war. We're just three people up against a fucking storm.

The next twenty minutes are filled with the boys going over every detail of the property that we can get our eyes and ears on. They watch the guards and figure out where they're stationed on the property, zero in on codes being punched into the front gate, and figure out where the weakest link is.

We study every angle of the property, and every now and then, a new question is thrown my way, but for the most part, my eyes remain locked on the screen that watches Levi, making sure he's still holding on.

A meticulous, detailed plan is put into place, and after giving Mick the rundown on the whole GPS tracker thing, instructions are given to clear out the warehouse and move all the boys' product and cash to a new location, ensuring the workers' silence and safety.

The warehouse turns into a buzz of movement, everyone doing what they need to do to get this place stripped while all the tech bunnies remain exactly where they are, having instructions not to move until Levi has been recovered and is safe. After that, they can do whatever the fuck they need to do to get out of here. The moment Gia realizes that we're coming, she'll use every last weapon in her artillery to win.

With everyone busy and preparing for what's going to go down in the dead of night, Roman and Marcus crowd around me, their faces grim. Nervousness weighs down on my chest as I watch them through narrowed eyes. "What?" I demand, getting to my feet while distantly aware of the way everyone in the room seems to ignore us, acting as though there aren't two psychotic serial killers moving in on me.

Roman glances at Marcus, a silent message passing between them, and after a beat, he turns back to me, a new determination written across his face. "You're not coming with us."

I stumble back a step, my brows furrowed as I look between them in confusion. Surely he just mixed up his words because there's no way he could possibly mean what he just said. "Excuse me?" I demand. "What the hell do you mean I'm not coming?"

Marcus takes a hesitant step toward me, slowly reaching for my hand, but I quickly pull away, knowing this bullshit idea would have belonged to him. "You know I think you're incredible, and if anyone can handle themselves during this, it's you. Don't get me wrong by assuming I think anything different, but you can't be there. Gia wants your head, and she will stop at nothing to get it. Every one of those men will have kill orders on you, on all of us, and we can't go into this worried about you. You'll be staying here with Mick. He'll give you a head piece so that you can communicate with us and watch the live feed, but you won't be coming."

I stare at him, my heart slowly cracking right down the center before turning back to Roman. "And you agree with this?"

His gaze drops, usually being the one to break whatever news needs to be broken, only when he can see my heart shattering before him, his determination wavers. "I do," he finally says.

Letting out a heavy breath, I nod and turn away, hating the feel of their laser-sharp gazes locked on my back.

I didn't think that it would come down to this, but nothing, not even Roman and Marcus, will keep me from getting to Levi. He needs me more than ever, and after the stupid amount of times Levi has had my back, it's a damn guarantee that I will have his. I know Roman and Marcus are simply trying to protect me, and I know they have a really good reason to do so, but I will give up my life if it means saving Levi's.

Nothing is going to stop me.

Not Roman. Not Marcus. And not Gia Fucking Moretti.

They leave me no choice.

# TWENTY-THREE

**N**erves rattle me, but they're nothing quite like the guilt that sears me from the inside out.

They're going to kill me. Hell, I'm going to kill myself. But no one, not even Marcus and Roman are going to keep me grounded. This is too important. Levi needs me. He needs something to fight for. He needs a ray of hope to shine through the bullshit and get him through this until the guys can help free him. But right now, this whole waiting until the middle of the night bullshit to make a move, this shit isn't sitting well with me. In fact, just the thought of waiting another minute tears me to shreds.

I stare up at the ceiling of the dumpster fire motel room the boys and I have been shacking up in since leaving the warehouse four hours ago. They're dead to the world, deep asleep, with the intention to regain as much energy as possible for the raid on Gia's home. They're going to need it, especially being down one brother.

Time is ticking so damn slowly.

I haven't slept a wink, but I knew that before we even came here. How could I sleep after seeing that live feed? In the hours that I sat in front of that screen, Levi didn't get assaulted again, but the way he held his body made it clear that he was ready and prepared for more.

Glancing out the window, I decide that I've waited long enough. It's after eleven, and the sky is as dark as it's going to get. The majority of cars have cleared off the roads and Gia's night shift would have well and truly taken over.

I have no plan. No solid idea of how I'm supposed to get in there and find my way to Levi, but I have to try. The boys aren't planning on leaving until just after two in the morning, and by the time they wake up, they'll find me long gone. They'll race after me, and if everything goes as well as I hope, I'll already be with Levi when they arrive, then they can help us get out of there. Sure, I'll probably get the worst kind of lecture and be hate fucked afterward, but I'm not leaving Levi for one more second.

They can hate me all they want. They can rant and rave at me until their throats are bleeding, but they can't possibly deny the fact that if it had been me in that padded cell beneath Gia's home, they would have done the exact same thing. Hell, I just raced back into the lion's den to save their bitch asses from their father, risking it all. If they don't expect me to try something, then they mustn't know me well enough.

With the guilt riding high, I slip off the uncomfortable double bed and silently kneel, pulling the rolled-up hoodie out from under the bed. I'd stashed it under here the moment I pushed my way through the cheap motel door. Marcus had slipped into the bathroom while Roman stayed out front talking to Mick on the phone, and I took my shot. I couldn't risk them seeing what I'd stolen from the warehouse. If they knew what I was about to do … fuck.

My hand slips inside the fabric of the hoodie, and my stomach twists as my fingers brush over the cold metal of the handcuffs.

They're legit going to kill me, and Marcus might even enjoy it.

Anxiety pulses through my veins, and I blow my cheeks out in a heavy breath before finally finding the nerves to get back to my feet. I rub the cuffs between my hands, trying to warm the cool metal before leaning over the cramped double bed. I hold my breath, and before I back out like the chicken shit that I am, I hook the cuff over Marcus' wrist and slowly clamp it shut. The metal jingles, and I swear I could either faint or throw up. I don't even want to begin to think what Marcus could do in a split second, getting woken and assuming I was an intruder.

I close the cuff around the heavy bed frame before turning my attention on Roman across the room. He's sprawled out on the couch and a part of me dies. The guy hasn't slept in a proper bed for at least two weeks. We had ridiculous little beds in the bunker, a couch at his burned down mega-mansion, and nothing but a dirty cell floor at the castle playground. They're going to need a vacation once they finally get through all of this bullshit … assuming we all get through this alive.

Padding across the shitty motel room, I creep up to Roman and try not to stare. Roman is some kind of super-human, and I don't doubt that my stare lingering on his face for a moment too long could probably wake him.

I move extra carefully, sweat beginning to coat my skin. I could hurl. Hell, once I get through the door and into the car, maybe I just might. Fuck, I've wandered through his bedroom a million times while he's slept and not woken him, even had nights of tossing and turning right next to him, probably kicked him in the shins a few times too, so why the hell does this time feel so risky?

Reaching his side, I take the cuffs and slowly thread it over his wide wrist, feeling like absolute shit about it. The cuffs aren't going to hold them back. They'll probably tear straight through them, and assuming there's a gun shoved in their pants or below their pillows, they'll shoot their way out, but it's enough to get me out of the door.

I frantically search around for something to attach Roman to, but all I've got is the lamp bolted to the ground. It won't bring much of a challenge, but for now, it's the only chance I've got.

Moving toward the door, I glance back at my sleeping soldiers, knowing without a doubt that I'll be seeing them soon.

Slipping out of the room, I run.

My gaze lingers on the Escalade, and I shake off the thought for the millionth time. Roman and Marcus are going to need it. It has all their weapons and plans. Without it … well, they won't entirely be fucked. They're the kind to go into a situation blind and come out looking like gods. They don't need the car, but it'll definitely help, and I don't doubt that there will come a time during my night where I'll need that help. So, instead, I run for the main road.

There's a gas station a mile down the street, and by the time I reach it, my heart is pounding. I'm not a runner, but tonight, I'm a fucking track star whether I like it or not.

I hide in the bushes, impatiently waiting. This isn't exactly my brightest idea to date, but when a girl is desperate, there's no saying what she might do.

A black Dodge RAM comes hurtling into the gas station and pulls up beside the pump as a grin tears across my face. The guy who falls out of the driver's seat looks as though he's on his tenth bourbon for the night, and the desperation in his eyes suggests that maybe some chick just agreed to let him rail her for the whole four seconds that it'll take for him to come and grunt the wrong name.

Bingo.

I watch, waiting for my chance to strike, and because I'm a classy bitch, I make sure he's pumped enough gas to get me where I need to go. Minutes pass and the moment he turns his back to his Dodge RAM and heads into the store I pump my fist like a fucking loser and make my move.

I race across the lot doing my best to keep quiet, and as I reach the big truck, I start praying to Taylor Swift that there isn't a passenger in the cab.

Yanking the door open, I do a quick scan before diving headfirst into the truck. The cab is empty and as my heart races, I frantically bring the seat as far forward as it'll allow before pressing the push start button and feeling the monster of a truck come alive beneath me.

It's loud and the whole thing vibrates with power. My head snaps up, watching the guy through the dirty windows. He's too occupied scanning through rows of condoms and knowing my shot isn't going to get any better than this, I hit the gas and take off like a bat out of hell.

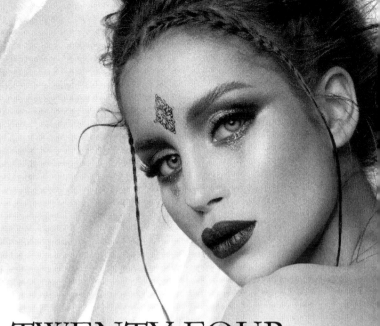

# TWENTY-FOUR

## MARCUS

"**M**OTHERFUCKER!**"** Roman's voice booms through the small motel room, and my head snaps up from the pillow, my eyes springing open, ready for any threat. My arm immediately pulls back in a jarring yank, my wrist screaming from a sharp cool metal.

The room is pitch black, and I instantly search for the threat before my gaze flicks back to find my bed empty and my wrist cuffed to the fucking headboard. "FUCK," I roar, pulling on the cuff, testing its resistance.

"She took off," Roman spits, standing from the couch.

My hand falls to the sheets beside me, and I curse under my breath, struggling to control the rage pulsing through my veins. "The bed's cold. She's long gone."

A heavy thump sounds from the couch, and I take a moment to look him over, finding him in the same fucked-up situation, only cuffed to the damn lamp. He pulls on the cuff, anger radiating out of him like a fucking tsunami, destroying everything in its path.

"I'm going to fucking kill her," he spits, turning his gaze away from me to mask the panic in his eyes.

"Get in line," I spit back, sitting up and turning, trying to find a weakness in the headboard that I can use to my advantage. It's been too fucking long since I've spilled blood, and I'm getting a little antsy. I crave it, need it. It's my fucking elixir to life, and right now, the thought of spilling Shayne's is sitting high on my list of priorities.

Fuck her and her bullshit little games. Is this what it feels like to be played? I can't say I've ever let someone pull one over on me like that, never allowed someone close enough to even try. Fucking sneaky brat. Her perky ass is going to be stinging when I'm through with her.

Roman quickly grows impatient with the lamp and tears the whole fucking thing right out of the ground before holding it up and letting the cuff fall off the bottom. He throws what's left of the lamp across the room, taking his anger out on the cheap metal before trying his luck at squeezing his hand through the cuff on his wrist.

I scoff. Every fucking idiot in cuffs always tries that shit. He should know better.

Quickly realizing his attempts are useless, he strides over to the small double bed and scans the headboard with a keen eye, trying to figure out how the fuck to get me out of here. I'm not gonna lie, it's not the first time Roman has had to save me from some crazy chick who handcuffed me to a bed, but it's the first time he's not been laughing about it.

"I should have fucking known," he grunts, gripping on to the headboard and pulling it away from the wall, pressing his whole weight over the narrow bars that keep me bound and grunting as he forces them down. "She accepted it too easily. Back at the warehouse. It didn't feel right."

The bars give way under his weight but not enough to free me. "I know," I mutter, recalling the moment we cornered her in the tech room only for her to agree too quickly. Roman and I had questioned it between ourselves, but ultimately, we decided that she understood the risks. "She could be fucking …"

I cut myself off, not wanting to imagine what could be happening to her right now.

"She couldn't have been gone for more than an hour, maybe two at the absolute most," Roman says, prompting me to turn to the old digital clock bolted to the bedside table. It's just after midnight, but that's far too late. If she's already made it back to Gia's home, then the scene we turn up to could be something none of us could possibly move on from.

As if that same thought circles Roman's head, he presses all his weight down on the metal bar once more and it caves again, snapping under the pressure. Without skipping a beat, I slide the cuff from the bar and grab my fucking shirt. I yank it over my head and have my gear in my hands before the hem has even fallen to my waist.

It's a shitload earlier than when we'd planned to do this, but when the hell have our plans ever gone right? Hell, I don't think we've ever seen a plan through. In our world, we're all too used to shit blowing up in our faces, but when it comes to Shayne Mariano—or Shayne Fucking DeAngelis as she's legally known as of now—we can't fucking handle it. She has us all wrapped around her pinky, and as much as we hate to admit it, she's the one pulling the strings here.

We're out the door in two fucking seconds, and I let out a breath after finding the Escalade right where we left it. My brows furrow as I tear the door open and fly up into the passenger seat. "Why would she leave the car?" I bite out as Roman climbs in beside me and slams his door with a heavy thump.

He shakes his head as he backs out of the parking space and takes off like a fucking rocket, tires screeching against the asphalt, leaving thick black lines of rubber in his wake. "My guess is that whatever fucked-up plan is going through her head, she still needs us to come and save her ass."

"She would have had to steal a ride," I muse out loud, unable to focus on the road in front of us. "That could buy us some time."

"Maybe," he says, an edge in his voice that tells me he doesn't feel good about this, a feeling that's all too mutual. "We can only hope that she was listening to the plan and knows where to get in. If she's beaten us there and goes in gun blazing through the front fucking gates …"

"She's not suicidal," I remind him. "A fucking brat with a death wish, but not suicidal. She'll play it safe. At least until she's got Levi right where she wants him. After that, there's no telling what she'll do to try and get them out."

"Fuck," he mutters, clenching his jaw. "Then we better make sure we're there when this shit goes south. I can't fucking lose her. Not like this."

The thought to console him filters through my head. I should tell him we're going to get her back, that we're going to save them both and somehow come out of this unscathed. But that's not the relationship I share with my brothers. Never has been. To sit here and discuss how our hearts are breaking at the idea of Shayne falling captive to the Moretti family feels weak, feels wrong. Roman knows where my head is just as I know where his fucked-up one is. We're both ready, and that's all that counts.

I shake my head, the disbelief clouding my mind and making it hard to focus. I turn to Roman and an involuntary grin tears across my face. "She fucking cuffed us, man," I say with a breathy scoff, lightening the mood in the cab, trying to pull him out of the hole his mind is dragging him into. "How the fuck did we let her get away with that?"

His eyes sparkle for just a moment before he schools his features. "More like how the fuck did she manage to find two sets of handcuffs and smuggle them out of the warehouse?" He laughs to himself before letting it fade away. "If she somehow survives this, then she's definitely got a career in smuggling if she wants one. Clearly, she's got talent."

"No shit," I mutter, the words choking me up.

She's going to be okay. If she felt out of her league, she would have waited with us.

Fucking hell. I can't even lie to myself. She wouldn't have waited for us. Her mind is set on getting to Levi no matter what. I should have known the second we had a firm location, she would have been out the fucking door, and that's on us.

Shayne is the type of chick to fall hard, and that's exactly what she did with each of us. She loves fiercely and proudly, without question or hesitation. She's accepted what we are, what we've done, and for that, she's the whole fucking world to me. She would do anything for us, and any other time, I'd worship her for that very thought. But right now, her hero complex is really pissing me off.

If Shayne wants to survive in this world and wants to thrive at our sides, then she's going to have to learn how to look out for herself, and she's going to have to learn it fast.

A moment passes when Roman is clear-headed enough to pull his phone from the center console. He presses a few buttons before the call picks up over the Bluetooth and Mick's deep voice fills the cab. "What do you need?" he questions.

"Get your boys ready," Roman tells him. "Plans have changed."

"We're ready," he says, and without another word, Roman ends the call and presses harder on the gas.

The hour drive out of the city feels like it drags on forever. Roman hasn't said a word since ending the call, and I haven't bothered to either. My mind is focused. Set and ready. I'm craving the bloodshed like never before, and the sooner I get in there and find my girl, the better.

My chest aches for her, screams for her, and I can only hope that she knows what she's doing.

The Escalade pulls to a stop a few streets away from the entrance of the gated community where a black Dodge RAM stands out like dog's balls. We have no clue what the gate code is, nor do we feel it's a good idea to play guessing games with that one and set off every alarm system in the area.

Guns are loaded, earpieces inserted, and knives strapped to every available inch of skin. I hear Mick in my ear testing the earpiece while Roman straps a bulletproof vest to his chest. Can't say we've ever worn them before, but tonight is a fucking war. It's Roman and me up against the fucking Moretti army, and with that thought circling my mind, I reach for the other vest and strap it on.

Letting out a breath, I meet Roman's heavy stare. "You good?" he asks me.

Find Shayne. Save Levi. Get the fuck out of there without dying in the process.

Easy. What could I possibly have to worry about?

I give him a curt nod, determination deep in my eyes. "I'm good." I tell him, not bothering to ask the same in return. I know he's ready; I see it in the way he holds himself, the way his chin lowers and his eyes darken like two storm clouds rolling in to destroy everything in their path.

Roman holds my stare a moment longer, each of us knowing the risks all too well, knowing that one wrong move could see either of us spending eternity in a shallow grave. And with that, we take off toward the gated community, more than ready to spill Moretti blood.

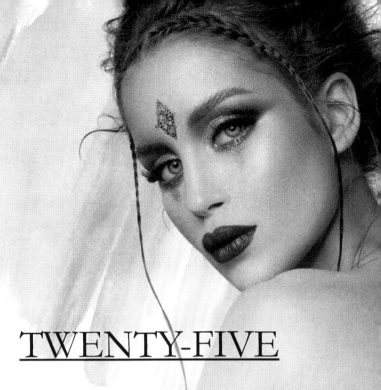

# TWENTY-FIVE

## SHAYNE

Fuck. Fuck. Fuck. Fuck.

What was I thinking?

My elbows hit the hard earth as I crawl through the thick bushy hedges that surround Gia's property. It's already been a nightmare getting to this point. Scaling the fence of the outer community was a joke and then ending up in some rich dude's backyard wasn't pleasant either. His dog wasn't exactly happy to see me, but lucky the poor thing was overfed, old, and had short legs. I got away with nothing but a small nip to my ass as I tried to fly over the side entrance.

Really not my finest hour, but things could have been worse.

I stuck to the shadows, all too aware of how much time I was wasting. It took nearly thirty minutes to navigate my way to the big Moretti mansion, each passing second closing the gap until Roman and Marcus come and whoop my ass for cuffing them in that shitty motel.

They're never going to forgive me for that one. Well, Roman won't. Marcus will probably just get payback by using it in some kinky sex games, and honestly, I'm down for whatever he wants to put out.

I made my way around to the side of Gia's property, right where the boys had planned on making their grand entrance, which is exactly how I got here. Commando crawling under the thick hedges, my elbows digging into the mud, and my hair catching in the hedges above me. Not gonna lie, chilling with the spiders isn't exactly my idea of fun, but if it means getting to Levi, then I'll do it.

It's the thickest hedge I've ever come across, and after what feels like a lifetime, my head peeks out the other side, giving me the worst possible view of the property, but right now, I'll take anything I can get.

There are guards everywhere, each of them evenly scattered, watching their designated section. The property is huge, but from the ground, it looks a million times bigger than I remember. Though when I was here last, I wasn't exactly focusing on the manicured gardens. I was in a state of mourning followed by a state of pissed-off, raging anger. It was like the worst kind of PMS.

Big lights cover every section of the property, and I let out a shaky breath. Running across that is going to be like bolting through a minefield while escaping a prison, guards more than ready to shoot me down. The sky is still overcast with big dark clouds, making the night sky seem so much darker but thankfully working for me, the angles of the lights leave long shadows that are dark enough for me to slip through … at least, I hope.

Swallowing down the nerves and anxiety, I figure there's no better time than the present. Keeping as quiet as a mouse, I slip out from under the thick hedge and plaster my back to the bush, stepping back into it to keep myself concealed.

A guard walks the perimeter, and I remind myself that I'm the same girl who broke out of Lucas Miller's fucked-up bathtub with severe stab wounds. I'm the girl who escaped Giovanni's desert cells and slaughtered the men holding me captive. I chainsawed a rapist in half without even blinking.

I've got this. I just need to call on that crazy bitch who lives inside me.

With every step the guard gets closer to me, I feel that bitch rising up inside me. I forget all the little things that make this guard human, forget about the family who might be waiting on him, forget about the student loans that he never planned on paying back, forget about the Great Dane in his too-small backyard that he needs, not because he loves him as a pet, but because he's overcompensating for something else.

I forget it all.

The only thing that matters is that this guard is just one more hurdle keeping me from Levi.

And with that, I pounce.

My arm locks around his throat, my hand clamping over his mouth to keep him silent. I drag him back into the thick bushes as my hand falls to his thigh, tearing the knife out of its sheath. He stumbles back, taken by surprise, and in a half-assed attempt to save himself, he roars against my hand, trying to grip me as we disappear into the hedges. Out of sight, out of mind, but it's already too late for him.

I bring the knife down in a deep arc across the front of his throat, and blood immediately pours out like a fountain over his chest. He fights me for a moment but quickly grows weak, and I lower his heavy body to the ground, doing what I can to keep concealed and quiet.

His eyes go glassy as I look away, not ready to feel like shit about this just yet. Once I have all three of the boys back in the safety of our home—wherever that might be—then I can allow myself to grieve over the lives I've destroyed here tonight, but not a second before.

Needing to blend in, my lips pull into a cringe. "Sorry, dude," I mutter, slipping the cap off his head and fixing it to mine. I consider taking his uniform too, but like … yuck. It's blood soaked and ruined, and while I'm desperate, I'm not *that* desperate.

I take his weapons, unclasping the holsters from his thighs and strapping them to mine before taking the gun at his hip and jamming it into the waistband of my pants.

Wanting to get out of here before anyone realizes this guy is missing, I slip out of the bushes, pull the cap down over my face and keep my head down. I follow the path the guard was expected to walk, sticking to the shadows, which is harder than it sounds.

Nerves wreak havoc over my body, my hands quickly growing

clammy, and I can't help the feeling that every single guard on the property is watching me. In reality, they're minding their own damn business, probably wondering why the fuck they've been called to walk circles around the property all night.

A pathway comes up and I hesitate. If I take it, I draw attention to myself, but if I don't, I'm going to end up walking the same path for hours. It's mostly masked in shadow, and I realize that this could very well be my only shot at this.

My knees shake but I keep putting one foot in front of the other until I'm moving onto the path. I start walking up toward the mansion at the top of the hill, bypassing other guards and keeping my head down. No one pays attention to me, and I sure as fuck don't raise my head to pay any to them.

The pathway is long, and just when I think I'm getting away with it, a voice cuts through the silence. "Yo, where the fuck do you think you're going?" a guard questions from his post to the side of the path.

My eyes bug out of my head, and I scramble for anything to say as I spare a sideways glance, trying to keep my face concealed. I'm supposed to be playing the role of a guard, and for a moment, I consider telling him that I'm due for my break, but that's a risk in itself. Gia probably doesn't offer her guards breaks. So instead, I lower my voice and do my best Marcus impression. "Gotta spring a leak."

The guard grunts, clearly not impressed, but he lets me pass. "Make it quick. Boss bitch will have your ass if she catches you slacking."

I force a scoff through my throat. "Yeah, man. I'll make it quick."

I pass by him like a fucking tornado tearing through a quiet town.

Fast and straight to the fucking point. I don't know how the hell I got away with that one. It must be the late hour and the double shift this guy is probably pulling. Either way, I don't plan to linger.

Moving up the pathway, I finally reach the main house. I stand around the back of the property, not daring to plaster myself so obviously at the front of the home. The property has been done up with spectacular gardens and a pool that I would die for. There are three separate outdoor dining areas just on this side of the property, and I realize that during my week here, I really didn't take enough time to appreciate everything that Gia built. Not going to lie, had she had a heart inside that chest of hers and if she was a decent person, maybe I would have enjoyed being her daughter. Might have even visited every now and then.

Fuck that. I learned a while ago that people are never who they appear to be, and Gia is the perfect example of that.

Moving deeper through the outdoor entertaining area, I try to figure out a plan. I can't exactly smash my way through a window like I did at the DeAngelis mansion. I mean, why do all these asshole mafia bosses have to have mega-mansions, and why do I feel the need to keep breaking into them? This is so fucked up and definitely not the life I dreamed of while I was in high school. But then, what girl wouldn't dream of having fiercely loyal men like the DeAngelis brothers railing her every night? Not gonna lie, if breaking into homes is what I have to do to keep the wicked, kinky railing going, then that's what I'm going to do.

I sidle right up against the side of the house and try to put together a plan. I'm not so stupid to walk straight through the back door, so it has to be a window. But which one to tackle is the ultimate question. Which one is going to cause the least amount of trouble for me?

My stomach clenches and twists with nervous anticipation as I pass by one of the many formal living rooms and come to a stop as a guard stands out on the back porch, a puff of smoke blowing out in front of him. The side door is open just a fraction and hope surges through me.

I can't say I've ever caught myself being thankful for cigarettes. It's always been drummed into me that cigarettes will kill me, but tonight, one of those little cancer sticks might just save my life.

The guard stands a little further out from the building, not wanting the smoke to blow back into the mansion and get caught. Something tells me that Gia isn't one of those bosses to be overly happy about her guards slacking on the job and taking cigarette breaks, but the fact he's chosen this particular spot suggests that perhaps there may be a blind spot in her security surveillance, and I intend to take full advantage of it.

Sneaking closer to the guard, I keep my wits about me, using the stealth and silence the boys trained me with while drawing my trusty knife. I'm not going to lie, I wish I had the strength to simply snap a grown man's spine with a twist of his neck like the boys do, but it's just not in the cards for me. So, until I find something easier, I'm left with the good old slit throat. It's messy, but it'll have to do.

The asshole doesn't even see me coming. One second, he's puffing away on his cigarette, his attention focused on his phone, the next, my hand is knotted in his hair, yanking his head back and the sharp blade is sailing across his throat.

He drops like a heavy sack of shit, and I groan at the mess he leaves behind. He's out in the open and anyone could come by his body, but what choice do I have? If I drag him away and hide his body, there's going to be a long ass trail of blood left behind which is going to be just as obvious as stumbling across the body.

Oh well, I'm damned if I do, damned if I don't. It's not like I'm about to go searching for a garden hose and spend an insane amount of time cleaning up after myself. That's simply not on the agenda tonight.

Not wanting to waste any more time on it, I leave the guy to be found and slip in through the back door, making sure to pull it closed behind me. The formal living room I step into is beautiful. Everywhere I look is white marble, and the plush white carpet beneath my shoes is the best kind of carpet money can buy.

The thought has my gaze drifting down to my feet, and I gape at the blood I've just marched across the room, the blood staining my fingers and destroying literally every object I've come in contact with.

Well, shit. That also hadn't been on the agenda today.

Going against everything I believe in, I scuff my shoes against the white carpet, wiping off every little smear of blood, rubbing until the soles of my shoes are crystal clear and absolutely destroying the expensive carpet in the process. Then just to add salt to the wound, I crouch down and wipe the blood from my hands as well.

It's a necessary evil. I can't afford to make tracks and have someone follow me through the mansion. It's the same as drawing a target in the center of my forehead and firing a gun in the middle of the place to draw attention to myself. Covering my tracks is common sense, and with everything already working against me, I have to do what little I can to protect myself. Plus, I can just hear the bullshit Roman would have thrown at me had I allowed that to happen.

Certain that I won't be making any more tracks, I make my way through the formal living room, stopping behind oversized vases and curtains to get a feel for the rooms I'm about to enter. I hear guards and staff deeper in the house, but from where I'm standing, I don't see anything.

I'm not foolish enough to believe that Gia is fast asleep in her bed all the way upstairs. She's making her way around here somewhere. My only hope is that she's holed up in her office, leaving her guards to do all her dirty work.

Convinced that the coast is clear, I sprint through the formal living room and through the adjoining foyers before finding the main entrance with the double staircase that I'd once thought was the best feature of the mansion. Taking a risk, I circle right around the over-done staircase and let out a shaky breath. I've been out in the open for far too long, taking too many risks, but I'm so close. I have to keep going.

Moving around the final corner of the grand staircase, just as I'd done a million times during my week here, I sail through the adjoining hallway and bring myself to a stop outside the elevator that goes down into the training facility below.

I always assumed the training room was the lowest part of the mansion. Zeke was always the one to press the button, and I never took it upon myself to notice if there were any levels below, but this elevator has to be the way down there. I spent hours searching this place before getting sidetracked learning that the boys were still alive, and during my searching, I didn't find anything else that could possibly suggest another way down to the cells below.

My hand slams down over the call button as my heart races. The stupid thing moves like a fucking snail, and I look back over my shoulder, certain that if I'm going to get sprung, now is going to be the time.

I bounce on my toes, my knees shaking with anticipation as my hand hovers over the gun in the back waistband of my pants.

Come on. Come on. Come on.

Anyone would think that a woman with a shitload of cash ready to burn would be able to afford an elevator fit for a queen. It's not like we're back in the early days where an elevator attendant would literally stand inside with you, closing gates and pulling a chain to bring us up and down.

What feels like a million years later, the elevator *dings*, and I curse it to hell. It's the softest ding I've ever heard, but right now it sounds like a fucking wrecking ball smashing through the walls.

The door opens, and I hastily get in before turning around and slamming my hand over the close door button, all too aware that there could have been someone waiting for me inside.

I scan the buttons. There are two upper levels which would lead to the bedrooms and living suites, the current level I'm on, and then the training room below. My brows furrow and I shake my head. There has to be something more. Some way to get down to Gia's cells below.

I spin around, taking in every corner of the elevator when I find a single black button on the wall. It's much smaller than the other buttons and mostly hidden by the interior design of the elevator. My finger retracts, nerves pulsing through me. There's a good chance that button lets off some kind of alarm and will screw me over in the worst way, but what do I have to lose? I'm not leaving this place without Levi, and it won't be long until the boys are storming in here to save my stupid ass.

Letting out a shaky breath, my finger strikes out, hitting the button with a fierce determination.

The elevator starts moving down, and I grip my gun, certain that if I'm right and the door opens to Gia's hidden cells, there will be guards lying in wait, and I'm going to be ready. I hold the gun out in front of me, my finger hovering over the trigger.

The further the elevator descends, the more my stomach fills with unease, but the second the soft *ding* sounds through the small metal box and the door slides open, every bit of hesitation dissolves within me.

Three guards stand inside the darkened room, one looking my way, his brows furrowed while the other two keep their stares on whatever the fuck they're doing.

My gun rings out.

A bullet plunges deep into the first guard's chest as I move like lightning, sprinting forward and adjusting my arm to the right before they get a chance to react. Their sharp gazes whip toward me, their eyes wide with fear as the gun sings out again. *BANG! BANG!*

One bullet pierces through the closer guard's skull, sending him flailing backward, while the other collides with the further guard's shoulder. He cries out, and I take another shot—BANG! My arm flinches with the powerful shot, but I keep moving forward, watching as he falls, one bullet in his shoulder, the other straight through his chest.

I don't stop to make sure they're dead because the second I look down at them and see them as humans bleeding out on the ground, I'll break. My conscience will come up and crush me, and I can't afford that right now. All that matters is racing around the corner and finding the man I've been desperate to see for the past three days.

My feet move like lightning, rushing across the dark flooring, barely touching the ground. I race around the corner and into a wide-open room with black walls and chains hanging from bars across the ceiling, and right there in the center of the room is the reason I'm here.

I pull myself to a stop, my greedy gaze sailing over every inch of his body, taking in the angry whip marks across his wide chest. He looks strong but exhausted. His chest rises with heavy breaths, and I don't doubt that every movement kills him just a little bit more.

"Well, well," I mutter, a wicked grin spreading across my face. The relief is like nothing I've ever felt before. "If it isn't my favorite DeAngelis."

A relieved sigh escapes through Levi's lips as he slowly raises his head to meet my eyes, and the pain I see reflected in his is nearly enough to drop me to my knees. "You better not let Marcus hear you utter those words."

I race toward him, my desperation knowing no bounds. "You've got it all wrong," I tell him, scanning over his binds and trying to figure out how the hell to get him out of here. It won't be long until someone finds me on the camera feed and decides to do something about it. After all, those gunshots couldn't have gone unnoticed. "If I tell him you're my favorite, then he might just spend the rest of his life trying to convince me otherwise … and the sex when that man is on a mission. Daaaaamn. That might just be the best idea I've ever had."

Levi shakes his head, a small smile playing on his lips, but his exhaustion is quickly catching up to him. "Get me the fuck out of here, babe," he mutters, pulling against the chains as he glances around the room. "Where are the boys?"

My lips twist into a cringe and I let out a shaky breath. "You see, here's the thing…"

Levi fixes me with a hard stare, the look in his eyes making my words fall away. "What the fuck did you do?"

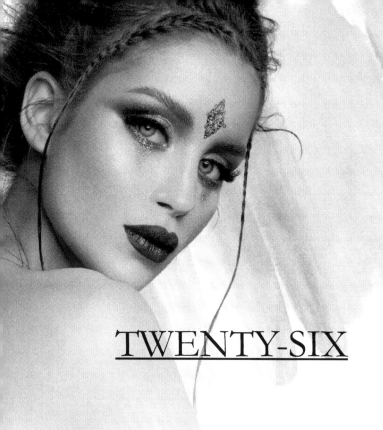

# TWENTY-SIX

"Can you bitch at me later?" I question, meeting Levi's dark eyes. "Now really isn't the best time. We have to get out of here."

"No shit," he mutters. "You snuck all the way in here and decided to let off four fucking gunshots at the very last moment. Are you trying to get every last guard down here?"

"Would you have preferred that I took on all three of those guards with my bare hands?" I question, searching around for some kind of release for the chains.

Levi smirks. "Why not? I've seen you take on three men plenty of times and you've never had an issue handling yourself. In fact—"

I give him a blank stare. "Seriously? Sex jokes right now?"

His brows bounce, and despite the agony tearing through his body, he's doing everything he can to keep in good spirits. "Whoever said that being held captive was supposed to be boring?" he questions. "Though, I'm not going to lie, I'm surprised to see you, little one. Imagine all the fun we could have down here together."

My face scrunches as I study him a little closer. "Did they give you something?"

He rolls his eyes. "Nope. This is all me, baby. Now, if you wouldn't mind kindly releasing me from these fucking chains, I'd really appreciate it."

"How?" I spit, frantically searching around, all too aware of the time quickly ticking by. "I've got a gun, but I'm not sure I can make the shot."

He shakes his head. "No, the chains are too thick. If anything, it'll ricochet and hit us both, or you'll just shoot me by accident."

"If you don't start being a little more helpful, I might just shoot you on purpose," I throw back at him, my gaze lingering on the welts across his chest, already trying to think of what creams I'll need to go searching for the moment we get out of here. "What do I do?"

He swallows hard and lets out a heavy breath that has his lips twisting into a pained cringe. "Out where the guards were. There's some kind of closet or storage area where they keep all their fucked-up little toys. Check in there."

I rush out into the hallway to where the guards were watching over Levi and find the storage room just as Levi had said and tear the door open. There's all sorts of shit, but the industrial bolt cutters are what have my attention. I don't know if I'll be strong enough to cut through it, but I've got to try.

Hurrying back into Levi's strange cell, I get straight to work, struggling with the weight of the cutters let alone making them do what they're supposed to do. "What's the plan?" Levi questions, grunting as my movements pull against the chains and rub at his bloodied wrists. "Have you got weapons? Gia's not going to let us just walk out of here."

I swallow hard and refuse to meet his stare, concentrating on the chains above his head. "The plan is to get out and we have whatever weapons we can pull off those assholes out there."

"Fuck, babe. Did you honestly just come storming in here without thinking this through?"

"It was no better than the plan your brothers put together," I throw back at him. "They were going to leave me behind. Make me hang out with Mick like a little bitch who can't handle herself. And for the record, I think I'm doing pretty fucking well to have made it this far. Marcus wouldn't have been able to resist slaughtering every guard in sight. It would have been noisy and messy, which would have only seen a war out on the lawn and given Gia all the time she needed to get down here and finish you before they even made it through the front door. So, feel free to thank me at any time."

Levi shakes his head, and I can't tell if he's frustrated or just knows that I'm right ... maybe both. But either way, it's not important right now. "I can't break through the chains," I tell him. "I'm not strong enough."

"You are," he tells me, conviction shining in his dark eyes. "Keep trying. You've got this. Besides, when my brothers inevitably show up, do you really want to tell them that you got this far and then gave up? Marcus would never let you live it down and Roman would have you doing push-ups every day for the rest of your life. Now break the damn chains."

Groaning, I try again, straining my muscles until they ache, trying to snap through the heavy chain. The metal puts up a good fight, but with the image of Marcus laughing at me in my head, I give it that little bit more until the chain finally breaks under the pressure. The bolt cutters fall and narrowly miss Levi's head as the chains give out, releasing him from their hold. He drops heavily to the ground, and I go down with him.

"Are you alright?" I rush out, my eyes wide. His arms are probably aching. He hasn't been able to stand properly for days, dangling here with no relief. I can't even imagine how his shoulders feel. He takes a deep breath, slowly bringing his arms around in circles, testing the joints while his muscles more than likely scream for relief. "Levi?"

He shakes his head. "My shoulders are fucked. It's gonna be weeks before they're back to normal."

"Can I do anything?"

He pushes to his feet, his face showing every ounce of agony that his body has suffered through as he grips on to me. It takes a moment to get his balance, but the second he does, he looks just like the fierce asshole who stormed through my shitty apartment all those months ago, intent on raising the dead. "Nah, there's nothing we can do right now. Let's just get out of here and figure out our next step."

Gripping his hand, I lead him out of the cell, and as we stride past the guards slowly bleeding out on the floor, Levi pulls me up short. "Well, hey there, Larry. Fancy seeing you down here." He crouches down and pulls the gun from Larry's hip. "Did you guys get a chance to meet? This is my girl, Shayne. You know, the one you said you were going to fuck right there in front of me." He looks over the bullet wound in his chest and presses the tip of the gun into the hole and listens to his scream. "You'll have to forgive Shayne, she's new to this whole killing people thing, but it's cool. Not everyone just gets it, you know. She'll learn to take better kill shots, she just needs a little more practice."

I cross my arms over my chest, sighing as he uses my pathetic skills as an excuse to torture this guy as he slowly bleeds out.

"Anyway," he continues. "It's been really nice chilling with you these past few days, but I really must be going. Though don't stress, I haven't forgotten about my promise to end your life. So, just to wrap this up, it's been fun, glad you met Shayne, and I'll see you in hell." And with that, Levi stands before letting out two shots straight through the hole in his chest that I'd already put there while listening to his sweet screams. He smiles as if getting some sort of peace before moving the gun to the guard's face and taking a perfect shot right through his eye.

Levi turns the gun on the other two guards, taking the kill shots that I clearly hadn't been able to make before indicating for me to collect as many of their weapons as possible. "You good?" he questions, cringing as he rolls his shoulder, the shots having irritated his joints.

I scoff, looking back up at him as I hand him a bunch of guns and knives. "I should be asking you the same thing."

He looks back at me as though unsure why I would feel the need to ask him how he is, and with a bonus eye roll, I let out a heavy sigh, making my way over to the elevator. I press the call button, and Levi moves to my side, checking over the guns and counting bullets. "Prepare yourself," he says, handing one to me. "It could be an ambush."

Levi discreetly moves a step in front of me, and I resist the need to curse him out when the doors open, and we're met with nothing but an empty elevator.

"Huh?" I grunt, my lips pulling into an ugly sneer. "Why aren't they coming?"

Levi shakes his head. "I don't know. They could be waiting for us up top. Don't drop your guard."

Nervously moving into the elevator, the door closes behind us and I press the button for the main floor. We start moving up, and Levi quickly rolls out his shoulders once again, his face contorted with pain. "You know that really fucking sucked," he murmurs. "I had to start meditating just to try and forget the pain."

I glance across at him. "You know how to meditate?"

His lips pull into a cheesy grin, and I see laughter flashing in his eyes. "Absolutely not. It didn't fucking work and only managed to frustrate me some more."

"Serves you right for walking away—"

"Uh-uh," he says, wagging his fingers just as the elevator dings our arrival. He indicates for me to focus on the door while adjusting his stance. "No time for '*I told you so*' in battle, my deadly little assassin."

"Deadly little assassin?" I scoff as the door slowly begins to draw back. Surely he could come up with a name a little more … scary than that. I mean, I'm really rocking this whole slitting throats thing. If I'm going to get a serial killer name, I want it to be something cool.

"Well, *mostly* deadly assassin," he teases, his eyes lighting with excitement at the thought of destroying the Moretti empire from within its very walls.

The door opens and Levi and I stand in silence, staring out at the empty hallway. "What the fuck?" he sighs. "Why aren't people trying to kill us?"

There's a hint of irritation and annoyance in his tone, sounding like an eight-year-old who just learned he has to share his ice cream with his baby sister. "I'm sorry," I murmur, peeking out the elevator to the empty hallway beyond. "Were you hoping for an ambush?"

He shrugs his shoulders and presses his hand to my lower back, casually leading me out of the elevator as though we were in the lobby of a fancy five-star hotel, not in the heart of his enemy's lair. We get all of three steps before we hear the shooting coming from outside and a grin tears across Levi's face. "Guess our back up finally arrived."

I scoff, shaking my head while letting out a sigh. "I told you they wouldn't be able to get through the front door without causing a scene."

As if on cue, an army of guards rush through the open foyer of the mega-mansion and if we were just a few steps ahead in the hallway, we would have been sprung for sure. "I suppose we should go and help them."

"I mean, what's the rush?" I murmur, a smile playing on my lips. "Marcus hasn't killed anyone in like … weeks. He's probably out there having the time of his life. If we go, we're only taking away from his body count."

Levi shakes his head and nods up toward the floor-to-ceiling front door across the foyer. "Quit stalling. Get your ass out the door and … fuck."

Without warning, Levi throws his hand up and two loud shots echo through the hallway behind me. A sharp gasp tears from the back of my throat as I spin around to find two guards bleeding out on the ground, knives in their hands, barely a step behind us.

"Holy shit," I breathe, realizing just how close I'd come to having a knife through my spine. "I guess I should thank you for that."

"No shit," he says, his voice in a hushed whisper just like mine. "I accept sexual favors in the form of blow jobs. Now, if you're gonna deep throat that shit, I'll let you right off the ho—"

The sight of six armed guards moving toward us from the foyer is enough to stop Levi mid-sentence. "Well, this just got a little more interesting," he mutters, moving with me further into the foyer to meet them head on, rather than leaving us backed into the hallway.

The guards circle us from every angle as I hear the battle raging outside, gunshots screaming through the night as men scream for freedom. The boys must be doing well out there, which means there's no reason why we shouldn't do the same here. "Know what you're doing?" Levi questions, putting us back-to-back, naturally choosing the side he believes would have the toughest opponents while leaving me to deal with the scraps.

A grin pulls at my face as I watch the three men who I'm about to slaughter. "Of course," I tell him, not prepared to admit that I'm more interested in hearing more about this whole deep throating situation than what I'm about to face down. "I was trained by none other than DeAngelis royalty."

And just like that, the guards storm toward us.

I'm not here to fuck around, so instead of bothering with this hand-to-hand combat bullshit, I raise my right hand and let off three shots directly in front of me. The guard in the center drops to the ground as the other two run at me from the side. I try to get off another shot but they're too close and the gun is knocked right out of my hand and slides across the marble floor.

Frustration burns through my veins. I haven't had any sleep and am really not in the mood to be fucked with, but if these guys are willing to dust off my skills, I'm more than happy to come to the party.

Knifed fists come hurtling toward my face, and I pull away, my back pressing up against Levi's. His hand shoots out behind him, steadying my body without sparing me a single glance. I throw myself forward, one hand snapping down to my thigh, gripping the knife with a ferocity that I wasn't prepared for.

My hand strikes out, curving a bloodied arc through the arm of the guard on the right before it continues its arc straight back, stabbing into the gut of the other. They both cry out in rage and my adrenaline spikes, a part of me wanting to deal with these guys before Levi gets through his. Though from what I can hear of the noises coming from behind me, Levi isn't taking any prisoners.

I keep focus and lash out, preferring to be on the offense rather than stuck defending. Flying forward, my foot kicks out in a low sweep, giving the guard on my left a hard shove and knocking him back. He tumbles, but I don't get a second to hesitate as the other on my right comes at me. His fist flies forward and he gets only a step closer when Levi's hand curls into his hair from behind and yanks him back onto the tip of his knife, spearing him through the back of his spine and out the front of his throat. "Sorry, man. No hard feelings."

Levi looks at me, a sickly-sweet smile spreading across his gorgeous face. "That makes two," he says. "Maybe I'm gonna need a little something more than just a wicked round of deep throating."

His eyes widen, and before I can even flinch away, his hand rises and a perfectly round bullet whooshes past my shoulder and plunges deep inside the skull of the last remaining guard. My head whips back to see the guard dropping to his knees before his body collapses with a heavy thump. "Oh, come on," I groan, throwing my hands up in frustration. "I had that one."

"Right," he scoffs, hearing the guys' fight outside starting to die down. "Come on, we should—"

A slow clap sounds through the big foyer and both our heads snap across the room to find Gia standing on the bottom step of the grand staircase with Zeke right by her side. A flicker of relief washes through me. I wasn't sure Zeke had made it after being shot in the chest, but he looks more than fine to me. Perhaps he was wearing some kind of bulletproof vest or maybe the shot to his chest simply wasn't as bad as I'd thought.

"Impressive," Gia says, her eyes raking over Levi with disinterest before falling on me and slowly beginning to move toward us.

Levi crowds me, his big shoulder pushing in front of me in a half-assed attempt to protect me from the woman who wants my head on a stake.

"Your training is lacking," Gia says. "You should have been able to take out those guards in half that time. I'm disappointed, but I suppose it's a little late for training tips because you're not going to live long enough for it to matter. You'll never stand in my position, never be good enough. What a joke." She lets out a sigh, hitting the bottom step and moving in even closer, her heels clicking against the expensive white marble. "You know, for a moment there, I considered allowing you to continue here, to become my heir and take over my empire, but it didn't take long for me to realize that you were weak. You never had what it takes to rise up, never will."

My hand falls to Levi's back, brushing down his skin until my fingers are digging into the waistband of his low riding pants, holding him close.

Gia continues toward us, her gaze falling back to Zeke. "Do away with the DeAngelis," she says. "I want to end my daughter myself."

Panic tears through me and I shake my head, needing more time. "What was the point?"

"The point of what?" she fires back as Zeke awkwardly pauses, unsure if he should keep moving.

"Sending me to live with my father," I say. "Spending years funding what you believed was a good life for me. Why not just abort the pregnancy if you didn't want an heir?"

A slow smile creeps across her face and a flash of pity makes my stomach twist. I know exactly what she's going to say before the words are even out of her mouth. "You believed all of that? After everything you've learned over the past few weeks, you're going to stand before me and ask such foolish questions?" She laughs to herself. "Oh, God, it's almost comical to imagine such a daft child trying to rule over my empire. If you must know, it was Maxwell that wanted you so much. It never made sense to me when he promised I'd never have to see the two of you again. But your father was like the shit on the bottom of my shoe, no matter how much you scrub them clean, the smell just keeps coming back. He used you as a bargaining chip for twenty-two years. If I didn't pay, Giovanni would."

Not gonna lie, that one stings. But she's right, I needed to believe that she wanted the best life for me. I had such a shitty childhood, and I clung to the idea that it should have been better, that I wasn't meant to suffer the way I did.

I should have known better. I was never more than a pawn or a paycheck to anyone that was supposed to love and protect me.

Before Gia gets a chance to take this further, Roman strides into the big foyer at my right, having come in through a side entrance. His gaze sweeps over my body before falling on Levi, and while his face remains a complete mask, concealing his emotions, I feel the relief washing over him.

Roman stops to my right, leaving a few feet between us, giving Gia two separate targets rather than one big one, and I watch the way Gia watches us. Her eyes flicker from side to side, trying to figure out how to play us now that her chances of survival are beginning to plummet. She can send Zeke in, but there's no way he can take out one of the brothers before the other makes a laughingstock out of her.

"Decisions, decisions," I taunt, knowing the ball lies in our court.

Her jaw clenches, and just as she goes to spit what I'm assuming is another bullshit insult, a velvety voice comes pouring in from the left. "Sorry I'm late to the party," Marcus muses, making my lips pull into a wide grin. He strides into the foyer, spinning a knife between his fingers, the blade catching on the chandelier light directly above Gia.

His sharp stare locks onto mine. "Shayne," he says, his eyes darkening and sending me one hell of a nasty reminder that I'm right at the top of his shit list. "You're fucking lucky that you're all the way across the room and that all this bloodshed has managed to sedate me because I'm fucking fuming at you, babe."

I clench my jaw. "Really? You want to talk about this right now?"

Marcus stops directly opposite Roman, the four of us creating a semi-circle around Gia and he doesn't say another word, just focuses on the matter at hand.

Gia looks nervous, and she should be. Her guards are dead and we have her surrounded.

She has one final lifeline, and as she turns to Zeke and nods, she realizes all too quickly that she doesn't even have that. Zeke silently steps away from her side and moves back toward the grand staircase, completing the circle.

She looks at him in horror. "What the hell is the meaning of this?" she seethes. "What are you doing?"

His lips pull into a crooked grin, and he nods his head as if in greeting. "Pleasure to meet your acquaintance," he says. "The name's Agent Byron Davidson, FBI, but feel free to keep referring to me as the best fuck of your life. I know how much you like to get screwed."

"Well, shit," I laugh, drawing her attention back to me. "I bet you didn't expect your day to end up like this when you woke up this morning."

Gia's eyes blaze, and just like three nights ago, standing out on the manicured lawn before the charred remains of Roman's home, she loses control. "YOU," she spits, her hand falling to her hip and gripping her gun. She whips it out from the holster and holds it out. "Say goodbye, bitch. You'll never get what's mine."

Her hand flinches, her finger squeezing the trigger in the same moment that I drop to the ground. The bullet sails over my head as Marcus' hand snakes out with the kind of power no man should be capable of, his knife hurtling from his fingers with perfect skill and precision.

The bullet penetrates the heavy front door before the loud *BANG* has even finished echoing through the expansive foyer, and in that very same moment, the tip of Marcus' knife glides straight through her back, severing her spinal cord.

Gia's eyes widen in shock before she slowly falls to her knees, barely holding on. Silence fills the room, this moment changing the whole fucking game.

My heart races erratically as Levi offers me his hand and pulls me to my feet. Gia's eyes remain locked on mine, and I see in her wicked stare that she truly thought she was going to survive this. I move forward, unsure of what to say in her final moment, but as I take my last step and position myself right in front of her, I realize there is nothing I can say. She was nothing short of a monster with no heart and a black, rotting soul.

"I'll be seeing you," I remind her. "One of these days, I'm going to join you in hell, and I'm going to enjoy watching you burn, but not as much as I'm going to enjoy burning your empire to the ground."

And with that, my arm stretches up above my head and I squeeze the trigger one final time. Stepping back, I watch as the heavy chandelier drops from the high ceiling. Thick glass splinters drive deep into her skin, ending her life and cascading across the foyer like a wave of shimmering diamonds.

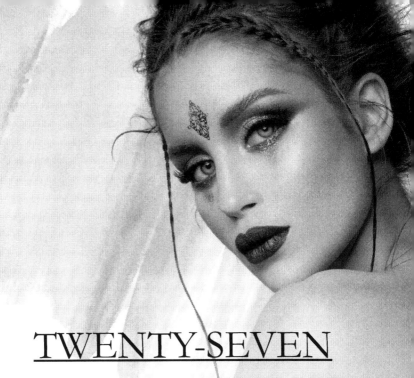

# TWENTY-SEVEN

A stray diamond glimmers up at me, and I scoop it out of the rubble, completely mesmerized by the way it sparkles yet screams of vengeance as a single drop of blood falls from its sharp edges.

The dust has barely settled before Roman and Marcus make their way to me, their feet crunching over the shattered diamond remains of the chandelier. Zeke—or Agent Davidson—stands back with his arms crossed over his wide chest, looking down at the woman who he's shared a bed with for who the fuck knows how long. His expression is unreadable, but I'm sure a million things are coursing through his mind, while probably also irritated that however many years of hard work are all washed away. I bet there's going to be one hell of a report for him to fill out come Monday morning.

Marcus reaches me first, and his tight grip instantly circles my throat, drawing me into him as his hard stare bores into mine. He doesn't look away, doesn't blink, just keeps staring, his wild emotions burning through his stare. He's more unhinged than I've ever seen him, and fuck, I think I like it. I've always loved that wild intoxication from Marcus. He's unpredictable and relentless. I never know what to expect from him, but add this dangerous desperation, and my heart is racing just as fast as his.

Roman moves to Levi's side, seeing that Marcus is going to need a moment to calm down. He leads him out of the bloodstained rubble and Zeke follows them out of the room, leaving me with the man who first captured my soul. "I'm okay," I choke out.

His chin lowers as his eyes go far away, giving me that same wild look he used to give me when I first arrived at the castle and he didn't know what this pull was between us, back when he had no idea why the fuck his heart used to race so hard every time he was around me.

"You think you can cuff me and then bat your fucking eyelashes like the very thought of you running away from me didn't destroy me?" he growls, his voice so low that I feel its vibration rocking against my chest.

He pulls his hand up, squeezing my throat just a bit tighter. "Don't act like you don't know why I did it," I spit back at him, holding his stare just as profusely as he holds mine, refusing to break. Not now, not ever.

A deep growl rumbles through his chest as my lungs begin to scream, but I don't dare gasp for breath. Marcus knows my limits, and while he'll sure as hell push them, he won't ever cross them.

Heat floods me, my pussy throbbing for this wild man, and seeing the desperation and desire burning in my heated stare, his mouth drops to my throat, his hand releasing me and falling to my ass. He bites my neck, not hard enough to draw blood but enough to make me gasp.

Pain flares at the base of my throat, immediately replaced with the most overwhelming pleasure as he kisses me there, his tongue rolling over my skin with practiced skill. His hand grips my ass, squeezing it tight, and I push back against it, wanting more. It's been too long since I've felt him. I need him more than I need to breathe.

He spins me around, plastering my back to his wide chest as I gasp for air, already missing the feel of his lips on my neck, but here, like this, I feel his raging erection grinding against my ass. Marcus grips my chin and forces my head back, and before I can even demand that he takes whatever he needs from me, his mouth is closing over mine.

His tongue dives into my mouth, and I melt into him as his hand curls around my body, sliding up the thin material of my tank and gripping my tit. He rubs my nipple between his fingers before giving it a sharp pinch, and I gasp into his mouth as the need grows wildly between my legs.

If he doesn't touch me soon … fuck.

As if reading my every need, his other hand glides down my body and slips between my legs, cupping my pussy and giving it a firm squeeze, relieving only a fraction of the pressure until he uses the palm of his hand to grind against me.

I groan into his mouth, already panting and desperate for more while fearing that he's going to go easy on me because of what happened with his father. I don't know what it is. I don't know if I've suddenly managed to forget the trauma or if I've just put it aside for now, all I know is that I need to feel him inside me, need to feel his touch, need him to make me come alive again.

The beauty of Marcus DeAngelis is that he's going to take whatever the fuck I'm giving out, and damn it, I'm giving out everything I've got. My body is his, I'm his salvation just as he is mine.

He releases our kiss and I gasp for breath as his mouth returns to the side of my throat and my gaze lands on the mess of blood and diamonds scattered at my feet. "I fucking love you, Shayne," he growls as if in this very moment, the thought of loving me is wreaking havoc over his soul. He releases my pussy and I cry out, but all too soon, his hand is slipping inside my pants and grazing over my clit. "Don't ever fuck with me like that again."

"You know I can't make promises like that," I warn him, telling him what he already knows.

A ferocious growl tears through him again and without warning, two thick fingers push up inside of me, deep and raw. I gasp out and immediately grind against him before his thumb finds my clit and rubs tight little circles, just the way I like it.

"You'll do what I fucking ask of you."

My hand slams back against his cock and he grunts in pain before grinding against my palm and allowing me to release him from the confines of his pants. His heavy cock falls into my hand, and I squeeze him tight, pausing at the very tip and grinning at the way his breath catches, hostage to nothing but my grip. "And become your little *yes, bitch?*" I scoff. "Please, you'll be bored in a matter of seconds."

He growls against my skin, and I begin pumping my hand up and down his thick, veiny shaft, giving him exactly what he wants as I ride his fingers. His intensity grows, pumping into me faster and harder as I cry out in need. "Fuck me, Marc," I pant.

His fingers curl at the perfect angle moving against that one spot deep inside me that drives me insane. "No," he demands, his tone suggesting this is some form of punishment as he hits that spot again, his fingers like the deadliest dark magic moving inside of me.

My hand squeezes at the base of his thick cock. "Fuck me, or one of your brothers will."

His eyes blaze with startling amounts of need and desire and within seconds, his fingers tear out of my cunt and my pants are down just enough for Marcus to get exactly what he wants as he bends me over, his hand pressing against my back to keep me down.

He slams deep into my cunt, and I cry out, the pleasure rocking through my body and filling me. "Oh, fuck," I cry, looking back up at Marc to find his eyes already on mine, blazing like molten lava as he groans in deep pleasure. He holds my stare as he brings his fingers to his mouth and sucks them dry before pulling back slowly.

My body shakes, the anticipation building as he holds my hungry stare. "Fuck, Marc. Give it to me."

He slams into me again and we each groan, both of us needing this more than we could have known. He fucks me hard, fast, and wild, stretching my walls and taking me deep. His fingers fall to my hips, digging painfully into my skin and I cry out for more.

My orgasm builds and builds, getting more intense by the second, and all too soon it's rocking through me, filling my body with undeniable pleasure, burning every little nerve ending and making me come alive. "MARC," I cry, reaching up and gripping on to his fingers at my hip.

My pussy clenches around his thick cock, spasming as he takes me harder, refusing to stop as I ride out the high. I pant, struggling to catch my breath as my knees threaten to give out from under me, but he holds me up, slamming deep inside of me, his balls rocking against my clit and sending sharp jolts of electrifying pleasure shooting through my core until finally, he comes hard, spilling his hot seed deep inside of me.

"Fuck, Shayne," he pants, his fingers loosening on my hips as he slowly moves back and forth, trying to ease my bruised skin. I come up, plastering my back to his wide chest as he remains buried deep in my core. "I don't know what the fuck it is about seeing you covered in death, but it brings me to my knees every goddamn time."

Turning my head, I raise my chin and capture his lips in mine. "You know there's nothing I wouldn't do for you," I murmur. "You and your brothers, you're my home now. I belong to you. If one of you is in trouble, then I'm going to be right there, fighting at your side. Don't try to silence me like that again, Marc, because this is how it's going to end every fucking time. Do you hear me?"

He lets out a deep breath, his hand curling around my body and holding me close to his chest. "I hear you, babe. We were wrong to demand you stay behind. We saw that reckless need for blood in Gia's eyes and she wasn't going to stop until she had your heart beating in the palm of her hand. I couldn't see past that. I'm sure Roman has his own reasons for wanting to keep you away from all of this, but where you're concerned, I can't see reason."

His forehead drops to mine, and I breathe him in, my knees shaking beneath me. "I know," I murmur before awkwardly pulling away from him and fixing my pants around my waist.

Marcus tucks his cock back inside his pants, doing up the fly as I move back into him and capture his lips once more. "Come on," I whisper, dreading what comes next before indicating to Gia's body sprawled beneath the heavy frame of the shattered chandelier, her eyes wide and staring straight back at me. "We need to figure out what the hell all of this means for us."

Marc nods and slips his hand into mine before pulling the lone diamond out of the palm of my hands. "What's this?" he questions, looking it over, the smear of blood now long gone.

I shake my head while shrugging my shoulders. "Don't know," I mutter as he leads me through the wreckage. "It was just sparkling and for some reason, I felt the need to pick it up. I don't know, consider it the first thing to go up on my trophy shelf."

His jaw drops and he looks at me as though he's just seen a ghost. "Nu-uh. You only get a trophy if you were responsible for the death, and as I recall, it was my knife that got lodged in her spine."

I stare back at him. "No way," I say, snatching the lonely diamond out of his hand. "That's bullshit and you know it. My bullet is what dropped the chandelier and crushed her. All you did was paralyze the bitch. Besides, if that were the rule, then by all rights, I should be able to take your cousin's tongue off your shelf."

Marcus watches me through a narrowed gaze. "I knew you played dirty, but I didn't know you were quite so ruthless," he tells me. "I earned that tongue fair and square."

"You weren't even there," I mutter under my breath as he leads me through to the kitchen where Agent Davidson leans against the counter, a mug of steaming coffee in his hands and a first aid kit spilled out over the expensive granite.

Roman hovers over Levi, whose wounds have been cleaned and bandaged, and digs his fingers into Levi's shoulder, getting a good feel for the damage as Levi's face twists with pain. "Fuck, alright," Levi spits, pulling away from Roman's poking and prodding. "This ain't helping shit."

"Makes me feel better," Roman mutters under his breath before noticing me and Marcus moving into the room.

All three of them raise their heads, a strange hesitance in their eyes. "What?" I demand, stopping by the entrance, having seen that look more than enough times over the past few months to know it means nothing but bad news. "Spit it out. I haven't slept in what feels like a lifetime. Let's just get this over and done with."

Roman goes to speak when Agent Davidson pushes off the counter and places himself between us, stealing the spotlight. "Congratulations," he says with a tone that fills me with unease. "You are now the most powerful woman in the country."

My gaze sweeps to Roman and Levi while gripping tighter onto Marcus' hand. "Elaborate."

Roman lets out a heavy breath and looks as though he's about to take a bath in acid. "Gia's dead, Empress. You're her heir."

I shake my head, knowing what they're suggesting but not liking it. The whole point of this was because I didn't want anything to do with her or her empire, and now they're trying to tell me …

"Say the words," I beg him, an unknown heaviness settling into my chest. "I need to hear it. I need to know exactly what you're telling me."

"Shayne," Roman says. "You are Gia's heir. You're the leader of the Moretti family."

Marcus scoffs beside me, shaking his head. "Every empire must have its Empress."

"No, no, no, no," I say, shaking my head as bile rises in my throat. "This is a sick joke, right? I can't rule over the Moretti empire. That's … it's fucking ridiculous. I'm twenty-two and have connections to you guys. There will be a massive target on my head."

Levi nods as if already coming to this concussion a million times over. "Yep."

I begin to pace.

Agent Davidson steps toward me, his eyes softening in a way I never once saw while staying here, and I can't help but wonder how he feels about all of this. "I can assure you, Shayne, this is certainly no joke. I've been undercover here for over six years, and this is about as serious as it's going to get. You need to be prepared. They are going to make you choose—your family or them."

"They?" I ask. "Who is they?"

"The Moretti family," Davidson says. "Just as the DeAngelis family has all of its members, so does the Moretti family. They are just as awful as you can imagine, probably a lot like the extended members of the DeAngelis family. They don't even know about you yet, and the moment they become aware of Gia's death, it will turn into a race for her position. She has been holding the reins of this family for far too long, and these men have been terrified of her, but you … you're just a girl, mixed up with the DeAngelis family who hasn't had a chance to prove herself. They won't like you, and they'll do whatever it takes to knock the crown right off your head."

I search his eyes, desperate for some way out of this. "Can't I just … give it to them? Walk away?"

Levi shakes his head, his big, dark eyes coming to mine. "Doesn't work like that, babe. If my father came to us and said here, I don't want it anymore. We'd take it from him and put a bullet in his back the second he walked away to ensure he never came back to lay claim over leadership. You're not any different."

"So, what am I supposed to do?"

"Do what any one of us would do," Roman tells me. "Take it by the horns and shoot down anyone who dares to question you."

"They're not going to like us together."

"Fuck them," Marcus says. "They don't like it, I'll let them choose the bullet that gets loaded in my gun."

My hands shake and I pull out a chair, needing to sit. Hell, the mess Marcus left between my legs doesn't even bother me right now. I try to go over everything, try to remember the small snippets of information Gia taught me while I was here, but knowing that she had every intention of killing me kind of makes all of that information unreliable. I can't trust anything I already know.

I'm the motherfucking queen of the Moretti empire.

I'm one of the richest, most powerful women walking the planet, and the second news gets out about this, I'll also have the biggest target to ever exist on my back.

Shit.

Just another day in the life of Shayne Mariano ... Moretti ... DeAngelis.

Trying to come to terms with everything, I turn back to Agent Davidson and let him see the very real fear in my eyes. "What's going to happen from here?"

"In Gia's office, there is a pre-programmed cell phone. You will need to use that to call an urgent family meeting. Choose a time and date, the sooner the better as you can't risk news of this getting out before you have a chance to introduce yourself. Family members will ask what the meeting is in regard to, but you must not say anything or give away your identity until they are here in this home."

I nod, understanding all of that all too clear. "What happens at the meeting?"

"That's up to you," he says, raising his gaze to Roman's. "Might I suggest that you three make yourselves sparse for this meeting. Your presence will not be tolerated."

"Absolutely not," Roman says. "Where Shayne goes, we go. They'll have to drag us out of there."

"Dragging won't be your issue. It'll be the bullet through your head that you'll struggle with," Agent Davidson says before shrugging his shoulders, not really giving a shit if the boys were to get hurt. They've made their decision, and it's not up to Agent Davidson to change their minds. He's given them fair warning and that's all he needs to live with a clear conscience.

"Okay," I say, thinking of the few meetings the boys held after running out their father. It can't be much different than that. I just have to act like I belong until they finally accept it. "I think I can handle it."

"The meeting isn't your biggest problem," Roman adds, making my head snap up as Agent Davidson's brows furrow in confusion. "You're legally married to my father," he reminds me, as if I needed that bucket of cold water dumped over my head. Seeing the irritation in my eyes and clearly wanting me to understand something that I'm simply not getting, he walks across to me, crouching down in front of my seat and gripping my hands. "Your marriage to my father means that if you were to fall, the whole Moretti empire would legally be his. Do you understand what that means? What kind of power he would wield?"

Dread sinks heavily into my veins and all color washes from my face. "Holy shit," I breathe, the weight of just how serious this is falling onto my shoulder. "I need to get this marriage annulled as soon as possible."

"Exactly," he tells me, a grim expression falling over his dark features. "And you need to do it without getting a bullet shot straight between your eyes."

Well, fuck.

# TWENTY-EIGHT

The formal dining room is packed with bodies, each of them more powerful than the next. My nerves are shot. I would be fine had this been a normal meeting with Gia not being a crazy psycho bitch and introducing her long-lost daughter to her family, but this is something much different. Plus, they're already apprehensive due to the stack of bodies they passed by on their way to the door.

I'm not going to lie, the dead guards inside the foyer were nothing compared to the massacre Roman and Marcus created out on the lawn. I mean, daaaaamn. They worked hard. Marcus in particular. It was almost comical looking over the differences in the kills. Roman's were quick kill shots, easy and less messy, where Marcus was carving initials and decapitating heads left, right, and center. Asshole was probably having the time of his life.

Come to think of it, I should have demanded that he showered before touching me.

Gross.

I stand with Agent Davidson and the boys in the sitting room adjoining the formal dining hall, and I hear them getting rowdier by the minute, wondering what this is all about. Hell, half of them are furious about the call that came through at four in the morning and are demanding answers, but they won't be making demands from me.

I need to go into this with my head held high, and I need to lay down the law from the beginning, otherwise, they'll never respect me, never see me as their true leader.

Crap. How are they supposed to see me as their leader when I barely see myself that way? This is going to be a shitshow, especially considering the boys walking in behind me. I need to be honest with the Moretti family about my relationship with the boys, and they're going to have to learn to accept it, or they can walk. It's not going to be easy, but I have to hope that the Moretti family is a little more lenient than the DeAngelis assholes the boys have to deal with on a daily basis.

Fuck me in the ass and call me Fred. This is going to be hell.

Agent Davidson pushes off the side of the small armchair. "It's time," he tells me, somehow holding his nerves better than anyone considering the fact that his cover has now been blown and he's about to walk into a room full of powerful criminals, possible rapists, and murderers. His only hope is that word hasn't spread about his identity, but considering we were the only ones in the room at the time, I doubt it. But who knows what ears could have been listening in, what conversations Gia's security system caught. "You don't want to keep these assholes waiting."

My shoulders bounce with anticipation until Levi presses his hand over them and holds me still. "Professional bitches don't bounce," he tells me as his hand slips around to my chin and forces it up. "Chin high, shoulders back, and use that tone you use on Marcus when putting him in his place. They'll have no fucking idea that you're riddled with nerves."

"Easier said than done," I tell him, certain that he knows the feeling all too well. I move across the room, my eyes tired but my body alive with nerves. "Let's do this."

Finding the courage deep inside of me, I push through the big double doors and enter the crowded dining room. Men in expensive suits fill every space, and as I make my entrance known, every single one of their eyes fall to me.

Brows furrow and confusion laces their dark eyes, having expected Gia in her ridiculous heels and tight business dress, but instead, they get a younger, less put together version of her, probably wondering why I seem so familiar.

Their gazes linger on me for barely a breath before taking in the three men at my back. With guns drawn and nasty comments flying, the room erupts into total chaos.

Holding my head high, just as Levi told me, I keep myself moving, and as far as I can tell, the DeAngelis Grim Reapers at my back don't even flinch under the weight of facing their enemy.

Moving into the space at the head of the table, I keep myself standing and prepare for the worst.

"What is the meaning of this?" an older gentleman spits from my immediate left, while another growls, "What have you done with Gia?"

I hold my hands up as if to silence them, and I'm surprised when they actually oblige. "For a group of men who are supposed to lead the largest mafia family in the world, I am disappointed," I muse, scanning over each of their faces and trying to decipher who's the biggest threat in the room. "I believed I was attending a meeting with men who understood the importance of professionalism, yet all I hear are tantrums and outbursts from way down the hall."

"Who do you think you are?" that same older gentleman demands, his gaze cold and calculated. "You come in here uninvited, wielding the most pitiful of DeAngelis mafia at your back."

Instead of rising to the bait, I lay my hands down on the table, intrigued by the way their guns slowly begin to fall. "Take your seats, gentleman," I start. "And then I can explain to you all why you've been called here this morning."

I wait a moment, watching as they all take their seats, their sharp gazes warily flicking between me and the boys, but Agent Davidson's presence goes a long way in gaining what little trust I can. They've known him for many years, watched him thrive at Gia's side, gain her trust, and become her most important player. If I were some kind of threat to them, he wouldn't be standing with me … at least, they think.

Chairs scrape against the marble, and after a few short moments, their reluctant gazes turn back to me. "My name is Shayne Moretti, and I am the biological daughter of Gia Moretti."

Gasps and outrage pour through the room, some men shocked to find that Gia had harbored such a scandalous secret, others immediately assuming I'm lying, while the few closest to me realize that their claim to the top spot just got a little bit harder. It doesn't take a genius to figure out that these men are the ones I need to be wary of.

The older gentleman to my right stands, slamming his hand down on the table. "Zeke, is this true? Does this … this woman speak the truth?"

Zeke—or Agent Davidson as I now know him—steps closer to the table, his face a mask of indifference, completely unreadable. "Yes, Alec, this is Gia's biological daughter. She sent her away as a newborn because she knew the risks of bringing a child into this world," he says, my birth certificate appearing between his fingers before he places it on the table. He slides it across the polished oak toward Alec. "Gia kept her away as a precaution."

Alec studies the birth certificate before pushing it aside, letting the other men around him feast their eyes on it. He raises his head, his eyes full of skepticism as he scans over me before flicking straight to my back, his lips pulling up in a disgusted sneer. "So, why the hell would Gia's sole heir be standing at our meeting table with the DeAngelis brothers at her back? Brothers who are rumored to have perished at their fathers' hand?"

I hold my hand up, silencing his question. "We'll get to that, and I'm sure all will be cleared up in a timely manner. However, the reason why I am here holds a greater importance," I go on, holding his stare for a moment longer before addressing the rest of the table. "In the early hours of this morning, my mother—Gia Moretti—was slaughtered here in her very own home."

Men fly up out of their chairs, their guns held firmly once again, all eyes going straight to the boys with heavy accusation. Chaos breaks out, and within the blink of an eye, a gun is pressed against my temple as men storm toward the boys.

The boys don't fight back, just stand there as Moretti men move in on them. I turn toward Alec who stands with his finger on the trigger, his wicked plan for his future flashing in his mind. He can't kill me, not without confirming my identity. After all, if he pulls the trigger and finds that I am who I say I am, meaning he kills the only true heir to the Moretti empire, he will be hunted out of nothing but sheer loyalty to Gia.

"Why don't you go ahead and call off your hounds so that I may explain everything that has been going on over the past couple of weeks?" I suggest, raising my brow and not daring to flinch at the cool barrel pressed up against my head. "Or would you prefer to keep making a fool of yourself by showcasing an award-winning tantrum?"

Alec glares at me, not liking me one bit, but ultimately pulls the gun from my head before nodding to the men surrounding Roman, Levi, and Marcus. "We can talk," Alec spits. "But DeAngelis scum will not be privy to our family meetings. They are unpredictable and not worthy of our trust. They will be held in our cells until further notice."

The boys tense, their bodies ready for a fight, not in the least pleased with the idea of leaving me here undefended, but there's no way around this. If I keep them here, the Moretti family won't hear me, won't even give me a chance to explain, but if they go, I might just be able to gain their trust.

"Fine," I say, nodding to the men who surround my boys. "Take them to the cells. However, if any of them are harmed in even the slightest way, I will personally see to it that your lives are not worth living."

The boys are captured, their arms restrained behind their back. "Shayne," Roman warns, holding back as the two men at his sides try to force him away. He holds my stare but I nod, letting him know that I'm alright and that I know what I'm doing, but I know he sees the nervousness in my eyes, the fear that this could all go wrong in a matter of seconds.

Roman reluctantly allows them to take him, and my heart shatters at having to send them to yet another cell, but they'll be okay. The moment this meeting is over, I'll be straight down there, freeing them from the confines of those four small walls.

With the boys out of the way, I turn my gaze back to Alec and wave my hand out in front of me in a challenge. "Go ahead and take your seat," I tell him, remaining on my feet to address them.

He reluctantly goes, and I press my hands back to the polished oak table. "Okay, where shall I start?"

"Why not start at the beginning?" Alec suggests, a snide tone to his response.

I nod before looking out at the sea of faces, none of which I can trust. "Very well," I say, going right back to the beginning. "A little over nine months ago, I was kidnapped out of my city apartment by DeAngelis forces," I say, skimming over a few of the details that probably won't bode well for me. "At the time, I was unaware of my lineage, in fact, I had no idea who or what the Moretti family even was, but Giovanni DeAngelis knew who I was. He had somehow discovered that Gia was harboring a daughter and saw that as his way in. He plans on infiltrating the Moretti empire and using me to do so."

"How?" Alec spit, fury blazing in his eyes.

I hold back my temper, knowing a snide remark isn't going to get me far right now.

"I am sure you are all aware who those three men at my back were. They are the DeAngelis Grim Reapers, Giovanni's own sons— Roman, Marcus, and Levi. Giovanni feared his sons so much that he imprisoned them in a castle, and to gain their cooperation, he *gifted* me to them to hold until he was ready to use me for whatever sick games he had planned. From what you just witnessed, it is clear I have formed a bond with the three DeAngelis brothers who share the same mutual hatred for their father as you do. They have suffered under his hold, as have I."

I let out a shaky breath before quickly reeling it in, terrified of showing any weakness and having it exploited. Pulling my shoulders back, I continue. "Coming up on three weeks ago, Giovanni brought a battle to his sons' front door. Many lives were lost that night and resulted in his sons suffering once again. They were stabbed and thrown in cells, left for days as infection began to eat at them—"

"Why should we care about DeAngelis civil affairs?" A man to my right throws out. "That is none of our concern."

"If it involves me, then you can guarantee it is our concern," I bite back, hating the feel of the words preparing to come out of my mouth, "especially considering that the week Giovanni's sons were locked down in those cells, Giovanni forced me into a marriage and then raped me to make it binding."

Shock rumbles through the room, but I forge on, not willing to linger on the details of that day. "Giovanni plans to use his marriage to me as a way to infiltrate the Moretti empire. He sees this as some kind of gateway. If I were to die while Giovanni is my legal spouse—"

"The family will fall," Alec murmurs, realizing the severity of the situation.

"Exactly," I say, my voice lowering. "It is believed that Giovanni's forces were at action this morning. Gia's blood is on his hands."

Murmurs fill the room and I briefly glance at Agent Davidson and catch his eye. He nods as if to tell me that I'm doing a good job before keeping his attention on the table. "Kill them," someone cries out. "Kill them all."

I raise my voice again, unsure of the politics and rules I'm supposed to be following, though assuming it would run in a similar way to how the boys went about dealing with their family. "I am unsure how this is supposed to play out," I admit. "I assume that we are to vote on an appropriate course of action."

Alec scoffs. "We will vote once we have confirmed your identity.

MANIACS

This birth certificate is pitiful at most. I demand full DNA testing."

"I am more than happy to supply anything that this family sees fit. However, that will take days, and I am not willing to stand around twiddling my thumbs in the meantime while Giovanni goes about his plans to infiltrate this family, and I hope, out of your loyalty to Gia, that you would not feel any different."

A heavy silence fills the room as all eyes turn to Alec, waiting for his response, but all I get is a sharp glare that makes victory swarm through my chest. *Take that, asshole.* "Alright, then it's settled. All in favor of protecting the Moretti empire by eliminating Giovanni DeAngelis, raise your hand."

It's unanimous. Every hand in the room silently raises and I nod. "Good," I say, before feeling a flutter of nerves rushing through me once again. "I feel that I must also inform you that Giovanni has a newborn son. The mother of this child has importance to me, and I made a promise to her that I will not break. I fully intend on taking that child for myself and raising him, whether that be as his mother or simply as a guardian, that is undecided."

"Will this child become your son for all Moretti purposes, your heir?" Alec questions, watching me through a narrowed gaze.

"No," I tell him. "It has not yet been discussed but considering that DeAngelis blood runs through his veins and that his older brothers bore no children of their own, he will more than likely become the next DeAngelis heir. However, having said that, you should all be aware that any attack on this child will be seen as a personal attack upon both me and the DeAngelis family, and the full force of both families will come

329

down on those responsible. Is that understood?"

Heads nod around the room, and I finally begin to feel the unease shifting out of my chest, loosening enough to allow me to take a proper breath. "Perfect," I say, more than ready to dismiss this. "In the meantime, we will work on funeral arrangements for Gia. If anyone knew her on a personal level and would like to offer suggestions on what she might like, I would appreciate that. I will have a pathologist called here within the hour to have my DNA tested on a rush order and confirm it with you as soon as the results come in. Is there anything I am missing?"

"What is to happen to the DeAngelis sons once Giovanni is … dealt with?"

I shrug my shoulders. "That is their business, however I assume that they will rise up in their father's position just as they always intended. However, with me standing at the head of this family, it is a guarantee that there will no longer be hostility between the families. My relationship with the boys is not going anywhere, nor am I. It is, and forever will be, set in stone. If anyone has any issue with that, then you are welcome to leave."

Alec stands once again, his stare on me. "You would choose those degenerate murderers over your duty to this family?"

I stare straight back at him, not wavering for a damn second. "If you are asking me if I would choose happiness and love over a lifetime of murder, fear, and betrayal, then you're absolutely right, I would."

And with that, I turn on my heel and stalk toward the exit. "Now, if you'll excuse me, there are three men down in our cells who need my attention. You may all be dismissed."

# TWENTY-NINE

T he elevator *dings* its arrival, and I can barely wait for the door to fully open before I barrel out into the small hallway and step over the three bodies that we'd clearly forgotten to clean up earlier. "HOLY SHIT," I call, rushing through to the cell to find the three guys slouched against the darkened walls. Levi's stare is focused heavily on his hands and not the chains that lay in a heap in the center of the room. "I SURVIVED."

Marcus flies to his feet as Roman's head snaps toward me, his dark gaze trailing over my body, but Levi just keeps staring at his hands.

I move across the cell, crouching down before him and forcing his eyes to mine. "Come on," I tell him. "Let's get out of here."

His brows furrow as he looks at me with a heavy gaze that seems so far away. He looks as though he's caught in a world of pain, reliving those awful few days he was chained here, remembering the sting of the whip as it cracked against his chest. I reach down, brushing my fingers over the side of his face, and with a single blink of his eyes, he's back to the guy I last saw upstairs trying to defend me from their sworn enemies. "Yeah," he says, taking my hands and allowing me to pull him up, visibly shaken by the thirty minutes down here. "Let's go."

We make our way back upstairs, and having nowhere else to go, nowhere that feels safe, we stay put, willing to call this home for now. I give the boys the breakdown of everything that happened during the meeting and breathe a sigh of relief as they confirm that everything I mentioned about the DeAngelis family and their newborn brother was right.

"I think we need to have another meeting with the remaining DeAngelis family members," Roman mutters, as I lead them through the mega-mansion despite them having already studied the layout like they've studied the curves of my body. "They need to be ready, and we need to confirm whose side they're fighting on."

I scoff. "Do I need to remind you that every last one of those bastards stood by and watched as your father forced me into a marriage and didn't do shit about it? They knew exactly what he intended to do to me over the next few hours."

"Trust me," Roman says, stopping in the middle of the hallway and turning into me, taking my chin and forcing my stare to meet his. "I haven't forgotten, and they will all suffer consequences for their actions. But we have priorities, and we can't burn the few remaining bridges we have until we're certain we don't need them anymore."

I pull my chin out of his soft grip and avert my eyes. I know he's right and completely agree with his reasoning, but that doesn't mean I have to like it.

"Whatever," I mutter like a pissed-off teenager. "But for the record, your grandfather is getting my stiletto heel shoved right up his ass. I really don't like that guy."

Marcus stifles a laugh as his gaze sweeps the surrounding rooms, making sure we're actually alone in here. "Get in line," he says before indicating deeper into the house with a flick of his chin. "If we're staying here, I want this place swept twice over."

Without another word, Roman and Marcus take off around the property, making sure that none of the Moretti family has made themselves at home, hiding under my bed with a knife.

Levi stays with me, not willing to leave my side, and as long as he's with me, I see no reason not to get him cleaned up. There's still dried blood matted in his hair and covering his body, and at this point, it's hard to tell if it's his from his time down in that cell, or if it's just the aftermath of killing Gia's guards in the foyer.

There's also the untreated bullet wound in his shoulder courtesy of Gia from the night she took him, and while it's not bad, mainly just a flesh wound, I'd hate for it to get infected and cause him even more pain.

This war between Gia, Giovanni, and us has left the boys with the kinds of scars that no man should have to bear, but it's coming to a close. I feel it in my blood. Before we know it, we'll be chilling on a private island, soaking up some rays while the boys fight over who gets to fuck me first. In the end, it'll probably turn into another epic four-way, but hell, a girl can only dream.

Levi grips on to my hand as I lead him up the stairs to the room I'd used for the week I'd been staying here. The room is alien, too clean, too clinical, and holds absolutely no sense of home. It's not exactly going to be nice staying here for … hell, I don't know how long, but it'll definitely help me with the transition into filling Gia's role at the top of the Moretti family food chain. In this home, I have exclusive access to all of Gia's files and the Moretti family with just the touch of a button. Plus, the awesome training room and armory Gia built won't go astray.

Leading Levi into the private bathroom, I lean into the shower and turn the faucet until hot water is spraying down and steam is beginning to cloud around us. I move into Levi, my hands falling to the bandages over his chest. "Are you okay?" I ask, slowly peeling them off and cringing as the stickiness pulls on his open wounds.

Levi nods as his lips press into a hard line, waiting for me to hurry up and pull the bandages off. A grin stretches across my face, and I can't help but tease him. "You've fought battles, been stabbed, shot, and faced down the worst kinds of people, but a sticky bandage is what's going to drag you down?"

His hand curls around my waist as I tear the rest of the bandage from his skin and toss it into the basin. "You better watch that mouth, brat."

A thrill pulses deep in my core, but I push it away. This is hardly the time and place for me to be thinking with my lady boner. Levi's been through hell. The only thought in my head should be trying to figure out what's best for him right now.

My fingers brush down his strong body until they fall to the top of his pants and quickly pop the button. He ate while waiting for the Moretti family to turn up, but after three days of hanging from chains and a week down in the playground, I'm not surprised to find his pants slip straight off his narrow hips. He's lost weight. They all have, but it won't be long until they're back to normal, dominating the world and reminding wives, husbands, and children why they rule over their every nightmare.

Levi steps out of his pants and grips the hem of my tank before pulling it up over my head. He tosses it behind us, and it lands somewhere on the ground, but he is my only focus. He keeps one hand on my waist as his other reaches for the waistband of my leggings, but as a grimace crosses his face, I quickly take over, pushing them down over my hips until they fall the rest of the way.

"Come on," I murmur, taking his hand and leading him into the hot shower. His thumb rubs back and forth over my knuckles as if trying to soothe me, when I should be the one helping him. Always the selfless one. His pain doesn't matter to him, doesn't even register in his mind when he thinks someone else might need him more.

God, I love him. He's just that little bit wrong, just a little bit broken, but that's what makes him so damn incredible, so strong and everything I have always needed. Even through the suffering and pain, he never gave up hope for something better, never gave himself over to the darkness.

Water cascades over both of us, and his eyes close, letting the pain wash away. I take a washcloth and soap it up before gently pressing it to his tanned skin. My eyes linger on his strong, sculpted body, gazing over his tattoos and scars, washing away every drop of blood and reminder of the torture he's suffered over the past few weeks.

He deserves so much more. He deserves to be worshipped and exalted. He and his brothers are kings in my eyes, and despite society's views on them, they will always be held in the highest regard to me. I don't know what I would have done had I lost any of them. My heart still pounds with agony at the thought of almost losing Marcus.

But I didn't feel a damn thing when I ended Gia's life … what does that make me?

Shit.

Levi's fingers tighten on my waist as his other hand comes to my chin, softly raising my head until he finds my eyes. "What's wrong?"

A moment passes before I take a breath and let the words I fear fly free. "Am I a bad person?" I ask him. "Before finding you guys, the thought of ending someone's life would have made me sick. If I knew all of that was my future, I would have ended my own life. But nine months down the track, I've never been happier. Countless men have perished by my hand, and I don't feel anything for them. I know that months down the track, I wouldn't have given it another thought. Then Gia … I didn't even flinch. This is the woman who gave me life and I didn't even care—still don't care."

He shakes his head as my hand pauses on his arm, the suds slowly trailing down over his toned muscles. "You're not a bad person, Shayne. You're just a different one than you used to be. You need to remember that you have seen and experienced things that normal people simply aren't witness to. They could go lifetimes before encountering the type of callous slaughter you'll become accustomed to. You've adjusted and because of that, you've built a shield around your heart, holding off anyone who doesn't belong and not allowing them the ability to hurt you." He pauses a moment, a smile pulling at his lips. "It's ironic. You've had to learn how to keep people out, where me and my brothers have had to learn how to let you in."

I move into him, and he curls his hand around the back of my neck before pulling me against his chest. I gasp, not wanting to touch the angry welts scarring his skin, but he holds me to him, nonetheless. A silent moment passes between us where we just stand in each other's arms, slowly taking deep breaths and coming to terms with everything that has happened. "I hate that you're hurting," I tell him, devastation swelling in my chest.

"And that right there is why you could never be a bad person," he tells me. "You've got the biggest heart I've ever known. You're strong and fearless, and the perfect balance for me and my brothers. You're going to thrive as the leader of the Moretti family. You're going to be the most powerful woman on earth, but we already knew that."

A smile pulls at my lips as I move back and meet his gorgeous eyes, sparkling in the dim light of the bathroom. "You know I love you, right?"

"I know," he says, his grin pulling even wider. "You screamed out for the whole world to hear. Kinda hard to ignore that one." I narrow my eyes and a soft laugh rumbles through his chest. "I fucking love you too, little one, even despite your many flaws."

"Flaws?" I laugh. "Pray tell, what are these horrendous flaws that have so disgustingly caught your attention?"

"Simple," he tells me, gripping my waist and pulling me back in, leaning down until his lips are hovering just over mine. "You're a brat. You don't know how to just sit still and do what you're told, and for fuck's sake, how hard is it for you to just get through one day without making me want to see my handprint across that perfect ass?"

His cock stiffens between us, and I raise a brow, glancing up at him as heat floods my core. My eyes darken with desire, and I let him see the overwhelming need beginning to cause havoc on my body. "You'll have to forgive me, Daddy," I purr, watching his eyes widen with a ferocious hunger. "I didn't realize all my flaws were bothering you so much. How will I ever make it up to you?"

A deep growl tears through his chest, and it speaks right to the vixen living inside of me. I've never been one for the whole daddy kink, but I teased it with him once before and his eyes lit up like the fourth of July, just like they are right now, and if this is what he wants, then that's exactly what he'll get.

His jaw ticks as a deadly seriousness comes over him, making my heart race even faster. "Get on your knees," he spits, gripping his rock-hard cock in his tight fist.

Despite how badly I want to do just that, the need to push him flutters through my chest, testing these new limits and figuring out where our boundaries lie. "And if I say no?"

Fire flares through his eyes, and just seeing how hot this gets him has me so turned on, I'm practically salivating at the thought of his heavy cock in my mouth, but it's nothing compared to the rush and throbbing between my legs. God, I need him to touch me.

His hand curls around my body, slowly trailing down to my ass. He squeezes tight, and just as I groan and push back against his hand wanting more, he releases me and comes down in a sharp stinging spank. I gasp, my eyes widening as his gaze blazes like molten lava.

"Holy fuck," I breathe, panting for more, the shock and desire in my eyes matching the coursing need shining through his.

"Knees," he says, the word filled with authority, telling me that he won't tolerate any more resistance.

Without uttering a single word, I drop to my knees, his veiny, thick cock right in front of my face. Oh, fuck, I need to taste him, need to drive him wild with need, need to show him just how good it can really be and exactly what he's been missing over the past few weeks.

This whole daddy thing could really work for me. I wonder how Roman and Marcus would feel about this. All three of them making demands like the fucking devils they are.

Oh, God. My pussy clenches at the delicious thought.

Too hungry to waste another second, my tongue rolls over my lips before I open my mouth and lean in. He releases his cock, and it bounces heavily in front of me, the tip brushing against my wet lips. I take him in my hand while looking up at those dark, heated eyes and slowly close my mouth over him.

Pleasure washes over his face, and it's already worth every last second even though I've barely moved. Wanting so much more, I begin moving up and down his thick cock, having to keep my hand around his base, pumping up and down and matching my rhythm.

My tongue rolls over his tip, and I groan, tasting that small bead of moisture that makes hunger flare within me. I need to have more, need to take everything he's willing to give.

Levi's hand curls into my hair, moving me up and down and forcing me deeper onto his cock until I feel him in the back of my throat. My pussy aches, my walls clenching around sweet nothing, desperate to be filled and stretched until I can't possibly take anymore.

My tongue works over his tip and down his shaft as I reach lower and cup his balls, giving a firm squeeze just the way he likes it. "Fuck, Shayne," he moans, his hand tightening in my hair. "Show me what you can do."

Damn, he knows how much I like a challenge.

I rise to the fucking bait and give him exactly what he needs and more, his low growls and grunts spurring me on. Up, down, cup, and squeeze. It's intoxicating, but nothing gets me wetter than his hand tightening around my hair and his body clenching.

I grin against his cock like a hungry fucking lion and wait to be served, then just as I knew he would, he gives me exactly what I've been waiting for and pours hot spurts of cum down my throat. "Oh, fuck," he moans, the sound like music to my ears.

Not wasting a damn drop, I swallow him down and look up to find his eyes filled with awe, already locked on mine. I slowly release him but refuse to uncurl my fingers from the base of his cock—because why the hell not. "Good girl," he breathes, and damn the thrill that shoots through me and sails down to my needy cunt is so much more than I could have imagined.

Levi reaches down and grips my chin between his strong fingers, drawing me up to my feet and keeping his deadly stare locked on my heated gaze. "Tell me what you want."

My voice comes out like a breathy whisper, and I'm shocked. Every other time I've told him what I wanted, I've been more than vocal about it. "I want you to fill my pussy and fuck me like there's no tomorrow."

The corner of his mouth pulls up into a cocky smirk, and for a moment, I forget about everything, forget the reason why we're even in this shower to begin with. Nothing else matters. "Oh, I will, my little devil. I'm going to fuck you until you're raw," he tells me, his tone deep and filled with a low growl. "But not before I've tasted your cum on my tongue and felt you come undone around my fingers."

Oh, dear God.

My breath catches in my throat as my stomach clenches, burning with a fiery desire so intense that I know I'm not going to be able to handle it, but hell, I'm down for absolutely anything this beast of a man is willing to put down.

His hand presses back behind him and shuts off the water before both his hands are on my ass, lifting me into his arms. My legs wrap around his waist, and before he's even stepped out of the shower, his lips are crushing down on mine.

Levi kisses me deeply as he walks out to the main room and drops my ass right into the armchair in front of the floor-to-ceiling window. The cool air brushes against my skin and my nipples instantly harden, which only has that hunger in his eyes intensifying.

He's going to tear me apart, and it's going to be the best thing I've ever endured.

Levi drops to his knees, his gaze roaming over my body as though he has no idea where he wants to start until his deep voice fills the silent room. "Spread them."

Oh, God.

My knees part, and I watch the way his gaze travels down to my pussy, his tongue rolling over his bottom lip, more than ready to devour me. "Wider, Shayne," he orders. "I want to see everything."

A thrill fires through me, and I scoot down in the armchair, giving me space to widen my legs as far as they'll go. As I feel a cool breeze against my most intimate parts, I know I'm as exposed as humanly possible and that he's getting absolutely everything he's asking for and more.

Levi groans and the sound sets me on fire, but not as much as the feel of his fingers pressing to my clit and slowly trailing down and mixing with my wetness. He gets to my core and watches closely as he pushes two thick fingers inside of me.

He draws them back out, and his eyes blaze as he takes them in, seeing how they're coated in my arousal. He pushes up on his knees, indicating for me to meet him in the middle, and I do just that before he guides his fingers into my mouth. I suck them dry and before I even get a chance to swallow, his mouth is on mine, his tongue diving in and sharing the taste.

He doesn't release the kiss as his fingers push back inside of me, and I gasp into his mouth, my eyes rolling into the back of my head as the pleasure rocks through me like a powerful storm.

"Oh, fuck, Levi," I groan into his kiss before he slowly pulls back and lowers down, always wanting to have that up-close-and-personal view of his most prized work.

I fall back into my chair, my hands roaming over my body as every nerve ending comes alive, but damn it, if he doesn't—

"OH, FUCK," I groan, throwing my head back as his warm mouth closes over my clit, his tongue flicking the tight bud with skilled precision.

I reach forward and knot my hands into his hair, holding him right there as he starts to work me, his fingers moving in and out, his tongue circling as he sucks and sends me into a world of sweet bliss. I groan and gasp, unable to keep myself still. His fingers stroke over my G-spot, moving back and forth, and my pussy clenches around them, desperate for the release that's quickly building.

"Fuck," I groan. "Fuck, fuck, fuck."

It doesn't get better than this.

His tongue flicks over my clit one more time, and I come undone in a fit of explosive pleasure that rocks through my body, coursing through my veins like an electric current, soaring to all my most sensitive spots. My toes curl and my eyes clench, throwing my head back in irrevocable pleasure.

But he doesn't dare stop. His fingers keep moving, his tongue still working as I ride out my high while my walls spasm around him.

Holy hell. Why have I been holding out on this? Well … I know exactly why and for a damn good reason, but daaaaaamn. I knew he'd take care of me, never make me feel the way that he who shall not be named made me feel while his son's mouth is still enclosed around my clit.

When I finally come down from my high, his eyes are sparkling and he pulls back, releasing me from his intense touch and giving me a chance to breathe. I sit up in the armchair, my body utterly spent but still craving that fullness of his thick cock, especially after he made me a promise to fuck me until I was raw.

My eyes linger on his but movement down low catches my attention, and I find him rock hard once again, his cock held firmly in his grasp. He goes to make a move and I shake my head. "Don't even fucking think about it," I tell him, moving off the armchair and lowering myself on top of him, slowly dropping down over his cock and feeling that delicious intrusion as he stretches my walls, his breathy groan in my ear. Once I'm fully seated over him, I clench around him, loving just how deep he gets. "I'm running this show."

And without a second thought, I ride his cock like a fucking cowgirl giving it her all.

# THIRTY

We pull up outside the DeAngelis mansion at precisely two in the afternoon, and up until now, I thought I was going to be fine. Hell, I might have even been a little too cocky about being able to face my demons, but now that the Escalade is pulling to a stop, the very real possibility that Giovanni could be inside is seriously fucking with my head. I'm crumbling like a little bitch.

Expensive cars are littered around the circular driveway, and I don't see a body in sight. The meeting was called for one o'clock, so I suppose we're a little bit late, but who can fault us? It's been a rough twenty-four hours.

The boys take their time getting out of the car, and a smirk settles over my face at how they simply don't give a shit. If their disloyal family members have to wait, then so be it. It doesn't mean anything to them, but I want it known for the record that if they ever pull this shit with me, it's their balls on the line.

Letting out a shaky breath, I fall in line with the boys, the four of us moving toward the mansion like a force to be reckoned with. Only the closer we get, the more I start to fall behind.

The steps leading to the front door feel as though I'm walking up the steepest mountain, each step weighing me down, but I push on, knowing the boys would never allow that to happen again. Hell, the likelihood of him being here … my husband. Gag. The mere thought of being connected to him like that makes me want to hurl.

Roman slams through the front doors and I grin as the heavy oak crashes against the marble tiled walls, a resounding BANG echoing through the whole mansion. I mean, when the boys make an entrance, they really make an entrance. I know that all too well. They're particularly good at walking into a room and making a woman believe she's about to live through the most excruciating moments of her life.

Ahh, sweet memories.

We barely get through the door when the crammed bodies in the foyer turn our way, their eyes wide and their jaws slackening in shock, quickly realizing that the great battle from two weeks ago didn't claim their lives, just as Giovanni had them all believe.

I resist the urge to shout 'SURPRISE' and simply follow the boys as they make their way through the foyer, a clear path forming before them. Roman pauses by the door and turns to a much younger version of him, a kid who's maybe in his late teens, probably one of the many cousins or second cousins—it's too hard to tell. "I want the whole property swept for my father. Take Trevor and Julio and make it quick. I want a full report in five minutes."

The kid nods and immediately turns on his heel, stalking away, his fingers already curled around the grip of his gun, and despite him being just a kid, a sense of safety comes over me, and I find it easier to put one foot in front of the other.

We stride in through the big doors of the formal meeting room, and I'm not surprised to find the boys' grandfather sitting right at the head of the table, just as he'd been last time.

Marcus scoffs, not in the mood for his grandfather's bullshit, and rather than making a big scene and dealing with the back-and-forth insults and death glares, Marcus simply pulls his gun and holds it to his grandfather's head. "Don't try me today, pops. I'm not in the mood."

A hint of fear flashes through the old man's eyes and as he glares at Marcus and sees just how ready he is to pull the trigger, he scoops his tumbler of whiskey off the table, throws back what's left, and slowly pushes the chair back. He moves around to the side of the table, taking the space reserved for the second in command—who apparently is still me, but I'm not about to fight him for it. Besides, there's no way in hell I'm about to step away from their side to join the rest of them, especially with the idea of Giovanni on the loose.

Any one of the assholes about to join us in the meeting room would no doubt like to get their hands on me, only to offer me up to

Giovanni in return for immunity ... or at least, the short-lived safety that he would offer them, something he won't be able to come through on anyway.

The rest of the family follows us into the meeting room, quickly taking their places at the table while keeping their curious stares on the boys. It hasn't been that long since the last meeting, and I feel as though I barely recognize a single face. Though, I suppose that happens when the boys tend to slaughter anyone who dares stand against them. Hazard of the job, I suppose.

"Thank you for coming," Roman starts, taking the lead as usual.

"What is this about?" the boys' grandfather questions, his empty tumbler resting in the palm of his hand. "You have kept us waiting for an hour. Do you assume that you can click your fingers and we will fall to our knees?"

Levi shoots a sharp glare at his grandfather. "That's exactly what we expect," he states. "The moment this family pledged their loyalty to us, your time became ours. Do you need me to remind you of your place, old man? After the hell I've been through just to make it here today, I wouldn't mind making an example of you."

Roman watches the exchange before slowly turning his attention back to the table, making it known that his grandfather's questions are not worth his time. "We did not intend to keep you waiting," Roman says. "However, there are a few things that require our immediate attention."

Soft murmurs rumble through the room and it takes only one venomous glare from Marcus to shut them all up. Roman continues.

"Those of you who were in attendance at my father's wedding three weeks ago, please stand."

As one, every last man at the table stands and their eyes go wide, already knowing where this is going. Roman goes to say something when the young look-alike and two others walk into the room and meet Roman's heavy stare. "It's clean," one of the other dudes says with a sharp nod before falling into their place around the table.

Roman waits until they're comfortable and quiet before going on. "Those of you who attempted to put a stop to the wedding, take your seat."

Terror rips across the table, the tension in the room thickening until it's nearly impossible to breathe. "Roman," a guy to his left says, a few seats down. "You must understand, we thought you were dead. We were left with no choice, and Giovanni insisted that your girl was a Moretti."

All three of the boys watch the man, but it's Marcus who speaks up. "So, what you're telling me, Frances, is that if I came into your home in the middle of the night and slit your throat, you'd be okay with me taking your wife as my own?"

Frances doesn't respond, but the fear in his eyes makes his thoughts on the question well known. Marcus winks. "Nothing to say?" he questions. "You're either a loyal servant, willing to give up your most beloved treasure for the head of this family, or you're just fucking stupid. Which is it?"

Frances averts his eyes, his stare heavy on the big table. "You're right," he murmurs. "I apologize. I'm fucking stupid."

"That's what I thought."

Roman grows tired of Marcus' line of questioning and continues with his inquisition. "Those of you who even questioned my father of his intentions, take your seat."

Three men take their seats, one of them being Roman's younger look-alike, making me wonder if I should like the guy. After all, if he had the balls to question Giovanni on his intentions at such a young age, then he's already proving that he's going to be a force to be reckoned with. Given the years and experience, I'm sure he'll dominate in this world.

Roman nods, not liking what he's seeing. "Final question," he states. "Those of you who stood by your vow of loyalty to me and my brothers and even considered saving the woman we love, take your seats."

One more man takes his seat, and Roman lets out a heavy breath, disappointed in the lack of fight shown by his family. "I'm sure that you are all aware of the repercussions that will follow. Whether you thought my brothers and I had perished at our father's hand or not, no bodies had been found, no confirmation of death was made. At that point, your loyalty still belonged to us, and we consider your failure to save Shayne from the clutches of Giovanni DeAngelis a direct betrayal."

I can practically hear every heart beginning to race through the room, see the sweat coating their foreheads while hands flinch at their sides, ready to lunge for their guns if that's what it comes down to. "Take your seats," Roman says.

They all slowly do as they've been asked like a bunch of delinquent kids in the principal's office. Nervous glances fill the room, terrified stares searching out others who feel that same sense of impending doom. They fucked up and they know it. But just to add that extra punch to the unspoken threat, Marcus and Levi begin making their way around the table, walking slowly behind their backs. Men flinch as they pass, knowing they could end them with their bare hands in a matter of seconds.

I hide my smirk and try to appear as the badass I want to be. It's not exactly going to help my case if I'm caught grinning like a fox in the hen house.

"Why would your father claim that she is a Moretti then? Why should we believe anything different?"

Roman scoffs and discreetly takes my hand, out of sight from the prying eyes in the room. "When did I give you reason to believe otherwise?" he questions. "Shayne is a Moretti. My father was right. But she is not just any Moretti, she is the Moretti."

Confused murmurs flow through the room as sharp eyes come to me, each of them filled with ugly promises and silent vows to end my life. "Four nights ago, Gia Moretti attacked our home. She got away with Levi and spent the next three days torturing him."

Their grandfather slams his hand down on the table, the glass tumbler cracking with the force. "Why are we only just hearing of this now?"

"Because it was not necessary for you to know until now," Roman throws back at him, irritated by his interruption. "Last night, we infiltrated Gia Moretti's private residence and got Levi out of there. It wasn't easy. She anticipated our arrival and had guards lying in wait. She drew us out just as she intended to do, but she was not prepared as well as she should have been. In the early hours of the morning, Shayne Moretti, this woman standing right beside me, the woman whom not one of you deemed worthy enough to save from my father's clutches, slaughtered our greatest enemy with nothing but a flick of her wrist."

"What?" the boys' grandfather says, standing and gaping at me. "Gia Moretti is dead?"

I step forward, releasing Roman's hand. "Yes. I ended her life, just as simply as I will end yours if you continue to doubt me and your grandsons."

He swallows hard. "The Moretti empire has fallen," he comments, almost in awe. "Who will rise in her place? She has no known heirs."

"Think about it, grandfather," Marcus says from across the room. "Why else would my father have such an interest in forcing a marriage to Shayne?"

All heads whip toward me again, and I raise my chin, knowing this can either go one of two ways. "My name is Shayne Moretti, and I am the only living heir of Gia Moretti. I am the new ruler of the Moretti empire."

It's a fucking uproar. Men throw themselves to their feet as Levi circles back around and moves in behind me, his hands at my hips. "Just give them a moment," he murmurs. "They just need a moment to feel like their opinions matter."

I nod, resting back into him as I watch Roman silently take his gun from the waistband of his pants and lay it carefully on the table before him, and just like that, silence follows. He leans onto the table, not even bothering to hold the gun, its presence is enough of a threat. The men in this room know just how fast he is and just how lethal he can be. "From this moment forward, I declare that the Moretti family is no longer our enemy. Any move against them is a direct move against myself and my brothers."

A scoff comes from the far end of the table. "So, all of a sudden, you meet a bitch with a magical pussy and you forget what really matters? Where's your fucking loyalty? The Morettis have been our enemies for over a century and you expect us to just fall in line because you're banging their new leader?"

The gun snaps out, a bullet firing through the room, and just like that, the voice is silenced. "Anybody else have an issue with us finding peace with the Morettis?"

Silence. Pure fucking silence.

"Good, now that brings us to the matter of our father—"

"STOP," a sharp cry sounds through the room as a woman comes storming in, Phillip DeAngelis standing at her back. Her eyes are red and she looks as though her world has been torn out from under her. "IT WAS ALL THEM, RIGHT FROM THE BEGINNING. THEY PLANNED IT ALL. ALL THE MURDERS."

The boys' grandfather gets to his feet, anger staining his features. "What is the meaning of this?" he spits, glaring at his son across the room. "Not only are you late to our family meeting, you bring your wife? Do you have no respect for our laws?"

The woman strides deeper into the room, every eye on her as Phillip remains hovering behind her like a scared little bitch. "I don't give a shit about your family rules. Your stupid family has destroyed my life, ruled over every last second of it, and now I've lost my children because of this goddamn war. A war that was created by those … those three monsters," she spits, pointing toward Roman and Levi. "I want them held accountable. I WANT THEIR HEADS."

Roman glances toward the little-Roman-look-alike and with nothing but a simple nod, he, Trevor, and Julio stand and make their way toward the woman. She instantly begins to back up, seeing the threat for what it is, all while Phillip just stands there, not even bothering to defend his wife. That spineless piece of shit. I knew we should have killed him when we had the chance, but the boys just had to go show him mercy.

Stupid boys. He should have died, especially after what he did to Ariana. If this were the Moretti family and I had the final call, a bullet between the eyes would have been the only acceptable response. I won't tolerate that kind of bullshit, not under my roof. Things are going to change and I don't doubt that there will be a few ruffled feathers because of it … but that's for another day to worry about. Right now, I want to know why the hell this crazy ass bitch is accusing my men of having anything to do with her daughters.

The three stooges grab the woman and force her forward, pushing her down to her knees as they hold her arms. Roman moves around the table, watching her through narrowed eyes as the men at the table watch with curious stares.

"Because I am feeling generous, I am going to give you a chance to explain yourself before deciding how hard I will come down on you."

"You murdered Antonio, you and your spineless brothers. You killed him and led everyone to believe that Ronaldo had done it because of his relationship with his wife." Gasps sound throughout the room, but she's not even close to finished. "You orchestrated it all. You knew that Victor was going to go after Ronaldo, but you didn't care. You let him slaughter an innocent man, all for what? For the two seconds standing at the top? You're pathetic, all three of you. You should be ashamed of yourselves."

"Have you had enough?" Roman questions, his tone full of boredom.

"Please," she scoffs. "Why don't you tell them all how you killed Victor in his home and burned it down? Or how about the way you slaughtered Louis right here outside these very walls. You annihilated every major player and kept the rest busy while you swept in and stole the leadership for yourselves."

Their grandfather stands, rage pouring over his features. "Did you murder my sons?" he demands, his hands balled into tight fists at his sides.

Roman shrugs it off, his face twisting with irritation as he looks back at the woman on her knees. "I don't know where the fuck you're getting your information, but unless you've been living in a cave, you would be well aware that my father had my brothers and I held as prisoners in our castle home. When Antonio was slaughtered, may he rest in peace, we were trapped within the very solid walls of that castle."

The grandfather scoffs and mutters something under his breath about the boys being more than capable of escaping the confines of their prison, while the woman shakes her head, her eyes going wide with uncertainty, wide with the fear of believing that she just accused the DeAngelis Grim Reapers of something they didn't do. "No," she says in a fluster. "He told me. He said it was you three all along."

"Who said?" Levi spits. "My father?"

"Yes," she cries. "He told us to come here, to tell them all the truth. He wants them to turn on you, to believe how truly vile you all are. He took my girls. Please. He's going to kill them if they don't believe me."

Roman's back stiffens, his eyes narrowing on the woman. "When did he take them?"

"In the early hours of this morning," she says. "Please, they're just babies. Innocent children."

Heavy sobs tear from her throat, and Roman indicates to his little followers to release her, allowing her to crumble into a ball at his feet as she cries. He raises his head to Phillip who still hovers by the door, staring straight ahead at nothing in particular and looking as though he's about to lose it all. "How could you let him take your children?" Roman spits, anger burning in his features. "Are you that starved for his approval, you'd give up everything that matters? You saw how he treated me and my brothers when we were younger, before he learned to fear us. They're young girls. Do you know what will become of them in his hands, what he will use them for?"

Phillip's face turns green, and I watch in horror as he turns and doubles over, gripping on to a large vase and hurling until he falls to his knees.

Roman turns and meets Marcus' stare from across the room before turning to Levi, the three of them doing that fucked-up silent conversation shit that I've always wanted to decode. Hell, if I could, it'd make my life a shitload easier.

Roman looks back at Phillip. "If we do this, you disappear. You take your family and you forget the DeAngelis name. You turn your back on everything you've ever known. Take your wife's maiden name and leave. Return here again, even to check in, and we will see you punished appropriately for your acts against Ariana. Is that clear?"

Phillip nods, swallowing hard. "Anything."

A moment of silence passes, the only noise coming from the weeping mother on the ground. "Okay," Roman finally says, turning back toward the men gathered around the table. "Every single man who sits around this table is guilty of betraying our trust for your spineless actions during my father's wedding to Shayne Moretti. Do not be fooled, guilty men suffer gruesome consequences, but I am offering you the chance to earn back my trust."

Backs stiffen around the room, eyes wide with fear, unsure what Roman is asking of them. I doubt these boys have ever asked their family for anything in their lives, but to stand here and ask for help, it's gonna be one hell of a big request.

"From this point on, Giovanni's newborn son will be seen as my own. That child is mine to raise, and I will do so in my own image.

Right now, my son is held captive at his hands along with Phillip's two daughters, and we are going to get them back. The DeAngelis army will rise again. However, we do not hold the necessary equipment to track him. At least, not fast enough."

"What are you suggesting?" the man who spoke earlier questions.

"The Moretti's have the technology that we need. I put forward that we unite our forces, for just this one mission to get children back where they belong and to put Giovanni in the ground where he belongs."

And just like that, the room turns into a fucking warzone.

# THIRTY-ONE

**M**arcus stands by my side, rolling his eyes as the masses pour out of the room. There was an hour of arguing until the boys finally put their foot down and made it a little more obvious that uniting our people for this mission wasn't so much of a suggestion and more like a hostile demand.

Those that refused will face the boys in person, and that one little threat held the weight of the world. But what it all comes down to is my ability to do the same with the Moretti family. They already don't like me, and now I have to stand before them and suggest working side-by-side with the family who has been responsible for raining hell over their world countless times.

Great. Sounds like fun.

Levi walks with an older gentleman, showing him out as Marcus mumbles something about checking on something in his bedroom upstairs. I watch him step away from me and stride to the door, my brows furrowed in concern. "What could he possibly need from his room?" I question, turning to look at Roman.

He shakes his head, laughter sparkling in his obsidian eyes. "His bed," he mutters as though it's an obvious answer, one I should have been able to figure out on my own.

"He's sleeping?" I ask, my brows rising with interest as the exhaustion of the past few days creeps up on me even more than it already has. "Well, shit. I might just join him."

Moving toward the door, I'm pulled back with a hand on my wrist. "Shayne, wait," Roman says, drawing me back. I turn and meet his stare to find a hint of nervousness swimming deep in those dark eyes. He glances away, his lips pressing into a cringe. "I um … I've been meaning to talk to you about something."

My brows furrow and I move closer, searching his stare for even the tiniest hint of what this could be about. "What's up?" I ask, my hand falling to his chest.

Roman takes my waist, the nerves only seeming to get stronger. "Come on." He leads me toward the big table before lifting me up and placing me onto it. He hovers between my knees, his hands resting on my thighs as I patiently wait for him to figure out how to word whatever it is he needs to say.

His lips press into a hard line before taking a deep breath and slowly letting it out. He meets my waiting stare. "Have I ever told you that Roman isn't my first name?"

"Uuuuhhhhhmmmmm …. no?" I say, my confusion coming out as a question, not understanding what could possibly have him acting like this, especially considering he's opening with a line like that. "What's this about?"

His shoulders pull back as if finding the nerve to be strong and face his demons. "My full name is Giovanni Roman DeAngelis the second," he tells me, watching as my brows shoot up in surprise, my body unintentionally flinching at the sound of that name, bringing back memories I don't care to think about. "Ever since I was a kid, I rejected my name and went by Roman instead. I didn't want to be associated with him like that because … well, I think you can figure that out."

"Okaaaay," I say slowly, narrowing my eyes. "I think I'm missing some vital pieces of information here." A small smile cracks across Roman's face. "Alright," he says. "I'm just going to come right out and say it." I wait patiently, my eyebrow slowly rising in anticipation. "The name on your wedding certificate, the name on the license and all the paperwork is 'Giovanni Roman DeAngelis.' What I'm getting at is … what if there happened to be some way to change the paperwork to add 'the second'?"

My brows furrow, watching him closely as the pieces finally begin to fall into place. "Then … I'd be married to you. Not your father."

He nods, watching me warily, waiting for the moment I either laugh in his face or tell him there's no way in hell I'd want that, but I don't dare because the idea of severing that connection to his father means the whole fucking world to me. "What do you think?" he asks after a moment, my silence probably sending him into an anxiety induced coma.

"I … can you even do that?"

He shrugs his shoulders again. "Fucked if I know. It's not like I've ever had to manipulate marriage documents before, but I'm sure where there's a will, there's a way."

"But then we'd be married …"

I let the thought linger in the air, positive that this isn't what he really wants. Now, if it had been Marcus standing before me asking to do this massive thing, then I'd believe it, but Roman … I don't know if he understands what he's really getting himself into.

The silence gets heavier, and I watch him as he watches me. That nervous energy begins to cloud his stare once again, and when he shakes his head and looks away, I know he's preparing to shut this down. Gripping his chin, I force him to deal with this right here, right now, just as he would do if the positions were turned. "Why do you look like you're about to shit yourself? You don't need to be nervous about this."

An incredulous expression rips across his face and he laughs before leaning into me, pressing his hands on the table on either side of my thighs. "There are so many fucking reasons to be wary of what I'm asking you."

"Oh, yeah?" I challenge. "Like what?"

"Where do I even start?" he says, before hitting me with the list that he's no doubt been torturing himself with since this little idea fell into his calloused hands. "First up, I'm a killer, a cold-blooded murderer. I'm on every single most-wanted list in the country, and you … you're innocence wrapped up in a pretty bow. I don't want to be the reason that you get dragged down, plus, we both know you deserve a man whose reputation alone isn't going to place a target on your back. Second, I don't fucking deserve this. Do I want to be married to you? Hell fucking yes, but I think Marcus needs this more. Levi probably wouldn't give a shit. He's not sentimental like that, so as long as nothing changes between you two and your relationship, then he wouldn't care, but Marcus would see this as me taking something from him, a betrayal of the worst kind, and I'm not sure that I could do that to him … but for you, I fucking would."

My fingers caress the side of his face, beginning to feel the weight of what he's asking me, what it would really mean. "Roman," I start before getting cut off again.

"Don't," he says. "Don't give me whatever bullshit you were about to spew. You and I both know that after Felicity, the idea of getting married isn't something I'd have considered again, especially considering our … unique relationship. But Marcus sure as fuck would. He'd give you the greatest fucking proposal a girl could want, he'd get you the ring and be down on one knee. He'd make you feel like a goddamn princess. And this … this right here, this would crush him, and the fact that I'm even asking you is going to be a slap in the face to him.

"Not to mention," he goes on, "at some point, my father is going to die, and you're going to be free of that marriage anyway."

"But I'll forever hold the title of being Giovanni's widow. I don't want to be connected to him in any little way, even in death."

"Exactly," he says. "So, you have a choice to make. I can fuck with that paperwork and you can officially call me your husband, or we can walk out this door and never speak of it again."

My heart races. A year ago, the thought of being married to one of the DeAngelis brothers would have scared the crap out of me … well, if I'm being completely honest, the thought of being married to anyone scares me. I'm only twenty-two, not nearly ready for such a big step in my life, but what choice have I been left with? Remain married to Giovanni, or become Roman's wife?

There is no fucking choice.

My fingers drop to the waistband of his pants and I pull him in closer. "You really want to be married to me, Roman DeAngelis?"

"I'd burn in hell for eternity at just the mere shot of being able to call you my wife."

A bundle of nerves settles deep in my stomach and quickly begins to grow before turning into fully grown butterflies wreaking havoc over my gut. "I mean, you know I can be a bitch first thing in the morning, right? And I don't take demands very well, plus I'm sleeping with your brothers so I can't guarantee that it's your bed I'll be in every night. Are you sure that's what you really want in a wife?"

Roman takes my chin, raising it up until our lips are barely a breath apart. "You're everything that I want," he whispers. "You make me feel whole again, and just being near you reminds me that I have something to live for. All the suffering and pain from my past doesn't matter when I'm with you, Shayne Moretti. You are my fucking ride or die, whether we're hitched or not."

I nod and lean in that little bit more, brushing my lips over his in a gentle kiss. "And the baby?" I ask him, pulling back to meet his eyes. "At the end of that meeting you said you were going to raise him as your own. I love you, and I know I already have a soft spot for that baby, but I don't think I'm going to make a very good mother."

"I'm not asking you to be his mother. Whatever role you want to play in his life is perfectly fine by me, but you and I both know that once he comes home and you're holding him in your arms, knowing there's nothing you wouldn't do to protect him, you're going to slip into that role because that's just who you are."

My eyes widen with fear. Be his mom? Holy crap. I can't be responsible for screwing up another human being, I can barely manage myself. Shit, I've been kidnapped at least five times over the past year. Surely Roman doesn't see me as a good role model for his child. "Are you sure?"

Roman nods. "I see it in the way you adopted Dill and Doe. You've become their family. You care for them and protect them. When Dill was hurt, it nearly killed you too," he insists. "I know you're not ready, and if you decide it's too much for you, I won't force it. Whatever role you want to play is completely up to you. I just think you'll fall into it without even thinking about it. It'll be as natural as waking up in the morning."

"Will he have to call me mom?"

Roman laughs and shakes his head. "You can have him refer to you as the motherfucking queen for all I care."

A grin pulls at my lips and I lean in again, letting him capture my lips and hold them hostage for however long he wants. "So … we're doing this?" he questions after pulling back. "I'm going to amend the paperwork?"

I swallow hard, a thrill pulsing through my veins. "Yeah," I tell him. "We're doing this, but not before speaking to your brothers about it first."

True fear rocks through his eyes and I laugh, pulling him in again. "If you want to be technical about this. We were married nearly three weeks ago, which means that we also haven't consummated our marriage, and honestly, I'm surprised, husband," I tease. "I always picked you as the type to get that over and done with before the ceremony has even ended."

A deep growl tears through his chest as his hand falls to the back of my neck. He pulls me in and crushes his lips to mine as his other hand curls around my lower back, scooting me right to the edge of the table until I feel him pressed up against my core.

I groan into his mouth, the intense need for him slamming into me like a fucking wrecking ball. I feel his cock hardening behind his pants, and he grinds it against me, only making the need burn so much brighter.

He grips the hem of my shirt and tears it over my head, his eyes dropping to my body and flaming with desire. His mouth finds my neck and I gasp in pleasure as his skilled lips trail over my sensitive skin. "Oh, fuck, Roman. I need to feel you inside me."

His hands roam over my body as I reach for his shirt, tearing it over his head. I throw it over his shoulder as my greedy eyes linger on his warm skin. He's everything, his perfect tattoos dancing across his body with each movement, the sharp lines of his abs and pecs, the bulging muscles in his arms, and fuck me, that V.

My mouth waters, and I force myself not to linger on the angry red scar on his abdomen. Instead, I close my eyes and just feel.

Roman's hands curl around my body, and with a simple flick of his wrist, my bra comes loose and the straps quickly fall down my arms. He rips the lacy material away and pulls back from my neck as his cock continues to grind against my core. "These fucking tits," he murmurs, his tone tortured with desire as his fingers trail down and brush past the curve of my breast, his thumb pausing to run over my pert nipple. "Fucking gorgeous."

Goosebumps rise on my skin at his touch, and a breathy moan slips from between my lips, the anticipation of what's to come heating me from the inside out. Unable to wait any longer, I reach down, my fingers finding the button of his pants and quickly releasing it before pushing his pants down over his narrow hips.

His raging, thick cock springs free, and I grip on to it greedily, loving the deep growl that rumbles through his chest mixed with the fire burning in his eyes. My hand immediately begins pumping up and down, my thumb skimming over his tip. "Fucking hell," he grunts, pressing his fists against the table beside my thighs and dropping his head to my shoulder. He groans, his soft breath brushing against my skin, and barely a moment passes before it's too much and his hands are back on me.

Roman pulls me in hard against his body, his lips crushing to mine as his hands find the waistband of my pants. He pushes them down, curling his arm around my waist and lifting me enough to get them down past my ass. My panties go right with them, and in a moment, they're strewn across the meeting room and I'm bare before him, ready to take whatever he's willing to give.

His fingers trail down my body to my spread thighs and find my core, brushing against my sensitive clit and making me jolt as electricity fires through my body. I gasp, spreading my legs wider, desperate for more as Roman grins against my lips.

He circles my clit again, and I tighten my grip on his veiny cock, my eyes rolling with undeniable pleasure, but he's not even close to finished. His fingers go lower, mixing with the wetness right at the center of my core before slowly pushing deep inside me. "Oh, God, Roman," I groan into his mouth, feeling the way he curls his fingers, moving against my walls as they clench around him, trying to hold him hostage.

He goes again and again, his thumb pressing against my clit and keeping that fire burning deep within me. "You're going to be my wife, Shayne," he says against my lips, his tone deep and hungry. "All fucking mine."

"All yours," I tell him, my other hand curling around the back of his neck and gripping on to him, my nails digging into the back of his shoulder. "Now fucking take me, Roman. Make me yours."

Hunger pulses through his dark eyes, and in an instant, he curls his hand around me and scoots me closer to the edge just as he pulls his fingers out of me and lines his cock up with my entrance, all but impaling me on him. He pushes in deep, and I throw my head back as he stretches my walls, making me gasp with need as he fills me to capacity. "Oh, fuck," I cry out, my hand dropping to the big table to keep me from falling back.

Roman pauses for just a moment, each of us getting used to his delicious intrusion, and as my pussy clenches around him, he groans low, his eyes telling me just how desperate he is. He holds me tight, keeping our bodies plastered to one another and only then does he release our kiss and meet my eye.

His fingers brush down the side of my face in a gentle caress and I lean into his touch, watching as his need to claim control takes over. "You ready, Empress?" he questions, his lips pulling into a cocky grin as his other hand slips between our bodies and slowly begins to massage my clit, making me gasp as my pussy clenches around him again.

I meet his eyes, letting him see the hunger burning through my own. "Give me all you've got."

He doesn't dare hold back.

Roman fucks me like a damn god, slamming deep inside of me as his fingers work my clit, teasing, massaging, rubbing, and grinding. I gasp into him, our bodies growing sweaty as they press together. I cry out, my hands curling around him as he worships every inch of my body.

My teeth sink into his shoulder and he groans as my pussy squeezes around his thick cock. His fingers dig into my skin as a tortured breath escapes his lips, a breath that sounds a lot like my name. I squeeze him hard and in turn, he fucks me harder, taking me deeper and faster as he pinches my clit between his fingers.

My legs curl around his waist, holding him tighter, and he doesn't hesitate, grabbing one of my legs and hooking it over his elbow, pulling it up higher and fucking me at a whole new level. "Fuck, Roman," I pant, my orgasm beginning to creep up on me. "More."

He grins against my skin before pulling back and meeting my eye. "Is that an order?"

I shake my head and grin. "It's a fucking dare."

And within only a moment, my knees are planted on the ground as he presses my chest into the cold marble tiles, my ass high in the air. He takes my hips and I cry out as he slams that thick cock deep inside me once again. "FUCK, YES."

I reach down between my spread thighs and rub tight little circles against my clit as Roman's fingers mix into the wetness coated between us. He draws his fingers back to my ass and presses into me, making me groan as a shudder travels through my body.

Holy fuck.

My eyes roll to the back of my head. I'm not going to last.

His fingers at my hips bite into my skin and I push back against him, taking him deeper as my orgasm builds, threatening to send me into a world of bliss. Roman pushes me to the breaking point, taking me deep as I furiously circle my clit. He pushes against my ass, filling me more, and just as he thrusts into me one more time, my orgasm explodes within me.

I cry out, squishing my face into the cold marble as my pussy comes undone, shattering into a quivering mess around him. I squeeze him as I ride out my high, every nerve ending coming alive with pure satisfaction.

He keeps moving as I'm shattered with ecstasy, and then with a low guttural groan, he comes hard, spilling hot spurts of cum deep into my cunt, slowing his movements to a lazy caress. He comes down over me, his cock still buried deep in my cunt. "Was that more *enough* for ya?"

I look back over my shoulder and capture his lips in mine while pushing back against him and circling my hips. "You're damn right, it was," I murmur as he curls his arm around me and slowly begins circling my clit again, sending that familiar electricity pulsing through my veins. "But now I'm wondering what that tongue can do."

He growls deep in his chest and captures my lips in his. "Prepare to be blown the fuck away."

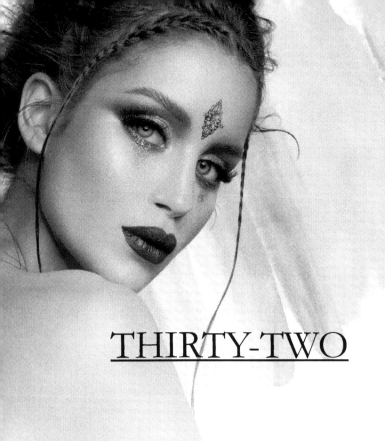

# THIRTY-TWO

S till tasting Roman in my mouth, we walk hand in hand out into the oversized living room that we'd all but made our own in the short time we've lived here. Levi's drums are set up in the corner and all the boys' favorite drinks are still piled high in the adjoining bar. Not going to lie, I was certain that Giovanni would have done away with all this shit, but I suppose the future ex-husband doesn't really have time between trying to raise his empire and avoid being slaughtered by his sons.

There's no sign of Levi or Marcus, and I'm not surprised. Marcus is probably deep in the middle of a sex-murder dream, while Levi is ... actually, I have no idea where he could be, but I'm sure it's not far.

Roman releases my hand and makes his way across the room to the fully stocked bar. "We're celebrating," he tells me. "What can I get you?"

I gape at him. "Celebrating?" I laugh. "More like preparing for battle. I'm more terrified of telling Marcus that we're going to be married than I was when Giovanni showed up here with all his soldiers."

Roman shrugs his shoulders. "No matter how you look at it, we're still celebrating. You're going to be free of my father and no longer hold his name. Plus, everything else. Gia is dead, you're the leader of the Moretti empire, and we're a million steps closer to slitting my father's throat. Not to mention, you just got fucked within an inch of your life and I think that's something to celebrate."

I roll my eyes and shake my head, trying to hide the smirk stretching across my face. The guy has a point—a really good fucking point. "Just pour me whatever you feel is appropriate," I tell him as I wander toward the drums in the corner of the room. My fingers trail over the high hats before dropping to the snare.

"What are you doing?" Roman asks warily, watching me out of the corner of his eyes.

I avert my eyes as I circle around and spy the little seat. "Nothing."

"Don't do it," he warns, watching me reach back for the sticks. "It's not worth it."

A grin cuts across my face as I adjust the sticks in my hands. What can I say? I'm taking all sorts of risks today. "Weren't you just telling me how I'm the new leader of the Moretti empire?" I question. "And doesn't that make me the most powerful woman in the country?"

Roman shakes his head. "You may be the most powerful woman in the country, but if you touch his drums, he'll bring down a whole fucking war on your shoulders."

My grin widens, my eyes sparkling as he slowly shakes his head in warning from the bar, his hands pausing as he pours our drinks. "Eenie, meanie, miny, moe," I say, taking on their father's sick little game. "Just how far will I go?"

And not a moment later, I live out every child's rockstar dreams. Bringing the sticks down on the drums, I perform to the best of my ability, letting the sound echo through the mansion. I smash down on the high hats while stomping the bass, and I'm not gonna lie, I'm pretty good at this.

A wicked grin cuts across my face, and just as I raise my eyes to meet Roman's stare, Levi comes storming into the living room, his fingers closing around the door frame to propel him faster into the room.

Anger burns through his stare as he bolts toward the drum set, ready to tear me in two. "THE FUCK DO YOU THINK YOU'RE— oh," his voice dies and he pulls himself to a stop, eyes wide as he takes me in. "It's just you."

Levi stops, doubles over to catch his breath, and something tells me that he might have been way over on the opposite side of the mansion but I don't get a chance to question it as Marcus comes flying in behind him, panic written across his face. "ROMAN, STOP. DON'T FUCKING—"

His words fade away just as Levi's had, spying Roman safely across the room. His head whips toward me, both his and Levi's eyes locked on mine. "The fuck is going on in here?" Marcus grunts, moving toward the bar as Levi saunters closer to me, his eyes heating at seeing me behind his drums.

Roman scoffs. "More importantly, why the fuck isn't he tearing her a new asshole like he did to you?"

Levi glances back at his brothers, his eyes dancing with laughter. "Because unlike Marcus, she looks fucking hot doing it. Besides, as long as she'll allow me to keep fucking that tight little cunt, then I'm gonna let her play. Hell, if she wanted to drop her pants and take a shit on them, I'm gonna stand back and applaud and let her know how much of a masterpiece she just created."

My jaw goes slack and I stare at him in disgust. "Okay," I say, placing the sticks back down. "Why do you guys always insist on taking things too far?"

Levi grins as though he just won some kind of game I didn't know we were playing. "It got you off my drums, didn't it?"

That fucker.

He takes my hand and hooks our joined fingers over my head before leading me over to the bar and grabbing our drinks. He pulls me down onto his lap and I cringe, feeling Roman still between my legs. "I'm curious," I say, glancing up at Marcus. "What did Roman mean when he said Levi ripped you a new asshole? What exactly happened? I mean, you came storming in here like you were petrified of history repeating itself."

Marcus shakes his head. "No. Absolutely not. We're not discussing that."

Levi scoffs, his hand falling to my thigh. "You got to tell her about Roman being shot in the ass and when I got caught jerking off and you assumed I was getting hard over a fucking clown, so why shouldn't we share this particular story?"

Marcus' cheeks go bright freaking red and I gape at him in shock. "ARE YOU BLUSHING?" I screech, my eyes wide as a wicked grin cuts across my face. "No fucking way. The great Marcus DeAngelis is actually blushing! Now you have to tell me what happened."

Marcus looks to Roman for help, but he should know better. Roman just grins back at him. "What's the problem, little brother?" he questions, his brows bouncing as his eyes sparkle with laughter. "Don't have the balls to tell her?"

Levi laughs and I can't help but feel as though I just missed some kind of inside joke.

Marcus sighs and drops down onto one of the bar stools. "Fine," he mutters, throwing back his drink and handing it back to Roman for a refill. "I was sixteen and Levi was in his 'fucking angry about everything' phase and so naturally, as his big brother, I took it upon myself to fuck with him as much as I could," he explains. "One night, he was particularly crabby, so I stripped down to my birthday suit and went to town on his drums."

My eyes bug out of my head. "Do I even want to know what that really means?" I question.

He shakes his head, his eyes lighting with the memory. "No,

probably not," he says as Levi's hand bunches into a fist on my thigh, the story clearly still having an effect on him. "Anyway, Levi came after me and I fucking took off like a bullet. I was just getting my boxers back on when the fucker came up behind me and gave me the ultimate atomic wedgie."

A gasp slips from between my lips as I watch the humiliation washing over Marcus' face. I never had siblings to do that sort of shit to me growing up and have thankfully never experienced even a small wedgie that wasn't self-inflicted by an ill-fitting thong, but I can only imagine what that would have felt like. "What exactly entails a wedgie to become an ultimate atomic one?"

"Put it this way," he says, throwing back his second glass of whiskey. "The fabric pulled right up to my head before it tore to shreds. I got rug burn to my asshole and the fucker nearly severed my right testicle."

I suck in a loud gasp, my eyes wide as my hand flies to my mouth. "NOOOOOOOOOO."

His head falls, his lips pressing into a hard line. "Yep. I was out all summer and couldn't walk properly for weeks."

"Well, shit."

Levi scoffs behind me. "Serves you right, brother. I warned you that you'd regret fucking with my drums and you just had to test me."

Marcus rolls his eyes, shoving his glass at Roman for another top-up and I press my lips into a hard line, feeling sick with what I have to tell them, while also a little excited. I don't know how this is going to go, but either way, none of us are leaving this room until I've said what needs to be said. "Umm … anyway, so Roman and I kinda wanted to run something by you."

Roman's eyes bug out of his head as he holds back Marcus' drink, refusing to put anything in his hands that could be used as a weapon. "Now?" he questions. "After he just had to share that story? Nah, pick another time, Empress. Now ain't it."

Marcus snatches the glass tumbler from Roman and looks back at me through narrowed eyes. "You even think about holding out on me and I'll withhold every fucking orgasm until you tell me what the fuck is going on."

I glance nervously at Roman who just shrugs as though this is my mess and now it's my problem to dig myself out of it. "Ummm … so Roman thinks he might have found a loophole to get me out of the marriage to your father."

Marcus' hand pauses halfway to his face, the glass hovering in the air above the bar. "Really?" he questions, his eyes brightening with hope.

"Yeah," I say slowly, hating to be the one to crush that hope within him. "Ummmm … it's not so much of a loophole, rather an amendment." His brows furrow and he looks at me in confusion as Levi stiffens beneath me, already figuring out where this is going. "So, I'm sure you're aware that Roman shares a name with your father and what we were thinking is that—"

"FUCK NO. ABSOLUTELY NOT," Marcus spits, throwing himself to his feet and immediately starting to pace. "You wanna be married to this asshole? FUCK." He turns toward Roman and I see the anger building in his eyes, but before I can do a damn thing about it, Marcus has already propelled himself over the bar with his fist currently sailing right toward his eldest brother's jaw.

There's a sickening crunch before Roman shoves Marcus hard, pushing him a step away and allowing him that moment of clarity to find control. He glares at his brother, shaking his head as he clenches his jaw. "I should have fucking known you'd put that fucking idea in her head."

Roman rubs his jaw and spits a mouthful of blood into the bar sink. "It's not about me trying to steal her away. Fuck, Marc. You should know her better than that. If that were the case, she'd never even consider it. It's about releasing her from the marriage to our father."

Marcus shakes his head, grabbing himself another drink and throwing it back. The glass slams down on the bar and quickly shatters with the force. "I don't fucking like it."

"No shit," Roman says. "You made that clear."

Levi's fingers gently squeeze my thigh, bringing my attention back to him. "Are you sure about this? My father could be dead in as little as a few days. We're going to have both families working together. The moment he's gone, your marriage won't matter."

"Not technically," I tell him, knowing that Marcus is listening intently, "but I will still be considered Giovanni's widow. Even in death, I won't be able to escape that connection to him. Now if I weren't married to him at all, if he weren't legally my husband …"

I leave the words hanging and Levi slowly nods. "Look, I'm not going to lie," he starts. "If any of us were lucky enough to have your hand in marriage, I always thought it'd probably be Marc, but if this is what you want, if you can walk away from this decision and be happy with it, then you'll have my blessing."

"You're not upset or anything like that?"

"Tell me this," he starts. "Will being married to Roman have any effect on our relationship? Will you be any less mine?"

I shake my head, horrified by the idea. "Absolutely not. It's just a piece of paper," I say, turning back to Marcus. "Same goes for you. Yes, I'll be technically married to him, but it's not like I asked for this. It's not like he got down on one knee and demanded exclusivity. All we're doing is making an already shitty situation better. And if I'm completely honest, if I had my own way, I wouldn't be married to any of you. I love you all equally, and I don't believe that having our names written on a piece of paper is any kind of endgame, especially in our situation. It would never work."

Seeing the indecision still on his face, I get up and move across the bar until I'm leaning against it and reaching over to grip his warm hands. "What's going to make this okay for you?" I ask him, meeting his dark eyes.

He watches me closely and a flicker of nervousness flashes through his eyes. "After all is said and done, when everything has calmed down, I want a vow ceremony. All three of us, and you. We lay it all out on the table and you officially become all of ours."

My brows furrow. "Like a wedding, but without the marriage certificate at the end?" I question.

"Exactly. We make our vows in front of the priest, in front of our families, and we combine as one."

My heart flutters wildly in my chest. "You really want that?" I question, pushing up against the bar to get closer to him. He nods. "I do," he says. "You'll technically be married to Roman, but you'll also have equal ties to me and Levi. I mean, if you're down for that."

Warmth spreads through my veins, lighting every nerve with adrenaline until I find myself climbing up over the bar and planting myself in front of him. "Of course, I'm down for that. I'm so fucking down it's insane."

Marcus grins and fuses his mouth to mine, kissing me deeply as his arms curl around my body. His tongue sweeps into my mouth and I moan into him, feeling more at home in his arms than I ever felt in any of the places we've stayed since meeting them.

He pulls away from me, his forehead tipping to mine. "For what it's worth, if that asshole gets to refer to you as 'wife' and I don't, I'm going to castrate him while he sleeps."

I shake my head and laugh before turning back and meeting Levi's dark eyes. "Are you down for a vow ceremony?"

His lips twist as he lets out a heavy sigh. "Would I have to wear a suit?"

"No," I laugh. "Come in your bare-ass naked glory for all I care."

Levi groans. "Fine, I suppose," he says, "but there better be a fucking epic party afterward."

Rolling my eyes, I turn to my almost husband. "And you?" I question, unsure why I feel so nervous about the guys' responses to this.

"You fucking know it, babe. Now—"

A loud buzzing sounds through the mansion and Roman cuts off his sentence, his gaze snapping to Levi's. "That's the front door. Someone's trying to get in."

All conversations of weddings and marriages fall away as Roman's hands fly under the bar, pulling out weapons and handing them to his brothers. A shitty little gun is placed into my hand and I glare at Roman. "Sorry," he says before launching himself over the bar and landing right beside me. "That's all I got left under here."

He grips my hand, and as one, the four of us fly out of the living room, Marcus in front, leading the pack with Levi behind, protecting our backs. "So, ahh … I'm assuming I need to make the call?"

"Huh?" I grunt, far too preoccupied with whoever is trying to break into the mansion.

He rolls his eyes. "To amend the paperwork. To officially become married."

"Oh yeah," I say as my eyes dart from left to right, certain that someone is going to jump out at us at any second. "Make the call, but for the record, I'm going to need some shiny diamonds to go along with that bullshit non-existent proposal, and they better be brand spanking new. I don't want any of your twisted ex's hand-me-downs."

Roman groans and rolls his eyes as both Levi and Marcus scoff. "Fine."

We storm through the mansion, more than under prepared for this particular attack, but as we enter into the massive foyer and Marcus moves toward the front window, his brows raise before he starts shaking his head. "Fucking hell," he mutters, not pleased by whoever stands at the door.

He lets out a frustrated groan and just like that, Roman and Levi seem to relax as we watch Marcus move to the front door and tear it open without even a hint of warning. His gun remains up, holding steady and strong, making him look like the twisted psychopath that I've come to love. "What in the ever-loving fuck do you think you're doing?"

Well, well … speaking of Roman's twisted exes.

Ariana's hands snap up, her eyes going wide as she takes in Marcus. Fear sweeps through her stare as she watches over his shoulder, taking in the scene behind him, Roman's hand in mine, the weapons, and Levi to our left.

A hint of jealousy courses through her eyes and I smirk, wondering just what she'd think of Roman's very untraditional proposal. Hell, the whole vow ceremony. After all, Ariana lives by the theory that any DeAngelis dick is good dick. Fucking cow, and to think I actually wanted to help her.

She closes her mouth, unsure of how to respond to this welcoming, as by the looks of it, she assumed she was coming to an empty house. Marcus moves forward, the barrel of his gun pressing against her head. "I'm not going to ask you again, Ariana. What the fuck are you doing here?"

She swallows hard, indecision in her eyes. "I know where Giovanni is."

And just like that, Marcus lowers the gun and welcomes her into the mansion.

# THIRTY-THREE

Ariana lasted all of three minutes before Roman had every bit of information out of her and sent her straight back out the door with a reminder of what was to happen to her if she ever showed up here again. She cried like a whiny little bitch and was sent away without even a second glance, and I'm not going to lie, I was all too smug during the whole thing.

Best three minutes of my life.

We stand in the training room of the Moretti private residence with the best Moretti soldiers around us. They aren't exactly thrilled to have Roman, Marcus, and Levi standing in their space, and they were even less thrilled to learn that we'd invited the best of the DeAngelis men to join us. But that's the beauty of being in my position. What I say goes, and they can either learn to accept it, or find out what kind of leader I will be when they step against me.

Agent Davidson has quietly slipped away, not interested in being involved with a war that he doesn't have to be a part of, especially now that Gia is dead and his assignment is officially coming to a close. Though I'm sure it won't be long until the Moretti men begin to notice his absence.

The boys are busy searching through the armory, checking over what kind of weapons we have access to when they step out as one, leaving the other Moretti men behind to finish cataloging everything we have. "They're here," Marcus says, nodding toward the elevator.

I nod and let out a nervous breath. The last time I saw these men, they weren't entirely down with the idea of working side-by-side with us, but we all have a mutual enemy who needs to be taken out. After that, I have no idea what's supposed to happen, but I'm sure whatever it is will be ugly. I've come to learn that nothing is easy in this world, and when asking grown ass men to play nice, it generally doesn't go as planned.

We take the elevator up to the main floor and step out into the foyer just as the DeAngelis men make their way through the front door. "What is this place?" the little Roman-look-alike asks with his henchmen, Trevor and Julio, at his sides.

"This," I say, spreading my arms out wide as Mick and his tech team file in behind them carrying boxes of tech that I can't even begin to understand, "was Gia Moretti's personal residence, and this here," I add, pointing out the crack in the marble where the chandelier fell and eliminated Gia for good, "is where the bitch died."

Eyebrows shoot up into hairlines while others just simply gape, staring at the spot on the expensive marble as though it's some kind of magical place that will offer them the supernatural powers of the gods.

"Okaaaaay," Marcus says after a moment of awkward silence. "Fighters with me, tech dudes with Roman. Everyone else … fucked if I know. Figure it out yourselves." And just like that, Marcus saunters off with a handful of fighters following behind him.

I look up at Levi and Roman. "Is it really such a good idea to have Marcus do the introductions between the DeAngelis and Moretti fighters? He'll probably encourage some kind of bloodbath."

Levi presses his lips into a hard line before cursing. "Fuck."

He turns on his heel and jogs after Marcus as Roman glances down at me. "Guess you're stuck with me," he says before turning to Mick and his team. He indicates with a nod of his head and the group of overqualified men follow us through the mansion.

We lead them through the maze of hallways until finally pushing through to the massive tech room Gia had set up. The Moretti team is already busy doing their searches, and when Roman steps through the door, they barely glance up.

The team leader is Lennox who stands at attention, waiting on instructions from me, which only manages to send a wave of unease through my system. I'm not used to this kind of attention, but I have to get used to it. "Lennox," I say, indicating to Mick, "this is Mick and his team. He's the DeAngelis tech dude. He's a computer wizard so I'm sure between everyone, it shouldn't be a problem finding the information we need."

"Of course," Lennox says, turning to Mick. "I know your work. It's impressive."

"Same to you," Mick responds with a curt nod of his head.

Lennox gives an awkward smile before stepping back and indicating to the spare tables and chairs throughout the room. "Make yourselves at home and I'll show you our tech."

And just like that, Mick's eyes light up like it's Christmas morning and his team flies in like toy soldiers and starts setting up their equipment before we can even step out of their way. They all seem to get along, and I quickly realize they don't hold that same animosity as what the fighters and the direct family members do. These guys are more like brains for hire. They come, they do their job, and they get the fuck out before they can get dragged deeper into this bullshit world.

Roman and I walk out after giving instructions to get us the information we need as soon as possible, and just as expected, an hour later, we have a full map of Giovanni's estranged mother's property and details on how to infiltrate it.

Lennox is still working on getting heat signatures and has promised that by the time we get there, we'll have that information. In the meantime, Mick has set everyone up with communication devices and explained how they'll be watching our backs and guiding us through, while also demanding this upgraded tech for the DeAngelis warehouse.

Within ten minutes, there's a convoy of SUVs peeling out of the Moretti residence. I sit beside Marcus in the backseat, Roman and Levi in front, the four of us sitting in silence as our bodies don every type of weapon that could possibly fit on our black tactical uniforms. Well mostly, I stuck with the pants and boots because they look fucking fire and paired them with a cropped black tank.

Holsters curl around my arms and thighs while my hair is pulled back into a high pony, plaited right down to the very end. I feel like I just stepped out of a sexy assassin movie—but the boys. Holy mother of all things sweet and sexy! They look like sex on legs, I can barely keep focus. I've never wanted to jump them more.

Apparently, I have a thing for men in uniform. Who would have known.

With Giovanni's estranged mother's property being heavily guarded, we don't dare pass the property, instead we pull off into the nearby forest, our headlights going off as our convoy of SUVs trail through the too narrow hiking trail.

We come to a stop, and as we wait for our teams to come together and wait for instruction, I notice the very moment the sun dips down behind the mountains in the distance. It won't be long until we lose what little light remains, and while attacking in the dead of night holds all too many memories for me, it's exactly what Giovanni expects of us.

Roman holds his hand to his ear. "Mick, you hear me?"

There's a short pause as the soldiers around us fall into silence. "Right. Where's Lennox at with the heat signatures?" Roman questions, his gaze off into the distance, staring toward the home where his son—*our son*—is being kept.

"Good, and the kids?"

Another pause.

"Okay. I'll check in when we're at the boundary."

Mick mustn't reply as Roman immediately addresses the waiting army. "Heat signatures suggest possibly fifty armed guards surrounding the immediate house, a further twenty-five inside the home, and a few sporadically outside of the property gates. Giovanni was last seen two hours ago in the main dining hall. However, he has not been detected on any of the surveillance cameras since. If you find him, the goal is to capture him alive and bring him back to either myself or my brothers. If your life is in immediate danger and it is imperative to make a kill shot, then take it."

"The children?" one of the Moretti soldiers asks.

Roman nods. "Lennox has determined through heat signatures that the three children are located in the upper west wing of the property. You're looking for two girls, ages eight and ten, and a newborn, less than three months. There seems to be someone watching over them. At this stage, it can not be determined whether this is an innocent nursemaid hired solely to tend to the children, or if this is a trained guard. Keep your eyes open. Are there any questions?"

"If we get our hands on one of these kids? What do you want us to do? Keep them safe while helping our brothers or bail?"

"Bail," Marcus says as though his soldier should have known better. "You have been brought here to do two things—find Giovanni and save those children. If you happen to get your hands on them, you communicate through your earpiece with a confirmation of the child and give your location. The men closest to you will be responsible for watching your back to ensure you get out of there with the child unharmed. If you have one of those three children in your arms, your job is not to watch your brother's back. It is to take care of your own."

The soldiers nod, understanding it for what it is—the children's lives above theirs—and not one of them disagrees.

"Alright," Roman says, keeping his eye on the dimming daylight. "I trust everyone studied the blueprint of the property on the ride over and knows where they need to be?" Every last man confirms just as we all knew they would, and with a determined nod, Roman says, "Good. Let's move."

The soldiers take off into the thick trees, moving with the kind of stealth that the boys were trained to have. They break off into small attack groups and I watch with awe. They take their mission seriously, and it's clear that they were trained by only the best this world has to offer—both the DeAngelis family and the Morettis.

There's no doubt in my mind that tonight, we're going to win. There's no way we can't. We have surprise on our side and come fully loaded with a team that Giovanni would never be able to obtain, no matter how hard he searched and who he had to threaten to make it happen.

I stick between Levi and Marcus, and a thrill travels down my spine watching Marcus' eyes light with the excitement of the impending bloodbath he's about to create. Hell, with each step he takes, I'm almost certain that he forgets about the reason we're here just a little bit more. But I know that when it comes down to it, Marcus will do whatever it takes to save those kids, even if it means escaping without spilling even a single drop of blood, no matter how much he might hate that.

Roman walks ahead of us, his shoulders back and his head held high with fierce determination. He won't fail tonight. Not after everything he's suffered through to bring him to this point, his head is in the game, and no matter what risks he has to take, he will get what's rightfully his.

The trees begin to thin and as I look left and right, I don't see a single body, but I know they're there, completely surrounding the property and waiting on Roman's instructions. There are twenty small groups and we stand in silence, listening through our small earpieces waiting for confirmation that every last group is exactly where it needs to be. The wait seems to go on forever as some of those groups have to make it the whole way around the perimeter of the property and to the other side, but we'll wait as long as it takes.

As we stand hidden in the bushes, we get a good feel for the property, watching the guards who stand on the outskirts of the gates, peering into the trees and missing every last one of us. Lights are on inside the house, and we take note of where people are inside as Mick and Lennox feed information back to us, detailing the location of all the guards.

A grin pulls at the corner of my lips and Levi glances down at me. "What's funny?" he murmurs, keeping his voice low.

I shake my head. "They're telling us exactly where they are," I comment. "Where's the fun in that? They're making it too easy."

Marcus scoffs, and I know without a doubt that he agrees

wholeheartedly. He likes the chase, he likes the opportunity to play with his food before destroying it. Levi on the other hand just rolls his eyes, more than happy to know where his targets are so he can sneak up on them and take them out without the risk of sounding the alarm.

"You ready?" Marcus asks. "Gun loaded? Checked?"

I glare up at him. "You honestly think after everything, I haven't checked my gun?"

He arches a brow and I try to hold my glare, but that nagging thought in the back of my head that usually tells me I forgot to turn off my hair straightener even though I checked it twenty times, insists that maybe I did forget. My eye twitches as the need to recheck it fires through me, but I won't dare, not as long as his eyes are still on me.

His lips begin to pull into a wicked smirk, knowing exactly what he's doing to me, and after a long pause, Roman sighs in front of us, not even bothering to look back. "Shayne, check your fucking gun, and Marc, stop making her doubt herself. You know she checked it when she first got it, when we got in the car, and again when she got out just like we trained her."

The need to poke out my tongue fires through me, but I'll save it for a time when there's no risk of Roman turning around and knocking me out. I'd miss all the fun and he'd claim it was a 'safety measure.'

The final confirmation comes from the group of guards directly across the property from us, and my shoulders immediately pull back, all ridiculous light conversation fading away. Roman presses his hand to his ear and his voice sails through to the small piece of tech in my ear. "Let's move in three … two … one."

Despite not being able to see them, I know that every small group of soldiers swiftly steps out of the trees, moving silently toward the property without raising suspicion until the very last minute, which is exactly what we do as we move toward the two guards standing outside the front gates.

We're on the left of the oversized, wrought-iron gates and we head for the guard standing closest to us. Moving silently through the shadows, both Roman and Marcus prepare themselves, watching their targets closely.

The guard closest to us turns his back and Roman strikes, rushing in behind him and slapping his hand down over his mouth. The guard doesn't even get a chance to scream before Roman's knife strikes across his throat. The guard falls, and just as the other on the right of the gate spins around, Marcus is there, slamming him back against the big pillar. Marcus snaps his neck, clean and effortlessly, and with a heavy thump, the guard falls to Marcus' feet.

The boys drag the bodies into the small guard booth beside the big iron gate and we each step over them, slipping through the booth to gain access to the property, rather than drawing attention by trying to scale the tall gate or moronically opening it.

"Did you guys even know about this property?" I murmur, keeping my voice as low as humanly possible.

"No fucking idea," Marcus murmurs behind me. "Never even met the woman. Don't even know her name."

Great. This should be interesting.

The night is silent, telling me that our men are doing their job flawlessly, and as I scan the property, I watch with amusement as guards are snatched out of the shadows and seamlessly dealt with.

We move out from the booth and glance back as Marcus' hand falls to my thigh, gripping my knife and pulling it from its sheath. He keeps his eyes trained on the property, and without even glancing at me, he presses the handle into the palm of my hand, a silent message to be ready for whatever might come at us.

"Three guards approaching the front gate," I hear through the small piece of tech in my ear. Excitement drums into me and I clutch my knife a little tighter. Hearing the soft rustling of feet in the grass, I grin and turn toward the approaching men. Ready to leave my mark, I move forward to strike, only three giant assholes move in front of me, blocking my view as they take care of business.

I sheath my knife and stand back, crossing my arms over my chest, impatiently waiting.

They take the guards out in record time before turning and glancing back at me as though they're some kind of heroes. "Seriously?" I question, eyeing the three of them and ignoring the fact that I'm super impressed with how they managed to dispose of the three guards in a matter of seconds while also avoiding being splattered with blood. "Why am I even here? Do you just want someone to watch you make your kills? I mean, what's the point if you're going to step in front of me like egotistical asshats? I can take care of myself. I've had good training and made plenty of kills against men twice my size. I think I've more than proven myself. So, let's summarize, shall we? Step in front of me and block me from doing my job, and I won't be marrying a damn one of you."

Guilt flashes in their eyes and there's no doubt in my mind they knew exactly what they were doing when they moved in front of me like that. I narrow my gaze and Roman lets out a sigh. "Fine," he says, pointing to my right. "Then this guy is all yours."

I spin on my heel, my knife already in my hand to find a guy stepping out from behind the booth, his brows furrowed, probably trying to figure out where the hell all the other guards disappeared to.

I pounce like a fucking tiger, not even giving him a chance to react.

He's tall and beyond round, and I know without a doubt I won't have a chance in hell of getting him on his ass, so I scale the fucker like a cat climbing a tree. He cries out like a little bitch, and I curse the asshole. The sound wasn't loud enough to catch the attention of the other guards, but it was enough for the guys to know I'm not getting this done fast enough.

I don't waste my time glancing back at them, but I sense them preparing to step in, which only pisses me off more. I get up high on his body, my head hovering over his and forcing him to look up as he grabs me. His nails dig into my skin in an attempt to throw me off, but my reflexes are too fast and as he goes to roar out, sounding the alarm, I sink my knife straight down his open throat.

He gurgles on the blood pouring down his throat, and I quickly tear my knife out before slashing it across the front of his neck, the angle of his body ensuring that the boys are drenched in his blood like a waterfall.

He slowly falls forward and I prepare myself on the way down to simply step off and plant myself in front of the boys.

Marcus grins at me like he just met an angel, while Roman and Levi look anything but pleased. "That was fun," I tell them, seeing another group of our men approaching from behind the guys. "Now can we get on with it? We've got a baby to save."

With that, the boys wipe the blood from their faces and just as the other soldiers meet us, a gunshot sounds through the property. "Fuck," Roman curses just as gunfire returns twofold. "They know we're here. Go hard. No prisoners."

# THIRTY-FOUR

We race toward the house, the soldiers taking the lead to clear the path so that we can make it to the house without anything slowing us down. Guards race toward us and bullets whiz past my face. Months ago, those bullets would have scared the shit out of me, but tonight, they're just pissing me off.

Pulling my gun, I fire back, trying not to shoot the boys or any of our men in the process. More guards join and Marcus curses, pulling his own gun. "You guys go on, I'll hold them off."

We don't even get a chance to respond before he lets off two perfect kill shots, his impeccable skill like no other. We take off at a sprint, and I feel sick leaving him behind, but the middle of the war zone is where Marcus thrives, and with the other soldiers at his back, I know he's going to be alright.

A few guards meet us as we storm up the grand stairs leading to the front door, and Roman lets off quick shots, not bothering with the dramatic slaughtering as we're now in a time crunch. Every moment the guards are aware of our presence is another moment that allows them to slip away ... allows Giovanni to slip away, and that is simply not acceptable.

Getting past the armed guards, Levi shoots out the lock for the floor-to-ceiling front door, and as he gives it a hard shove, we find guards already waiting for us. They attack immediately, not allowing us the chance to get the upper hand, but unfortunately for them, they underestimated the power that Levi and Roman wield.

This foyer isn't as grand as the ones I've been fighting in over the past few months and doesn't allow much breathing space, and despite the raging need to join in and end these guys, I'm only going to be in the way. So instead, I slip out behind the boys and bolt for the stairs.

I get halfway up the staircase when I hear the familiar sound of flesh being beaten and my head whips to the left, peering over the railing to find that some of the Moretti soldiers have already made it through the maze of guards. One of them glances up, more than aware of his surroundings, and upon finding me, his gaze sweeps over my body to check that I'm unharmed. In that moment, a sliver of camaraderie passes between us, so much so that not a moment later, my knife flies through the air and plunges deep into the stomach of the guard who moves at his back.

His eyes widen and he quickly sends a nod of thanks, but I don't linger on it, having more than enough already on my plate. I soar up the stairs, getting right near the top when Roman's voice booms through the foyer. "SHAYNE, ON YOUR SIX."

I whip around and immediately duck as a set of strong hands reach for me. My eyes widen and the guard tumbles, slightly off balance from missing his mark, and I shift out of the way, gaining just enough space to kick my booted foot out and slam it into his chest. The guard falls back and tumbles down the impressive staircase, coming to a stop at the bottom where Roman is waiting and ready for him. He doesn't last another fucking second.

With Roman and Levi clearing out the foyer and the extra soldiers to our left, Roman leaves Levi to finish off the remaining guards and sprints up the stairs after me. "Mick," I say, hoping to God that he hears me. "We're on the stairs. Where do we go?"

"To the west wing," he says, his voice sharp and loud in my ear.

My head whips left to right as Roman quickly gains on me. "West?" I question in a panic. "I was raised with left or right. WHICH WAY, MICK?"

"Left," he rushes out. "Take the hallway to the end. We're still getting four heat signatures from the room. Two children, one baby, and an adult. The hallway is clear as are adjoining rooms."

I take off at a sprint as Roman comes up after me, his gaze sharp as he scans the space in front of us, searching for threats despite Mick's assurances. "Anything on my father?" Roman questions. "Anyone found him yet?"

"Negative," Mick responds. "We've got nothing. All heat signatures have been confirmed as guards. I'm sorry, man. He slipped us again. He must have known we were coming. There are still bound to be family members who remain loyal, but we knew that was a possibility."

"FUCK," Roman spits, stopping toward the end of the hallway, his frustration getting the best of him. "FIND HIM," Roman demands. "You have the best fucking technology at your fingertips. Track the bastard with whatever means necessary. I want him dead."

"Yes, sir," Mick responds, his voice fading to a distant murmur as he relays their orders to Lennox and the rest of the tech team.

My hand presses to his shoulder, drawing his attention back to the here and now. "We'll focus on your father later, for now, we need to get those kids, and you need to meet your son."

As if those words spark a fire deep inside of him. His head snaps up and he looks toward the door at the end of the long hallway, and without hesitation, he moves toward it, his gun in hand. I stand by his side and get the awful sense of déjà vu. I've been here twice before, certain that I was about to push open a door and put an end to this, only to have my hopes crushed. "You ready?" I ask him, my gun in hand.

He nods. "Just like last time," he tells me. "I go for the threat, you go for the baby."

He sees the conviction in my eyes and I can practically hear the countdown inside his head.

Three.

Two.

One.

Roman storms in first, his gun held high, ready to take out whatever threat lies in our way as I dart below his arm into the room.

A woman stands before us, her arms up and tears streaming down her face. The baby cries in the corner as Phillip's two daughters crouch down in the farthest corner, holding on to one another and silently weeping, absolutely terrified.

I immediately recognize the woman who'd helped me flee Giovanni's clutches, who told me to run and never look back. She knew I'd come for the baby at some point, but finding her like this, her life flashing before her eyes as the bomb strapped to her chest slowly counts down.

Four minutes and thirty-six seconds.

Thirty-five.

Thirty-four.

"May," Roman breathes, taking in the woman before him, the woman who silently cared for the boys, a prisoner to that castle just as much as they were, despite her freedom to come and go.

"Just go," she begs, tears streaming down her face. "Take the children and go. There's nothing left for me here. If you try to disable it, the timer will stop and we will all perish. You must take the children, Roman."

"May," he repeats, shaking his head. Leaving her to die is not something he's capable of doing.

"Roman DeAngelis," she snaps. "Don't you dare start going soft on me now. These children need you. Take them out of here. Do it now."

"Shayne," Roman demands, the rest of his orders not needing to be spoken out loud. My heart races with fear, even just knocking her could set it off. I can't risk it. I have to get them and leave, and as much as it kills me, I'm going to walk out of this door with those children in my arms and not look back.

I race toward the crib in the corner of the room and reach down toward the screaming baby, cradling him in my arms. "There's a go bag in the closet," May instructs. "Take it."

I do as I'm told, my gaze snapping back to the timer.

Four minutes and three seconds.

Fuck. I still have to get them out of the house and far enough away not to be impacted by the bomb.

Grabbing the baby's go bag, I hook it over my shoulder and glance across the room to the two girls. "I need you two to walk very slowly toward me," I tell them, meeting their horrified stares as Roman continues to skillfully gaze over the bomb that could blast us all to pieces.

Three minutes and forty-eight seconds.

The girls nod, gripping on to one another's hands as they begin to make their way toward me, tiptoeing across the room as though they're scared to even breathe, and hell, I think they just might be. Fuck, I am too. The baby squeals in my arms, probably past due for a sleep or a feed. Hell, maybe the little dude just needs to take a shit but it's not something I can deal with now.

The girls safely make it to my side, and I awkwardly hold on to the baby as I move toward the door. "Let's go," I tell Roman, hating the way he stands like a statue watching the timer slowly counting down. "ROMAN," I demand.

He doesn't move and May shakes her head. "Don't be a fool, Roman DeAngelis. Get out of here while you still can."

He doesn't budge and tears spring to my eyes as I release the little girl's hand and grip Roman's chin. "Snap the fuck out of it, Roman. That bomb is going to go off the second you touch it. You're not fucking leaving me like that, do you hear me? You can't save everyone, but these kids? You sure as fuck can save them. I can't get them out of here and far enough away by myself." The tears spill down my face as I watch the moment realization dawns on him and his heart falls right out of his chest, shattering into a million pieces on the ground before me. "I can't do this without you, Roman. Please, we have to walk away."

Roman's gaze falls to the baby cradled in my arms before turning back to the time.

Three minutes and twelve seconds.

Devastation pours out of him as he meets May's pained stare. "I'm sorry," he breathes, his voice breaking as he grips the elbow of the little girl at his side and slowly begins retreating out of the room.

May presses her lips into a tight line and nods her head. "It's alright, Roman. I always knew you had the biggest heart out of all of them. I don't hold this against you. I'm not angry with you, but you need to go, and you need to go now."

Roman nods, and with one final step, we cross the threshold of the bedroom and Roman turns to me, panic in his eyes. "Get the fuck out of here."

We run, booming down the hallway as Roman grips onto both of the girls, the younger one in his arms while the older sister stumbles trying to keep up with our speed, but Roman doesn't dare let her fall. "MICK," Roman calls. "EVACUATION ORDER. NOW! GET THEM OUT OF HERE. WE'VE GOT A LIVE BOMB AND IT'S GOING TO FUCKING BLOW."

"Done," Mick fires back before I hear him in my ear, the same message being relayed to every last soldier in our team. "ABORT MISSION. LIVE BOMB. I REPEAT. ABORT MISSION. GET OUT AND SAVE YOURSELVES."

I clutch the baby, holding him tight to my chest as we hit the top of the stairs. I try to keep him from jostling around, unsure just how fragile they are. He keeps crying, and damn, if I could, I'd be screaming my fucking lungs out too, but it'll have to wait until we get out of here and to the safety of the surrounding forest.

We storm down the staircase, and as soldiers run for their lives, racing out the doors and smashing their way out through the windows, only two fuckknuckles are running in the opposite direction, their eyes wide as they search us out.

Levi waits at the bottom of the stairs, collecting the older sister as Marcus scoops me into his arms, slipping the bag off my shoulder and lightening my load as we bolt for the stairs. I have no fucking idea how much time we have left to spare, but it can't be good. We got up eight flights of stairs and a block down the street in the space of two minutes, so surely we can do it again with three children.

Fuck.

We break out into the cold night and bodies litter every inch of the grass, blood running down the path and staining the manicured lawn, but I don't dare hang around to check just how many of the bodies belong to us. We can do a headcount when we get back to the Moretti residence, assuming we make it back.

My heavy boots slap against the hard ground and I cringe realizing that we have to leave the way we came in. We can't possibly scale the high gates with the children. We'd have to physically pass them over and that would take too much time. We have to risk detouring past the guard booth before doubling back toward the thick bushes.

Shit. Shit. Shit.

I push myself faster, all too aware of the screaming baby in my arms. We hit the guard booth a moment later, and getting through it and stepping over the dead bodies takes precious seconds that we don't have. Getting back past the gates, I smell sweet freedom, and we run as fast as we can, the other soldiers already deep into the safety of the thick forest.

The trees loom up ahead and every step I take feels as though it takes a lifetime and—

*BOOM!*

My body is catapulted up off the ground, and I fly through the air as a raging heat hits my back. The ground comes up fast as arms lock around my body, holding me close, and just as quickly as it happened, I'm slamming down against the ground, my hip hitting the hard earth as the majority of my body is protected by Marcus.

The BOOM echoes through my ears and my head spins as hands begin pulling at me. "SHAYNE," Marcus yells, shaking me. "Is the baby alright? SHAYNE. FUCK."

Shit. The baby.

I wriggle out of Marcus' tight grip, my head snapping down to the baby in my arms. He's silent and my heart races with terror. He hasn't been silent since the second we stormed into that room. My arms are clean of dirt so I don't think he hit the ground, but he sure as fuck could have been jostled around from the impact of our fall.

"Fuck, fuck, fuck, fuck," I cry as Roman rushes into my side, dropping to his knees beside me. "Come on, baby. Be okay. Please be okay."

I cradle his tiny body, holding him gently. I can see the quick thrum of his pulse through his fragile skin, so I know he's alive, but his eyes are closed and he's not making a damn sound.

"Why won't he cry?"

Roman's eyes are wide and he takes the baby from my arms, stroking the side of his face. "Come on, little man," he begs, his tone tortured and full of a heart wrenching fear that makes me want to break down and scream. Roman leans into him and blows against his face, and just like that, his little obsidian eyes spring open and the loudest screech tears through the fiery night.

"Holy fuck," Roman says, meeting my horrified stare. "I thought—"

"I know," I tell him. "Me too."

"Come on," Levi says, the girls hovering by his side as the mansion burns behind us. "We need to get out of here."

And just like that, we storm back through the thick trees and barrel into the SUV to lead our men home and figure out how the fuck we're going to find Giovanni.

# THIRTY-FIVE

"What the fuck do we do with it?" Marcus asks, his lips twisting in confusion as we each stare over the side of the crib, looking in at the baby who we've moved heaven and hell to bring home. He lays at the bottom of the crib, his arms spread wide as he sleeps soundly.

It took us all of two seconds after returning back to the Moretti residence to realize that we were going to have to call in a professional to teach us how to care for this little creature, and we made sure to pay whatever fees she asked for if it meant she could show up within the next ten minutes with every last thing we could possibly need. Though, to be fair, most of it we had to wait for, but she was able to grab formula, bottles, and diapers on her way. Apparently that's all we needed to make it through the night. The rest, Levi was sent to get the second the sun peeked above the horizon.

Our nanny taught me and Roman how to prepare a bottle and how to change his diaper, and despite seeing the concern deep in her eyes, she didn't dare question what two clueless idiots did to end up with a baby in their care. Hell, she didn't even seem intimidated by the boys despite knowing exactly who they were the moment she walked through the door. All she cared about was making sure the baby got the best possible care, and that's exactly what she focused on.

We may keep her hostage here for a few weeks, that's still undecided. To be honest, I'm terrified of letting her walk out the door and forcing me to adult all by myself, but Roman seems to get this as though he was born for it.

Levi tilts his head to the side in an eerily similar way to how he tilts it right before he decides to kill something, and I watch him a little more closely. "I think he needs a blanket," Levi says, quickly nodding as if agreeing with his own conclusion. "Yes, he definitely needs a blanket."

"No," I call out, my hand snapping up and catching the blanket just as it flies through the air toward the crib. "The lady said he can't have loose blankets, or toys, or pillows in his crib. It's dangerous."

"What?" Levi grunts, twisting his face in the same way that Marcus has been doing for the last hour. "That's ridiculous. Everyone likes a pillow on their bed."

I roll my eyes and throw the blanket right across the other side of the room as if to make a point. "I know, pillows are amazing, but what if he manages to roll onto his tummy and his face gets pressed up against the pillow and he can't move. He'll suffocate himself. Or … or what if the blanket gets caught over his little face and he can't breathe?"

Levi's eyes bug out of his head as he looks down at the little guy. "Fuck, are you sure?" he questions. "How are we supposed to know that shit? Do regular people just know that? Or is there like … a Mom course you're supposed to do when you're pregnant?"

"I, uhhhh … I don't actually know. The baby lady told me."

"Shit, well … what else?"

"Umm … I guess, there are lots of things to know. Like, you have to make him burp after he has a bottle so he doesn't get a sore tummy and—"

"Make him burp?" Marcus questions, his face blank apart from his eyes that look slightly terrified. "How the fuck are we supposed to do that? Punch the little dude in the stomach?"

"Holy shit," I breathe, staring at him in horror before slowly turning my gaze on Levi and then Roman across the big room. "Let's make a pact to never leave Marcus alone with the baby until he can at least walk—NO. No, until he's five and going to school. That should be enough time."

Marcus looks back at me, his brows furrowed in confusion. "I don't get it … what's wrong with that? It was a serious question? It's not like I was going to do it hard, you know, just a little love tap to the gut."

"Unless you'd like him to projectile vomit on you," Roman mutters moving across the room to stare over the side of the crib again, "then I suggest that's not such a bright idea."

Marcus nods as though the thought of vomit hadn't even occurred to him, and he's more than grossed out by the topic. "Fair call," he says, backing away from the sleeping baby, realizing he's not just a little bit out of his league on this one, but that he doesn't even have his foot through the door. Levi though, there might be hope for him. Maybe supervised visitation.

The little guy begins to wake and a soft smile spreads across my face watching as Levi leans down into the crib and scoops him into his arms. The baby instantly begins to cry and Levi's face fills with a sick, panicked fear. "Oh, fuck," he rushes out before thrusting the baby right into my arms as though I'm supposed to know any better.

It hasn't even been a full day yet, and already I'm so attached. It's not hard to understand why Roman insisted that I'll want to be in his life as some form of motherly figure. I just gotta figure out how to hold him without him screeching like a banshee.

I panic and Roman saves me, taking the baby into his capable arms and watching as he calms. "Hey there, little man," Roman says as the baby stretches in his arms and immediately snuggles into his hold, soaking up the affection as though he's been starved of it. "Do you need a bottle?"

My heart legit melts, like holy fuck, but side note, how does he do that?

I thought seeing the boys in uniform was the most delicious

thing I'd ever seen, but apparently watching them care for this sweet, innocent baby is what really gets me. At least, watching Roman like this does. If Marcus were to pick him up, I'd probably die of fear.

The baby begins to cry and Roman gently sways as I hurry across the room and quickly scoop up the bottle we'd made just before striding in here as though we knew what the hell we were doing. I pop the lid and hand him the bottle, watching as Roman effortlessly glides the teat into the baby's mouth.

He sucks hard and his eyes close in satisfaction before going to town on the bottle.

My fingers brush over his head, feeling the soft hairs beneath my skin. "Have you figured out his name yet?"

Roman shakes his head. "I have no fucking idea," he says. "Normal parents get nine months' notice to think of the perfect name, but I've had literally one day. It's too much pressure. What if I choose something that sounds kind of cool for a kid, but as an adult, would have people thinking he's a douche? I don't want that for my kid." He pauses and looks up at me with a terrified stare, something I don't think I've ever seen from him. "What if I fuck up my kid?"

I shake my head. "Look at you, Roman. Look how much you already care for him. You're a natural at this and he can sense that. I don't think it's possible for you to fuck this up. You're going to make a great Father to him. Hell, I'm jealous. My father was awful, and so was yours. You know what a shitty parent looks like, so you know exactly what not to do."

Roman's lips press into a tight line as his gaze drops back to the baby, watching him take big gulps of his milk as though he can't possibly get enough. "You sure about that?" he questions, taking a heavy breath.

"Positive," I tell him before looking back at the boys. "Actually, while you're all here, there's something I wanted to run by you."

Marcus narrows his stare, already suspicious. "Last time you said you wanted to talk, you dropped a fucking 'I'm gonna marry your bitch of a brother' bomb on my ass. This better not be like that."

A grin cuts across my face and I laugh, moving across the room to stand directly between them all so I can see the three of them at the same time. "No, it's definitely not that," I tell him, hoping to somehow relieve the panic soaring through his chest. "It kinda occurred to me that we don't really have a home," I tell them. "I don't want to live at the castle because for ten years, that was your prison, and with how much you've all seemed to keep away, I don't think you want to be there either. Then there's the DeAngelis mansion and well …" my gaze drops away and my voice lowers. "That's where your father—"

"I know," Levi says, his voice soothing and making me feel alright again. "That's where he abused us too."

I nod. "I don't want to live there either, which only leaves here, in the Moretti residence, but I'm just not sure how you guys might feel about that." I glance toward Levi again, my gaze drifting toward his scarred chest that's covered with clothing. "I know you've got particularly nasty memories of being here. Not to mention this was the home of your enemy for so long. If you guys aren't cool with it, then I'll push the idea aside, no questions asked, but I guess … I wondered how you felt about making this our home?"

Marcus leans back against the crib, crossing his ankles as he watches me carefully. "What do you want, Shayne? Do you actually want to live here, or is this just the lesser of three evils?"

"I …" I pause, shrugging my shoulders as I truly think about it. "I mean, I guess I don't really know. This home is beautiful, but every time I walk through the foyer, I see Gia's face right before I shot down the chandelier."

"Then this isn't your home," Marcus says just as Roman's phone rings and he awkwardly adjusts the baby to pull it out of his pocket. He's been waiting for Mick's call, telling us that he's got something, but judging by the disappointment on his face, I can only assume that the number flashing on his screen is anyone but Mick.

Roman strides toward the door, bringing the phone to his ear. "You better have good news for me," he says, his voice fading away as he moves further down the hall, the baby happy to go along for the stroll.

"What's that all about?" I question, watching as they shrug their shoulders, not caring to get involved in Roman's business, not that he'd actually care to share unless it had something to do with them or me. Anything else is his business.

Marcus keeps his stare on me and my brows furrow, watching him back. "What?" I say slowly.

His lips press into a hard line as though he's concocting some sort of top-secret plan. "What if we didn't live at any of those places?" he throws out. "I mean, we'll have to choose one and stay there for a bit, but what if we completely knocked down the home that Roman built and re-do it as our own?"

My brows instantly shoot up, my back straightening as my eyes widen with hope. "Are … can … is that even possible? Like, can we do that?"

He shrugs his shoulders. "I don't see why not. Roman built it once before, why can't he do it again? We can all put in the things that we want, and Roman can design it around that. Besides, it looks like he's got some sleepless nights in his future, so it'll give him a project to work on."

"What will he say about this?"

"What would who say about what?" Roman questions, striding back into the room with the baby up over his shoulder and his phone slipped away into his pocket. He rubs the baby's back, and I grin as the little dude lets out an almighty burp. "We were just discussing the possibility of maybe knocking down what was left of the home you built and rebuilding it, making it our new home."

Roman stops in the middle of the room, his hand pausing on the baby's back. His eyes widen slightly as he turns to take me in, looking a little unsure. "You'd want that?" he questions. "You don't want to live here?"

"I want to live where you guys are, in a home that doesn't harbor secrets and lies, somewhere we can all feel safe and allow the baby to grow and run without fearing that someone could sneak onto the property and hurt him, and somewhere none of us have been brutally tortured."

His lips start pulling into a wide grin. "You're sure?" he questions. "Because I've been thinking about rebuilding that thing ever since it burned down, but if you really want it, I'll start putting plans into place."

"I really want it," I tell him, moving into him and pushing up onto my tippy toes to brush my lips over his. "I only have one requirement … No, two. Two requirements." Roman watches, his brow arching with impatience. "I want a sex room," I tell him. "Nothing creepy or anything like that … actually, maybe that's a shitty idea. I mean, what am I supposed to tell people when I give them the grand tour *'and this is where I get thoroughly fucked.'* No, that can't happen."

Marcus scoffs, a smirk resting on his lips. "Dare I ask your second requirement?"

A hunger spreads through me, heating me from the inside out as I glance across the room to Levi, watching the way he reads the hunger in my eyes for exactly what it is. "I want drums in every fucking room."

Marcus and Roman just stare, not understanding the fascination, but Levi … he gets it. He groans low and I bite down on my bottom lip, just thinking of all the fun we could have with all those drum sets.

Roman shakes his head. "No way in hell am I having drums in every room, we'd never have a moment of silence. What if we just had them in every main living area, but no dining rooms or bathrooms, and definitely not in my bedroom."

I cross my arms over my chest and take a step back, narrowing my eyes. "I see your drums only in living spaces, and I raise you a soft serve machine in the kitchen and a pizza oven … OH, and a popcorn maker for movie night. And can we have bean bags in the theater room? Like those ginormous ones where you practically disappear when you jump into them. OH!" I add, the excitement quickly taking control. "And a slide into the pool? Wouldn't that be awesome? I've always dreamed about having a pool."

"Okay," Levi laughs, moving across the room and pulling me into his arms, his chest pressed against my back. He leans down and presses his lips to my temple. "Would you prefer if you just made the designs with Roman?"

My eyes bug out of my head and I gape at him before turning my stare on Roman, positive that he's going to shut down the idea before it even gets started. My heart races with excitement, quickly building higher with every passing moment. "Is that ... Can I? Would you mind?"

"Would I mind?" Roman laughs. "I'd like nothing more than to build a home with you."

Warmth spreads through my chest, mixing with the pure joy that already resides. "I don't think you have any idea what you just got yourself into."

His phone rings again and he sighs, digging into his pocket again. "Hold that thought," he tells me before his back stiffens and he turns toward his brothers, watching them intently. "Mick, talk to me."

Silence fills the room except for the soft coos of the baby. It feels like a lifetime passes before Roman ends the call and tells us exactly what we've been waiting for. "We've got him."

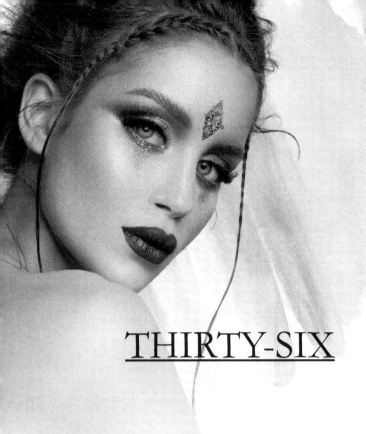

# THIRTY-SIX

A light shower rains down over the deserted street, the sole street light casting a glow across the cracked pavement. We're well out of the city now, in bum-fuck nowhere with nothing but ourselves to watch out for.

We sit in the black Escalade, covered in shadows with the headlights turned off, watching the rundown motel across the street.

This is it.

Giovanni DeAngelis paces in front of the window, moving back and forth, over and over again with the dim room lighting casting his shadow against the old curtains.

The second we got the call from Mick, we made our move. We

weren't letting the asshole get away again. We got our intel, got his location, and quickly learned that he was alone. He has nothing; no guards, no children held hostage to use against us. Just him and justice waiting to be served.

Fuck, I can't wait. I feel as though I've been waiting for this moment since the second he stormed into the castle and demanded I strip for him. He's nothing but an egotistical pig who thinks way too highly of himself, but without his army of guards at his back, without his precious DeAngelis mafia ready to back him up, and without the fear of his threats hanging over our heads, he's nothing but tonight's entertainment.

This is going to be good.

The things he did to me, the things he forced me into, the pain and suffering he's caused, it's all going to come to an end. No other woman will suffer at his hands, no other child will bear the scars of his abuse. There's no amount of pain we can inflict on him that would ever make up for the torment he's rained down over the people closest to him, but we're sure as hell going to try.

I bet the asshole is pacing back and forth, trying to figure out how he's going to see this through, how he's going to rise again, how he's going to put himself back at the top of the food chain. I bet he's panicking, bet he's frothing at the mouth with fear. After all, only a pussy would have run from that mansion after strapping a bomb to his child's nursemaid. He knew we were coming, knew we were going to defeat him, and he was a bitch who slipped away, too scared to face the wrath of what he'd done.

Not anymore. It ends here.

If he knew we were just outside, ready and waiting to make our move, I'm sure he would run. He would slip his bitch ass through the small bathroom window and make a break for it, but he thinks he's safe, thinks he's gotten away with something. Proving him wrong is going to be the highlight of my night.

I can't wait to see the fear in his eyes. This is going to be one of those sweet bedtime stories that I'm going to share with the baby, and he's going to grow, learning of the wonders of this night, and knowing every damn moment of it was nothing short of perfection.

I mean, does that make me a bad sort-of-mom? Maybe telling him bedtimes stories about murdering his rapist sperm-donor isn't exactly a decision other Moms would make. Though, I can't say other Moms are really in our unique situation with two psychopathic uncles who thrive on bloodlust and a Father who can snap a neck in two seconds flat.

Yeah, there's no doubt about it. This child is going to be raised in Roman's image and hone that same incredible skill set to ensure he thrives when it comes his time to rule over the DeAngelis mafia. And I don't doubt that it will happen. I'm sure of it. He will rise just as the boys have. However, he will do it with warmth in his heart and pride for his family, and when that day comes, the boys will happily hand him the reins knowing he will take this family to new heights. Though, he sure as fuck has big shoes to fill.

By the time this baby is grown and taking over, the boys will have taken the DeAngelis family to heights they never thought possible. They're going to exceed the expectations of the Moretti family and dominate. They will be the most powerful family in the world and nothing can change my mind.

"Alright," Levi says. "We've got the drop on him. He doesn't know we're here. Let's take our shot before he decides to look out the window."

Not gonna lie, the guy has a good fucking point.

My hand curves into the small door lever, and I pop it open, holding my breath as if that's going to somehow make the sound of the car door opening any less loud. I mean, damn. It sounds like a fucking gunshot in the night.

I gently close the door, holding up the handle as I push it closed before carefully releasing the lever, a smile pulling at my lips remembering how I'd done this exact thing when the baby had his first sleep after getting him home.

We left him at home, obviously. I mean, we're not the world's most experienced baby watchers, but we're not about to drag him to his first murder at such a young age. We might wait a few years before corrupting his little mind. At least, I know most of us will. Marcus on the other hand … I'm not so sure about that one.

We left the baby in the care of our new nanny with strict instructions to the Moretti men remaining at the mansion to watch her with a keen eye. While she's already proven to be some kind of epic baby whisperer, she's still someone I haven't learned to trust yet.

Slipping through the silent night, we keep to the shadows, moving around the sole street light as the rain kisses my skin. We hurry across the cracked pavement, our black hoodies pulled high over our heads.

Roman and Marcus slip deeper into the night before taking off at a run down the side alley, out of sight, out of mind, while Levi and I stick like glue to the side of the building.

Giovanni is up on the second level of the rundown motel, and to be honest, it seems like a risky move. If he needed to make a quick getaway, a ground level room would have been more appropriate. But who am I to judge the actions of men who should know better?

Gripping on to the handle of the old metal staircase, I launch myself up them two at a time. Levi follows closely on my heels, and my heart hammers erratically, despite knowing just how simple this is going to be. The idea of seeing his face again has haunted me since the night he stole what innocence I had left, and now, I'll be taking whatever pathetic shreds of life he holds on to.

I can't wait. It's like going to the circus for the first time and not knowing what to expect. The blood rushes through my veins, pumping adrenaline and making my heart race with excitement. My hands shake and I feel jittery, but right now, I feel more alive than when the boys are buried deep inside of me.

Tonight, Giovanni DeAngelis becomes our bitch.

Despite skipping the steps two at a time, Levi beats me to the top, somehow managing to do it in complete silence while I sound like a fucking truck bogged down in wet concrete. We hit the top level and I keep close on his heels as we propel ourselves around the corner and disappear into the shadows of the building.

All the other rooms seem somewhat deserted, but we keep quiet anyway, not willing to risk giving ourselves away at such a crucial time.

We creep toward the door with the number 14 plastered on the front.

The curtains are doing a shit job of keeping him concealed and cast a dim glow across the pavement in front of his room. He's still pacing, and as we position ourselves in front of his door, I can't help but glance up at Levi to find that same twisted excitement shining through his eyes.

He grins down at me and damn it, why do I want to fuck him so bad right now?

*Time and place, Shayne, and this seriously isn't it.*

*Don't think about drums. Don't think about drums. Don't think about drums.*

Without wasting another second, Levi brings his heavy boot up and slams it against the cheap wooden door. It splinters perfectly under his force, flying off the hinges and sailing right into the room. We storm through the small opening just as Giovanni spins around, his eyes wide.

His hand automatically goes for a gun, but the fuckhead has left it on the nightstand across the room, but I suppose that's what you expect from a man who has never dealt with his own dirty work.

We've barely even made our move and the asshole is already cornered. Giovanni stands in front of the bed, just a few steps away from the bathroom, and without a moment of hesitation, he takes off like a bat out of hell.

Levi doesn't even bother going after him as Roman and Marcus stride out of the bathroom, smug, shit-eating grins wide on their faces. Giovanni skids to a halt, his eyes wide with fear as he quickly backs up, desperately searching for some other way out, but he's got nowhere to go. We have him completely surrounded, and my heart has never been so happy.

"Well, well," Roman says from behind him as he begins to back up against the wall, putting himself in a position to see each of us at the same time. "You certainly are a hard man to track down. Hard—" he continues, "but not impossible."

Color drains from Giovanni's face and panic flares from his eyes as we all begin to creep toward him. "You're going to regret this," he spits.

Marcus howls with laughter. "Regret, Father? Was it not you who taught us to regret nothing? Congratulations, all your hard learned lessons are about to pay off. We're exactly what you created us to be."

His gaze snaps to me, fury boiling in his eyes. "YOU. This is all your doing. If you hadn't corrupted their minds with your bullshit, they'd be the perfect soldiers. Now they're nothing but lap dogs," Giovanni spits at me and I laugh.

"Oh, my wicked little husband, your sons would have destroyed you with or without me. Don't pretend like you haven't seen this coming for years. It was only a matter of time, but now that time has come, and there's nothing standing in our way. You've abused them all their lives, you locked them up and tormented them in the worst ways, but now, the tables have turned and all that pent up aggression and rage they feel toward you is finally going to be set free. I'd prepare myself if I were you," I taunt, "because until the moment they finally bless you with death, you're going to experience the most excruciating pain of your life. You're going to beg for death, you're going to weep for forgiveness, and you're going to regret ever crossing your sons."

And with that, Marcus moves toward his father, his fist cracking out like lightning and knocking him out cold. He spins around, a grin ripping across his face as he takes in his cracked knuckles, his eyes sparkling with excitement. "Oooh, that felt good."

----------

Giovanni hangs in the padded cell that Levi was held captive in only a few short nights ago. His body hangs limply and I'm not going to lie, there's already a foul stench coming off him. If we had our own way, we would have driven back out to the castle to use the boys' playground. It's filled with all the finest toys, and I'm sure the boys would have enjoyed using every single one of them, but that's an extra two hours away and we simply couldn't wait to get our hands on him.

Levi steps forward with a bucket of ice water and throws it at his father, watching with a satisfied smirk at the way Giovanni gasps and his head snaps up. His eyes widen with fear as he pulls against his binds and I see the very moment he realizes that this wasn't some fucked-up dream.

"Ahh," Marcus says, casually leaning against the back wall, a knife flipping between his fingers. "So nice of you to join us." He pushes off the wall and slowly walks toward his father. "You just know how much I love doing things as a family. Good times."

Giovanni spits at him. "I will end you, boy. Release me now."

"Even in death, you think you hold power over us," Marc muses. "It's nice to see that some things never change."

"The family won't stand for this," Giovanni growls, anger flashing in his eyes as he pulls against the binds again. "They'll have your heads for this and they won't stop until you're buried, your little bitch too."

Marc laughs and moves in closer to his face before pointing to the small space above the door. "You mean the family who gave their full support?" he questions before sending a cheesy as fuck grin toward the camera. "Say hi, they're all watching. The Morettis too. It's like their own personal snuff film, though I have to admit, it's a lot of pressure, all those eyes on us. But don't worry, I have a few tricks up my sleeve. I'm sure they'll be thoroughly entertained."

Roman stands by my side, looking bored with Marcus' theatrics, but I know deep down he's getting a wicked kick out of it, just as I am. "Come on, brother. There's only so long I will wait before stepping in."

Marcus tsks him, holding up a finger and wagging it at him. "Now, now, Roman. Play fair. You know the rules," he taunts. "The laws of rock, paper, scissors must be upheld."

Roman rolls his eyes and Marcus turns his attention back to his father. "Do you remember when I was six? That was the first time you beat me black and blue. For what? Mouthing off like every kid is supposed to do." Marcus' fist slams into Giovanni's gut, winding him, and the sound is like music to my ears. He hits him again, his fist striking out across his jaw and colliding with his face with the force of a freight train, knocking his teeth right out of his mouth.

Marcus laughs, getting the sickest enjoyment out of this, and all I can do is smile. It's such a precious moment. I hope he pressed record on the live stream because there's no doubt in my mind that he'll want to watch this back.

Giovanni spits a mouthful of blood at Marcus and Marcus just laughs a little louder. "I'm surprised father, you've always been so put together. Surely you're not going to resort to spitting now?"

He walks around him and Giovanni keeps his stare straight ahead, refusing to let Marcus break him, but it won't be long. He'll be nothing but a shell before Marcus is even close to handing him over to Levi.

Marcus moves back in front of his father. "What about when I was eight and I found that stray puppy?" he says, a hint of anger in his obsidian eyes. The tip of his knife presses to Giovanni's stomach, and I catch my breath, watching with wide eyes. "He had a broken leg and I nursed him back to health. He was the first thing I loved and you held a knife to my throat while forcing me to snap his neck. It gutted me," Marcus says. "Do you know what that felt like?"

Without waiting for a response, Marcus slowly pushes against the knife, piercing through his stomach. Giovanni cries out in agony while Marcus relentlessly keeps going, his positioning perfect. Deep enough to cause the worst kind of agony, but not enough for him to bleed out before we've had our fun.

What can I say? Marcus is a gentleman like that.

Marcus goes on, tormenting his father in the worst way, burning him like he'd been burned, cutting him like he had been. Every foul memory living in the darkest parts of Marcus' mind are recreated and freed from ever tormenting him again.

Forty-five minutes pass before Giovanni is black and blue and the true horror of what Marcus has suffered at his father's hands comes to light. My heart shatters for him, but with each passing second, Marcus holds his head higher, the weight lifting off his shoulders.

Marcus steps aside, knowing if he doesn't stop now, he'll end up killing him before his brothers have had their chance to experience that same sense of relief. His eyes sparkling like it's Christmas morning, he asks, "Who's up next?"

Levi's tongue rolls over his bottom lip, his eyes darkening with murderous rage. He walks over to his father and just stares at him, his shoulders pulled back with pride. "You never held the power to break us," he tells him. "You tried. Fuck, did you try, but you never succeeded. All you did was ensure that when the time came, we were more than capable to see it through. You didn't just create soldiers, you turned us into weapons to use at your beck and call, but what's the first rule of playing with weapons, Father? Be sure of your target and what's beyond it. You were always our target, right from the start, and you were too damn self-involved to see it."

"Out of everything you want to say, boy," Giovanni spits. "That's the best you could come up with? You were never going to be strong enough for this life. You're weak."

He doesn't waste any more time before reaching up and releasing the chains that hold him up. Giovanni falls heavily to the ground, his bloodied body sprawling out as Marcus and Roman move in with heavy restraints. They're placed over Giovanni's wrists and ankles, and just like that, Giovanni is nothing but a demon with his wings pinned.

Levi settles himself over his father's chest, his knees on either side of Giovanni's face, those strong thighs making it impossible for Giovanni to turn away. And damn, I can't say he's ever sat on me like that, but I just know Giovanni's lungs are threatening to give out under the weight.

"That's just your issue, Father," Levi laughs, pulling a short dagger from the sheath at his side. "You've never *seen* us for what we are, but don't worry. We've always *seen* you." He leans forward, the tip of the knife dragging across his skin and leaving a trail of blood. "You've always been so blind to the world around you, but a blind man does not need his eyes to see."

And just like that, the tip of the sharp dagger hits his eye.

Levi digs into his socket, the knife working its magic as Giovanni screams out, the blood-curdling sound sending shivers crawling across my skin. Blood pours from his eye as Levi severs the ligaments and muscles attaching his eye to his face, and after getting bored with the knife, he throws it aside and replaces it with his fingers.

He pries his eyeball right out of his head as his father screams, and I swear that Levi doesn't even hear it. It's as though he's so taken with his task at hand that the rest of the world has fallen away, and I don't blame him.

A moment passes when Levi stands off his father's chest and holds the bloodied eyeball up to the light, a grin stretching across his face, pride settling into his handsome face. He nods to himself, as if completely satisfied and as he goes to toss the eyeball aside, a gasped squeak tears from the back of Marcus' throat.

Levi glances up at him to see his hand outstretched and a pleading desperation in his eyes. Levi sighs and tosses him the eyeball and Marcus scoops it out of the air before grinning manically and slipping the fucking thing straight into his pocket.

"That's it?" Roman questions as Levi falls back beside me. Levi nods and Roman grunts. "Huh, figured you'd be throwing punches for hours."

Levi shrugs before his eyes bug out of his head and he rushes forward before Roman gets a chance to take over. Levi crouches down and tears the family rings off his father's fingers. "You won't be needing these," he says, looking all too smug. I don't really understand the significance of the rings, but where Levi is involved, I'm sure it's just another knife right through the back.

Leaving his father for Roman, Levi moves away and I watch as Roman kicks the heavy restraints off his father's wrists and ankles. The fucker curls into a ball, gripping on to the worsening wounds at his waist, courtesy of Marcus.

Roman scoffs, looking down at the sight before him. "Pathetic."

He shakes his head, and I can practically see all the comments on the end of his tongue, yet none of them are worthy of being voiced, nothing strong enough to convey his intense disgust. So instead of giving a whole spiel about how his father has fucked with his life since the moment he could walk, Roman simply reaches for the heavy chain dangling from the ceiling.

He pulls it down and binds his wrists before nodding toward

Marcus, who hits a button. The chains immediately begin retracting, lifting Giovanni up until his feet are dangling above the blood-soaked ground.

Giovanni stares back at his eldest son through his one remaining eye, not even having the energy to spit at him. Blood trails down his face and I'm pretty damn sure he pissed his pants, but the way he looks at Roman, it's clear that he fears him most. Marcus is unhinged in the most brutal ways and Levi … Levi is as fucked as they come, but Roman … Roman plays the game. Roman is the silent one, always thinking, always planning. He's ruthless.

"You're done taking from me," Roman tells him. "Ariana. Felicity. Shayne. You took them from me and you poisoned them with yourself, but you underestimated Shayne. She can't be held down, and the only reason why I haven't ended your life yet is because I think she deserves it more."

Giovanni's eye flickers toward me and I'm met with nothing but fear. "Have you heard the news, father? The priest accidentally fucked up the paperwork. She was never yours. It's funny how easy it is to make just the slightest amendment to a marriage certificate. Though, I guess I've got you to thank for that. If you weren't so egotistical in giving me your name, it might not have been so easy."

Giovanni's face falls, realizing exactly what we've been up to, but Roman's not nearly done twisting the blade in his back. "You made the biggest mistake of your life the day you set your vile sights on her. Look at her, look how she shines. You didn't break her, you only made her realize just how fucking strong she is. Shayne's going to take your life and then she's going to be worshipped as the leader of the Moretti empire for the rest of her life. She holds the power, and you will die knowing that everything you worked toward, everything you poisoned with your venom was all for nothing."

Roman laughs and takes a step back before pulling his gun. He lets off two perfect shots and I jump with the suddenness, the sound booming through my chest. Giovanni cries out, heavy groans and whimpers filling the room as both his knees bleed.

Roman doesn't outright grin like his brothers had done, but I see the sick enjoyment in his eyes, and it gets me hot. There's nothing like these men when they're in the zone.

He walks across the room to a small table and scans over the selection of tools he placed there a little over an hour ago. He glances back at his father and considers his condition, knowing that whatever he does to him has to leave his heart beating, and if I'm completely honest, if I don't get to hear him scream when I put my hands on him, I'm going to be pissed.

Roman picks up sharp needle-like pins, at least thirty centimeters long while also reaching for a hammer. I don't see how many of the needle pins he grabs, but I hear the metal in his hands and know there's got to be at least four of them.

Stepping up in front of his father, he places the pins at his feet, keeping just one in his hand and the hammer in his other. He scans over his father's naked torso, looking past the wounds Marcus left behind. "I'm not going to lie, Father. This isn't going to be comfortable but please, be a good sport and try not to move."

Then without a second of hesitation, he presses the tip to his father's skin, directly between his ribs and slams the hammer against the end. The pin pierces through his skin and Roman hammers it again, letting the pin perforate his lung.

A giddy satisfaction tears through me and I peek toward Marcus and Levi who both watch with cocky, delighted grins on their handsome faces. I've seen the boys do some really fucked-up things, but this is a whole new level of twisted.

The pin protrudes from his body and even the slightest flinch would have agony tearing through his body. But Roman DeAngelis has never been the type to stop after one, trust me, I know.

He scoops another pin off the ground and presses it to the hollow just beneath his shoulder before going ham on his ass. The pin pierces through his shoulder and Roman keeps going until he sees the bloodied tip from his father's back.

Pin number three goes through his thigh while the fourth and final goes horizontally through his waist, starting above his left hip and piercing through to the right. It's a masterpiece, absolutely brilliant.

Considering himself thoroughly satisfied, Roman turns and meets my eyes. "You ready?"

I stare at him in wonder. "I'm gonna fuck you so hard when we're done here."

"Damn straight, you will."

And with that, Roman steps aside and lets me at him.

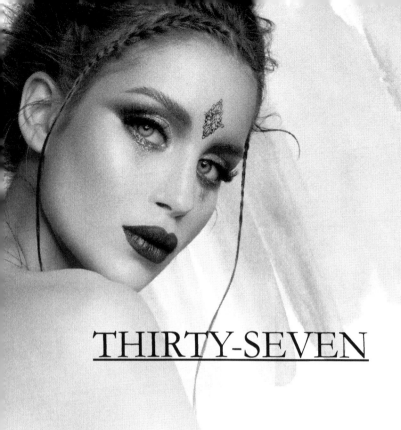

# THIRTY-SEVEN

Slipping my hand into big, thick rubber gloves and pulling them right up to my shoulders, I get myself ready to stare down the man who abused the boys, the man who caused them insufferable pain, murdered their mother, and stole from them for years. The man who locked them up and nearly slaughtered them on the lawn outside their family home.

This is the man who's raped multiple woman, slaughtered Ariana's family, forced her into a loveless marriage, and stole her away from Roman, breaking his heart for the first time. The man who forced himself on Felicity, who got her pregnant and locked her in a cell where she birthed her child in fear and bled out. The man who sold countless women and children into slavery, and the man who then forced himself on me.

He tried to own me like he's done in the past, tried to destroy me and plague my heart with fear, but he picked the wrong bitch to fuck with.

He hangs limply, pins sticking out all over his body, gaping bullet holes where his knees used to be, stab wounds, and a missing eye. And honestly, he's never looked so good. At least, through my eyes.

Giovanni doesn't have the energy to lift his head, but something tells me that when it comes down to it, he'll find whatever energy he needs to settle that raging need for anguish inside my chest.

Picking up my tool, I stride across the padded cell and grin at the fucker. "Well, hello there. Fancy meeting you down here," I say. "I trust your stay has been welcoming."

A deep growl tears through his chest and I laugh, searching the area around me. "You'll have to forgive me, I have so many things and nowhere to put them," I say, before looping the handle of the big scissors over the pin protruding from his ribs. I drop their weight against it and smile sweetly and he growls with agony. "Ahhh, yes. This is perfect."

I step in nice and close before gripping the front of his pants and tearing them open. The loose trousers fall to his ankles and I laugh, looking at the piss stains on the front of his old man boxers. "Ahhh, shit. Good thing I've got my gloves on," I tell him before winking, just to drive the humiliation home. "But it's okay, I'm sure it happens to everyone."

Gripping the edges of his boxers, I yank them down and expose his limp cock, not at all impressed with what I'm seeing. Though, I already knew that. I wasn't impressed then, and I'm sure as hell not impressed now. "Wow, you really don't have much in common with your sons, huh?" I ask, because why the hell not insult the size of his dick? "It's okay, between you and me, it's not like you're going to have much use for it anymore."

I go to grab it when it occurs to me that I really don't have much experience in this area. I whip around, meeting Marcus' heavy stare, and damn, the way he's looking at me, might just have me postponing this little adventure. But I won't dare. We've more than learned our lesson about following through. If I don't do this right now, there's a good chance when we return, one of his loyal followers would have figured out how to bust his stupid ass out of here, and that simply won't do.

Marcus arches his brow, wondering what I could possibly need. "If I just like … chop it off, is he going to bleed out too fast?"

Marcus nods and holds his hand up, making a tight circle between his fingers. "Clamp that thing like a cock ring and you shouldn't have any issues, plus you won't get as drenched in blood."

I give him a wide smile and bat my lashes, feeling all the love in the world. "Thanks."

Marcus winks and I turn back to Giovanni. "Well, I can't say that I've really gone fishing through Gia's bedside drawers but something tells me that she's a boring fuck, so we're probably shit outta luck with the whole cock ring thing," I tell him. "But never you mind, I'm crafty at the best of times."

Reaching up, I pull the hair elastic out of my hair and a shiver sails down my spine at the feel of the thick rubber moving against my hair. I hold his dick up and tie the elastic around it before deciding a second loop is needed. It sure ain't pretty, but it'll do.

Giovanni grunts and I laugh. "What's the matter, lover? I thought you liked it rough?" I question. "But just between you and me, if you hadn't touched me, I would have found some other way to end you. You could have died with your manhood right where it's supposed to be, but I don't belong to you, and men that touch what isn't theirs need to be taught a lesson, even if they won't be around to right their wrongs."

I flick the end of his tip, checking the blood flow and smirk as he flinches, making each of the pins adjust inside his body. I wait a moment for the elastic to do its thing and smile up at the asshole, playing his own twisted game. "Hickory dickory dock," I grin. "Giovanni's losing his cock."

Marcus muffles a laugh behind me, and I glance back over my shoulder meeting his stare again, my brows bouncing with smugness, and hell, if that makes me just as unhinged as he is, then so be it.

Roman crosses his arms over his chest and leans back against the wall, ready to watch his father perish, a bored expression on his chiseled face while Levi's hands fidget at his sides, the anticipation slowly killing him.

Turning back to Giovanni, I unhook the scissors from the pin sticking out between his ribs and slip my fingers into the holes. "Just so you know," I whisper, meeting his one-eyed terrified stare. "I'm going to take this nice and slow."

Gripping his dick, I open the scissors and press the cold metal against the base of his cock. After all, I want to get as much of it as I possibly can if it's going to have a special space up on my trophy shelf that Roman will no doubt build for me.

Giovanni sucks in a breath, his eye wide and filled with unshed tears and fear, and with that, I get this show on the road. I squeeze down on the scissors, watching the sharp blades dig into his flesh. Giovanni screams and it's like the sweetest music to my ears.

Blood pours and I cringe. Perhaps I should have waited a little longer for the elastic to do its thing, but hell, I have gloves. Reopening the scissors, I go again and again, and while the blades are sharp, I still need a few tries to get through the flesh and muscle.

It's a hack job at best, but it's the best fun I've ever had, and when his cock finally comes free in my hand, his balls still sadly attached, I glance up to find his face white as a ghost and on the brink of passing out. He's not going to last much longer and a part of me hates that it will happen so quickly. The whole point of the elastic was so I could drag this out, but it is what it is.

Turning around, I meet Roman's eyes before sending the amputated dick hurtling through the air. "Think quick."

His reflexes have his hand snapping out and catching the dick midair before his face pales and he throws it at Marcus, who clearly has no issues holding his father's limp cock. "Fucking hell, babe. Not cool," he says, his face scrunching in disgust. "Now I'm going to have to shower."

"Wait," I say, pausing as I stare at him in concern. "You weren't planning on showering after this? And you were going to let me fuck you? Gross, Roman."

He rolls his eyes and lets out a huff, probably with a smartass comment on the tip of his tongue, but Marcus laughs and holds the bloody cock up against Roman's forehead. "Look, babe. Roman really is a dickhead."

Roman's fist has never moved faster. He lands a brutal punch to Marcus' jaw, sending him flying across the room, but he doesn't dare drop the dick. I go to bitch out Roman but he's already across the padded cell, hurling his guts up into a basin, a splatter of blood across his forehead.

I shake my head and turn back to Giovanni as the boys right themselves. "To be honest," I say to the guys, "I haven't really put much thought into anything further than cutting off his dick, but it feels wrong to take the kill when you all deserve it so much more."

Levi moves into my back, his hands at my waist and he breathes me in, the smell of blood in the air. "What do you want to do? The call is yours."

All my options fly through my head as I watch Giovanni beginning to bleed out. He's weak and there's no way in hell he'll be able to fight back at this point. A kill from the boys almost seems merciful, too easy. "Dill," I finally say, remembering the day I ran after him into the woods around the DeAngelis mansion. "He deserves to get a piece of him too."

Levi nods and steps away from me. "Consider it done."

Levi moves out of the cell and I watch him walk toward the small elevator. He presses the button and within moments, he's gone.

Moving across the room, I pull the big black gloves off my arms and drop them to the ground before putting myself in front of Roman. I take his hand in mine and shake my head as I find his knuckles split and a trail of blood trickling down the length of his skilled fingers. "You know, I hate that you've probably bruised Marc's pretty little face, but you know how the violence turns me on."

Roman grips my chin, his fingers biting into my skin, and before I can even catch my breath, his mouth is crushing down on mine in a bruising, dominant kiss. His tongue pushes into my mouth and I plaster my body up against his, feeling his cock hardening against my waist.

I hear Marcus moving behind us just as the soft ding of the elevator sounds Levi's return. Roman breaks our kiss and I turn to find Giovanni in a broken heap on the ground as Levi strides into the cell with Dill on one side and Doe on the other.

Dill growls at seeing the man who put a bullet through his hip, and I watch as Levi makes a hand gesture that has Doe sitting at his side. Dill's growls become more vicious and without having to tell the giant wolf why he's here, he's already figured it out. "Dill," I say, gaining his attention as I stand back, giving him space to work. "He's all yours."

And just like that, Dill attacks, his ferocious sharp teeth snapping into Giovanni's flesh like a vise and tearing him into ribbons. Blood splatters wildly across the room, as gurgled cries tear through the cell.

His arm is torn clean off his body and not a moment later, Dill tears out his throat, his teeth piercing straight through the artery.

Blood spurts, and not a moment later, Giovanni DeAngelis is dead.

# THIRTY-EIGHT

S tepping out of my bathroom, I curl my hair up into a bun and secure it with a clip. It wasn't easy getting all of that blood out of my hair, but now that I have, I feel a million times better. I grab my champagne-colored silk robe and slip my arms inside before tying it loosely at my waist, a smile playing on my lips.

Giovanni DeAngelis is dead.

Roman, Levi, and Marcus are the leaders of the DeAngelis mafia family.

And I ... a shiver tracks down my spine. I mean, technically I know how I became the leader of the Moretti family, but HOW THE FUCK DID THIS HAPPEN? It's going to take me a long time to wrap my head around this one and become okay with it all. On the plus side, I will never have to starve again or worry about the electricity going out in the dead of winter.

The guys disappeared to shower and I'm almost certain that Marcus sped through his just to give himself a few extra minutes to prop his father's dick up in a display case. Though at some point, he's going to have to show me how to preserve this shit, especially if this is the way our lives are going to continue.

Padding out of my room, I venture downstairs and into the main living room before finding my way toward the bar. The boys are bound to be a minute longer. Roman went to check on the baby while Marcus is dealing with the floppy dick, and Levi, he just tends to take long showers. I can only imagine what he does in there, and honestly, I'm a little jealous every time I'm not invited.

Today is cause for celebration. The boys have been needing this for so long, way before I was even a thought inside their incredible heads, and after the hell they've suffered through, they more than deserve it.

Grabbing myself a champagne flute and a couple of tumblers, I fill them with all of our preferred drinks—only the best champagne for me, the most expensive whiskey for Roman and Marcus, and bourbon for Levi.

I've barely finished filling the glass when Levi strides through the door, his eyes coming directly to mine and filling my chest with the kind of warmth that only he and his brothers are capable of. I've never known this kind of love. I've had plenty of boyfriends and plenty of guys slipping into my bed, but not once did I ever feel the way that they make me feel. I will never give up on that, it's my addiction, my drug, and I'm all in.

"You good?" he asks, striding toward me, those tattoos peeking out of the top of his shirt and curling up around his strong neck. That just-showered, manly smell wraps around me, and my knees immediately go weak, a heaviness settling into the pit of my stomach, something only he can take away.

"Fine," I tell him, a slight blush spreading over my cheeks as my pussy begins to throb, needing his touch like never before. I don't remember a time where we haven't had bullshit or death threats resting on our shoulders, and now that it's just me and him, I truly get a chance to enjoy him, and damn it, tell me why the hell I feel so shy?

Levi steps right up to the bar, leaning across to take my chin between his fingers, forcing my stare back to his. "Are you blushing?" he murmurs, his deep tone wrapping around me and holding me hostage. "What have you got to be shy about? I have literally sat in front of you and watched the way you fuck yourself."

My cheeks redden further and his eyes blaze with desire. I lift my chin higher, silently begging for his kiss. "You like it when my skin reddens under your touch?" I tease.

Levi growls and releases my chin, and not a second later, he propels himself over the bar and plasters his body to mine, taking my waist in his strong, capable hands, my glass of champagne long forgotten. "I fucking love you," he murmurs. "You know that one of these days, I'm going to lock my brothers in that cell downstairs and have you to myself."

Raising my chin, I brush my lips over his. "I don't doubt it," I tell him. "I might just be the one locking the cuffs into place."

His lips capture mine and he kisses me deeply, his tongue fighting mine for dominance. I melt into him, my fingers knotting into the front of his shirt as I try to pull him in closer. I feel his heart beating through his chest and it's all I can do not to reach in and claim it for myself.

Footsteps pad across the room, but I don't dare take my attention off Levi, taking in his warm caresses against my skin, that manly scent holding me hostage and making a flood appear between my legs. His body is so big pressed up against mine, and I can't get enough.

I hear a glass sliding along the table and the way it's immediately slammed back down for more tells me it's Marcus. I reluctantly pull away to find him reaching for the whiskey and refilling his glass. "I was wondering if you'd come up for air," he murmurs, lifting his glass to his lips again.

My eyes sparkle as I lean against the bar, the shoulder of my silk gown slipping and exposing the freshly showered skin beneath. "Jealous?" I tease.

He captures my stare and holds it, his eyes darkening with hunger. "Immensely."

A shiver trails down my body and I groan at the way Levi's hand finds my ass and squeezes through the flimsy fabric. I press back into his touch as Marcus slowly stands, refusing to release my stare.

He holds me captive as he leans across the bar and I suck in a breath, the anticipation burning through my veins. His fingers brush across my shoulder and a shiver sails down my spine as his lips finally meet mine. He kisses me slowly, gently, and with the kind of passion that has my heart thundering in my chest. Droplets of water remain in his hair from his shower and drip onto my face just as his hand trails up from my shoulder and closes around the base of my throat.

Levi moves in closer, his hand dropping lower down the back of my thigh and bunching up the silk robe between his thick fingers. His fingers brush against my bare skin and I gasp into Marcus' mouth, groaning as his fingers sail straight back up my inner thigh.

A scoff comes from across the room and Roman's deep tone caresses my ears. "Couldn't fucking wait for two seconds."

I grin against Marcus' lips and he pulls back before turning to his eldest brother. "You snooze, you lose, bro," he says, throwing himself over the bar just as Levi's fingers brush against my core, making me gasp and push back against him, feeling the way he pushes those thick fingers into my cunt.

I bite down on my lip as my eyes roll in the back of my head. "Oh fuck, Levi," I groan, my approval pushing him deeper. "Yes."

Marcus moves to my other side, his hand going back to my throat and squeezing just enough to make me catch my breath. He uses his hold to draw me up off the edge of the bar, changing the angle in which Levi's fingers massage against my inner walls.

Marcus tilts my head back and captures my lips in his once again, this time kissing me deeper, hungrier, with a determination that has a delicious groan sounding from across the room. "Fuck, no," Roman murmurs, maybe to himself. "Not without me."

Roman strides across the room, launching himself over the bar just as his brothers had, and if I were in any state to think for myself, I'd probably be scolding them for not using the perfectly good entrance just a few steps away. But I'm not complaining, watching the way their muscles bulge when they do anything even a little athletic gets me wet—much like Levi's fingers buried deep in my pussy.

A deep hunger settles into my chest as I turn to Marcus and kiss him deeper. His hands skim along the edge of the fabric, roaming down until he reaches the loose knot barely holding the robe together. He gives it a gentle tug and it comes undone like putty in his hands, the silky fabric quickly parting and flowing down off my shoulders.

I let it fall to the floor and not a moment later, I feel Levi's warm chest against my back. His fingers pull out of me, drawing back to my ass as his head dips to my neck, his mouth closing over my skin. His tongue brushes over the thrumming pulse in my throat before working up to the sensitive skin below my ear. "Be a good girl and spread those pretty thighs," he murmurs.

Oh, dear God. If Levi brings out his daddy kink to play while both Marcus and Roman are already touching me, I'm going to come before I even let out another breath.

A shudder of raw anticipation trails down my spine, and I groan as I spread my thighs, opening up for them. Roman takes my chin, gently drawing my face to meet his, his eyes narrowed with curiosity as Marcus' fingers trail down my body, finding my clit and gently brushing over it.

My eyes remain locked on Roman's while all too focused on the feel of Marcus' fingers. "You liked that, didn't you?" Roman questions, his hungry stare eating me up. "When he called you a good girl."

I hold his stare, letting him see just how worked up his brothers have got me. "Only when I get to call him daddy."

A grin pulls at Roman's lips as Levi groans, his chest vibrating against my back, and damn it, my words have his fingers pressing into my ass. I gasp, my breath catching in my throat before a strangled groan tears from deep in my chest.

"Well, damn," Roman says, his gaze dropping with his hand, trailing down my sensitive skin and brushing over my pebbled nipples. He gives one a gentle squeeze before continuing down and making me suck in a gasp as his fingers tickle my waist.

Marcus moves his hand, making room for Roman as he travels down further. I groan as he pushes between my spread thighs and finds my clit impatiently waiting for his touch. He circles it with his skilled fingers and I grind down against him, needing so much more … needing all three of them.

"Patience, Empress. You'll get what you want."

Holy fuck. How do they do this to me?

His voice is like a purr in my ear, filled with the most delicious kind of promises, and I can't help but turn to him and capture his lips in mine. He kisses me greedily, and I remember the man from down in the cell, the man I'd promised to fuck hard, and I fully intend to come through on that.

Levi pushes into my ass deeper and I can't help but press back against him, taking more. "You want me to fuck your tight little ass, baby?"

I groan, my eyes rolling as Roman's fingers dive deeper, pressing up into my cunt, his thumb still working my clit. "You can fuck me any way you want," I say on a breathy moan, all three of them more than pleased by my answer.

Unbelievable pleasure rocks through me and I grip on to Marcus' shirt, my fingers knotted for only a brief second before sliding down his rock-hard abs to find his cock. He's in a pair of sweatpants that leave absolutely nothing to the imagination and are no obstacle when getting to what I want.

Pushing his pants down over his hips, his cock springs free, dropping heavily into my hands, and I instinctively roll my tongue over my lips. "Hungry, baby?"

My eyes burn with desire. "Famished."

"So, what are you waiting for?"

Goddamn.

Holding his stare with mine, I bend at my waist, spreading my legs wider until I feel his tip right at my lips. I open wide and guide him into my mouth, taking all of him until I feel him deep in my throat. He groans, and I roll my tongue over his tip, gripping his shaft with my tight fist.

I start moving up and down, my eyes watering with how deep I take him, and just when I think they have all their bases covered, Levi draws his fingers out of my ass before I feel his cock springing free against my cheek.

I groan as everything clenches, which only forces a soft chuckle out of Roman who can more than feel my excitement. Levi's fingers slip back under my ass and I feel them push up into my cunt, mixing with my wetness and brushing against Roman's fingers, stretching me wider, and all too soon, his fingers are back at my ass, making sure I'm good and ready.

He takes my hip with one hand while guiding his cock to my entrance, and I can feel the bead of cum on his tip pressing to my hole. Roman's fingers slow, curving deep inside of me, slowly massaging and helping me prepare for Levi's thick intrusion.

I pause bobbing up and down on Marcus as Levi begins to push into me. He stretches me wide, and as I catch my breath, he pushes deeper. Roman's thumb rubs against my clit, and I let out a breath, relaxing around Levi as my knees shake with anticipation.

Levi begins to move, holding my hips as he takes me deeper then slowly pulls back. I gasp against Marcus' cock, and with Levi holding me still, Marcus starts to move in and out of my mouth, fucking me exactly how he wants.

They take it easy, fucking me slow and letting me feel every slight movement, every brush of skin against my body, every last stroke. Roman's fingers curve just right, massaging that spot deep inside of me, and I clench around his fingers as his other hand slowly strokes his own cock, and damn it, if my hands weren't busy holding me up, I'd be all over it. Though, there's no denying that watching a man like Roman DeAngelis stroke himself is the most erotic thing I've ever seen, and judging by the heated look in his eyes, he knows exactly what he's doing to me.

That familiar pull starts to grow deep in my core and my eyes close, the sensation taking over me, but when Levi's fingers grip my hip harder and his cock presses into me one more time, it's all fucking over.

My orgasm takes me by surprise, exploding throughout my body. I gasp around Marcus' thick cock as my ass clenches around Levi's. Roman's fingers keep working my G-spot and my eyes roll, the three of them watching me come undone.

My cunt spasms, convulsing and squeezing as Levi slowly draws back and forth, making it all that much more intense. My high pulses through my body, rocketing through my veins and raining havoc over every last nerve ending.

And just when I thought it couldn't get any better, Marcus comes, and that deliciousness hits the back of my throat. I swallow him greedily, taking everything he can give me, sucking hard as he comes undone in my mouth.

He groans my name before slowly pulling out of my mouth and meeting my heated stare, but all too soon, Levi's hands are curling around my ribs, pulling me back up straight. "I'm not nearly done with you," he mutters, making my pussy clench as Roman steps directly in front of me.

Levi's lips fall to my neck as Roman moves in close. "You ready to come through on that promise, Empress?"

A wicked grin stretches across my face as hunger surges through me once again. "Oh, I don't know if you can handle it," I tease.

Roman growls deep, his fists squeezing down around his veiny, thick cock. He reaches down, gripping my thigh and hitching it up high and to the side, opening me wide and exposing my most intimate parts while Levi's strong arm tightens around my ribs, holding me up.

Roman's tip glides over my clit and I groan as he guides it toward my entrance. Levi pauses his movements, giving us a chance to make this work.

Roman pushes into me and I grip his shoulder, my nails digging in as he stretches me wide, both of their thick cocks filling me to the brim. "Oh, fuck," I groan, heavy panting taking over as Marcus takes his drink and moves across the living room, his eyes locked heavily on the show, hooded and getting hungrier by the second. I don't doubt that he'll be ready for more the second he finds the bottom of his expensive whiskey.

Roman presses deeper just as Levi pulls back. I suck in a breath and Roman meets my eye. "I'm not planning on being gentle."

I hold his stare, the thrill pulsing through me. "Then what the fuck are you waiting for?" Levi groans behind me, and I grip on to Roman's shoulder tighter as my other hand curls around Levi's by my ribs, more than ready for a thorough fucking, and that's exactly what they give me.

Roman begins to move, fucking me hard and Levi matches his pace, one pushing deep inside of me while the other draws back. It's an erotic dance that has my eyes rolling in my head. "Oh, fuck," I groan, tipping my head back to Levi's shoulder as he moves our joined hands up to grip my tit.

He squeezes as Roman adjusts his angle, his new position leaving his pelvic bone to press against my clit. "YES," I groan, watching

Roman's face, the hunger driving me wild with need.

My pussy throbs, and I notice Marcus from the corner of my eye, his hand slipping inside his sweats as he stares back at me. I shake my head. "Let me watch."

He fucking grins, his eyes sparkling with an intense, wicked thrill that has everything clenching. That asshole. He knows what that cocky smile does to me. He stands, letting his cock spring free of his sweats and I take him all in. He's so fucking big—all three of them are. It's amazing they all fit at once.

Levi grunts, his jaw clenching. "Fuck, babe. Clench that ass one more time and you're going to tear my cock right off."

"What can I say?" I grin, looking back at him. "That's my specialty."

He growls and just like that, they fuck me even harder until all four of us are coming, the boys shooting hot spurts of cum deep into me as Marcus groans from across the room, his cum spilling out over his hand. My cunt spasms wildly as my orgasm pulses through me, a million times more intense than the first one.

Roman curls his fingers around my neck, bringing my eyes to his as my high rocks through every cell of my body. "That's right, Empress," he pants, catching his breath. "Don't you ever forget how good we give it."

I lean into his touch, my lips brushing against his wrist. "Not possible."

Levi gently pulls out of me, and I sag against Roman's chest, his arms curling around my body and holding me up. He releases my leg but refuses to pull out of me before lifting my ass back onto the bar and slowly moving in and out as he passes me my drink. "You're my fucking queen," he tells me as Levi finishes cleaning himself up and moves in beside us, collecting his drink while Marcus comes back over for another refill.

I tip the glass to my lips and take a greedy sip, my body exhausted and worn out, but I'm not going to lie, I'm liking that slow movement from Roman.

I drop my head against his. "I love you," I murmur, before shifting just a little to take Levi's hand. "All three of you. I feel like we finally have our shot at living our lives the way we want. There are no threats hanging over our heads, your father is rotting in hell with Gia, and we have the baby. I don't ever want this to change."

"It won't," Marcus promises, resting his elbows against the bar, his big shoulder pressing against my ribs. "But don't assume we won't ever have threats hanging over our heads. It's going to be a constant battle. The FBI are only just learning your name, and they're going to come for you at some point, but we will always have your back just as you've always had ours. Without you …" he pauses, his tongue rolling over his bottom lip as his eyes soften, meeting mine. "Without you, nothing is worth living for. The fucking money, the head of the family, the bloodshed, it's not worth it to me anymore, not without you."

A smile spreads across my face, and he raises up just a bit to capture my lips in his before kissing me deeply.

Levi grunts, throwing his drink back. "Is this the part where I'm supposed to say something equally sappy? Because honestly, get fucked. It ain't happening."

I laugh and shake my head, pulling away from Marcus. Levi said everything he had to say before Marcus and Roman even walked in. He's not the kind to say sentimental crap, especially in front of his brothers. He prefers privacy and I love that about him. "You know you're an idiot, right?"

Levi rolls his eyes and grips my chin, forcing my mouth to his. He kisses me just as Marcus has, only pushing his tongue inside my mouth demanding dominance, and I can just imagine the praise he'll give for allowing him to take what he wants.

Roman's gaze is heavy on my face as he begins to harden within me, and I find myself laying back on the bar, Levi coming down with me and lowering his warm lips to my body, worshipping me with his mouth. Roman thumbs my clit as he continues moving in and out, and Marcus takes his shot, standing and meeting my eye. He kisses me upside down and all too soon, I'm reaching for his cock, more than ready for round three.

# EPILOGUE

## 10 MONTHS LATER

The blindfold falls from my eyes and I stare up at the beautiful home that I've been drooling over for the past ten months, seeing it only on paper and hearing absolutely nothing about, apart from when Roman had a question about color schemes and styling.

It's driven me crazy. I've wanted nothing more than to escape their hold and get my ass out here, but they haven't made it easy. They wanted this to be a surprise, and now that I'm here staring up at the stunning home, I'm so glad they did.

"Holy shit," I breathe as Marcus' thumb trails over my knuckles, running back and forth. It looks exactly like the drawing. Roman's team got it just right. "It's beautiful."

We stand at the top of the property as I look on in awe. Every single inch of land has been beautifully landscaped—including a long, curved driveway with trees lining either side leading to the big circle before the mansion. Not to mention, the most stunning water feature directly in the center that draws your eye up to the home. Gardens surround the property, all beautifully designed to complement the home, but I wouldn't expect anything else from a perfectionist like Roman.

It's huge. There's no other way to describe it. Simply huge.

The house is modern with a flare of the boys' gothic style, while also including that elegance I love about the home that Gia built … not that I'm thrilled about admitting to liking anything Gia did, but there's no denying the bitch had style.

Every light in the house is on, including the lights that line the driveway, and as the sun sinks low in the sky, the entire property glows. I don't doubt that the boys picked this exact moment to show off the home because there's no denying that this is as good as it's going to get.

"This is really our home?" I ask, inwardly scolding myself for the tears that threaten to fill my eyes. I'm supposed to be at the top of the Moretti empire. I can't cry about this shit, but damn it, the tears are coming.

"Yep," Roman says, pressing his hand to my lower back and leading me toward the big house. "We each have our own wing—a private residence within our home, filled with everything we could need.

Three ballrooms, meeting rooms for family business, fully equipped training areas—one underground, plus another up on the rooftop. Fully stocked armory, garage big enough to fit both of our fleets, and of course, prison cells—one for people who mildly piss us off and another for those who will die at our hands."

"And what about a new and improved playground?" Roman's eyes sparkle and I don't need an answer to know that he went all out on it, probably the space he spent the most attention on with his brothers nit-picking over every little detail. "Shit, you didn't hold back."

"You deserve the best," Levi tells me. "The fucker even remembered my drums. At least, everywhere throughout my wing, plus a handful in our more common areas."

My pussy throbs to find and christen every last one of them, and judging by the look in Levi's eyes, he's thinking about the exact same thing. Fuck, there's nothing quite like drum sex. You know, apart from bar sex, and chain sex, rooftop sex, and being fucked with the handle of a knife sex.

The boys lead me toward the grand entrance, and I gaze up at the home that sits at the top of the stairs. There must be at least fifty steps leading just to the front door, and I gape at its beauty. I'm going to get a workout making my way up and down these stairs every day, but at least I can be certain that I won't get any random people knocking on my door trying to sell me shit.

Reaching the top step, I find myself thinking about just how much we've managed to achieve. Our lives haven't exactly been stress free. Claiming our titles within our families is one thing … but maintaining them and reaching expectations is another. I never realized how much politics were included in all of this. I figured I told people what I expected of them and then they killed themselves to make it happen … apparently there's a little more to it than that.

Not to mention the uproar when I suggested merging our two families to create the world's most unstoppable, lethal force. Some were down, others may have pulled guns and tried to make their disapproval a little too obvious. I was quick to make an example out of them and since then, we've slowly started the merge.

It's not going well. The Moretti and DeAngelis men are pig-headed. They're assholes and don't like to share. Who would have known, right? We're getting there though, and when we do, we'll be unstoppable.

I haven't seen Zeke—Agent Davidson—since before the war that saved our baby boy, but every now and then, I hear whispers about the FBI trying to move in on us, and I can't help but wonder if that's Agent Davidson sending me a message. I like to believe it. I like to think that after all of this, he still has my back, but I wouldn't blame him if he were to leave me to face the firing squad. He deserves to wash his hands of this shit and never look back. All those years standing at Gia's side and taking on tasks that went against everything he believes in … yeah, that couldn't have been easy.

Roman opens the floor-to-ceiling double doors and I gasp as I take in the unbelievable entrance. "Oh, my God," I breathe, stepping through to the circular foyer and taking it all in. There's a beautiful pattern in the marble tiles and stunning pillars framing the room and accentuating the high ceilings. A big double staircase curves around the edges of the foyer leading up to an open loft with stunning wrought-iron railings that I can't wait to explore, but for now, I move straight ahead, slowly scanning over every fine detail, and wondering who the hell the boys had to threaten to get this completed so quickly.

We walk straight ahead, leading under the stairs and into a formal living area where I assume our guests will wait to be blessed with our presence. The space is open and light, big windows in every possible space, such a stark contrast to the darkness of the castle that it breaks my heart. The boys were locked up tight in there, deprived of the simplest things that life has to offer—like sunlight. But not here. In our home, they will have everything they never knew they needed.

Pillars surround the room, and I follow them through to their adjoining spaces, scanning over the meeting rooms and wandering down to one of the many ballrooms, unable to stop imagining the parties we can hold.

The grand tour takes nearly an hour, and by the time I've seen everything and drooled over our pool, my thighs are beginning to burn. Our home is perfect, and so much more than I could have ever imagined despite having agonized over every last inch of the blueprints and designs. But it's becoming startlingly clear that the design plans I was offered weren't exactly the ones they were looking at. This here before me is a million times better, a million times bigger, and a million times more perfect.

They were holding out on me, but I'm really not surprised.

We're up in my private suite—something that I feel isn't actually going to be as private as we'd intended—looking out over the property, the soft breeze brushing through my hair. We stand out on my balcony, my suite directly in the center, allowing me the most stunning views of both the front and back of the property. "Come on," Marcus says, his eyes sparkling with whatever the big secret is that I know they've been hiding from me for the past ten months. "There's something we want to show you."

My brows furrow as I let Marcus take my hand and lead me through my wing, bypassing my private theater room, stocked to the brim with bean bags, cushions, and blankets to snuggle into, even in the hottest summers. I try to go over the blueprints in my head, trying to figure out what room we haven't visited yet, but I'm positive that I've already seen it all. "Where are we going?"

"Fuck, you suck at accepting surprises," Levi murmurs, his eyes sparkling with laughter. "Would you just let us show you instead of trying to figure it out?"

I roll my eyes and zip my lips, allowing Marcus to lead me along the main hallway in my suite. He walks right to the end of an empty hallway, and for a moment, I think he's fucking insane, that is until he presses his hand against the wall and the whole thing shifts back and opens. "What is this?" I breathe, my eyes bugging out of my head.

Marcus glances back at me, his eyes shimmering with desire. "Why don't you come on in and see."

The challenge in his tone has me striding straight past him and into the darkened room. There are no windows in here and it takes a moment for my eyes to adjust. There's a big bed in the center of the room, a bar and small seating area with only enough chairs for the four of us, not including the long, narrow couch across the room. My brows furrow, wondering what the hell this is, but as I take in the finer details, the strategically placed pieces of furniture, the full frame around the bed, the metal hooks and harnesses, it finally clicks.

"Holy fuck," I gasp. "What in the fifty shades of kinky-fuckery is this? You made us a sex room?"

Roman laughs, his wide grin confirmation enough. "Would you expect anything less?" he questions before pointing out some things in the room. "We're directly in the center of the mansion, each of our own private suites connecting to this very room." He walks around, pointing out all the separate doors which no doubt have secret entrances. "We wanted a place where we could come together, the four of us to do whatever the fuck it is that we need to do. Don't get me wrong, if we happen to be out by the pool and the moment strikes, then so be it. I just thought with so many people coming in and out of our home, guards, and family members, plus Sebastian running around, we needed somewhere we could slip away without anyone barging in on us."

I nod, totally getting it. "I'm assuming that each of your entrances also have super-secret hidden doors?"

Boyish grins settle across their faces, and I roll my eyes as Marcus moves forward. "In here, we can play out our darkest desires, not that we haven't already done that," he says, leading me around the room, indicating to the harness above the bed and the thick metal hooks on the headboard. "With Sebastian due to start walking in the next few months, we didn't want to risk him walking into one of our rooms and wondering why his mom was naked and hanging from chains with her legs spread apart, so … all that shit can go down in here."

He moves toward the bed and I realize that behind the wall, there's some sort of open closet. "Come check it out," he says, a hint of nervousness in his eyes. I follow him around the bed and into the closet and gape at the collection of sex toys. "Anything you want, baby. I got you."

"Holy crap," I breathe, knowing without a doubt that Marcus was completely responsible for the contents of this closet. Levi's never been one for all the extra stuff. I mean, if it's on offer, he's not going to say no, but it's not what he seeks out. As long as I call him daddy and he gets to bite back with his snarky attitude and call me a brat, then he's guaranteed to come. Roman, on the other hand, is down for a bit of kinky-fuckery. He'll put anything anywhere and watch me come undone. But Marcus, my dark and twisted broken soul of a man loves to explore the darker side of sex, loves to fuck me hard while my hands are tied behind my back, loves to chain me and take my freedom just as he did that very first time. He'll never cross the line though, always making sure that I know what he's going to do when that desire strikes, always making sure that he has my consent.

The three of them are so different and yes, it just works. I would never have it any other way.

A smile breaks across my face as my fingers brush over the array of things laid out before me, half of them things I've never come across before, though I'm sure Marcus is all too eager to teach me.

My fingers catch against a rope and I pick it up before turning back to Marcus. "I mean, this is all great and I can't wait to explore it all with you, but I can't get past the thought of you three tying me to that bed and fucking me senseless."

He gapes at me for a moment, not having expected that to come out of my mouth right now. He was probably waiting for me to demand answers, to gawk at the insane instruments around us and beg for explanations on how each of them work, but we told the nanny we'd be back to collect Sebastian in two hours, and we've already wasted one of them looking around our new home.

Time is of the essence.

Marcus steps into me, taking the rope from my hand, his cock already bulging at the front of his pants. "Your wish is my fucking command," he murmurs, looking at me in awe. "But can you do me one little favor?"

I watch him carefully, tracking his every step through the narrow closet until he stops in front of a set of built-in glass drawers. He presses on the front of the drawer and it quickly pops open and displays the most jaw-dropping lingerie sets I've ever seen.

Marcus scans through them before pulling out a black lacy piece with straps going everywhere. Picking it up out of the drawer and clutching it between his strong fingers, he moves across the room until he's standing right in front of me, forcing me to tilt my neck to peer up at his dark, hungry eyes. He presses the flimsy lingerie into my hands, his voice lowering to a deep growl. "Wear this so I can tear it off with my teeth."

And just like that, I'm soaking wet, gasping as he steps around me, rope in hand, more than ready to tie my ass to that bed and fuck me senseless.

----------

We emerge from our sex dungeon an hour later and I can barely walk in a straight line. My knees shake and I hold on to Levi, trying to catch my breath. I feel each of them between my legs, leaking out of me and smearing between my thighs.

Roman glances back at me, a smug smile resting on his warm lips. "You alright, Empress?" he questions. "Looks like you're struggling to keep yourself upright."

I flip him off. "I can handle myself just fine, thank you very much. Though, if I'm completely honest, after letting the three of you fuck me like that, I shouldn't be able to walk at all. I'm disappointed."

The smug grin falls away, and I plaster one of my own across my face as Marcus laughs, not even my endless teasing is able to fuck with his satisfaction. There's nothing quite like tying your girl to the bed and turning her into a cream donut. He'll be smiling for the rest of the night.

Roman rolls his eyes, more than certain he gave me everything I needed and so much more. He's never disappointed me during sex … except that one time in the beginning, but I'm partly at fault for that. "Why don't you go and shower?" he suggests. "There's a bunch of clothes in your walk-in. I thought we could swing by the Moretti residence, grab Sebastian, and take you out. After all, it's your birthday."

"Wow," I grin. "Birthday sex and a dinner date with my favorite boys? Shit, I must be a lucky girl." I pause, thinking it over and letting my brows furrow. "Wait, a dinner date? Like you actually want to go somewhere to have a meal … in public … where literally everyone wants us cuffed and sentenced? What's going on? Is it the local police department's night off? The FBI too busy with a raid?"

Levi groans and pulls me away, his hand coming down on my ass with a smack, the sound ringing in the air just right. "Would you just go and get yourself ready?"

Rolling my eyes, I make my way down to my private bathroom, a little too excited to test it out. There's a waterfall shower head and a bath that looks divine. I could probably spend hours in here just relaxing as I stare out the big window at the view of the rolling mountains and the stars twinkling in the night sky. But as it is, I'm too eager to get back to my little guy.

Sebastian is thirteen months old now, and he's already the coolest little guy I know. I officially became his mom last month and have the adoption papers to prove it, but in all honesty, I became his mom the moment I picked him up out of that crib and ran for our lives.

Being a parent alongside Roman has been a bit of a learning curve. I'm overprotective and terrified of him getting hurt, while Roman is pushing him toward every experience and eager to show him everything that this life has to offer, even if it means running and bombing into the deep end of the pool in the dead of night just to make him laugh. There's no doubt about it, we both made the right decision taking him on as our own. Even if something happens and our relationship crumbles, I will always be Sebastian's mom, through thick and thin.

Getting out of the shower, I walk through to the closet and gape at it. I hadn't looked in here when we did the grand tour, assuming it was just like every other mansion closet I've experienced over the past year and a half, but I was wrong. This closet is as big as my old apartment. It has separate rooms—one for bags, then shoes, gowns, accessories, and everyday wear. This is insane. No one could ever need this many clothes, but then, with the way the boys tend to tear them off me, I might just need them after all.

I get myself all dolled up in a silver bandage dress that hugs my body just right, showing off my subtle curves and pushing my tits up. After slipping my feet into a pair of red-bottom heels and finding a purse to match, I make my way out of my private suite and try to figure out how the hell I'm going to find the boys.

Soft music comes from downstairs, and I grip the wrought-iron railing—still so freaking impressed by it—before carefully making my way down the stairs and following the soft murmured voices out into the night.

As I step through the big doors and onto the patio looking over our stunning property, I find my boys in suits, little Sebastian on Roman's hip, and a priest standing between them.

I suck in a gasp as all of my boys stare up at me with proud smiles across their faces, Dill and Doe racing through the trees in the distance. "What in the ever-loving hell is this?" I whisper, already knowing all too well, but the shock coursing through my system forces the words out of my mouth.

Marcus makes his way toward me, his eyes sparkling as his brothers and Sebastian watch, already in on the secret. I go to take Marcus' hand, but he stops just out of reach before dropping to his knee and staring up at me, his heart shining through his eyes. "Shayne Alexandra Moretti, I know I can't spend my days loving you as your husband, may never receive the honor of calling you my wife, but that's exactly who you are to me. I love you with every part of my being, you are an extension of me, my soul, my other half, and the light that dragged me out of the darkness. You saved me, Shayne Moretti. You saved me from myself and from the hell I was living. You taught me what it meant to love, to allow light into my life, and taught me that there is good in this world. I don't know where I would be without you, and so I ask you, Shayne, the love of my life, to allow me to make solemn vows to you, to stand before my brothers and offer myself to you in every way humanly possible. I am yours wholeheartedly, and it's about damn time that I scream it for the fucking world to hear."

I drop down in front of him, tears welling in my eyes. "Absolutely yes," I tell him, capturing his face between my palms and crushing my lips to his.

"I love you so freaking much, Marcus DeAngelis," I tell him, my lips moving against his. "It would be my greatest honor to stand before you and the eyes of the world and vow my love to you."

He kisses me again before pulling back and slipping his hand into his pocket and producing a diamond ring. "I had this made for you," he says. "I don't know how this whole vow ceremony is supposed to go and that you can't exactly wear three diamond rings on one finger, but I want to offer this to you all the same."

Taking my hand in his, he slides the ring into place and my heart explodes with joy. "It's stunning," I tell him. "And you're wrong. I will wear every diamond you want to give me if it means getting to keep you forever."

Marcus grins as I hear Sebastian's soft laughter behind us, and he takes my hand and raises it to his lips. He kisses the back of my hand, his eyes warm and full of life. "Do you remember that diamond chandelier that you shot out of the sky?"

"How could I not? I have one of them perched up on my trophy shelf."

Marcus grins at the fond memory before indicating to the ring. "I stole the diamonds for you, all of them," he says. "I didn't want anyone else to get their hands on them, so I had them collected and stored away with the intent to have each one forged into the most priceless piece of jewelry. I hired a full time jeweler solely to create pieces for you. Earrings, necklaces, rings, anything you desire is yours."

I stare at him in shock. "You did all of that for me?"

"Of course, I did," he tells me. "These diamonds are rightfully yours. They're a part of your story and it wouldn't be right for anyone else to have them. One day when the time comes, they can be a part of your legacy, something you tell your children about and pass down through generations."

I throw my arms around him and hold him to me, my heart booming in my chest. I've never been one for wearing heaps of jewelry, but that doesn't mean I don't love to gawk at it every chance I get. "Thank you so much," I whisper. "Before meeting you three, no one had ever done anything for me, never went out of their way to love me, never cared enough, but you … you're out here on your knees wearing your heart on your sleeve, asking me to love you for the rest of my life. No girl could ever be this lucky, Marcus. I love you so damn much."

He smiles and draws me in. "Then what the hell are we waiting for? Let's get this ceremony over and done with so I can officially call you mine."

Marcus leads me down the aisle and I meet Roman's stare, my husband. We've talked about this ceremony a million times over, and as much as we have committed to it, it was always something that we never got around to doing. There was always something else that demanded our attention, but now that it's here and the boys are ready and waiting, I couldn't be more excited.

Sebastian immediately flies out of Roman's arms, diving toward mine, and I catch him before he gets a chance to fall. "Hello my sweet boy," I coo, my heart shattering with overwhelming love as I take in his tiny little suit that has his dinner smeared across the front. "You look so handsome."

"Mama," he babbles as Roman puts his arm around my waist and presses a kiss to my forehead.

"Are you surprised?" he murmurs against my skin.

"Surprised is an understatement," I tell him, meeting his warm stare. "Are you ready to be technically married to me?"

"Damn fucking straight, I am," he says, his eyes sparkling with laughter as he turns his attention to Levi. "The question is, is he ready to sound like a sappy bitch, pouring his heart out on the ground for the world to see?"

Levi shoots his brother a lethal glare and I step out of Roman's arms before walking directly into Levi's and tilting my head. They don't know him like I do, don't know the private conversations we've shared, don't know just how gentle his heart can be. He might not be sentimental in the same overwhelming, scream it from the rooftops type of way that Marcus is, but that doesn't mean he doesn't feel it just as strongly as I do.

Levi wraps his warm arms around me and brushes his lips over mine. "Too fucking right, I'm ready," he murmurs against my lips before raising his head and glancing toward the priest. "Let's get the show on the road before the next sorry asshole decides to paint a target on her back."

And no sooner do the words come falling out of his mouth does the property light up in red and blue flashing lights, sirens echoing through the mountains. "Well, fuck," Levi says, switching out my hand for a gun. "I suppose I spoke too soon."

My red-bottom heels are kicked off as Sebastian is handed over to the priest and directed to our safe room and just as the heavy door of the bulletproof chamber closes behind them, the FBI come tearing through our brand new home.

Our guns go up as wicked grins stretch across our faces.

Happy fucking birthday to me.

# THANKS FOR READING

If you enjoyed reading this book as much as I enjoyed writing it, please consider leaving an Amazon review to let me know.
https://www.amazon.com/dp/B09R4NS8NG

# STALK ME

Facebook Page

www.facebook.com/SheridanAnneAuthor

Facebook Reader Group

www.facebook.com/SheridansBookishBabes

Instagram

www.instagram.com/Sheridan.Anne.Author

# <u>OTHER SERIES</u>
www.amazon.com/Sheridan-Anne/e/B079TLXN6K

## <u>YOUNG ADULT / NEW ADULT DARK ROMANCE</u>
The Broken Hill High Series | Haven Falls | Broken Hill Boys | Aston Creek High | Rejects Paradise | Boys of Winter | Depraved Sinners

## <u>NEW ADULT SPORTS ROMANCE</u>
Kings of Denver | Denver Royalty | Rebels Advocate

## <u>CONTEMPORARY ROMANCE</u> (standalones)
Play With Fire | Until Autumn (Happily Eva Alpha World)

## <u>URBAN FANTASY - PEN NAME: CASSIDY SUMMERS</u>
Slayer Academy